CH01278686

Blos on the Thorn

Book 3 in the Out of Time series

1194-1195

Loretta Livingstone

Copyright © 2018 Loretta Livingstone

Cover Design by Cathy Helms Avalon Graphics

The moral right of Loretta Livingstone to be identified as the
author has been asserted by her in accordance with the
Copyright, Designs and Patents Act, 1988.

This book is sold subject to the condition that it shall not, by
way of trade or otherwise, be lent, resold, hired out, or otherwise
circulated without the author's prior consent in form of binding
or cover other than that in which it is published and without a
similar condition including this condition being imposed on the
subsequent purchaser.

All rights reserved. No part of this publication may be
reproduced, stored in a retrieval system, or transmitted, in any
form or by any means without the prior written permission of
the author.

All characters in this publication are fictitious apart from those
in the public domain, and any resemblance to real persons, living
or dead, is purely coincidental.

A copy of this book will be available from the British Library.

All rights reserved.

ISBN: 1790808529

ISBN-13: 9781790808526

DEDICATION

To my dad, Ian David Robinson, without whose legacy these books might never have been written.

.

ACKNOWLEDGMENTS

Thanks to my wonderful husband, Iain, whose unfailing support and encouragement, not to mention his willingness to have new chapters read aloud to him for his opinion and to accept late or burnt dinners when I was so deeply in the zone, I forgot the time, has been my mainstay since I started writing.

Also to those members of my family who have cheered me on, my fab beta readers, Heidi, Marie and Dominique, my equally fab editor, Nicolette Galliers, of Sic Est Verum (Sic Est Verum, Twitter) without whose knowledge of all things medieval, I would have been lost. Last, but by no means least, thanks to my cover designer, Cathy Helms. I couldn't have done it without any of you – quite literally. Also to Helen Hollick, whom I am proud to call my friend.

.

CHAPTER 1

Late October 1194

The hunters gave wild yells of glee. The alaunts barked with excitement as they found their quarry and held it at bay. Matthew, the hunt master, blew his horn to call them back, and his men waded amongst them, seeking to leash them before they should be killed themselves or spoil Lord Baldwin's sport. Baldwin and his entourage dismounted, for true boar hunting should be done afoot and he would not sully his reputation for courage by remaining ahorse. They moved in warily, spears at the ready.

Flushed from the nearby cover by the hounds, as the boar emerged, the men gave startled gasps at the size of the thing. Baldwin drew in his breath – this was a truly royal beast, fit for a king or even an emperor. Its eyes were red with fury and it squealed with rage as it made ready to charge. A rare black creature this, not the usual brown ones found hereabouts. Baldwin's blood sang in his veins with exhilaration. He hurled the spear at the same instant the beast charged. His aim was true, catching it in the throat as it launched itself upon him. It dropped to the ground, and the metallic smell of the blood gushing from its throat filled Baldwin's nostrils. But as it kicked in its death throes, a second one, even larger, almost measuring to the top of a man's thigh, dashed from the undergrowth beside them. Why had they not seen it? It must have been nearby, disturbed by the furious barking of the dogs.

"'Ware, lord!" Matthew cried a warning. Another spear flashed but it was too late. Baldwin had no time for more than the briefest flare of alarm before the tusks sliced into his gut. The weight of the creature flung him backwards onto the cold hard ground, and although he felt no pain, he knew he was badly injured. The boar, slain by the spear, pinned him down and he struggled to draw breath. A roaring was in his ears, and blood – his own, or that of the brute atop him? – puddled around him. If he could but see or even put a hand to where he was injured, but the boar was crushing him; he could not move.

Matthew bent over him, the others peering over the man's shoulder, and Baldwin swore at the horror on their faces. What were they about? He had healed of serious wounds before. If they could get him home quickly… And if they would just remove the beast before his chest was stoved in! Their panicked shouts seemed to come from a great distance; the stink of the boar was strong. Frost-rimed grass stood out sharply against the pale blue of the winter sky, and he felt the heat of the body pinning him to the earth. The sharp clarity astounded him, then the edges of his vision blurred and an agony such as he had never known seared through him.

He could not be dying. He wasn't dying. He strained for breath but it only increased the pain. He would *not* die. He opened his mouth but no words came out, just a gush of blood before his eyes dimmed. All he could hear now was that roaring in his ears. He tried to draw breath once more, then the last of the light faded.

The wind whistled through the chinks in the closed shutters. Isabella plied her needle with listless fingers which she flexed surreptitiously, hoping no one would notice. Oh, to be able to hold them to the flames, even for a moment.

The fire flickered as the draught from the chimney stirred it and cast its smoke sulkily across the room. Her hands were numb with cold and she longed to cast her work aside and move closer to the hearth, but the sharp gaze of her husband's mother was upon her.

Adelaide sniffed. "I told Baldwin chimneys were a mistake, but he would have his way. Girl!" She beckoned to one of the maids. "Stir that fire and bring hot spiced wine." It seemed that today even her son could not please her.

Isabella swallowed and hoped Evelina would bring her some, too, for the cold had seeped into her bones. If even Adelaide was feeling it, it must be bitter indeed.

"And light the braziers."

Isabella dared to glance at the woman, who was looking even paler than usual, her skin tight to her skull, her lips pressed together in a forbidding line. "Ma mère, are you unwell?" she ventured.

Adelaide gave a snort. "Is it not enough that this wind gives me the headache? Must I also answer your foolish questions?" Her voice was colder than the ice that formed on the edges of the castle moat.

Isabella dropped her gaze back to her embroidery so Adelaide would not see the surge of hate that blazed in her eyes.

There came a clattering outside the door, raised voices and shouts of alarm, and Matthew burst into the room. Adelaide looked down her haughty nose at him, but at the expression on his face, she rose with a cry of concern.

"My lady!" Aenor, her senior woman, took an anxious step towards her but stopped as a ferocious glare was directed at her.

"What is it? Are we under siege? Speak, man!"

Matthew hesitated a moment before meeting those fierce eyes. "It is your son, Lord Baldwin." He paused. "An accident…the boar–"

She cut him off, her voice sharp. "My son? He is hurt?"

"My lady," the man's eyes flickered away and back again, "Lord Baldwin is dead."

At his words, Adelaide stood as though turned to stone, her face like bleached linen, before giving a hoarse cry. Then, so slowly that, at first, Isabella did not realise what was happening, Adelaide crumpled towards the floor, falling against the newly-lit brazier.

Pandemonium reigned. Matthew caught her and lifted her before the hot coals that brushed the skirt of her gown could catch.

Men surged in behind him, righting the brazier, stamping out the flames that had begun to lick the floor rushes; women screamed, and amid the chaos, Isabella stood perfectly still, clasping her embroidery to her, eyes downcast to hide the wild surge of joy that ripped through her.

She was conscious of one thought only. *Free! I'm free!*

CHAPTER 2

Ignoring the malevolent glare directed at her, Isabella touched the spoon of broth to Adelaide's lips. The twisted mouth clenched a little tighter, and something resembling a snarl came from her throat. Isabella pressed the spoon to her lips. "Ma mère, you must eat."

In truth, she would be happy to let the woman die if that was what she wished. Not a shred of kindness had she ever shown since the day Isabella had arrived, a stick-thin, terrified wisp of a girl with huge, frightened eyes. But to do so, to allow Adelaide to kill herself in such a way, would stain her own soul, and why should this witch doom Isabella also? Although, and she shuddered, mentally making the sign of the cross, belike she was already damned. Had her desperate prayers caused Baldwin's death? If so, no amount of false contrition would save her. It might be that it was already too late, that her soul was already cursed, but nursing this evil-tempered sow would surely be considered at least a partial penance.

The broth trickled down Adelaide's chin; Isabella put the bowl aside and, with a tenderness she did not feel, wiped the grey face with a moistened napkin. Then she reluctantly picked up the spoon and made a second attempt. As she tried to force nourishment between the wretched woman's lips, Adelaide's arm, the one limb that retained some movement, shot out, sending the bowl crashing to the floor where the broth, that which had not landed on Isabella, seeped into the rushes. *The evil old…!*

Isabella was glad she had covered her gown with a piece of sacking, already stained and fit only for rags. She bent to retrieve the bowl and, as she straightened, met the red-rimmed eyes of Adelaide's senior woman who glowered at her, curling her hands like claws. Why she cared for the venomous hag in the bed was beyond Isabella. Even Aenor had barely been treated with courtesy.

"My poor lady has nothing left to live for," Aenor hissed. "Had you done your duty in Lord Baldwin's embrace, I doubt not a grandchild would have given her reason enough to live."

Isabella ground her teeth but did not respond. If Lord Baldwin had not used her so ill, mayhap her womb would have quickened. Could any woman retain a child when they were treated so brutally? It would have made more sense had he cosseted her, given the seed a chance to settle in her womb. Mayhap then he would have had the child for which he and Adelaide longed. And it must have been the same for his first wife, poor wight. Surely his attentions had been the death of her. Isabella would not hold herself responsible. If the hellspawn Adelaide called son had been a better husband, she might not now bear the stigma of barrenness.

"Ma mère," her voice was cold, no longer the coaxing tones she had tried earlier, "if you do not eat, you condemn your soul to Hell. Is that what you want? Is it?"

A single tear coursed down the withered cheek and almost, *almost,* Isabella could feel for her. "I will arrange for more broth, and Aenor will aid you if you do not wish for my help." She turned, stripping off the grease-stained sacking as she did so. Enough! She had done her duty. If the old besom would not eat, let her starve. As she left the room, she spoke to her once more. "I will send your confessor to you, Madame. Perhaps he can convince you."

She tossed the sacking to Evelina as she walked back down the narrow passageway. The maid pressed against the wall to allow her to pass. "Dispose of this, Evelina, and find me a fresh one for when I next attend upon Lord Baldwin's mother." She rolled her shoulders to alleviate the tension which had built up in them and rubbed at the stiff tendons in her neck.

"Yes, my lady. It's a thankless task, isn't it? And I'm sorry for your loss."

Isabella, who had been about to walk on, stopped and looked at Evelina, brows raised in disbelief. The girl coloured. "Er… I mean–" She broke off, floundering, looking as though she wished she'd not spoken.

Isabella regarded her steadily, which seemed to add to her discomfiture; her face, already pink, turned fiery. "My lady, I'm sorry, I know I've not been…um…" She bowed her head. "While my lady was alive–"

"She is not dead, yet, Evelina."

Evelina squirmed visibly. "Yes, my lady. Sorry, my lady. I wanted to be more help to you, my lady, but she watched me…us…all the time. I couldn't afford to lose my place here." She gave an apologetic grimace. "My father can't afford me to. I…" she paused before continuing, "I just couldn't. I did want to."

Isabella softened her heart. It was not fair to blame the girl. She, too, was skinny and half-starved, but doubtless her family would have struggled to cope if she had been dismissed. She gave a half-smile and Evelina's face showed relief.

"I understand. It has not been easy for most of us. I shall speak for you before I leave. I would suggest you come with me, but my own future is far from certain."

The maid's face lifted. "Thank you, my lady."

"And, until then, perhaps you might like to be my senior maid?"

Evelina looked radiant – for half a moment. Then sobered. "My lady, there are others more senior than me. Well, they're all more senior. They'll not be pleased."

It was a considerable understatement. Isabella was certain they would be furious, but none of them had cared a silver fourthing for her while Baldwin lived. Evelina, little though she knew her, would be capable of doing as she was bid, would not raise haughty eyebrows and sniff superciliously at each of Isabella's requests. She might even be a pleasant companion.

Certainly, that cat, Aenor, was not going to serve her, even if the woman wished to, which was doubtful. "I do not care. Whilst I am lady here, however short that time may be, I'll have whom I please to serve me. Give that rag to Maud to get rid of and then come to my chamber. We'll find you something more fitting to wear."

The maid looked nervous but glowing. Doubtless, if she could screw up her courage to face down the older women, she would take the same pleasure in it that Isabella was taking now. "And I shall see your wage increased. Make sure you save it; you may have need of it."

When she reached her chamber, Isabella threw herself down on the bed with a bounce and a sigh that would have called curses on her head from Adelaide and scorn from the other women. She did not care. This would not, could not, continue long, but for the short while she had her freedom, she would enjoy it.

Ripping the veil from her head, she called Sybilla to comb and rebraid her hair, rebuking the woman when she deliberately caught the comb in a knot, enjoying the look of chagrin on her face. Isabella did not care if she had offended Sybilla, any of them, come to that. If they would not serve with good grace, then why should she behave with grace in return? For the time being, the rule here was hers, outside from the steward's responsibilities. Which reminded her, she needed to speak with him about Baldwin's effigy.

She replaced her veil and wimple, leaving Sybilla to tidy the chamber, mouth turned down in a sullen arc, and went to find the steward, only to discover him deep in conversation with Adelaide's chaplain. It seemed the effigy was already decided. She had no interest in it anyway. Soon, that mother of his would be lying beside him. God grant she was far from here when her own time came, for she had no wish to lie beside her husband even in death.

She stalked back to the bower. Isabella was finding that, young as she was, subservient as she had been, if she could stand her ground and speak commandingly, her women, at least could be made to serve her, even if the men paid her no heed. And, truth to tell, it was rather heady. A pity it could not last.

CHAPTER 3

Isabella cursed beneath her breath as Godfroi de Bourne and his entourage clattered through into the bailey. She'd known he was coming – the messenger had been quite specific. De Bourne was to be appointed as new castellan. Unrelated to Baldwin, he had been given charge of the castle by William Longchamp, Chancellor of England. Isabella did not know why, neither did she care, so long as her dower lands weren't affected. It made little difference to her, unless she was to be given to any new castellan as bride, and since she'd been told de Bourne was wed, that was no cause for her concern.

Foolishly, she had put off thinking about her own situation. She should not have waited so long after Adelaide had been laid to rest. Now, it was too late – or was it? If only she were a more proficient rider, she could have set off for her dower lands. But then, she could scarcely have travelled unaccompanied, even if she could have carried sufficient of her possessions. And if she did arrive safely, her father would soon sniff her out and insist she return to live under his 'protection', at least until he could find her another husband.

What if she could reach a convent? Taking the veil would surely be a better option than having another man submit her to the treatment she'd received at Baldwin's hands. She could suffer the act itself if she must, but the rest?

And were not all men alike? Certainly, from the little she remembered, her mother's life with her father had brought few pleasures. Surely life in the convent, however barren, however joyless, would at least bring peace. And there would be no man to beat her or to abuse her. Surely, too, she could find some comfort amongst those she would call sister.

But she was dreaming. It would never be permitted. Listlessly accepting her fate – for what else could she do? – she massaged her temples, pinned on her veil and went to greet the newcomers, treading firmly, head held high, a smile of welcome fastened determinedly to her face. At least she could act the part of châtelaine and perchance win some respect from the man who would oust her from what, after all, had barely been a home.

De Bourne had already dismounted when she reached the bailey. Hugh Corbyn, the steward, somewhat tardily, was hurrying across from the barns. Why had he been there? She shrugged. As though she couldn't guess. To Isabella's annoyance, Aenor had reached de Bourne first and was greeting him as though she, not Isabella, was châtelaine.

Gliding forwards, she reached de Bourne as Aenor rose from a deep curtsey. Isabella shot her a warning from narrowed eyes, cutting off the words of welcome the woman had been about to utter with a sharp, "That will do, Aenor. Please ensure all is ready inside for my Lord de Bourne's comfort," leaving Aenor with little choice but to grudgingly obey. From the look on her face, it would add another notch on her tally stick of grievances.

Isabella curtseyed to de Bourne and the short, plump woman whom he had helped dismount from an elegant grey palfrey. De Bourne bowed, offering his hand to raise her, smiling courteously, saying, "My lady, I am sorry for your loss."

She was unimpressed. Had not Baldwin also possessed charm when the whim took him? The smile remained on her face, although a careful observer would have noted the lines of strain around the edges of her lips.

De Bourne, however, appeared to take it at face value, turning to introduce his companion. "My wife, the Lady Mabille. She will be glad to be shown to a chamber; the journey has been long and irksome."

Isabella inclined her head. "I shall be happy to do so, my lord." And if it was not precisely true, who would accuse her of lying?

As Hugh stepped forward, de Bourne engaged him in conversation, and the two men moved away. Isabella and de Bourne's wife surveyed each other for a moment until Mabille stepped forward and enveloped Isabella in a hug. Isabella stiffened at first; it had been long since she'd been embraced so warmly. Then, as Mabille patted her shoulders, she relaxed into the plump, motherly arms that enfolded her.

"Oh, my poor dear, this is a sad state of affairs. I hope we may be able to bring some ease to you." She stepped back, looking up slightly to meet Isabella's gaze. "And my lord will take all the burden of charge from your young shoulders, which will be a relief to you, I'm sure." She pressed her hand to her eyes. "But, as my husband says, the journey has been long and tiring. I should appreciate the chance to rest a little before

I take up my duties. Will you escort me to a chamber, my dear?"

Her short rule over, Isabella realised she must relinquish her own room, unless Mabille and de Bourne were pleased to share Lady Adelaide's chamber. By the looks of them, they would not wish to sleep apart, and Adelaide's chamber was slightly larger than the room she and Baldwin had slept in. No need for her to remove her belongings just yet.

"My lady, please come this way. I will show you to the lord's chamber." After all, this was the one that should have been the lord's chamber, had it not been for his mother. And at least that had been cleared, already. "It will be prepared for you immediately. I hope that will be satisfactory. Sybilla!" She caught the woman slinking away down an inner passage, and Sybilla turned back, the glare she aimed at Isabella slithering into an ingratiating smile as she saw the Lady Mabille. "Sybilla, please bring fresh linen for Sir Godfroi and his wife."

Water brought for washing, the linen changed and fresh herbs strewn on the rushes, de Bourne's wife proclaimed herself satisfied with the arrangements before eyeing Isabella, who, having dismissed Sybilla, now waited, fingers fluttering nervously about her skirts. The older woman smiled. "I suppose you're wondering what's to become of you."

"Yes, my lady, although I have my dower lands. I would be happy to remove to those, if I may."

The older woman shook her head. "You know better than that, my dear. A widow as young as you has no option. Normally, my husband would arrange for you to be escorted back to your father. And then, I'm afraid, you would once more do your duty by marrying to oblige your family."

Isabella could retain the forced smile no longer. It dropped from her face as she acknowledged the truth she'd been trying to ignore. A cold emptiness washed over her, yet after all, she'd known there could be no real escape for such as her. But Mabille was still speaking. "However, Lady Isabella, it seems the queen wishes to have you serve as one of her ladies."

The queen? Why would she be interested in me? Her puzzlement showed briefly before her habitual blank mask came down. She curtseyed. "As the queen wishes. How soon shall I prepare to leave? Will I have an escort?"

Mabille chuckled. "Be calm, my dear, there is no urgency. She had not even left Fontevrault when we set out. My lord husband has arrangements to make here. Once all meets his approval, likely after Martinmas, he'll accompany you. For the meantime, you'll be our guest. You may retain whichever maid you wish to serve you. Perhaps, when I've rested, you'll send the others to me?" She turned, as the door opened and a middle-aged woman came in bearing a tray. "Ah, Basilea, thank you." Then, waving her plump arm at Isabella in dismissal, she plopped down on the end of the bed as Basilea poured a cup of wine.

Isabella ordered food to be sent from the kitchen and walked thoughtfully back to her room, where she caught Aenor in the process of removing her gowns from the clothing poles.

"You may put those back, Aenor." Her voice was tight with annoyance. "For the time being, I shall be remaining here. Take yourself off and await Lady Mabille's summons. And please send Evelina to me."

Aenor glowered as she replaced them, then flounced from the room.

Isabella threw herself on the bed and lay there pondering her future. To serve the queen. She'd not thought of that, could not have imagined the likelihood. For all she was a lady, she was not in an exalted enough position, however highly her father thought of himself, to be considered for such a role. How had it come about? She could not imagine. And there would be no need to return to her father, for he could not gainsay this. It was a pity he would be as delighted as she was, but even that thought could not quench her joy.

She sat back up, her face glowing, her world suddenly alight with possibilities.

CHAPTER 4

Three scant weeks later, Isabella was seated on Mabille de Bourne's docile grey palfrey. It stood patiently whilst Godfroi took time to embrace his wife before mounting his own glossy, high-spirited horse which tossed its head, snorting as though it could not wait to be off.

Isabella raised her hand in farewell to Mabille, who was sniffing and wiping the corner of her eye. She had quite won Isabella's heart with her kindness. A time that could have been trying had turned into an enjoyable interlude. And now she would see what fate had in store for her next. A shiver of anticipation ran through her.

Evelina, who had pleaded to be allowed to accompany her, rode in the entourage seated behind one of the serjeants, her upturned nose almost quivering with excitement at the adventure.

Fortunate Evelina to have a say in her own destiny.

A sigh escaped Isabella, and de Bourne wheeled his horse around to see what was distressing her. His courtesy had proved to be quite as genuine as his wife's – if Isabella was given to such as he, she thought she could bear it. But she would not, could not allow herself to hope. For now, she straightened her spine and smiled back at de Bourne.

"It's nothing, my lord," she assured him. "Merely that I'm contemplating my future." He nodded his comprehension. Indeed, what could he have said? Acknowledging her words with a slight gesture of his hand, he dropped back to ride beside her, and she found his silent understanding companionable.

There could be no guarantees for her happiness; to imply otherwise would have been pointless, but now she had so much more hope she would not allow herself to think on anything but the thrill of being one of the queen's ladies. The day was light, and to be out of the bower was somewhat of a novelty for her. Birds warbled and called from the now nearly bare trees which stretched their bony fingers to the pale sky, fluttering like little flags the handful of bright leaves which still clung to them. The sights and sounds and the pleasure of being treated kindly, all were soothing.

However, after the first couple of hours, she started to sag slightly. The seat was only lightly padded, and the bones of her behind began to feel bruised. She ached from trying to look ahead whilst her body faced sideways and observing the set shoulders of the young squire who held her leading reins, she guessed he bitterly resented the duty. Furthermore, the chill of the day, which initially had not seemed too bad, was beginning to cling to her, seeping beneath her skin.

By crooking her neck painfully, she could see Evelina was still looking fresh as a daisy. Likely her position astride was more comfortable than this wretched throne-like outward-facing contraption. Likely, too, that Evelina was gaining some warmth from the body of the serjeant, to whom she was clinging a little more tightly than Isabella thought seemly.

De Bourne, who had ridden ahead again, fell back. She knew he was watching so forced her aching back upright again and held her head high but doubted she had fooled him, for he called a halt at the next inn they passed, escorting her to a table outside and sending for wine and food.

As he stood beside her, he said, to her disappointment, "Cold out here, my dear, but better chilled than exposed to the company within."

A gust of wind rustled the leaves around her feet, and Isabella shivered. Well for de Bourne to say, but she would rather have her senses assaulted and be huddling beside the fire than sit outside and freeze.

He must have noticed the shiver for, relenting, he said, "Ah, happen it would be better to warm ourselves. There's a fair way to go yet. Wait here, Lady Isabella."

He disappeared inside the shabby hostelry. Isabella heard his voice raised, then he came back and escorted her within to a bench placed close to the hearth. A hush fell when she walked in. Partly blinkered by her hood, which she kept close about her face, she slid her gaze discreetly around, unwilling to catch the eye of any of the villeins and cottars who glowered sullenly from the other benches.

The light inside was dim, mostly coming from the fire in the hearth, and the smell of unwashed bodies was strong. The reeds were rank, and she understood why de Bourne had been reluctant for her to enter; however, it was warm and so great was her need to drive the ice from her bones, all other considerations could be ignored.

As she sat, she was conscious of malevolent eyes watching from beneath bent heads. It seemed the occupants had been moved to make an acceptable distance between them and her. She did not care, happy just to hold her hands to the flames. Ignoring the resentful faces, she kept her gaze downcast, glad of de Bourne's protective presence and that of his men.

The proprietor, happy to welcome any member of the moneyed classes to his hovel, brought wine, heating it with the poker which he thrust into the fire then into the cups where it hissed and sizzled.

The wine tasted sour, as did the greasy stew which he served, but it warmed her, and she was reluctant to leave when de Bourne indicated they must be off.

The break had revived her slightly, but before they had gone more than a couple of miles, she felt herself starting to droop again as the ache in her muscles, so unaccustomed to this exercise, increased, and she dismounted gratefully when they clattered through the gates of Sparnstow Abbey where they would make an overnight stop.

After showing her to one of the private guest chambers, the hosteller fluttered around Isabella trying to ensure her comfort and producing a soothing balm sent by the infirmaress, which she gave to Evelina with instructions to rub it into her lady's skin. Evelina divested Isabella of her outer clothing, and Isabella relaxed as she felt the maid's firm hands massaging her aching body.

Afterwards, resting on the curtained bed, watching Evelina anoint her own aches and pains, Isabella wondered how the abbess would react if she were to throw herself on her mercy. The nuns had been all smiles, and she envied them the peace she had seen on their faces. If not for the fact that she was now to serve the queen, she could be happy here – well, content, at least – she knew it. Almost, with the assurance of her dower lands, she could bring herself to believe she would be welcomed as one of them.

While she was here, she would ask for their prayers for her future. To have God's blessing would be a good thing. And to reserve a place for herself in case things should go wrong in her new life if, Heaven forfend, it ever became necessary.

It was probably foolishness; things would not go wrong, of course they would not, but there was a small niggle of doubt that would not quite leave her.

As though aware of her thoughts, Evelina ceased her activity, adjusted her garments and stood before her mistress, hands folded neatly. Grasping the moment, Isabella said, "Come with me, Evelina, I wish to pray, then I must speak with the abbess."

Abbess Hildegarde prayed silently as she studied the thin girl who stood before her, noting how her fingers pleated and unpleated the fabric of her gown. She indicated a high-backed chair, and Isabella sat, her spine rigid, her hands clasped tightly on her lap – to stop them shaking if Hildegarde was any judge.

At a guess, Isabella was seeking an escape, and the abbess wished with all her heart she could offer the sanctuary she expected the girl was about to request, but in all conscience, she could not, for she did not believe there was a genuine vocation. This request to take the veil would be merely a desperate attempt to escape. That her first marriage had brought her un-happiness was evident, but she would not be allowed to remain here.

Hildegarde was wrong. Lady Isabella was not, it seemed, seeking sanctuary, not yet. Only God's blessing on her future and the possibility of sanc-tuary if she ever had need of it.

Relieved, the abbess gestured at the cup of hot spiced wine on the table; she had great belief in the efficacy of a warm drink. If only she could offer a cup of tea – she still had some of her precious leaves left – but how could she explain that without giving her own secrets away? The elixir she had missed so much had found its way to her through devious means, and now, she delighted in it. But it was not only her secret, and could not be shared.

How she hated the trade in fresh young women to satisfy greedy men, for Hildegarde was an enigma, a paradox. She did not come from this age. Thirty years ago, she had fallen through a chink in time and found herself at Sparnstow. Here it was she had come to know God, and here it was she had made a life for herself, choosing not to return to her own time when she had opportunity. Yet for all she was happy at the abbey, her years in this century could not make her acceptance of the prevailing customs any easier. But to fight against the order of things would do no good and so, however unwillingly, she had accepted the strictures placed upon her. As for the tea – well, she was not the only one who knew both sides of the divide.

She shook her head regretfully. "My child, we can certainly pray for your future, but as for Sparnstow becoming a refuge, it cannot be, and you know that is so. If the occasion should ever arise, even if I permitted you to remain, you would be taken from here by others."

Lady Isabella chewed her bottom lip with small, white, slightly uneven teeth and the glimmer of a tear on her lashes tugged at Hildegarde's heart. She had only one small crumb of comfort to offer. "Come, in all probability, things will go well for you, and you will not need an escape. We shall go to the Lady Chapel and seek God's blessing on your new life."

Isabella found the abbess's words discouraging. Yes, Hildegarde was probably right, yet she would have liked the security of an escape, just in case. Her first marriage had taught her that. *Ah well,* she shook herself mentally. In all likelihood, she would not need succour. She was a foolish wight, for was not a brighter future beckoning her now? Still not entirely satisfied, she set her mind firmly to the future and followed the abbess obediently to the chapel.

CHAPTER 5

The road seemed endless. Isabella, who was unused to being anywhere but in the bower or the great hall, felt weak with fatigue and misery. The day was cold and drear, sleet stung her eyelids, and water dripped from her hood onto her nose and wormed its way down the front of her mantle. It seeped into her gown and the layers beneath, making them cling, clammy and chill, to her skin. The hems of both mantle and gown were sodden soon after leaving the abbey, and her feet were numb inside her soft leather boots even though they were fur lined. She envied the sturdy footwear of her travelling companions.

Even Evelina's pert nose seemed less cheery today, though she chatted brightly enough to the serjeant whose courser she shared. Godfroi de

Bourne made sporadic attempts at conversation, but for the most part, he was silent.

Approaching Berkhamsted, the clouds lightened somewhat, and Isabella arched her back and flexed her shoulders, relieved to be nearing the end of the journey.

As she turned to speak to Godfroi, her horse lost its footing and stumbled, throwing her off balance. She fought for a moment to stay upright, but her saddle allowed her little control. She made a sudden grab at the palfrey's mane but missed. She started to slip and tried to jump clear, but her foot caught in her gown, and she tumbled, landing on her hands and knees in a deep slick of mud.

De Bourne was at her side in an instant, tutting his concern as he lifted her to her feet before turning to viciously berate the sullen-faced squire leading the palfrey for his carelessness. Isabella was not entirely sure whether his greater concern was for her or the horse.

He held her as she steadied herself. "Any hurts, lass?" he asked as he looked her over.

She tried her limbs gingerly. "Nothing apart from some bruising, my lord. But…" and she surveyed herself with dismay, "just look at me." De Bourne raised his eyebrows but merely nodded as he lifted her back into the saddle, and she heard the wretched squire snigger.

So, apparently, had de Bourne, for without a word and without turning, he swung his arm in a backward arc felling the youth into the same slick of mud Isabella had landed in.

Isabella permitted herself the satisfaction of a small smirk when she saw he was even muddier than she, but it quickly faded as she looked down at her gown and mantle.

De Bourne must have guessed her thoughts as he took her leading rein himself and gave her a tight smile. "No harm done," he said. "Never fret, you'll have chance to change into clean attire before you're presented to the queen."

Isabella flushed with annoyance. Kind but stupid! He had completely overlooked the fact that she would first have to parade through the castle caked in filth! She needed to hold onto her pride – it was all she had. But she said nothing, for nothing could be done anyway.

As they picked their way through the town, Isabella thought even the street urchins and town drabs were pointing and laughing at her. Her only satisfaction was that the mud–covered squire seemed as uncomfortable as she. She straightened her back, put up her chin and assumed her most haughty expression – the one she'd been practising on Adelaide's ladies since Baldwin had died.

De Bourne looked at her with approval. "Good girl. Never let them see you care."

Nearing the castle, though, she found it harder to ignore the stares, and her chin went up a little higher. By the time they dismounted in the bailey, she felt as though everyone from the meanest scullion to the highest lord was laughing at her, and her face burned; nonetheless, she held herself proudly, gritting her teeth as she awaited the promised change of clothing.

It never came. A steward bustled up to them, unsuccessfully trying to hide his disapproval as he greeted them. He led them straight through the hall and up a twisting stairway before ushering them into an antechamber beyond which must be the queen's solar.

A cluster of ladies, all plying their needles, looked up, and Isabella fancied she saw pity, amusement and disdain flit across various faces before she was whisked past them towards the elegant elderly woman seated on a high-backed cushioned chair at the end of the chamber. The queen surveyed them with an inscrutable expression before turning her gaze on de Bourne, eyebrows raised, as Isabella sank into a deep curtsey, quaking inside.

De Bourne harrumphed and blustered. "An accident, your grace. I had expected the Lady

Isabella would be permitted to wash before being brought to you."

Eleanor studied him a few moments longer, enough that Isabella could almost feel the tension in him. At last, she inclined her head, saying frostily, "Indeed! It is a pity my steward did not think likewise." She gave the steward a scathing glance, and the colour rushed up his neck and over his face like a crimson tide. "Mayhap, you might consider common courtesy as much as speed another time." As the steward stumbled over his apology, she cut into it with some asperity, "Well, do not gawp, man. Remedy the matter." He bowed, flushing again as he turned away.

The queen held out her hands to raise Isabella up, saying, "Now, child, let me see you," but dropped them speedily when she saw the mud on the hands Isabella held uncertainly before her. "De Bourne," she snapped, "don't just stand there like a stuffed capon. Assist the girl to rise if you please."

CHAPTER 6

After the constraints laid upon her as Baldwin's wife, Isabella found herself quietly enjoying her first taste of court life. Arriving just a few weeks before Christmas, the gaiety and the festivities had been amusing.

Just now, she was watching the knights and ladies dancing carols when a voice at her side made her jump almost from her seat.

"Lady Isabella, forgive me. Did I startle you?"

Isabella found herself confronted by a slender man of middle height in his late twenties. Hazel eyes with green depths laughed down at her.

John! The queen's youngest son. Isabella had not been introduced but recognised him. Indeed, he needed no introduction, it seemed. Her heart gave a flutter of alarm as he stood before her holding out his hand.

"Will you dance this carol with me, my lady?"

"I…" The words of refusal would not come. She felt bewitched, unable to move, far less to speak.

John smiled, caressing his neat beard with his left hand as he watched her, holding out his right hand to her still. "Come, lady."

Isabella moistened her dry lips with her tongue, then wished she had not as John's own tongue flicked briefly over his teeth. "I…I do not dance, my lord."

His eyebrows rose. "You do not dance? What, never? You surprise me, Lady Isabella."

She blinked, forcing herself to speak again. Her voice sounded strained even to her. "I beg your forgiveness, my lord, but it would be unseemly. My husband is not long dead; I am still in mourning."

John took a step closer. "In mourning? For Baldwin FitzAubrey? Now, you astound me. I would have thought you might be more inclined to celebrate his loss, rather than mourn it."

Isabella swallowed. Of a surety, he was right, but not for anything would she admit it. John sat beside her, taking possession of her hand, and she tried not to flinch, but he did not seem threatening as he let her palm rest gently on his. Might it be that he wasn't the ogre he had seemed at her marriage to Baldwin? Had she misjudged him?

Misremembered? She had been so young and afraid, and so many faces had leered at her that night. Perhaps she had confused him with someone else. Certainly, he seemed different now. Courteous. Kindly, even.

At any rate, she found herself quite unable to pull away from him. She glanced behind her, but the queen was speaking to Saveric de Grenoble, laughing with him. Isabella could not hope for help there.

Meanwhile, John still watched her, those eyes of his now more green than hazel. Her mouth almost too dry to swallow, she tried not to tremble as he claimed her attention again.

"I understand you might feel you must appear to mourn, my lady, but I feel very sure that in your heart you do not."

The image of him she'd held since her fourteenth year was fading; in its place, a man who seemed friendly, understanding, and she felt herself beginning to relax a little.

John retained her hand, patting it gently. "I did know your husband, Isabella." His informality appeared genuine – perhaps the tales about him were wrong. At any rate, he continued, his tone soft, confiding. "It would be reasonable for you to rejoice at his demise. But," he paused, his lips moved silently as though in calculation, "it must be more than two months

since he died. You've done your wifely duty."
He stood, pulling her to her feet, laughing. "And
now is the time to dance!"

He tugged at her insistently, and she rose, allowing him to draw her into the circle of swaying, swirling men and women.

As they joined the other dancers, John
snapped his fingers at the musicians who had
been watching him nervously and the music
stopped. The dancers reformed and Isabella took
her place opposite John. He bowed, she curtseyed, and the dance began again.

Caught up in the music, Isabella found she
was starting to enjoy herself, despite her initial
trepidation. She circled to the left, then to the
right, clapped her hands and took small steps in
and out. She moved towards John, and he put an
arm about her waist, swinging her around,
chuckling. No, he could not be as bad as rumours
would have her believe; his behaviour was impeccable. Certainly, she did not feel afraid of
him. Returning his smile, she joined hands with
him, and he moved her one position round the
circle.

The music played on until the dancers had returned to their original partners. Isabella, flushed
with exertion, sank into another deep curtsey as
the carol ended, and John raised her to her feet,
leading her not back to her seat, but into an

antechamber which led off the hall. Not another soul was there, and she shrank back a little, but he led her to a bench saying, "You are over-heated, my lady, and it's so much cooler here."

It was true, she was uncomfortably hot, and the air was fresher, tingling pleasantly on her skin.

"You see, Lady Isabella, that was not so ter-rible, was it?" His eyes crinkled at the corners, and Isabella couldn't resist a small hiccup of laughter.

"Confess now, you enjoyed yourself, did you not?" He went to the door of the hall and signalled to a page, who brought wine.

Isabella laughed again and took a sip from the goblet he held out to her. "Indeed, my lord, I must admit I did."

John's smile broadened, and his voice became silky, almost caressing. "I daresay there are other things you might enjoy if you allowed yourself to do so."

She gazed up at him trying to gauge his meaning and started when he sat next to her, putting an arm around her waist. Before she could stop herself, she stiffened. He tightened his grip.

"Lady Isabella, you are indeed an innocent, aren't you? It might be a delight for me to be your tutor."

"My–?" Before she could finish, he caught her to himself, his lips on hers, his free hand sliding from her waist to her hip and down her leg, fondling her through the fine fabric of her gown.

For one brief moment, she was motionless, unable to think, unable to extricate herself, almost frozen with horror; then, as his hand continued its exploration, she came swiftly to her senses. He was treating her like a harlot. Manhandling her, and in a public place! She turned her head quickly away and pushed ineffectively at his arm. "My lord, you dishonour me to treat me so here."

John let her go so abruptly, she almost over-balanced. His voice, when he spoke, was cool. "You would rather I took you to my bedchamber?"

"No, of course not. I…" She tailed off, words failing her.

John stood, never taking his gaze from her, assessing her, judging her, and she prickled with shame beneath his stare. His voice hardened. "I see. I fear I've misjudged you, madame. And yet you danced willingly enough with me."

Isabella flushed from her neck to her veil, which was starting to come loose, sliding from her hair. When she answered him, her voice was barely above a whisper. A mistake, for John had to lean forward to hear her. "I'm…sorry, my lord, I mistook your intent. I…" She stumbled over the words. "I thought you merely wished to cheer me."

"Well, and so I did. Yet if you enjoyed the dance, surely you'll enjoy a dance of a more…intimate nature."

His eyes burned like coals, very green now, and glittering. Isabella recoiled from what she saw in them. "My lord, I thought you were just being kind."

John flashed a grin at her. "Oh, I was, sweeting. I was being very kind."

At that moment, a squire came up. John moved away a pace, and the man murmured something. John looked into the hall, grimacing, before turning back to Isabella.

"I fear this most entertaining discussion must be postponed. My mother wishes for her ladies to return to the bower. Her, er, timing, was ever out of kilter with my own."

He bowed and left her, and she pushed herself to her feet, trembling so hard she had to reach out and steady herself against the wall for a moment. She leaned against it, breathing deeply for the space of a few heartbeats before she pinned her veil on more tightly and forced her legs to carry her across the hall as though nothing untoward had happened. Joining the other women, she ignored the curious looks which met her as they left the hall. From the comments she heard, some of the women were more reluctant than others to leave the entertainment. For herself, she couldn't get away quickly enough. John had done one thing for her, though – showed her no man, no matter how pleasant he appeared at first, could really be trusted.

After that night, the queen had ensured all her ladies retired to the bower before the company became too boisterous. For this, Isabella was very grateful. John had convinced her she could join the fun but once he'd tarnished it for her, she'd retreated back inside herself, smiling when it was expected of her, saying little, avoiding notice.

However, now Twelfth Night had passed, the queen was preparing to move on. With that, and keeping a careful eye on John and any intrigues he might be involved in via her web of spies, she would have little time for aught else. It must be painful for her, Isabella thought, to know John would likely be happy to see his brother, the king, dead. At least according to the rumours, which flourished like weeds here. It seemed children were not always a blessing, at least not once they were grown.

It hadn't taken Isabella long to work out the pecking order. Marie, married to the castellan, was one of the queen's senior ladies, and, since her husband was not presently here, slept on a pallet beside Eleanor's bed at night. When the queen moved on, Marie would remain to supervise the castle and bower, and likely be grateful when her man returned, hopefully before her babe was birthed.

Of the demoiselles who dwelt in the bower at present, Isabella had come to know a few better than others. Hanild, for one, with her merry brown eyes and rich, curling hair which was constantly escaping from her braids. Pretty, cheerful Hanild was betrothed and would be wed by summer. Constance, silvery-fair, with eyes of slate grey, a ward of the court who came with a fortune for the man to whom she would eventually be given. He would doubtless pay well for the privilege; Constance would not come cheaply to marriage. Eleanor, regent in Richard's absence, would give her wardship where there was most to be gained. Constance was reed-slender, always nervous, always on edge. Barbette, another cheerful soul, was not to be with them for much longer, it was whispered. Although Barbette herself neither confirmed nor denied the rumours and seemed unperturbed by her future.

There were the older women, Eleanor's ladies who travelled with her, and who had formed a small internal clique, barely bothering to notice the bower maidens. Their talk was of their children, their menfolk, and other household matters pertaining to their service to the queen. The only one who occasionally smiled at the chatter of the younger ones was Lady Mathilde, who sometimes looked as though she would like to join them.

Then there were the maids who saw to all their needs. And, lastly, there was Rosamund, daughter of a recently deceased and extremely wealthy baron. She of the butter-blonde braids, alabaster skin and softly rounded curves, with a limpid gaze like that of a small white dove when any male was near. Beautiful, desirable, and well aware of her charms.

When men were near, no one could be sweeter than Rosamund. When in the bower where the women busied themselves with their small tasks, those same periwinkle-blue eyes looked disdainfully at her companions, spitting fire at imagined slights. The cherry-red, moistly plump lips which almost dripped honey when men were in her sights, curled with dissatisfaction when she was in the bower. Unless, of course, the queen was there to see, as she was now, in which case, Rosamund was all smiles, fawning upon Eleanor with a demeanour which slightly sickened Isabella. And, if she was not mistaken by the thin-lipped expression Eleanor wore now, the queen knew exactly how Rosamund behaved when she was not here.

As Isabella approached Eleanor with the unguents she had requested, Rosamund turned to take them from her, smiling cattily. Her lips drooped downwards as Eleanor said, "No, Rosamund, I would have Isabella serve me now. Run along, child. There are other matters for your attention."

Isabella almost shrank from the spite on Rosamund's face as the girl pushed past her and nearly stamped back to the far end of the chamber. The queen, however, ignored her, rising from the well-cushioned chair, passing her embroidery to Marie and drawing Isabella into the bedchamber. One of her other ladies, Dame Isolde, drew back the curtains, pulling them together again once Eleanor had passed through. Isabella imagined her standing on the other side as ferocious as a small hound, daring the women to try to eavesdrop.

Once inside the bedchamber, Eleanor sat on a chair beside her great, curtained bed, motioning Isabella to draw up a small stool and sit at her feet. She pulled off her rings, flexing her fingers as she did so, and held her hands out to Isabella who rubbed in the perfumed cream with small gentle movements and light pressure.

"Ah, that feels very good, child. When your hands are as old as mine, it helps to have them treated softly." She smiled as Isabella continued, working her fingers around the slightly swollen knuckles which were usually hidden by those heavy gold rings Eleanor habitually wore. As she stroked and massaged, Eleanor sat back in her chair and relaxed. Her eyes closed, and she gave a soft sigh.

A small pride glowed in Isabella, delight that her efforts were appreciated. She liked Eleanor. The woman had many burdens, Isabella realised that, yet she bore them lightly. Certainly, at times she could be sharp, yet she often took time to bestow encouraging comments on her ladies.

While she continued to work on the queen's hands and wrists, she gazed around the room. The garderobe, as far from the bed as possible, was heavily curtained. There was probably a door behind the curtain, she guessed, so no noxious vapours would offend the royal nostrils. The ladies of the bower did not use the royal garderobe. They had a privy the other side of the small landing at the top of the stairs. It was the only other room up here apart from the queen's solar, the bower, which also had two windows paned with glass, the bedchamber, and a private chamber at the far end of the bower where

Eleanor dealt with the more private concerns of her business.

Rich hangings adorned the painted walls, and the throne-like chair she sat on had thick cushions on it. The back had been covered by a heavy fur, but Eleanor was not a young woman; doubtless she found the padding necessary.

Still elegant, Isabella guessed that, in her seventies, the strain of maintaining that seemingly effortless grace cost her dear. Close to, she could see wrinkles she had barely noticed before, fanning out from Eleanor's eyes and disappearing into her wimple. There were now deep lines carved between her nose and mouth, with smaller ones feathering her lips as though, once she retreated into her private chamber, she could let down her guard and become the age she really was.

The floor rushes were strewn over with fragrant herbs, more so here than any other room in the castle, and the air was redolent with the perfume the queen wore – a blend of rose, musk, and spice. A laver and basin stood on an intricately carved table, and large chests stood against the walls. She was surprised to see screens against one wall. She was wondering what they hid when Eleanor's voice cut into her thoughts making her jump.

"Yes, indeed. My private entrance. Few know it's there, for you cannot see it from the stairs."

Isabella jerked her gaze upwards. The queen was watching her, a knowing smile on her lips. "And how are you settling in, child? I trust you're feeling more comfortable than on the day you arrived."

She blushed, remembering the mud-covered garments which had been ruined almost beyond hope. She'd been too embarrassed to give them to the laundress, so had gifted them to Evelina, who received them rapturously.

Evelina had settled in as one born here, re-maining with Isabella as a maid of the bower and carrying on a hopeful courtship with one of the more senior servants. Evelina was making the most of her opportunity and had confided that she hoped marriage would improve her own status. When Isabella had asked if she loved him, she'd screwed her face up and said, "Love? Maybe. At any rate, I like him. He's good to look at and treats me well."

Eleanor coughed, dragging her thoughts back to where she was, and Isabella smiled; for all the petty annoyances the other girls complained about, for one such as her, the freedom was a relief. No frowning Adelaide watching her every move, no bad-tempered husband demanding the use of her body, complaining because she still had not conceived from the seed which he so frequently and brutally sowed. No bruises. And the warmth here was wonderful. Braziers burned in every room.

She could look out of the glazed windows without being recalled to her duties, and although kept busy, she found time to lose herself between the pages of a book as often as she might spare a moment. The queen encouraged her ladies to read, the better to entertain her when she required it. If Isabella could not become a nun, she thought she'd be content to continue serving this woman.

Eleanor gave her another of those disconcerting knowing looks. "An improvement on your previous situation, I think."

"Oh, yes, my lady." She hesitated, wondering if she dare ask for permanence.

The queen gave another small sigh. "I'm glad, child. I am aware of the character of your former husband, and of his mother. I imagine life was not easy for you. Still, we all, even I, have to do our duty." She motioned Isabella to stop her labours and leaned forwards, taking the young face before her in her hands, looking deeply into her eyes. Isabella stared back fascinated. Eleanor had almost cat-like eyes, slightly slanted, sometimes green, sometimes almost hazel, sometimes with a hint of gold. Always knowing.

Eleanor let go and sat back, steepling her hands in a manner that reminded Isabella of the Abbess Hildegarde, saying, "And it has been pleasant to have your pretty face and sweet nature enhancing my bower. Almost, I would wish to keep you beside me."

Isabella's heart sank at the words. Was she to be sent back to her father? Not for anything did she want that. The queen continued, "But, in truth, I have a position which I think you will enjoy." She laughed at the look of hope which leapt back into Isabella's face. "Did you think I would send you back to your father?" Isabella nodded, and Eleanor's laugh rang out again. "Not for worlds, child. Your father had the temerity to, let us say, cross swords, metaphorically speaking of course, with me on more than one occasion. He has sent for you, for he wishes to arrange another marriage. What do you say to that?"

Isabella shrank. The queen patted her cheek. "Never worry, child. I find myself much inclined to disoblige him in this matter. And, indeed, the knight I have in mind for you will most certainly annoy him."

Isabella remained almost frozen where she was. A numbness crept over her, a dullness such as she had felt almost perpetually during her time with Baldwin. At least it was better than the terror she felt when he was angered.

She slumped and withdrew back into herself, for it seemed whether her father or the queen, she would marry to oblige one of them. Unless... She nerved herself to speak.

"I had hoped," her voice trembled slightly, "to maybe take the veil?" She knew her eyes were beseeching; she hoped Eleanor would take pity on her.

"Ah, child, how many women have wished that choice was open to them. But I have need of you. And, I fancy, you'll find this knight a very different proposition from your previous husband."

No! She would never...could never... She clasped her hands in front of her in a gesture of supplication and tried again. "My lady, I would rather by far continue to serve you. Indeed, I would be happy to spend my life in your service."

The queen leaned forward again, almost confidingly, those eyes fixed, watching her intently. "You say you wish to serve me?" Isabella nodded. "Then oblige me in this, child, for it is my will concerning you. And indeed," she gave an encouraging smile, "you'll find your new life to be a pleasant one. I cannot promise many things, but that I do swear to you."

Isabella bit her lip and blinked hard to stop the tears welling in her eyes from falling. "Your grace," she said, bowing her head submissively.

Eleanor patted her cheek again. "You do not believe me, but you would do well to trust me. I've had much time to learn about men; to learn well. The husband I would give you will not be wealthy. Indeed, your bride-portion will be considered rich by him. But, I do not think you're a woman who desires wealth and high station even though it's what you've been accustomed to. I believe you would find happiness in lesser things. And, Sir Giles has been promised an heiress."

She clapped her hands. "Come, child, smile for me. And, if you cannot find pleasure in the thought at the moment, consider how much better my choice will be than any man your father has in mind." Her eyes twinkled, and she suddenly looked ten years younger. "And imagine how angry your father will be to find your new marriage will neither be of his own arranging nor bring him the alliances he would wish. Let that, at least, give you some satisfaction. Now, off with you, Isabella. Try not to look so hopeless, child. It shows a deeply unflattering lack of faith in my judgement. Send Marie in to me."

Isabella had no choice. She forced a smile to her lips and went back through the curtain, telling Marie the queen required her.

Marie must have guessed what had passed between them, for she pulled her discreetly to one side, whispering, "You must be pleased, Isabella. He will suit you admirably."

Marie knew who he was then? At least, now, Isabella might be able to winkle the information out from her, since Eleanor had either forgotten or omitted to tell her just who this husband of hers was to be.

Isabella set another humourless curve to her mouth and returned to her place in the bower where Rosamund eyed her, wrinkling her nose.

"You were gone an age, Bella." She tittered. "We began to think her grace had dismissed you, did we not? Indeed, you seem so glum, perchance we were right."

Rosamund looked around her for support from the other damsels. None came; their faces were averted, heads bent industriously over their stitching. If their ears quivered, they did not betray it by so much as an upward glance, for she was not popular. Not that it seemed to bother her overmuch.

Isabella eyed her narrowly. "Not at all, Rosamund." She found pride was helping her rise above her misery and fixed the girl with a glittering smile. "Her grace was just telling me something of great import, and I'm assured she has my best welfare at heart."

She wished she'd remained silent. Now, all the girls focussed their attention on her, and she found herself wondering how much she wanted to tell them; indeed, how much she was allowed to tell them. And, after all, she did not know who this knight was yet, which would not impress Rosamund much.

She smiled slyly, deciding to at least get some pleasure from annoying the simpering blonde. "But, Rosamund, I don't know whether I'm permitted to share it with anyone yet."

Rosamund's eyes shot daggers at her, then her lip curled. "Oh well!" She tossed her head as though she did not give a fig. "I expect your 'news' is nothing that would interest me, anyway." And she turned her back and flounced to the window.

"And good riddance." It was said so quietly that Rosamund would not have heard it, but Isabella did and turned her head to catch a faint smile on the face of Lady Mathilde.

Isabella smiled back. Mathilde had found little to say to her until now, but she came and sat beside Isabella, murmuring, "The queen has told you of your marriage, then?"

Great Heaven, was she the only one not to have already known? Apart from Rosamund, all the other damsels and ladies wore knowing looks. Well, mayhap now she would find out who it was she would be tied to. Not that it would make a difference. Were not all men alike? Even so, she'd survived Baldwin and that witch of a mother of his. Maybe, this time, at least, she would be lady of her own castle. Or manor house.

She risked another smile, trying to ignore a feeling like that of a stone sinking heavily into the pit of her stomach, and turned to the older woman shyly. "What do you know of him?" Best not to say she herself did not even know who he was. Nothing would be forthcoming if they guessed that.

Mathilde put down the psalter she was holding and closed her eyes as though recalling pleasant memories. "He has hair as black as night." She sighed and opened them again. "His eyes are like slate in winter, but there is a twinkle lurking in their depths if you watch for it, unless he's angered. Ah, if he's angered, they seem to flash fire." Her lips curved in reminiscence, and it was clear to Isabella that, whoever this knight was, Mathilde held a candle for him.

Marie joined them. "He's tall and well built, and if not precisely handsome, he has a presence about him."

Mathilde seemed to drag herself back to the present with an effort. "Indeed, I would say he has something more attractive than mere looks. And he is puissant. You are fortunate, Isabella." Still with a slightly distracted air, she picked up her psalter and left them.

Fortunate? Isabella did not think so. And as for eyes that flashed with anger – the stone in her stomach turned to ice, and she clasped her hands tightly together to try to still their trembling. And still she did not know who he was, nor yet anything relevant about him, but Rosamund was watching now from the window seat and not for anything would Isabella give her the satisfaction of her own ignorance.

Depression settled over her like a dark cloud, and she picked up her embroidery and stitched as though her life depended on it. Anything to shut out thought.

Later, that night, when all were abed, she lay on her pallet in the bower considering her options – which, after all, were none too many. She could survive this. She would. Besides, once he found she was unfruitful, for which Baldwin had so often cursed her, like enough he would want the marriage annulled. She stared into the darkness. What man wanted a woman who could not bear him children? A tear, unbidden, slid down past her ear and into the sheet beneath her. Children would have made anything bearable. Baldwin had certainly tried to remedy her barrenness, claiming her so often he left her sore and dreading his attentions, cursing her for the dried-up thorn she was. Angular, sharp and infertile, he had called her; a pity he'd not felt like that before, for if he had, he would not have married her in the first place.

Almost, she wanted to pray, but she would not put her faith in God, for had He not mocked her by freeing her only to imprison her again? She sighed deeply and heard a tsk of annoyance from Rosamund's direction before she turned on her side and tried to sleep.

CHAPTER 7

January 1195

Giles de Soutenay swore and strode from the courtyard, where he had greeted his brother Ralph on his arrival, to the house, throwing his cloak carelessly on the floor and planting himself on a bench before the hearth. Ralph followed him, amused, pausing to take the cup of ale Giles' steward was holding out to him before placing himself firmly between Giles and the warmth of the fire. Giles glared at his older brother. "I had believed the queen to be in Fontevrault!"

Ralph's broad, genial face assumed an expression of injured innocence briefly before grinning. "She was."

"Then what is she doing at Berkhamsted?"

Ralph rolled his eyes. "You'd be as likely to know that as I. At any rate, she'll be returning soon." He thrust the missive from Eleanor back under Giles' nose, chuckling. "You may as well open it. It won't bite."

Giles remained on the bench, chin jutting, making no move to take the letter. Ralph dumped it on a stool before him, then pulled a chair closer to the flames and made himself comfortable. Giles picked the thing up with all the reluctance of a man being handed an angry snake. "If it has anything to do with John, it well might," he said with disfavour.

Ralph hid a smirk. Giles' reaction to the news was exactly what he'd expected. His younger brother's small unadorned hall usually encouraged over-familiarity from his household, but today, even the steward had kept his distance when he'd seen Giles' face. Ralph stretched his legs out in front of him. Giles was a decade younger, the brothers who came between them having died some years back. Had they not, there would have been no manor for Giles, but Ralph had plenty and, unlike many, was almost paternally fond of his sibling and had willingly given him this small manor.

He gestured to the letter. "Well, you'll not know by staring at it. Open it; it may put your fears to rest, or it may confirm them. There's only one way to find out." He snorted. "If you only knew the trouble I had keeping Maude from opening it for you."

"Maude would have been welcome to it." Giles broke the seal, his expression one of deep mistrust. "She wishes me to attend on her at court as soon as I may arrange it." His tone was neutral and he gazed pensively into the fire.

"No more?"

"Nothing. Did she give it to you herself?"

"Nay, one of her ladies brought it to Maude ere we left the court. We've been home but two days; I came to you as soon as I'd caught my breath."

Giles ran a hand through his hair, his face troubled. "I've done my annual service to John. He usually prefers me to stay out of his sight apart from that, and I can't say the feeling isn't mutual. What's the fool been up to now?"

Ralph frowned. "John's no fool, Giles."

"No? Then why does he turn men against him?"

Ralph mused for a moment then nodded. "Aye, you're in the right of it there. You want me to bear you company, little brother?"

Giles threw him a look of gratitude. "I confess, I like not the company at court; yours would help leaven it. Yes, Ralph, I'd be glad of you, if Maude will spare you again so soon after your return."

Ralph choked back a laugh, spraying Giles' plain tunic with the ale he'd been drinking. Giles got up and thumped him on the back as he wiped his mouth, grateful he'd missed his own elaborately embroidered blue one. "Spare me? Not she! She's already declared her intention to return with us."

"Has she naught else to meddle with? I would have thought she'd be glad to be home from that hotbed of innuendo and gossip."

"Who, Maude?" Ralph's eyes gleamed with mischief. "When her grace has entrusted her with news which she does not yet know?" He indicated the letter Giles still held. "You know her better than that, brother."

Giles shrugged. "Ah well, belike she'll improve the company for us, at any rate."

"That she will. How long before you can be ready? May as well get it over with."

"I suppose within the hour, if I must. As you say, best to get it done or, doubtless, it will hang over me like that legendary sword of Damocles. I may as well know the worst."

Ralph gave another bray of laughter. "I did not have you as a man who'd expect the worst."

Giles responded with a tight smile. "If John is involved, it would be folly to expect aught else. Still," he brightened, "at least there'll be time to take my ease at your hearth on the way."

"With Maude on hot coals to see why you've been summoned? Don't expect more than time to grab a cup of ale before she has us on our way."

With Maude and Ralph accompanying Giles, at least the journey was bearable, although the weather was inclement. Maude's light chatter kept the worst of his concerns at bay at first, although, as they neared the castle, she began to probe as to why the queen might want him. All her teasing was to no avail, for Giles neither would nor could hazard a guess.

Once at the castle, he had to cool his heels for several days until the call to present himself finally came. He tugged the neck of his shirt, which seemed suddenly to be choking him as he stood before Eleanor in her privy chamber and resisted the urge to fidget like some callow youth.

"Well now, de Soutenay." She rested her chin on her steepled fingers. Giles waited patiently.

The years had been kind to her – he supposed, though, she had fought it with all the unguents money could buy. Yet, she looked her age close to; her face was wrinkled and creases fanned outwards from her eyes – eyes which still held something of a youthful gleam. Close to, the depredations of time were more obvious, with folds around her lips and deep furrows on the part of her brow which showed beneath the wimple she wore.

Eleanor raised her eyes and caught him staring. Embarrassed, he dropped his gaze, studying the floor rushes.

"I believe I promised you an heiress, did I not?" Giles looked upwards quickly, startled, as she gave a soft laugh. "Don't look so surprised. You did not think I had forgotten, did you?"

He swallowed. "I…er…that is–"

She cut in, her voice half amused, yet with a hint of asperity. "De Soutenay, if I had reached my dotage, do you really think I would still be wielding the power I have?"

He gaped speechlessly at her.

Eleanor's lips curved in a sardonic smile. "I see."

Giles' heart sank. Foiled by his lack of courtly manners. A pity his usual quick wits and ability to dissemble had failed him now. He was out of practice, he supposed. That John wanted him at court only once a year these days had suited him, but being out of court circles had cost him some of his hard-won skills. Still, he consoled himself, this heiress who had been briefly dangled before him and now looked to be snatched away would probably not have been the sort of woman he wished to live with. For it was certain, the most desirable would go to those of higher rank and importance than he.

Eleanor rapped on his forehead with her index finger. "You have pre-empted me wrongly again. Of a surety, you are no courtier." She put her head on one side, holding his attention now, the enigmatic eyes searching his face.

He groaned inwardly, hoping others could not read his thoughts so easily.

She laughed again and looked suddenly ten years younger. "Oh, fret not, de Soutenay, I cannot read your thoughts, but I have trained myself to read faces. And," she paused, examining her rings thoughtfully, "it has proved a most useful art." Smiling again, she said, "I'm sorry, de Soutenay, I'm afraid I can seldom resist the urge to tease. It's time I put you out of your misery. I have found an heiress for you. I've not yet been able to secure the king's approval, but he trusts my judgement; he will not object.

"Anyway, let us return to the subject in hand. Of a surety, she is not overly wealthy, nor overly beautiful." She studied him, and he tried to keep his emotions from his face. "Oh, well done. Much better. Now, of course, you did not expect to be given a woman with castles or extensive lands. And besides, the cost of that would have beggared you. But do not be disappointed; the girl is comely enough. She has no squint, she's not horse-faced, and I do believe she has all her teeth. She also has lands double in size to your own. She is no maid, but a young widow."

Well, that was no problem. Giles did not want a fourteen-year-old virgin in his bed.

"Her father still lives."

That jolted him, and he tried to conceal his shock while those greenish eyes laughed at him. Giles completely understood why John always seemed slightly ill-at-ease in her presence. She could make a grown man feel like a foolish boy.

"He had in mind to reclaim both his daughter and her dower and bride-gift. I have dissuaded him." She tapped her nails on the desk before her. From her expression, Giles surmised that had not displeased her. "Of course, you'll have to pay for the privilege, for the money must come from somewhere, but trust me – within two years, you'll have reaped the cost back from her lands."

Giles hoped so. He had enough to run his estate and household, but there was little left for luxuries.

"I assure you, you will. Think of this as an investment."

He hid a nagging worry that he was so transparent to her. But how she could read him so easily? Doubtless the years of judging those who came before her had trained her in the art, he supposed.

But, he could not ignore his other concern; the man still lived. Giles looked down as a nagging suspicion assailed him, then raised his gaze to Eleanor again. "Her father will not make difficulties?"

"He will not!" Her mouth snapped shut, and Giles felt a moment's sympathy for him. Whatever the girl's father had done to irk Eleanor, he would pay for it. But now, Giles grappled with this new information. "And if he should beget another child?"

"It will make no difference. His daughter's bride-gift will not be returned to him, neither will her dowry. If he does manage," she gave him a knowing look, "to produce a son, which I doubt, you will not receive his wealth at his death, but his daughter's lands will be, by then, legally joined to yours and will remain so. I will have the deeds tied so tight they will never be unknotted."

She paused, eyeing her well-kept nails with a satisfied air, and Giles made a mental note never to disappoint her.

"And, if he does not, all his lands, except that which is owned by the crown, will eventually be yours. Does that satisfy you?"

He nodded. How could it not? In one fell swoop he would treble his lands and income. But where were these lands? Near enough that he would be easily able to add them to his own? Or would there be the cost of a second steward?

Eleanor appraised him with a cool smile. "Almost, I can see the workings of your brain," she remarked. "Very well, I shall put you out of your misery. She is le Gris' daughter, Baldwin FitzAubrey's widow."

He was digesting that when she spoke again. "Oh, and, de Soutenay, do not fear that her father will make problems. He is lucky certain things cannot be proven against him. That strutting peacock is not near so important as he thinks he is, else it would be more than his daughter's marriage he would have to worry about."

Giles swallowed as though he had a stone lodged in his throat. And what of the girl? A fine start if his new wife had something to hold against him before the marriage was even con-summated. What hope for amity in his home if that were the case? Try as he might, he could not raise enthusiasm for this match; however, the queen expected gratitude, so he managed to force something which might be construed as a smile to his lips.

"By the by," she continued. He gave her an enquiring look. "It's good that you're my son's liege man; however, I remind you to take care he does not embroil you in any treasonous plots, for he'll throw you to the wolves to save himself."

Giles had no worries about that; nothing could be less likely. John had no desire for his service except for the one thing that bound them. Indeed, he loathed the fact that Giles was the only one whom he could trust, the only one who could help him. Of a certainty, had the once yearly visits to court not been necessary, Giles might have been invisible for all John wanted him. Their unwilling, shared secret had freed him from all other obligations except for the necessary service, and he was glad. Working for John had soiled him. He gave her stare for stare and said, "It would be unlikely, Madame."

She nodded her understanding, eyes glinting. "A pity. If I thought you were much in his presence, I might ask you to send word to me if he were about to entangle himself in something unwise."

Giles felt a cold shudder run down his spine. To be a spy for Eleanor against John – should John discover that, his life would not be worth a clipped penny; pray God she would not decide it was possible.

A knock on the outer chamber door made the queen turn her head swiftly. Quiet voices could be heard and the door between the two rooms was opened. A knight whom Giles did not recognise entered, bowing, and her attention was lost. She waved him away with a dismissive, "We will speak more, later. Go now."

"Your grace." He bent his knee, then left, cudgelling his brains, trying to recall exactly what FitzAubrey's wife looked like.

He must have been at the marriage, but that had surely been some three years ago or more. He'd attended several around that time in John's wake. In most cases, the brides had been barely more than children, and his distaste for such couplings meant he'd paid scant attention to them, unlike his companions, whose behaviour disgusted him. Doubtless, she'd be changed by now, anyway. How old would she be? Seventeen? Eighteen?

As he moved into the other room, he was aware of a group of the queen's ladies observing him. Was his heiress among them? He swept his gaze quickly around the chamber.

One of them, a little plump dove of a girl with pink cheeks and eyes of periwinkle blue, darted to open the door for him, fluttering a wide-eyed gaze from beneath unlikely black lashes, butter-blonde braids hanging to her waist, covered lightly with a veil of blue silk. Pretty enough, but she looked to be inane. If she were the one, he would find her a disappointment. Worse, she was the type who would wish for frequent expensive trinkets.

He strode past her, noticing the inviting moue she formed with moist pink lips. Giles hoped it would not be her.

How long would it be before he could meet his new bride? He had no idea, for now he was gone from the queen's sight, how long before she bethought to set things in motion. On the other hand, he had underestimated Eleanor before.

Lost in his thoughts, he paused as the entrance of the great hall loomed before him. Maude would be waiting for him, and he knew she would be almost quivering with impatience. Fighting the grin which tugged at the corner of his mouth, he rearranged his features into those of a man who had been given a death sentence, unable to resist the temptation to tease her.

CHAPTER 8

Speculating as he moved up the stone stairs in obedience to the latest summons to Eleanor's apartments, Giles felt torn between relief that she had not forgotten him, and concern. Roger le Gris! Giles knew him – or, more accurately, knew of him. He vaguely called to mind that he'd accompanied John to the man's manor some years ago, remembering him as a disdainful, posturing braggart. Elegant, yes, but his brains had all the sharpness of a blunted axe.

Certainly, Giles recalled Roger sneering at him down that large nose of his, full of his own importance. Had his wits been as good as his opinion of himself, Roger might have been dangerous. Certainly, too, there had been some plot afoot – but, with John, when wasn't there?

Of the household, Giles could remember nothing, neither family nor yet surroundings. And, if John had been scheming, Giles would not have been privy to those details either.

Doubtless, Roger had been conniving with John. Doubtless too, that John had been unimpressed, for, after dining with him, they had ridden out almost immediately.

Giles racked his brains trying to remember either wife or daughter but had only the vaguest impression of a whey-faced woman of almost wraith-like qualities. That must have been Roger's wife. He hoped the daughter would have more substance.

He did, however, recall Baldwin FitzAubrey. Charming and suave, but Giles had taken care to remain downwind of him on the few occasions they met for his sour breath was enough to fell a man at ten paces. And beneath the outward pleasantries, Giles had seen a man quick to lash out and blame others. A man of violence. Not someone he would care to have as a friend; equally, not someone he would wish for an enemy.

He had rarely crossed paths with him and taken care never to cross swords. Baldwin's first wife had died some years ago. He remembered her as a mouse-like woman, who crept timidly around the place barely speaking. What would this young widow be like?

In truth, she might be less than happy to be wed to a mere knight after being the wife of a wealthy baron. Or was he so wealthy? Giles recalled a certain profligacy. It was possible the castle coffers were empty. Whether that were the case or not, she must find Giles a more pleasant option – and, at least, he would not poison her with his fumes, although his twenty-three tenants and five hundred acres would scarce impress either le Gris or his daughter.

Giles was happy enough not to be gaining a castle with his new wife. A man of simple tastes, he was content with his one manor, although the revenue from hers would certainly not come amiss. God grant her lands were in good heart, although with Baldwin as her husband, he had cause to doubt it.

No matter, he would attend to that all in good time. For now, he had a bride to meet.

What would it be like to be wed? he mused. It was long since he'd had a woman for, although there had been occasional amours in the past few years – and what man had not had those? – once he had outgrown his youth, the thought of a furtive coupling in the darkness of the great hall, both crammed onto a single straw mattress, had lost its allure. As for the whores who offered their services in the royal courts so freely, when Eleanor was not there, at least – somehow, the thought of paying good coin for the favours they spread about so widely did not appeal.

Giles wanted a marriage like Ralph and Maude possessed. Ah, now that was the sort of gold that made all else seem but dross. But those two were unusual, for theirs had been a love match. The unlikely truth was that his bluff, genial brother had been struck dumb by his first sight of Maude, and by great good fortune, not only had Maude's parents welcomed the match but Maude, sixteen and not yet betrothed, had lost her heart to Ralph's less than elegant wooing.

Although, at the time, Giles had teased Ralph mercilessly, the contentment he saw between them had made him hope for a similar happiness. He had not bargained on Eleanor herself taking an interest in his welfare.

Still, for better or worse, the dice had been cast. He straightened his shoulders and went to meet his fate, fidgeting as he waited outside the queen's privy chamber. Was he ready for this? He snorted. And if he did not like his chosen mate? Why, then, he would do as he had already determined and seek solace elsewhere. But, for the sake of a peaceful life, he hoped this young woman would at least be pleasant enough to live with.

As he prepared to take a step forward, the door opened, and a woman in, he supposed, her mid-twenties peered out. He suffered a jolt to the pit of his stomach when he realised she was pregnant, then jeered at himself for an oaf. Did he really think Eleanor would foist some other man's unborn brat on him? *Get a grip, man!*

She laughed up at him. "My lord, you did not think...? I swear you looked grim enough to do murder when you clapped eyes on me. I am Marie of Brent, come to take you to meet your betrothed." She curtseyed and he inclined his head, feeling like the fool he must appear, and followed her into the small room.

At first, he thought it was empty. Almost, he felt relieved. Hell's teeth, he was as nervous as a maiden. But then, it was no small thing to meet your future wife for the first time.

Then, he saw her. In green, with a yellow un-dergown, she stood in the window embrasure, gazing out as though she did not much like what she saw, turning as he approached her, watching him with a face that seemed carved from stone.

As Marie introduced him, she dropped into a curtsey, and he took her hand, lifting it to his lips, just barely grazing the cold skin before raising her up.

"My lady, I am most pleased to make your acquaintance." *Banal*, he thought. *Yet what else is there to be said?*

She gave him a small, chilly smile, barely quirking her lips, and eyed him without expression. It was impossible to read her thoughts. She stood at medium height, and he would judge her hair to be brown if her brows and lashes were anything to go by. Brown, too, were her eyes, but not just any brown; lucid and clear, almost the colour of dark honey. Her nose was not over-long, and straight, her lips a rosy pink. Had there been any warmth in her gaze, she would have been appealing; as it was, she seemed like some statue.

"My lord de Soutenay, the pleasure is mine." Her voice was as cool as her expression. Giles' spirits sank a little lower. How would this effigy bring any warmth to his hearth? Perhaps the difference in their circumstances was not to be overcome so easily. No matter if her father did not like it, but if the woman herself did not… Giles could not see himself getting any pleasure from this alliance.

He stood like an effigy himself. With such a discouraging reception, he was lost for words and took refuge in another platitude. Marie, watching the pair of them, took charge, herding them to a seat, bidding them sit, fetching wine.

After what seemed like several candle notches worth of time, Giles managed to get his befuddled wits into order.

"Madame, I fear this match is not to your liking." Better to have it out in the open. "If I'm so abhorrent to you, I will not hold you to it."

She lifted her head, looking at him as though she had not heard him before quirking her lips into what he assumed passed for a smile. A little colour washed into her cheeks, and her voice trembled slightly as she said, "Not at all, my lord. I am content enough. If it is your will we be wed, I shall endeavour to give you no cause for complaint."

By all the saints! he thought. *Am I really expected to live with this?* Then the import of her words hit him. She had, after all, been wed to that louse, FitzAubrey, he recalled. Knowing how the hellspawn treated his mistresses, even his horses, small wonder if she was afraid. She probably expected more of the same from him. And in that moment, he felt a nudge of hope. This thing might work if only he were able to show her she could trust him.

When he was younger, he'd once acquired a badly treated horse which shied away from all touch. It had taken a long time to win the mare over. Time and patience. These things he had.

Maybe he could break – no, not break, melt – through her defences. Eventually.

With this in his mind, he relaxed, and set out to at least thaw a little of the ice in the room. He poured a cup of wine, handing it to her with grace, smiling at her, saying, "We are in a cleft stick, you and I, but many have been wed knowing each other as little and have made a good fist of things. Think you we might do the same?"

She raised her eyes again; he noted she did not look much at him, only when he spoke. And only until she had answered, when she dropped her gaze back to her lap again. "I will endeavour to please you, my lord."

Her voice was still expressionless, as was her face. He refused to be daunted; what had probably been done to her could not be undone in a short time. Indeed, he acknowledged, it would require understanding as well as patience. He hoped he had enough of both.

Giles poured a cup of wine for Marie, who accompanied Isabella but did not remain close enough to hear the conversation, and handed her the brimming cup. She took it from him, but he could see her discomfort. Hardly surprising; even without being able to hear their words, the tension in the room was palpable. She probably felt as awkward as the pair of them.

Taking the remaining cup, he poured wine for himself and took a long draught before noticing Isabella had not touched hers.

"My lady, do drink. I think you'll find it puts fresh heart into you." He smiled confidingly at her, willing her to smile back.

He was unsuccessful. The straight lips barely quivered, but she did take a small sip, then another. He tried again. "I'm sure this awkwardness is quite natural between two who have never met."

"Oh, but we have." Her unexpected response startled him, and he steadied himself quickly before he could spill his wine like some half-trained page.

This time, she did assay a small smile. "You do not remember me, my lord?"

Had he been to her wedding? He was sure he must have but try as he might, he could not recall seeing her before. He bowed to hide his discomfiture. "I regret, the nature of any previous meeting eludes me for the moment."

"Indeed, I have changed somewhat since then. We have met twice," the bland voice continued. Was she taking pleasure in his lapse? He eyed her covertly – no, he thought not.

Twice? And she remembered both times? He felt utterly foolish but her face was completely unfamiliar to him. "I'm afraid you'll have to remind me, my lady. It's most discourteous, but I admit, I cannot place you at all."

"The first time," she said, her voice still as dispassionate as a chirurgeon, "I was but eight. Lord John had called on my father. I was in the hall of our manor and he gave me a silver ring. I thought he was the kindest, most handsome man I had ever seen."

He still did not remember, but was not surprised at her impression of John, who did have a way with children, for some strange reason. "And I was there?"

"Yes, my lord, but you did not speak. I thought you were displeased with me."

For a moment, he thought he saw a flash of something in her eyes, but decided he'd been mistaken. He shook his head. "I'm sorry. I'm afraid I still do not remember."

She looked him full in the face. This time, he was sure he saw a spark of resentment, swiftly hidden. "You accompanied him to my wedding, some six years later. He was not so kind, that day."

No, he wouldn't be. Giles was well aware how lascivious John could be at the weddings of his barons. He thought he could place her now. Her hair loosed around her face, her eyes terrified, chewing her lip with nerves. His gorge had risen watching FitzAubrey's attitude, knowing he would bed such a child without waiting for her to be grown, and not with gentleness. No wonder she did not now look forward to their approaching nuptials.

At the time, he realised, he would have eschewed the bedding ceremony and averted his eyes when the proof of her virginity was displayed the next morning, the sheet hung on the wall for all to see. He had ever found those occasions distasteful, especially when the brides were so young. He cudgelled his brain but could not quite recall which year it would have been. He had not thought it more than two or three years back but he must be wrong; judging by her appearance, he'd guess her to be at least eighteen. Not a child, thankfully.

He felt sympathy for her, knowing her former life must not have been easy, and touched her face gently, stroking his fingers down the contour of her cheeks. She blinked rapidly, and he felt a tremor run through her, but she did not flinch. She had courage, then. Good.

"My lady, I find I do recall you, after all. My apologies for my slowness. I believe your last husband may not have treated you as kindly as he might." *An understatement, belike.* "However, I promise you will find I am no FitzAubrey. I give you my word here and now that I will not use you as I suspect he has done."

She caught her breath and bit her lip like the scared fourteen-year-old she had been, then she dropped her gaze back down, almost whispering, "I thank you, my lord. You are kind."

Giles, too, had been holding his breath, and released it quietly, relieved that he'd made a breakthrough. Just a tiny one, perhaps, but with time and gentleness, he thought, just maybe, they could have a future together. And, under the circumstances, she'd be better off with him than some of the others who had doubtless been sniffing around her. It would do. For now.

He tossed back the last of his wine, replaced his cup on the table and took his leave of her, raising her to her feet and touching his lips to her hand. It felt cool and quivered slightly. No matter. He would not press her.

He turned back to the door and was about to take his leave when he suddenly recalled the fact he had given his betrothed no token. Frowning, he tugged at the ring he wore on the small finger of his left hand. He stood undecided for a moment, rubbing his thumb over the garnet set in the smooth gold, for it was the ring his father had commissioned for his knighting and therefore precious to him, but he must give his bride some gift and he had nothing else suitable.

Making his mind up, he turned back to Isabella and knelt before her, holding out his hand for hers. She let him take it and watched impassively as he pushed it over the knuckle of her thumb. Her fingers were too slender for such a heavy ring and even on her thumb, it hung loose.

"A betrothal ring, my lady. I pray you keep it safe; it was a gift from my father."

He rose, pressed another kiss onto the back of her hand, ran his fingers over her cheek once more and was gone.

Left alone, she twisted the ring round and round on her thumb. It felt strange there, like a manacle. She would have to wind thread around it to stop it slipping off. Much as she found it uncomfortable, it would not do to mislay it. It would be a bad start to wedded life if she lost it and incurred his wrath.

She could still feel the caress of his fingers on her cheeks. He had been gentle – but so had Baldwin when he'd first come to speak to her father. She could not allow herself to hope, for to hope would be to be disappointed. And indeed, she was too numb to feel anything – mayhap she truly was as cold as Baldwin had accused her of being.

Marie, having shut the door behind Giles, came and took both her hands, giving her a look which spoke volumes. Isabella shut her eyes before the moisture behind her lashes could escape.

"Isabella, you need to listen to me. I know you were unhappily wed before. I'm aware you have fears – and rightly so. Now, I know little of the man, but his brother, Ralph de Soutenay, is a most gentle lord to his wife. He's renowned for being uxorious. Some mock him for it, but most envy the happiness which emanates from the both of them like a cloud of content. It's likely that brother takes after brother, for by all accounts, their father was of the same ilk.

"And it's not as though he's old; I'd guess him to be in his early thirties. Fifteen or so years is not such a large gap. My Saer is nigh on eighteen years older than I, and you know how fond I am of him. Things could be so much worse for you."

She paused, then took Isabella by the shoulders and shook her lightly. Isabella offered no resistance. "Bella, heed my words. If you make an effort to find the man, you may be happier than many women. However, if you persist in remaining so distant, you may be dooming yourself before the knot is even tied. Sir Giles may well be kindly, indeed, I expect he is, but no man will be patient forever."

She shook her again. "Bella! Do you hear what I say? I– Oof!" She broke off and bent double, wrapping her arms across her middle.

Isabella came back to her senses instantly, leaping up to help Marie, aiding her to the settle and watching her anxiously.

Marie smiled faintly. "It's only the babe."

Isabella felt her already white face blanch a shade lighter. "It's coming? Is it not too early?"

Marie, seemingly recovered, sat upright again, giving an unexpected chuckle. "He kicked me. Hard. I do believe this child will be a puissant knight. Saer will be pleased." She chuckled again. "Take that frightened look off your face, Isabella. He is not due for at least two months; I would not be here else." She took Isabella's hand and placed it on her middle. "Can you feel him?"

Isabella felt a sharp jolt beneath her hand. "He is indeed a strong one. You're sure it will be a boy?"

"With a kick like that, it's to be hoped so, for if not, it must be a mule I'm harbouring. And Dame Gudrun has swung a wedding ring over him; she assures me the babe is a boy. I'll be black and blue inside if this keeps up."

Isabella was conscious of relief. She had no experience of childbirth but she thought that this early, there was more risk to mother and child. With the first genuine smile she'd bestowed on anyone that day, she gladly held Marie's arm as they left the chamber.

As they rose to go back into the bower, Isabella did not catch the sly look of satisfaction on Marie's face. Concerned by Isabella's lowness of spirits, she had insisted on accompanying her, unsure of how she would react. Her overriding impulse at first had been to shore up Isabella's fortitude. Perchance her presence had helped, but when de Soutenay left, Isabella was still so withdrawn. It would not do.

The child had indeed kicked – not when Marie had yelped, but, by good fortune, when Isabella's hand touched her belly. The first time was a ruse. Marie had wished to give Isabella's thoughts a new direction and take the frozen look from her face before she had to face the other women. She had racked her brains for a way to distract her. This was all she could come up with. It had worked; the colour was back in Isabella's cheeks, a more natural smile on her lips. She linked arms companionably as they returned to the inner chamber.

CHAPTER 9

Isabella woke on the morn of her wedding, dry of mouth and sick at heart, to Barbette's urgent shaking. Had she really slept? The last she remembered was lying on her narrow pallet, eyes wide open, unable to think, unable to sleep. And now, she tried to focus her bleary gaze in the thin early-morning light which did little to cheer the room.

"Wake up, Isabella! Come, there's much to do. Would you be late for your own wedding?"

Late? She'd happily miss the whole ceremony! She sat reluctantly as Barbette whisked the blanket from about her and some of the maids lugged steaming pails of water into the room.

Hanild was sprinkling rose oil into the round padded tub. The sweet scent filled the air, and Barbette sniffed rapturously as she urged Isabella towards it. Barbette and Constance stripped the shift from her and ushered her into the tub.

"Too hot?" asked Marie, as Isabella dipped her foot into the water, wincing. She shook her head. In fact, it was uncomfortably overheated, but she cared too little to bother complaining.

"Today it's your turn to be served." Hanild laughed, her eyes twinkling. She rolled her sleeves up and began to rinse Isabella's hair with rose-water, rubbing it dry with a piece of linen so vigorously that Isabella squeaked in protest.

Barbette held out a soft linen towel, and Isabella emerged, dripping, from the tub and was enveloped in it. She dried herself, and Hanild brought a mantle to wrap around her as Barbette chivvied her to a stool.

"Now, hold out your hands," Constance commanded.

Wordlessly, Isabella obeyed, and Constance knelt before her. Even she was pink-faced and smiling today.

Isabella felt like a wraith amongst the frivolity, as Constance massaged her hands with perfumed cream and buffed her nails. Barbette continued to rub her hair until it had stopped dripping, then combed it through with her own treasured ivory comb, and Hanild took a rich, ruby-red fine wool gown and rose-pink linen undergown from the clothing pole.

Isabella looked at it listlessly. The queen had ordered it made for her. It was elegant indeed, but for all the joy Isabella was feeling, it may as well have been her shroud.

Hanild pulled her to her feet. "Arms up, then."

Isabella raised them, and Hanild threw the undergown over her head, smoothing it across her hips, tutting and fussing until Isabella could have screamed. Her head ached as though someone had tied a cord too tightly around it, and the chatter of the women made her feel ill. She swallowed and rubbed her temples.

Marie, who had been supervising the proceedings from the comfort of a blanket-covered chest in the window embrasure while she worked on Isabella's wedding chaplet, eyed her solicitously. Catching her expression, Isabella said simply, "My head aches."

Marie called Rosamund, who was sitting moodily in a corner chewing the end of her braid. "Up, Rosamund. Fetch some willow bark." She glanced at her briefly before turning her attention back to Isabella. "Will you take it powdered in wine or do you need to chew it? If your head is very bad, it would be better to chew it. Or wait!" She snapped her fingers. "Feverfew in a ginger tisane with honey. Yes, that would be better if you feel nauseous too."

Rosamund didn't move from her cushion, examining her fingernails, mouth turned down.

"Rosamund!" Marie ordered.

The girl looked up, resentment oozing from every pore. "I'm not her servant!" she snapped.

"Today, we're *all* her servants. No exceptions. Move, girl!"

Rosamund slowly prised herself from her corner and slid out of the room.

"Hanild!" Marie ordered. "Best you go with her. I shouldn't have asked her. Likely, that's the last we'll see of her, and I don't trust her not to waste time ogling any knight who passes her."

Hanild pulled a face as she hurried after Rosamund, muttering beneath her breath.

"Like as not, she'd have forgotten to return," Marie grumbled. "It was foolish of me to insist she made herself useful, but she was marring the festivities, sitting there like a surly cow."

She gasped and doubled over as the babe kicked her, and all conversation stopped until she straightened, one hand still on her abdomen.

Then, she took over the comb from Barbette and, tutting, started to bind ribbons of yellow silk, her wedding gift, into Isabella's still damp hair. "Best do it now, ere it dries," she said. "Then, when you unbraid it at your bedding, it will wave and ripple enough to entrance your husband."

She gave another gasp, handed the comb back to Barbette and hurried to the privy, returning to sit back down with a grunt. "This babe feels as though he is jousting with my bladder." She grimaced, as Hanild bustled Rosamund back into the room with a cup of feverfew potion.

"The spiteful little witch," Hanild said in an undertone to Barbette. "She deliberately spilled the first cup."

She snatched it from Rosamund, forcing it into Isabella's stiff fingers, and Isabella drank it, barely noticing the taste. At least, it might help her get through the day without feeling any worse.

She distanced herself from the scene, drawing inward, focussing her eyes on the wall hangings, feeling like a mere spectator as they fussed about her, arranging her hair, dabbing oil of lilies on her neck and earlobes. All except for Rosamund, who rolled her eyes and turned her back, muttering beneath her breath as she stalked to the edge of the room, setting her plump arms upon the sill, gazing at the inner courtyard as though it held a far more fascinating view.

"Ignore her," whispered Barbette. "We all know she burns with jealousy."

Rosamund was welcome to him. If Isabella could have changed places with her, she would have. Doubtless, de Soutenay would rather have had Rosamund, anyway, with her fashionable golden hair, her pink-and-white complexion and blue eyes. And Rosamund would come to his bed a virgin. Her dowry was greater, too. And her importance.

Marie came to her holding out some bear's foot flowers and some fragile blooms that looked to Isabella like drops of snow. Fascinated by their beauty, for a moment they distracted her from her misery.

Constance went to finger the little petals, but Marie held them away. "Take care, Constance, for I only have a few, and they're delicate."

Constance stepped back, and Marie held the flowers out again for inspection.

"Ohhh, you're so fortunate, Isabella. These are beautiful. What are they, Marie? I've never seen aught like them."

"Her grace told me they are called Candlemas Bells. They are most rare, but they do grow in the garden here."

Constance tilted her head on one side. "How so?"

"They were a gift from the pope. He gave them to her when she attended his inauguration. We did not know whether they would grow, but it seems they feel content. Are they not lovely?"

Rosamund added her mite in a bored drawl. "I heard tell they represent the purity of our

Blessed Lady – singularly inappropriate for one who is no virgin, I would have said."

Hanild glowered and opened her mouth, but Marie got in first, her voice dripping with sarcasm. "Then perhaps you would like to apprise her grace of that fact, Rosamund, for it was she who suggested them." Ignoring Rosamund's narrowed eyes which shot daggers at her, she added tartly, "And, purity being as much of the heart as of the body, I suggest you hold your tongue."

Marie turned her back smartly on the furious Rosamund. Switching her attention to the flowers again, she twisted and pinned them in amongst the ivy leaves, holding up the chaplet to admire her handiwork.

Balked, Rosamund stalked over to the window embrasure, resting her arms on the sill, gazing moodily out, as Marie placed the chaplet carefully on Isabella's head, then held up a polished metal disc for her to admire the result.

"Look at yourself."

Isabella moved away sharply, not wanting to see her reflection, and Hanild gave a muffled shriek of dismay as the wedding chaplet shook loose and fell to the floor, breaking the head of one of the delicate flowers.

Rosamund padded back over, giving a syrupy smile. "I did hear broken flowers in a wedding chaplet bring bad luck," she purred. "Do have a care, Isabella."

She brimmed with mock sincerity as she picked up the chaplet from where it had fallen and handed it back to Hanild. As she did so, her nail appeared to snag another of the fragile blooms, leaving it bent forlornly. "Oh dear. So sorry."

Hanild snatched it from her. "Do not be such a bitch, Rosamund. We all know you seethe with envy because you cannot have him for yourself."

Rosamund shrugged a plump shoulder, and her eyes glittered. "Even if that were true–" She broke off as Barbette raised a knowing eyebrow. "Even if it *were* true, my uncle would not let me wed him. Bella is welcome to her poverty-stricken knight."

Marie surged over to her, gripping the younger woman by the shoulders. "Enough!" she spat. "Sheathe your claws, you cat, and get you gone. Mayhap they'll find a dish of milk for you in the dairy, for we do not need you here." As she spoke, she propelled Rosamund from the chamber, barring the door against her before turning back to Isabella.

"You look as though you're going to your doom, not your wedding. What if Sir Giles is not as fair of visage as some? He's attractive enough with those dark eyes of his, and I hear tell he's a man of honour." She gently pinched Isabella's pale cheeks to bring some colour into them and stood back assessing her.

"Bite your lips to redden them, girl. They look as enticing as marble as it is. Or wait!" Marie went to the niche above her coffer, selecting a small pot. "Lip rouge," she said. "Stand still, Isabella."

Isabella obeyed without enthusiasm, and Marie tsked between her teeth as she opened the pot, touched it, then smeared her finger lightly over Isabella's mouth. "Now, press your lips together."

Marie tilted her head to one side. "Hmm, better. It's no secret you'd rather be cloistered, Isabella, but that's not the way of things, as well you know. None of us have a say in whom we wed, so be grateful you've not been given to Roger le Clos. I hear he seeks a wife, too."

Constance shuddered and crossed herself. Le Clos was nearing sixty and had all the charm of a mange-ridden old badger, with a temper to match. "Marie speaks truth, Isabella. Make up your mind to consider yourself blessed. It'll not be such a hard bed you have to lie in. I just pray I don't get le Clos."

Before Isabella could answer, the door rattled, and Constance ran to unbar it, allowing two women entrance, one tall with eyes so dark, they seemed almost black and a handsome face rather than beautiful, the other silvery-fair and fey-like. Marie led them to Isabella saying, "The Lady Petronilla, Giles' sister, and Lady Maude, his brother's wife."

Isabella curtseyed, forcing her stiff lips into a smile of welcome as Maude put her hands beneath her elbows and raised her, a look of pleasure on her face.

"Greetings, Sister. Giles is indeed blessed. Is she not lovely, Petra?"

Petronilla also smiled, a dignified curve of her mouth, not as impetuous as Maude. "Indeed. We welcome you to our family, Sister."

Maude hugged Isabella. "Oh, you'll be perfect for Giles, I'm sure." The warmth of her embrace thawed a little of the ice from Isabella's heart. To be kin to this cheerful soul, she could almost be reconciled to the burden of a husband. She hoped she would see much of her.

"Don't be afraid," Maude whispered in her ear. "I see you're nervous, but you don't know Giles as I do. He will not be an onerous husband. Take heart, Isabella. He's a good man, and you are most fortunate. I promise you, he'll make you happy."

She and Petronilla handed Isabella gifts – an ivory comb and an amethyst paternoster with a silver cross. Isabella murmured words of thanks through lips she could barely move, trying to look grateful, and they seated themselves on two chairs which Barbette had brought for them.

The younger women, finally content with their labours, lifted her wedding gown over her head, tweaking it so it sat perfectly on her hips, lacing it around her, adjusting the sleeves, which were trimmed with embroidered braid and finally, tying a braid girdle around her waist, arranging the ends to fall just so. They pinned on her veil, Marie set the chaplet atop it, and they stood back, admiring their handiwork.

They finished their work none too soon, squeaking in alarm as the door opened, and Isabella's grim-faced father entered the room, greeting Petronilla and Maude briefly. Marie whispered, "Where's your cloak?" Isabella pointed to the chair where she had lain it – a bridal gift from the queen, a practical but rich garment of green and russet coloured wool warmly lined with budge and edged with fur.

Marie pulled a face. "I can't see it. Here, you may borrow mine instead." She snatched up her own mantle of warm blue wool lined with coney fur, wrapping it quickly around Isabella then dropping into curtsey as le Gris approached them. He acknowledged Marie with a curt bow before turning to Isabella.

"Daughter." He greeted her with a kiss from dry lips which barely touched her forehead, his voice as enthusiastic as Isabella's, and held his arm out to escort her, as the women behind her chattered and gossiped.

At the stone stairs, he gestured her to go before him. *As though he feared I might flee were he not to keep me in his sight,* she thought, curling her lip, since no one could see her face.

As he alighted at the foot of the stairs, he held out his arm again, and she replaced her hand dutifully, despite her loathing.

Isabella felt tension in the arm her hand was resting on. Her father's face was drawn, his lips set in a tight line. Indeed, she was surprised he'd been willing to attend but rightly guessed the queen had brought pressure to bear on him.

He led her, wordlessly, across the courtyard to the church door, and she shivered as much from fear as from the sudden gust of cold biting through her gown.

Giles awaited her, dressed in a court tunic of a deep green, richly embroidered with red and yellow lozenges. He looked ill-at-ease, she thought, not knowing whether to be offended or grateful to see a sign of nerves in him. But then, anyone being confronted by her father in this mood might well be uneasy.

She made her responses with a heavy heart; Giles answered in tones which were clear, and the deed was done. A brief mass consecrated their joining, then Giles turned to her and claimed her with a light kiss on her mouth, but before he could draw her arm into his, a man came from behind.

"My privilege, I think."

Giles glowered as Prince John stepped between them, and Isabella's heart nearly stopped beating. She flinched slightly as he slipped an arm round her waist, forcing her head up with his other hand, fastening his lips like a leech onto hers. Horror-stricken, she could do nothing but stand there as his hands fondled her waist then slid lower, but when his tongue started to force her lips apart, she pulled back, an expression of disgust on her face.

John looked at her with venom, before kissing her again, viciously, remorselessly, this time succeeding in his aims. She felt his tongue, slimy as a fat slug, exploring her mouth, not daring to pull back again, sick with revulsion, eyes tearing as she fought not to retch.

Her torment ended when he let her go, his eyes glittering with malice. "My lady." His voice was vindictive as he turned to Giles. "I wish you much joy of her. A shame you'll not be the first to have her. I trust she'll provide you with an heir, although," he smirked, "it seems the lady might be slow to quicken. Unless, of course, you can be sure she does not already have a brat in her womb of FitzAubrey's get."

Isabella, still wanting to vomit, cringed. Of course she had not. Did he think Eleanor had not made sure of that?

Fire flashed in Giles' eyes, but he replied levelly, "I'm grateful for your kind thoughts, my lord." He smiled at Isabella, taking her shaking hand and laying it lightly upon his arm, drawing her from the chapel. "Come, my wife. Let us attend our wedding feast."

He led her, still trembling, feeling as though her legs might give way beneath her, back across the courtyard and into the great hall.

The queen was not present. She had kissed Isabella a week ago, giving her the cloak before leaving to return to Fontevrault, where, she said, her heart felt most at home. Eleanor had taken most of her ladies with her, leaving the others in Marie's charge.

Rosamund had made no secret of her envy of that cloak, although she already possessed more than enough mantles. She, also, had disappeared. Doubtless, she was finding her own amusement elsewhere.

In fact, there was no wedding feast, merely a handful of dishes quickly produced by a somewhat surly cook, who had complained loudly about people wanting anything more fancy than bread, cheese and ale this early.

Giles' sister, his brother and Maude ate with them, and Giles' men. Her father had already taken his leave.

"It's a poor feast, my lady," Giles said, "but I wish to be away betimes. We have a full day's journey ahead of us. However, when we reach Sparnstow, I doubt not the abbess will make us welcome and provide a suitable wedding banquet. We shall make merry there." He glanced over at the other side of the hall where John hovered, apparently passing the time with some wench but watching the small wedding party through narrowed eyes.

Isabella toyed with the morsels of meat Giles placed on her plate; to eat would, she felt sure, make her lose the last shreds of her control.

Giles touched her hand. "Isabella, I know he has distressed you. Try not to let his manners overset you, for that is what he wished to do."

She looked at him, eyes wide. He nodded. "It's what he does. Come, laugh as though I've amused you. Let him think he's failed even if he has not."

Isabella drew in a deep breath. He was right – of course he was. She forced a smile to her lips and then managed a light laugh as though he'd said something funny.

"Good girl." He flicked one eyelid in an approving wink.

CHAPTER 10

"Almost I wish we were coming with you," Maude said as their platters were removed. She tilted her head at Ralph, who gave her a knowing smirk.

"Doubtless," was all he replied, but Maude grimaced and flicked him lightly with her hand.

Giles bent over her to kiss her, embraced his brother, then escorted Isabella back to the bower, saying, "I wish to leave as soon as possible, though since I gave you no warning, I dare say you've not yet prepared. Just pack enough for the horses, for I cannot take your coffers at present. I'll arrange for them to be sent on later." He kissed her cheek and turned, saying, "I'll wait for you in the bailey. Be sure to clad yourself warmly."

After he'd left, she exhaled in relief. The thought of her wedding night was bad enough, the idea of consummating their marriage within the castle walls with John probably deciding to attend the bedding ceremony made her feel physically ill. She had no wish to ever clap eyes on him again.

She changed quickly into more practical clothing, stowing the red gown in her bags, adding extra layers to help her stay warm. It was only when she looked up and noticed Hanild's shocked expression, she realised that she was scowling and swiftly curved her lips upwards. Better to look as though she was not already regretting her vows. Besides, Rosamund would be only too pleased to goad her.

She cast a glance around the chamber as she removed her chaplet, laying it down carefully. Where was Rosamund? Her tension eased a little as she realised the girl was not there. The others she would miss; Rosamund, she would be happy to leave behind.

Preoccupied, she handed back Marie's mantle, finished stowing her bride gifts, some silver pins for her veils from Hanild, a polished disc of metal for viewing herself in from Constance, some rose-scented salve in a painted pot from Barbette, a smaller one from Marie. "A soothing salve, for tonight," Marie had whispered as she pushed it into her hand when the others weren't looking. The brooch of silver-gilt set with a large stone of rock crystal from the other ladies she would use to fasten her cloak. However, when she went to don that, she realised it was still nowhere to be seen.

She clicked her tongue with annoyance. It must be somewhere. She must have a cloak, and since the one she'd brought with her had been spoiled, she had no other warm enough; besides, it was a rich gift and one she valued. She delved into the chest again, checking it was not beneath everything else, then scoured the chamber searching for it. Barbette and Hanild checked beneath pallets, behind chests, everywhere they could think of. The cloak was not to be seen.

Constance, returning from the latrine, said nervously, "Have you already packed it?"

Marie threw her hands up in disgust as Isabella tossed her gowns from her bags again, rummaging down to the bottom before shaking her head glumly.

Barbette stood by, her brow puckered. "I wonder…"

They all looked at her.

"I do wonder…" She chewed a fingernail before marching to the coffer where Rosamund stored her personal possessions, rattling the lid, only to discover it was locked. As she sat back on her heels in disgust, Marie pushed herself to her feet and pulled a pin out from her veil.

Constance gasped. "Marie! You can't!"

"I should not have to," snapped Marie. She sat on the lid, attempting to poke her pin into the lock, but gave an exasperated grunt. "This babe is getting in my way."

Pushing herself upright, she leaned heavily on the chest before plumping to her knees. The mechanism was simple enough, but getting back up was not. Marie pressed her hands to the floor groaning as she tried to right herself, before giving up and sitting back on her heels. Isabella and Hanild both took her hands and heaved her to her feet, laughing at the disgusted expression on her face.

"You may well laugh now. Just wait until it's your turn," she chided them, but a dimple twinkled from her cheek even though she tried to frown. "In truth, I shall be glad when this child is born." She sat back in the chair Constance had pulled to her. "Get on with it then, Barbette. Make haste."

Barbette, still chuckling, lifted the lid, sliding her hands inside carefully, barely disturbing the contents.

Constance backed to the door and peered out. "Hurry up," she hissed. "She might return."

Hanild looked out the window and smirked. "Not she. She's busy in the courtyard, beguiling Adam de Grosmont, that young knight of your husband's household, Isabella. I don't admire his taste."

About to make a scathing comment, Isabella was distracted by a smothered sound from Barbette, who was busy pulling out the furred cloak Eleanor had gifted her. Barbette stroked the soft lining before giving it to Isabella. "Who would have thought she would stoop so low as thievery?"

Marie calmly replaced the pin in her veil. "Not thievery so much as spite. Certainly, she would have found it after you'd gone and been full of remorse. I believe she would have ensured it was returned to you, but I suspect you'd have found some small break in the threads or gaps in the fur. She would have been amazed that she had it, of course." She tossed her head. "And *so* sorry about the damage."

She held her hand out for the mantle, inspecting it carefully before wrapping it around Isabella's shoulders, pulling her hood on, covering the cap Isabella had pulled over her wimple and kissing her. "No damage. By good fortune, we've found it before she had chance to do anything."

Constance gave a rare grin. "I should like to see her face when she searches for it."

Barbette was grim. "She'll know Isabella found it, but she'll not know which of us know, or whether we'll tell the queen. I suggest we leave her to stew over that; happen it will teach her a lesson for the future."

She looked at Isabella. "Do you have everything?" Isabella nodded, and Marie summoned one of de Soutenay's squires to carry her bags down.

Barbette squeezed her arm, Constance gave her a small hug, and the others clustered around her bidding her farewell.

Isabella sniffed and dashed a hand across her eyes. She would miss them and miss her life here. Although it was foolish to fret – for most of the others, too, this was just a temporary refuge.

CHAPTER 11

When Isabella reached the courtyard, the air hit her like a slap. It had been cold earlier; now it was bitter, and she was glad she had found her new mantle. She wrapped it more tightly around her, shivering into the warmth of the soft lining. It would help keep out the worst of the weather, and she wore two shifts, two gowns and two pairs of fine wool stockings inside her boots, but even with those, the chill was noticeable. The weak sun which shone palely in an ice-blue sky had no perceptible warmth in it.

Maude, who had followed her down, kissed her farewell, before retreating back into the castle, and Evelina came rushing out to drop a curtsey. Isabella raised her and kissed her on both cheeks, and the little maid gasped, "Oh, I hope you'll find happiness this time, my lady. I feel that bad I'm leaving you but…" She hung her head and the colour rose up her face.

"I know, Evelina. You want to wed your man, and he'll not come with you. I shall miss you, but you, too, deserve happiness."

Evelina blushed again and pushed an embroidered purse into her hand, a simple thing made of a scrap of linen, embroidered with daisies and tied with a cord. "It's not much, my lady."

Isabella was touched. "I'll treasure it, dear Evelina. Thank you."

Evelina smiled timidly and pulled her cloak close as a gust of wind tugged at it. Isabella embraced her briefly, saying "Go, Evelina, you'll catch your death out here." She watched the maid make her way back to the castle, dodging around the servants who scurried to and fro, then the squire led her across the yard to the outer bailey where Giles was waiting for her, his open smile the only cheerful thing about the day.

De Soutenay rubbed his hands, then turned to the groom who had appeared at his elbow. "Where's my lady's horse?"

The groom shuffled and stuttered until Isabella took pity on him. "I have no mount."

"No horse?" He looked taken aback.

"No. Godfroi de Bourne lent me his wife's palfrey."

Her husband frowned for a moment, and she waited for an outburst of rage. Baldwin would have kicked the groom then berated her for not telling him earlier, but the day had moved so fast, she'd not thought; neither had she realised they would be leaving so quickly. Instead of being angry, he gave a good-natured laugh.

"Well then, my wife, since I have no saddle suitable for a lady, it would seem you'll have to ride either astride or pillion. Which is it to be?"

Hot embarrassment coursed through her. The gown she wore was unsuitable for riding astride, it would not be decent, even if she had the skill, which she hadn't; her only alternative would be to ride pillion, and that was so intimate. Although, tonight, she thought, barely suppressing a shudder, would be worse by far. She shrugged. "Since I cannot ride astride, I suppose it must be pillion."

"Come then, place your foot on mine." He mounted and held out his hand, she grasped it, and one of his men stepped forwards and lifted her up behind him where she put her hands beneath his cloak, looped her fingers into his belt and fancied she could feel the warmth of him through the thick fabric he wore. Indeed, just to have her hands beneath his cloak, although uncomfortably close, was almost a relief from the cold.

He looked over his shoulder at her. "I suggest you lean closer, my wife. That way, we'll both be less chilled."

She moved a fraction nearer, not enough to feel his body against hers but enough that she had complied with his words, and she thought she heard him sigh. Around her, his men mounted up, and they moved out.

Outside the castle walls, the wind hit them with renewed vigour. It was not a day for travelling, but, she thought with another shrug, even in this biting cold it was still preferable to staying anywhere John was. And, if she died of cold, she would not have to face her wedding night.

Surprisingly, they made good progress. Giles was travelling light – most of the baggage on the horses was hers, and that was not distributed amongst pack ponies but on the horses of his mesnie. With no pack animals to slow them down, at least they might reach warmth before her toes fell off.

She glanced up at the skies and wished she hadn't; the sun was now obscured by heavy yellow clouds, and she saw snow starting to fall. An involuntary shiver shook her, and Giles once more turned his head.

"Move closer, ere you freeze to death. If you wait much longer, my cloak will be wet with snow and will give you no relief." It wasn't a suggestion; she could hear the impatience in his voice, and anyway, she was so cold, it would be a relief to do so.

He wasn't wearing a hauberk, just a padded gambeson. She slid closer, leaning against him, and found it did keep the wind from the front of her. Indeed, she discovered she did not mind resting her cheek against his back so much as she had expected, once she'd taken that first step. And after all, there were many layers between them; she doubted he could even feel her touch.

Giles felt her lean against him, and his own tension relaxed somewhat. It had not escaped his notice that she'd barely touched him until ordered to do so, but now, the warmth of her body against his back took some of the cold from his own bones also since it prevented the chill air gusting between them. He was glad of his thick gambeson – by all the saints, she must be half frozen. He should have thought of that, would remedy it at a break in their journey. They would have to detour to find a tavern en route – or would it be better to go a little faster and reach the comfort of Sparnstow Abbey more quickly?

Still in two minds, he kicked Troubadour into a canter. The horse responded as though he, too, wanted to reach the shelter of the abbey stables. And, of course, Troubadour knew Brother

Bernard would be there. The horse had developed a deep affinity for the large lay brother who returned his affection in full measure. And the thought of a bran mash and a thorough rub down had obviously not been forgotten.

Giles felt Isabella clinging more tightly as Troubadour increased his speed. Her hands slid to encircle his waist, and she gripped his belt as though she feared she might fall.

The journey took a full four candle notches even then, Giles reckoned as he felt Isabella's shivers intensifying, sensed her starting to sag. Had he made a mistake not to detour to an inn? He thought not; although they would have had a temporary reprieve, the snow was falling more heavily by now. Once it started to settle, as he thought it soon might, their journey would take longer. On the whole, although conditions were unpleasant, it was worth not stopping halfway. He had a longing for the abbey. He also had a feeling that meeting Abbess Hildegarde might be helpful for his new wife.

Wife! He shook his head, still feeling disbelief that he was now wed. And to a woman who more often than not seemed colder than the bitter wind. He could not even begin to imagine how his wedding night would be. His lips quirked up in a grim smile. It might be that he was more at risk of frostbite between the sheets than out here.

He had slowed to a walk for a short while and now kicked Troubadour into another canter. There was no banter between the men as there had been at the start of the journey. Eyes were narrowed against the swirling snow, faces were pinched, and he sensed their relief as the pace picked up again.

At last, he saw the abbey dimly outlined against the sky. He sought to slow Troubadour again, for the horse was beginning to tire, but, as though the sight of the abbey spurred him, Troubadour threw his head back, gave a whinny, and they arrived at the gallop instead.

As they pounded on the heavy gates, he turned his head to glance at Isabella; her face was ashen, her lips bloodless, her eyes red-rimmed and darkly shadowed. *Not a moment too soon, by the looks of her*, he thought, and then Sister Berthe, the porteress, was unlocking the gate, lifting the bars that held it secure, and they were in.

He slid from Troubadour and held his hands out for Isabella; she looked to be only half conscious – he had not realised. But, he supposed, life in the bower would not have fitted her for a journey like this.

She almost fell into his grasp but straightened herself before he could embrace her, and he let go, instead holding his hand out in a courtly manner. She placed her arm along his, took one step, and skidded on the frozen ground.

Before she could lose her balance entirely, he had jerked her from her feet and swung her into his arms, and he felt her tense. Enough of this nonsense! She was his wife, and she would do as he bid her. By the saints, what did the silly wight think? He was going to tear the clothes from her here and ravish her in the stableyard?

Brother Bernard appeared from a barn, and Troubadour, with no need of a word from Giles, trotted straight to him, whickering softly. The lay brother took his reins and, crooning to him and scratching the big horse's withers, led him into the stables. Giles left his men to make shift as best they might and carried Isabella into the abbey buildings, where Sister Joan, the cheery hosteller, arrived, clucking in anxiety as she saw the burden he bore.

He wanted to pay his respects to Hildegarde, but before that, he must take care of Isabella.

Sister Joan led the way to a small chamber, not the one they usually allotted to him, bemoaning the fact they'd not known he was coming, that they were packed to the rafters, and this poor room was all they had left. Her face was all consternation, and he cut into her soft twitterings about where they would house him, would he mind bedding down in the main guest hall?

"No matter, at least we'll have a bed, and I cannot always claim your best. No need to worry yourself, Sister Joan. I'll not be wanting separate lodgings; this lady is my wife."

Sister Joan started visibly and nearly dropped the horn lantern she was holding. "Your wife?" Her voice was louder than usual, her brow creased, her eyes round.

Giles would have been sharp with her. He was cold and hungry, and his patience was at a low ebb; she surely did not imagine he'd bring his leman here expecting to lie with her. But he had a soft spot for Joan, so contented himself with saying, "Indeed. I was most surprised myself. I'll explain later, but for now, she's frozen to the marrow."

The doubt dropped from Joan's face, and she hurried to open the door, lighting the rush lamps, which flickered over the interior of the dark room.

Giles lay Isabella on the bed, where she curled herself into a tight ball. Sister Joan peered at her. "Do you wish Sister Ursel to tend to her?"

Giles frowned. Did he? Happen not just now; later, a visit from the elderly infirmaress might be beneficial. For now, warmth was the thing. "I think not. But if you could arrange for a brazier?" He rubbed his hands, his breath came out in a white puff. The air was not much less frigid in here. He gave Joan a wheedling look. "Maybe two braziers?"

She twinkled at him. "On the instant. But, first, Sir Giles, I suggest you get those wet clothes off her before the bedlinen is soaked."

Twinkling again, she backed out of the room and left him with his wife, who shivered and turned her face away from him.

Isabella must have heard Joan, though, for she sat up, teeth chattering, plucking at her cloak, struggling with the brooch which fastened it, her fingers nearly blue with cold. Giles threw off his cloak and removed his gambeson – he was dry enough beneath that apart from his hose. Then, he knelt before her and took her icy hands into his own, which were not much warmer. She did not resist but did not meet his gaze, either. He put one finger beneath her chin and raised her head, and, at last, she looked into his eyes. Her lashes were wet, whether with tears or melted snow, he did not know.

"Come," he said, gently. "You cannot help yourself with hands as cold as this. Let me aid you."

Isabella had little choice. Her fumbling fingers were too numb to unfasten her cloak, too numb even to allow her to relieve herself, which she was desperate for. And she would not use the pot she knew would be beneath the bed. Not in front of him. She would have to wait until she could visit the privy.

Unable to help herself, she let him assist her. She squeezed her eyes closed – she would not look at him – and felt him struggling to undo her cloak brooch. He swore as he caught his finger on the pin, and, as she peeked, she saw him put it in his mouth, sucking the blood away. Then, he stood her up and removed the cloak from around her. It had kept her dry for part of the journey, but the wet had seeped into it, and it was now sodden. She shivered again as he removed it, then gasped as he took hold of her gown.

"My lord, I will freeze if you remove that." It was the truth. Wet though it was, she could not bear the thought of taking it off. Even the damp wool of her gown was better than nothing. "It will dry."

"It will not! And you'll be warmer without it. See, there's a blanket here. Trust me."

Isabella looked up, and he met her gaze. She had no option; he was her lord now. Squeezing her eyes tight shut again, she wished she could switch off her other senses as easily as he pulled off her hood, cap and wimple, and started to unlace her gown. He swore beneath his breath again as he pulled at the laces before tugging it over her head, and she raised her arms listlessly to aid him, hearing his huff of surprise as he discovered how many layers she wore beneath, gritting her teeth as he removed her second gown.

As she shivered in her two undershifts, he chuckled. "Well, lass, I see you took your own precautions against the cold." His voice was deep and strong but without the undertones of anger Baldwin's voice had mostly held. If she wasn't so predisposed to mistrust him, she supposed she would have liked the sound of it.

De Soutenay ran his hands over the fabric, brushing her body, and she felt a surge of revulsion before he said, "No need to strip you, then. This is dry enough. Sit down, Isabella."

She obeyed, her legs weak with relief, then she tensed again as she felt him unbraid her hair. *No!* She was not ready for this; did not think she would ever be ready. She bit back a sob and pressed her lips tightly together, terrified she would scream or cry and raise his ire.

Her fears were unrealised. He felt the length of her hair, then said, "Just a little damp. It will soon dry. The best thing for you and me both, lass, would be a hot bath."

She felt the colour flood her face and then, just as quickly, drain away, and knew she looked pinched and ill. A drum beat against her temples; if she did not soon lie down, she would be sick.

Although, that might quell any desires he might be feeling. But, she could not stand the thought of the beating that would inevitably result from vomiting, so swallowed down the bile that rose in her throat.

She clenched her teeth as he pushed her gently backwards onto the bed before he removed her boots. They had leaked, and her stockings, both pairs, clung sodden around her feet and legs. His fingers reached beneath her gown, and she repressed a shudder as she felt his hands on her cold bare skin, before he drew them off, tossed them aside and started to dry her feet with a linen towel. Once done, he began to move up her body, and she dug her nails into her palms until it felt as though they would draw blood.

A knock came at the door and, without a word, he took his hands from her and rose. She heard him open the door, muffled voices, and the door closed again. This was it, then. He was tugging at something, presumably his clothing, and she lay, unspeaking, dreading what she knew would follow.

Nothing happened. It unnerved her, and she peeked from beneath her lashes, to see him kneeling on the floor fumbling at the fastenings of one of his bags. Resisting the urge to move, which might attract his attention back to her, she lay mutely, waiting for him to finish whatever he was doing, then felt his hands on her feet again.

"This will warm you." Again, that smile in his voice. Well, he would smile, wouldn't he? It might not warm her, but doubtless the exercise would take the chill from him.

Then, she felt him pulling something rough over her ankles and up her legs, felt him fiddling with the string of the loincloth she had added to her assortment of clothes. What was he doing?

Unable to bear it any longer, she opened her eyes, and a muted squeak escaped her. He had pulled a pair of men's hose over her legs. She gulped. What perversion was this?

Her gaze flew to his face in disbelief, and she saw the twinkle in his eyes. He chuckled. "It may not be seemly, but I'll warrant you'll feel a good deal warmer in these."

She blinked.

"Come, Isabella, don't be shocked. It may be strange, but I promise you, it will help warm you. I should have thought of it ere we left but..." His forehead wrinkled and his voice trailed away before he rallied and said, "To tell truth, I'm not used to travelling with women in weather like this. And, I believe you'll be grateful for them when we set out again. Better by far to be practical." He winked at her. "Admit it, you feel warmer already."

He strode to the window and inched the shutter open; an icy draught found its way inside and made the dim light from the lamps gutter, and he shut it quickly. "Although, it doesn't look as though we'll be travelling further for several days, at least. The snow is settling, and I believe it will drift. Still, it will give us chance to get to know each other properly."

A grin lit up his saturnine features, and Isabella was surprised how much more youthful it made him look. Not that she felt much like responding. Doubtless, he meant but one thing. Still, possibly, here in the abbey where word might reach the nuns, he might resist the temptation to hurt her.

He looked at her expectantly, and she managed to quirk her lips into a small smile. His own smile dimmed for a moment, his brows snapped together, and Isabella knew she'd made an error. She forced herself to smile more broadly, allowing the tug of her lips to crinkle her eyes. She must look as though she at least liked him, she supposed, for she did not know how long his patience would last else, and she hoped he'd not notice how her lips trembled as she racked her scrambled wits for a suitable reply.

"That would be...pleasant, my lord," she murmured, sitting up as the door opened once more. As the hosteller came back in, accompanied by two of Giles' squires bearing a brazier, she saw their interested expressions at the sight of her oddly-clad legs and curled them beneath her quickly, pulling the blanket around her.

The brazier was lit and a second brought in, as Giles had requested, then a wrinkled, apple-cheeked old nun bustled in behind Sister Joan. Sister Ursel, hazel eyes bright, a beaming smile on her face, and two steaming cups in her hands. "Well, well! I hear felicitations are the order of the day," the dame cackled, as she placed one on a table by the brazier where Giles stood warming his hands.

She carried the second cup over to Isabella, limping slightly. "Oh, this cold. It gets into your very marrow when you're my age. Here, child, this will take the chill from your bones. We'd not expected to see you again so soon."

Giles quirked his head, and Ursel explained, "It was not so long since your lady stayed with us on her way to Berkhamsted."

Isabella wrapped her hands round the cup Ursel had given her, taking comfort from the heat, as the nun said, "You'll be a blessing to him, my lady. It's about time he was wed with a quiverful of childer. You'll have him beneath your thumb in no time, I don't doubt."

Giles snorted, and the nun turned towards him. "And don't you be taking that tone with me, my lord. I know full well you're softer than you look."

Isabella gave a soft cough, her discomfort by now intense. "My lord, I need…" He looked at her, raising his eyebrows, and her courage gave way. She turned to the hosteller. "Sister Joan, would you remind me, please, where the…" She flushed and dropped her voice another notch so it came out as a hoarse whisper. "The privy?"

"Why, bless you, child, of course; I should have thought. Come with me."

Isabella scrambled from the bed, making sure that her unusual undergarments were hidden beneath her shift. She looked down at herself. Even without her overgown, she decided, she was more or less decent. Still, to be sure, she wrapped the blanket about her like a cloak, then bundling her hair back into her still-wet wimple, she followed Joan, desperate to relieve her bladder before she disgraced herself.

CHAPTER 12

Hildegarde had sensibly requested Ursel give Giles and his new wife the night to recover from their journey before the old nun escorted them to her. Besides, by the time they had supped, there would have been little time yestereve before the grand silence fell. Fond as she was of Giles, she was delighted to hear he was wed, and now, she knew she need have no fear for Isabella. That young woman would doubtless be celebrating her good fortune.

She rose to her feet to greet them, her hands held out in welcome, a smile on her face. "Well, Lady Isabella, I had not expected to see you again so soon. And so," she turned to Giles, "you are wed. Such wonderful news."

If her smile faltered momentarily at the set expression on his face, she quickly recovered herself, turning back to Isabella. "And, did I not tell you prayer was the answer?"

Isabella gave a faint smile which faded almost immediately. This time, Hildegarde knew herself to be visibly taken aback and plumped into her seat heavily enough to jar her spine. Her face creased with pain for a moment, and she dipped her head to hide her confusion.

Something was not right here. No matter, surely they could get to the bottom of it. Giles was dear to her, and she'd been concerned for Isabella. Surely, they could find happiness together. *Although it is early for them to be quarrelling.* She almost shivered at the coldness she felt between them. Nevertheless, she ploughed on.

"You will sup with me?" She leaned forward, placing her elbows on the table, clasping her hands and watching them, eyes bright. Ursel followed suit. "And you were wed, when? I had no idea you were betrothed, my lord."

Giles' face held no trace of the pleasure she would have expected. "We were wed yesterday, Abbess."

"Yesterday? Well, what could be better than to have your wedding meal here? We shall hold a special feast to celebrate it on the morrow, but for now, the fare will be suitable for a preliminary occasion." She could hear herself babbling but could not stop for the life of her. Her words hung in the air unanswered. And their faces! Not what she would have expected.

Neither met her eyes. She poured them wine, and Giles downed his in one almost desperate gulp. Silently, she refilled his cup. It was emptied before she could put down the flagon, and she decided it might be unwise to offer more.

Isabella took the tiniest of sips through tight lips, head down, face unreadable. When the food was brought in, she toyed with it; Giles, on the other hand, ate like one trying to fill an empty chasm.

The meal was interminable. Never usually one to talk small inconsequentialities, Hildegarde found herself almost rambling as she groped her way through supper, glad when she could take their leave and go to Compline.

As they left, not quite banging the door behind them, she looked at Ursel whose face mirrored her own dismay. "Do you have any idea what's happening between those two?"

"None, Abbess, but give me time, and I'll find out."

Well, time she would have aplenty. This snow would likely lie thick for at least a sennight if Hildegarde was any judge. Surely they would not attempt to leave while it was so heavy on the ground.

Hildegarde was right. The snow was set, the weather far too severe for travelling. They were packed to overflowing; their resources would feel the pinch, but it could not be helped. At least they had plenty of salt beef and fish in their cellars plus hams and barrels of grain, preserved fruits. Enough, if they were careful, to feed their guests and still last them through the season.

Meantime, Ursel and Hildegarde were pressing Giles for details whenever they could catch him alone. After a week, he cracked.

He had joined them for supper again; Isabella had declined. Normally, Hildegarde would have given the other nuns invitation to join her instead of favouring Ursel, but on the off-chance of being able to help, she had taken the risk of upsetting the others while she and Ursel worked together on probing Giles. She would make up for it later.

"She seems like a...a...she seems a pleasant young woman," Hildegarde finished limply. It sounded ridiculous, but she could not think of anything else to say about someone with so little personality. Perhaps she had misread Isabella. She had met the girl for such a short time, and one could not always tell. Disturbed, desperate to say something useful, she kept trying. "I'm sure you'll be very happy together. And you can look forward to heirs, a family." That sounded even worse. *Pathetic!* she chided herself. *Can you not do better than that?* But in truth, she could not.

Giles gave a short, bitter laugh and then put his head in his hands. "You think so? It is like living with an alabaster statue! Hellfire, this is not what I expected of marriage. And as for children! Have you not noticed how she flinches when I touch her? What hope of children if she'll not even speak to me, not even meet me halfway? I do not ask her to bed me yet, just treat me as though I were not an ogre."

Hildegarde chewed the inside of her cheek, overcome with guilt. Had she heeded Isabella's request maybe these two would not have been knit together in such misery now. Had she judged wrongly? If so, then she was the one responsible for ruining these two young lives.

Before she could answer, however, Ursel leaned towards him, patting his hand, and he raised his head, staring at her with eyes devoid of hope.

"My lord, you must be patient. She had married badly before you, I believe?" He nodded. "Then she is wounded. Not in her body, not now, but spiritually and emotionally. Wounds which go as deep as that take long to heal. You need to give her time."

"Time? You think I've not been patient? I've tried everything. I've not forced her." His voice broke, and he swallowed hard before continuing, "I knew it would take time, but I had not expected her to be so…so unyielding. She barely looks at me, barely speaks to me, can't stand me to touch her even when I but offer my aid. What am I to do?" The shadows on his face made him look haunted.

Hildegarde was blunt. "You yourself must have agreed to this marriage, my lord. And you've already said it will take patience to win her. Did you really think a sennight would be sufficient time?"

Giles had the grace to look abashed, but that stubborn set of his chin was still there. "I've told you, Abbess, I don't expect to bed her yet, have not pushed her neither have I forced her." He ran his hands through his hair. "If she would but speak with me, I would have hope, but this…this silence! What if she never thaws? Have you thought on that?"

Hildegarde said nothing while she prayed for wisdom. And that was what was needed. He must pray. Whether he was a man who prayed much outside of church, she did not know, but prayer, she believed absolutely was the answer. Maybe they could not change Isabella until he himself had been given the wisdom to deal with the situation. And maybe patience was all that was required.

She spoke with firmness. "Sir Giles, we sympathise with you. We can offer our thoughts and prayers; we can, if you wish, speak to your wife ourselves, but we can do very little else. However, this is what I suggest. You should go to the abbey and seek answers from God and–"

"God? You think He actually answers?" His mouth twisted. "I should have had nothing to do with those accursed Angevins. I should have run like Hell in the opposite direction when Eleanor summoned me. I should have known anything to do with them would be tainted."

Hildegarde was taken aback but rallied quickly. "Sir Giles, have you asked Him?"

He looked at her; that thinning of his lips told her he had not.

"Well, if you've not asked, how can you expect an answer?" He opened his mouth to dispute with her, but she forestalled him. "No! I will not argue this with you. You will go and seek God's guidance. Meanwhile, we will speak to Lady Isabella, see if we can get beneath the surface of this.

"And, my lord, pray for your wife, for by praying for her, you may learn to understand her."

He did not acknowledge her but stood, pushing back his chair, which clattered to the floor. Ignoring it, he strode to the door and barged through, leaving it to crash shut behind him.

Ursel caught her eye. "Well that you are an abbess, my lady. If not, I think he would have been...how can I put this? Impolite."

Hildegarde's face twitched as she tried not to laugh. "I suspect, dear Ursel, he would have told me to go to Hell. But what think you? Can we help them?"

"I don't know; we can but try. And pray."

Hildegarde put her elbows on the table and rested her head in her hands. Ursel tapped her rather sharply on the arm, and Hildegarde raised tired eyes to her.

"Mother Abbess, it will do no good blaming yourself. Well you know you would not have been allowed to give that poor lass sanctuary. Sometimes," Ursel added sagely, "I believe you take too much upon yourself."

Hildegarde started, briefly offended, then responded, "Yet is it not our duty, dear Ursel, to bear one another's burdens?"

"In prayer, yes," the older nun agreed, "but having borne those burdens to our blessed Lord, we leave them there. He takes our burdens; He does not leave us to carry them alone. Or would you fight to retain possession of something that is too heavy for you? With respect, my lady, sometimes you need to follow the advice you give others."

And that is to put me in my place, thought Hildegarde, saying, "You keep me humble, dear Ursel. Sometimes, I wonder whether I was wise to have accepted the position of abbess." Ursel would surely have served here far better than she.

Sister Ursel did not bother to respond, merely snorting her derision.

CHAPTER 13

Hildegarde was sitting in her private chamber, absorbed in prayer when the door opened, and Ursel's face peered round. She motioned to the settle, and Ursel seated herself, puffing a little.

The abbess poured her a cup of watered wine, and Ursel took it gratefully, sipping at it until she recovered.

"You need not have hurried so, Sister Ursel. There is no immediate urgency. Sir Giles and Lady Isabella will not be leaving soon, not with this weather. Have you managed to prise anything out of her?"

"Oh, as to that," Ursel took another sip from her cup, then steadied it carefully beside her, "while I can still move these old bones, I'll not be idle."

Hildegarde would have remonstrated with her but was too anxious to hear what she'd discovered.

The old nun's eyes took on a baleful glint. "That poor young woman was wed to Baldwin FitzAubrey when she was but fourteen."

"Yes, but he surely did not take her so young."

Ursel pursed her lips as though to spit but took one look at Hildegarde's face and scowled instead. "I wouldn't be so sure." She stopped to scratch her nose, and Hildegarde clasped her hands, resisting the urge to hurry her. "I knew his sire, and his grandsire; they were brutes. A maid I knew years back was wed to the grandsire and dead within the year, may God assoil her."

Ursel sniffed and stopped to wipe a tear from the corner of her eye. "Baldwin's sire was of the same ilk, and I suppose that would be true of the son, too. As for that mother of his, she was a b–"

"Ursel!"

The older woman continued, not one whit discomposed. "You know I speak as I find, dear Mother Abbess, and in this case, there is no other word for her."

Hildegarde sighed. Ursel was still incorrigible, but she sounded as though she had the truth of it.

Perhaps, between them, they would be able to help Lady Isabella mend some of the damage that must have been done to her. If this marriage was not to bring both of them unhappiness, something must be attempted, but she would do nothing without seeking God first. With that in mind, she headed to the abbey to kneel in supplication.

Isabella felt hunted. She had been doing her best to avoid the abbess and the abbey infirmaress, but they finally cornered her in the guest refectory. She looked around her but could find no way to evade them, bearing down on her as they were from two different directions.

"Lady Isabella." Hildegarde moved towards her, hands outstretched. "We've been searching for you."

"Well, now you have found me."

It sounded somewhat ungracious, and she noticed Hildegarde hesitate and her jaw tighten a fraction before she continued her glide towards Isabella. "Will you not join Sister Ursel and me in my private chambers, my dear? It would be so nice to acquaint ourselves more with you since it is likely your husband will bring you to visit us often."

Isabella took a step backwards and half turned to find Ursel had reached her and was nodding enthusiastically. She gave them a tight smile and opened her mouth to plead a headache, only to hear herself say, "Thank you, Abbess." Her jaw hung slack with shock for a moment after the words came out. She'd not intended to do that – what had happened?

And now, it was too late to refuse; they had ranked themselves either side of her, and before she'd quite recovered her senses, she found herself once more in Hildegarde's small private chamber, pressed to sit on the cushioned settle, a cup of the abbey's best wine in her hand and some honeyed wafers on a platter before her.

Abbess Hildegarde had dragged her heavy chair over to sit opposite, and Sister Ursel had perched beside her. Isabella felt a tight band beginning to clamp around her head, but there could be no escape. *Sweet Mary, have mercy.*

Hildegarde began the attack. "My lady, we were so pleased to hear of your marriage. Sir Giles is dear to the sisters of this house, for he has been good to us. Indeed, we almost feel he is kin, do we not, Sister Ursel?"

Ursel beamed. Isabella could think of nothing to say. Nothing suitable, at any rate.

"And indeed," continued the abbess, "he has need of a woman in his life. You are most fortunate, Lady Isabella, for he will be an uxorious husband, I do believe, once you have won his heart."

"I…" Isabella, still unable to find anything to say, trailed off and took refuge in sipping the wine and nibbling a wafer, although, in truth, she did not wish for either.

"And, it must be a great relief to you, my lady, that you've been given to such a good man. I'm sorry to say it, but there are so many who cannot be relied upon to treat their wives with much respect."

Was it Isabella's imagination, or was the abbess beginning to gabble?

"Indeed, since you were previously wed to such a one, that would be why you felt the desire to find refuge when last you were here, I suppose. At the time, I wished I could oblige you, but now I see why that could not be, for your destiny was not with us; your fulfilment lies with your husband. We can always trust our dear Lord to know what is best for us, even though it oft-times does not seem clear at first." Hildegarde tilted her head on one side, obviously awaiting a response.

When none came, Ursel broke the awkward silence. "Yes, my lady, the relief of being wed to a man like your new husband must be great indeed."

"I…er…yes." Isabella took another sip of wine, wondering what this conversation was truly about. Either these nuns were half-besotted by their Sir Giles or… Had he asked them to speak to her? And did he really think nuns were able to plead his case? What could they know? Had they ever had to suffer the things she had endured? *Had they?* It was likely the Giles de Soutenay they knew was not the one she would be living with.

"And you must know by now that your fears were quite unfounded, for you will already have discovered what manner of man Sir Giles is," the infirmaress continued.

Isabella decided attack was the best form of defence. "And my husband is known to you – how?" she asked sweetly. Let them tell her more about the man, else their assurances were worth nothing. Surely that was not a discomfited look that flickered across their faces. Then it was as she thought; he had asked them to speak for him.

"We have known your husband only for the last three years or so." Hildegarde seemed to quickly recover her composure. Now, she chuckled. "Of a certainty, the first time we encountered him, it was not an auspicious occasion. Ask Sister Berthe for her opinion of that for I'm afraid he manhandled her and infuriated her."

They both glanced at each other, laughing, before Sister Ursel added, "But since then, he has become almost as a son to us. And we have known his elder brother for many years; he is our chief benefactor, and a man well-known for his love of his wife. Sir Giles is of the same character."

Again! Everyone connected with de Soutenay seemed to be telling her the same. But all of them were so partial to him, so biased, how could she trust their judgement? On the other hand, surely they knew him well enough to be able to speak from experience. But how could she *know*?

No. She compressed her lips determinedly. She would not allow herself to hope, for if they lied, she would not be able to bear the despair. Better to stay contained within herself. Where there was no hope, there could be no disappointment.

She nibbled another morsel of wafer, took another sip of wine, wiped her mouth on the napkin they had provided and stood before they could press her more. The look of dismay on their faces did afford her some amusement. And if she could not be anything but obedient with her husband, she owed these well-meaning nuns nothing but politeness.

"I thank you for your hospitality, Abbess, Sister Ursel; however, I have a headache. Please hold me excused." And with that, she held her head high, manoeuvred herself between them, and swept from the room, glancing over her shoulder to see Ursel and Hildegarde, mouths agape, staring after her.

As Isabella dithered between returning to her chamber or the guest house – where would she be least likely to encounter her husband? – Giles appeared from behind a pillar, and her heart sank. Why did he keep seeking her out? Surely, he did not merely wish for her company. She forced her lips upwards as though the sight of him afforded her pleasure.

"Ah, Isabella." He took her arm. "I've been looking for you. With this weather as it is, we'll be forced to seek refuge here for some days more. I must make sure the abbess is well recompensed."

Isabella's eyebrows rose, and he frowned. "I'm afraid most take the food and shelter for granted, and if they are forced to provide for so many without redress, their resources will be stretched to the limit."

Was this just to impress her? Baldwin would have accepted their hospitality as his due; he would not have offered them a clipped penny. But the nuns had spoken so very highly of de Soutenay, perhaps it was his wont to pay them. She resisted the urge to twist her lips in scorn.

Buying his way into Heaven, was he? Well for those who could afford it.

"Wife?" She saw Giles was looking at her and allowed him to lead her into the guest house where he drew her near to the fire, pulled out a merels board and lay out the counters whilst making light conversation with her, which she answered in monosyllables.

CHAPTER 14

Giles lay in the dark, listening to his new wife's breathing. He had put his best efforts into getting to know his reluctant bride. He wanted to give her time, but the thing must be done at some point. Besides, sharing a bed with this woman was disturbing his sleep. Despite her coldness, she stirred him, and he yearned to know her more fully. He grunted. Little chance of that, thus far.

To manage his desires, he had avoided their chamber until he was so weary he could barely stand. He'd risen before she woke and absented himself as much as possible, returning to escort her to the guest hall. He'd tried to interest her in chess, played tafl with her and let her win as though he was some dolt with straw for brains, and chatted about mundane things until he felt as though his tongue would fall out. Slowly, infinitesimally slowly, she began to thaw – but not much.

Now, she was feigning sleep again. *No!* He propped himself up on one elbow and sensed the change in rhythm of her breath. It was almost imperceptible, a slight catch, but he was more aware of her presence beside him than he thought he had ever been of anything else in his life.

Hell's teeth! It was like having an itch he couldn't scratch. The past few nights had almost been an agony for him. He'd tiptoed around her sensitivities like that accursed stable cat from his youth. Was this what it would be like for the rest of his life? An eternity would seem short in comparison.

And yet, what was it like for her? He tried to put himself in her position.

But he could not let this go on. Sometimes, the easiest way to overcome your fears was to face them. He'd had to do it himself when he was near enough her age, the first time he had spilled blood. He'd been so afraid, he could feel his knees knock beneath him, and afterwards, he'd puked his guts out, shaking like a willow in a storm, but he'd survived; so would she.

He caught himself on the thought. It was not the same. He'd been too long with John; it had affected his judgement. He was not John, nor would he be. No, to force her would not help her.

A lock of hair had worked loose from her tight braid. It lay curling on the pillow beside him as though daring him to touch it, and he reached out one lean finger. Again, he sensed that slight change in her breathing, and he withdrew. He looked more closely at her face but in this light, with one single candle in the room, could make out very little.

Giles continued to watch until his eyes adjusted to the dark. He thought her eyelids flickered briefly. Was she watching him? He could not tell for sure, the candle was too far from the bed, but he thought so.

He almost ground his teeth with frustration. How long could he cater to her fears without losing his mind? What if he were to make love to her? Not violently – gently, tenderly, like a lover. Would that convince her he was no FitzAubrey? For he did want her. Heaven help him, he knew not why; she was as inviting as marble. Yet he felt there was more to her than what he had seen so far, and if this ice around her could be melted, mayhap they could have some kind of life together.

He would hold back, but there must be a way round this. If he could but convince her the act was not something to be feared with all men, could convince her he could be trusted not to hurt her, it would be a start. The consummation itself must wait.

He reached out again and this time took her braid in his hands, untying the ribbons which held it so tightly. She must have sensed him, for now, her bottom lip was gripped by her teeth. He ignored her and continued to untangle the ribbons.

As her hair came loose from its bindings, he caught the fragrance of rose oil and buried his face in the lustrous strands, inhaling deeply.

Now, she was definitely awake, her eyes huge, watching him in the dark. He could just make out the glimmer of them, and he put his arm around her shoulders, pulling her to him, burying his face once more in her hair.

Giles raised himself again and gazed down on her. Hellfire, did she have to look at him like that? He was not an ogre, but he was mortal. He could not stand much more of this. He murmured soothingly, "Don't be afraid. We will do nothing yet; you're not ready, and I would not rush you. But we cannot continue like this, can we? The tension between us will never ease if you cannot bring yourself to trust me." It hurt that she did not. He was neither a FitzAubrey nor a John, and it galled him to be judged by their standards, by their sins.

He caressed the sharp contours of her face. A woman should be more softly rounded, but even so, she was comely. Not the preferred beauty of corn-fair hair, white skin, pink lips – had he wanted that, the plump little dove in the bower would have been more than willing to offer it to him, he'd warrant. Isabella's skin was pale honey, her hair a deep golden brown, her lips a little too thin, a little too wide, but by the saints, he wanted her.

As he continued to stroke her face, slowly allowing his hand to move towards her neck and then the soft skin at the hollow of her throat where a pulse beat wildly beneath his fingers, he watched her eyes. They were almost luminous in the candle-light. Those eyes alone could drive a man wild, but the hesitancy in them nearly made him give up there and then.

He ceased his stroking and placed his hands either side of her face so she could not turn her head away. Then he spoke, keeping his voice gentle, restraining the rising passion in him; this could not be rushed even now, or they would both be undone.

"Isabella."

Unable to look away, she closed her eyes.

He spoke a little more forcefully, "Isabella, look at me!"

Her eyes flickered open, then closed again. He let go of her and moved away a fraction.

Of a certainty, she was too thin, needed more flesh on her. Nevertheless, she still made him catch his breath.

"Come. I know you were not sleeping. Sit up. Lean against me." If he could but get her not to shrink from him, he could wait for the rest. But living with her fear was making him feel as though he was indeed a monster. She bit her lip again, and he forced himself not to lose patience. "This feeling between us, it is not comfortable."

Giles was not certain, but the way her chin jutted spoke of a stubbornness. Why would she not speak? Would she always be thus?

"I don't wish for it to be like this our whole lives. Can we not be, at the very least, friends?"

She made a small gesture which he took as agreement.

"Then sit with me. Let there at least be conversation between us. Wait." He rose from the bed, moving cautiously across the room in the guttering light from the candle, resisting the urge to swear as he stubbed his toe on something.

The light he had left burning, for he had wanted to be able to see her at least dimly, was almost out. He took a fresh candle, lighting it and fixing it to the pricket, bringing it to the bedside and placing it carefully upon a stool.

That was better, he could see more clearly.

He got back into bed and leaned upright against the head of it, stretching his arm across the back. "Come, Isabella, you'll be warmer if you lean against me." Hell's teeth! It was freezing. Was he mad not to just stay beneath the covers? But this was more intimate, yet in some way less threatening – he hoped.

He held Isabella's gaze with his own, and she shuffled over and leant against his arm, although there was still fully a hand's breadth between their bodies. He moved to fill the space and felt her stiffen, but he was not going to lose the ground he'd gained. Pulling the covers up to their shoulders with his right hand, he wrapped his left arm more tightly about her.

"Don't worry, Isabella, I'll not do more than this." Did she believe him? He thought not, but he would convince her. He must. He could not sleep, would not let her sleep until they had at least talked, until he felt she had more trust in him.

He turned his head so he could see the outline of her face. Her skin reflected the glow of the candle. But her lips were folded tightly. "Was it so very bad with your first husband?" A stupid question, clearly it had been, but let them bring it into the open. Sometimes boils had to be lanced.

She glanced sideways at him, and her expression said what she did not. She remained silent.

"Isabella, talk to me. I need to understand."

Her voice was husky and so low, he had to strain to hear her. "He was a monster."

"He was not kind?"

"You did not know him?"

"A little. I knew of him, though. A rough character, not to be trusted."

She compressed her mouth, then said, "He was not kind. Not to anyone. Especially not to women. The only one he had any care for was his mother."

"And was she kind?"

"She hated me. And I…" She shook her head. "It doesn't matter; they're both gone."

He pulled her a little closer so her head was touching his shoulder, and although she did not relax, neither did she flinch. It was a start.

"I know you fear me, but I swear to you, you have no need. I am not FitzAubrey." Again, she flicked her gaze sideways at him. "I know it will take time to trust me, but believe me, I will not use you as he did."

"You do not know how he used me." If her voice had not been so quiet, he would have sworn she was challenging him.

"No, I do not. But I know he hurt you, and I know it does not have to be like that. It can be…" He pondered. What word was best to use here? "…a delight. For the woman as well, I mean. If done right, if done without violence, gently, with tenderness, love, it can be something beautiful."

Now, her head turned and he saw something like scorn in her face. He took a breath and ploughed on, measuring his words. "If you've only known cruelty, then you cannot imagine aught else, but I promise you, it is not always thus. Why do you think the troubadours sing so, and ladies enjoy their songs? The queen herself loves their lays and tales of romance. Isabella, I am not a cruel man. We are not all the same." He racked his brains. "You say his mother hated you? That she was unkind?"

She nodded.

"And are all women like her? Are you?"

Isabella's head jerked from his shoulder. She did not answer, and he pulled her head back down to the warm spot where it had been. "It's late, my wife. Shall we try to sleep?"

Without waiting for her response, he slid back down into the bed, taking her with him, keeping his arm around her. Slowly, he felt the tension drain from her. It was enough. *For now,* he thought, drifting into sleep.

Isabella lay in the curl of Giles' arm, unsleeping. Could she trust him? It was unfair of him to point out all women were not the same. That was different. And yet, although she'd been sceptical at the time, thinking about it now, Mabille de Bourne had appeared content with her husband. Isabella had seen warmth in the looks they gave each other, and Mabille had sometimes appeared to almost tease him gently when she thought none could hear. Godfroi had not seemed to mind, chuckling and squeezing her to him.

It was true that the tension between them had been unbearable. Since their wedding, she'd been unable to loosen the tightness in her jaw and body. Her head had ached constantly, she'd been on edge, ready to cry or scream. He was right. It was not comfortable. Was he right about the other? Could it truly be pleasurable? She doubted it, but something within her seemed to nudge her to find out. What if there could truly be something more between them? And how would she know if she did not try?

CHAPTER 15

Isabella arched her neck, realising with a start that she must have slept. And she was still in Giles' embrace. She'd not expected to be able to rest while he held her. Opening her eyes, she discovered he was leaning over her, his right arm propping him up, a grimace on his face.

"Wife, I'm sorry to disturb you, but if you don't move, my left arm will fall off."

She responded hastily. Baldwin would have thrown her to the floor – had he ever embraced her like that in the first place. De Soutenay merely chuckled ruefully, rubbing his arm and wincing, saying, "I feel the fire of a thousand needles. You may not be heavy, but just at the moment, I'm glad to be rid of the weight of you."

He flexed his arm, and she could see the hard muscle in it. Lean it was, no fat. His body was taut and firm, the curls of dark hair on his chest springy. He stopped rubbing his arm and caught her eyes, and she flushed as though he'd read her thoughts. His gaze slid lower, and she realised her shift had slipped revealing her bare shoulder and the curve of her body. She pulled it back quickly, but it was too late. She could read the desire in his face, and his breathing had quickened.

Even in her flurry of nerves, she could see something different about this man. She'd been too afraid to notice before, but the expression in his eyes was warm, admiring. He lacked the vicious, feral look Baldwin had habitually worn. That had been predatory; she'd felt like a mouse beholding a hawk. What she was seeing in Giles' gaze seemed to spark something in her. The feeling of being precious, to be cherished, not devoured.

What should she do? If he just took her, all that had passed between them would be ruined. If she offered herself and he was as gentle as he'd promised, maybe the tension of the past few days would ease and the band that seemed to have knotted itself around her head so tightly be gone.

Giles tilted his head in an unspoken question. That look was still in his eyes – not just desire, something more subtle, as though he might actually care. She held herself still, watching him. Was this just for her? Her, Isabella, not just any woman. She didn't know why, she'd hardly given him reason.

She shivered as he stroked her bare shoulder; a smile came, tentatively, to her lips. He had waited – she must give him that. He'd been true to his word, had not forced her. Would Baldwin have waited as long? She nearly laughed aloud at the thought.

Her lips curved more warmly and she peered at him beneath lowered lashes, marvelling when she saw him hesitate before taking a deep breath. Such a small action to provoke him.

He bent as though to kiss her, then held back, saying, "It has not been comfortable between us, has it, Isabella?" His voice was soft.

She shook her head, and her lips trembled with the enormity of what she was about to commit herself to as she murmured, "No, my lord."

"Do you think we've reached an understanding now?"

She could not speak again. Her throat was too tight with the conflicting emotions of fear and wonder to let the words out, but she nodded breathlessly.

"Then shall we break down this last barrier between us? I promise you, I'll not hurt you."

The uncomfortable feeling inside her had not gone, despite his soft words. Speaking of hurting was meat for her fear. And yet, what was inside her was not the same; fear yes, but something more, something brighter, so strange and almost unknown – hope. How long since she had felt that? And this man, this husband of hers, had gifted that to her, for, so far, he had asked little in return, except her body. Even that, with her new-found hope, did not seem so much to ask. It was his anyway, before the law and church, and yet he asked, not demanded; offered something of himself and did not snatch at her.

Maybe, she would even discover this delight he spoke of. She swallowed once, closed her eyes and nodded, letting go of the trepidation that had held her back.

He lowered his lips to hers; she braced herself, but they weren't hard and bruising as she'd expected. They were warm and pliant, gentle, and she found her own lips parting in response. He tasted of wine and fennel seeds; she had noted his use of the hazel twigs provided for them. Baldwin's breath had been so sour, she'd had to force herself not to retch. Giles' mouth lingered a moment on hers then moved over her face exploring her eyelids, her ears, her jaw and the hollow of her neck, the bristles of his beard scratching slightly. Almost involuntarily, her fingers entwined themselves in his hair, and although she was still nervous of what was to come, she felt a sudden bud of pride as she recognised his need for her.

Giles moved away from Isabella, a light sheen of sweat glistening on his chest, as she watched him through half-closed lids. Her face gave away nothing. Had he hurt her?

In truth, he'd not known what to expect from her. Now, he thought there was hope for, in repose, the tautness had left her face, and he could see the promise of the young woman she might become if he trod carefully. And how could she know how to respond to him so soon? It was very early days yet. Her confidence would grow, he hoped.

Her gaze was still upon him; he rearranged his features into a smile.

There was cause for optimism, of a surety, for despite her evident nervousness, she'd not resisted him. He hoped so or, he mused ruefully, their future yawned ahead like a chasm, long, cold and lonely, but it still could not be rushed. *A good thing I'm a patient man.*

For Isabella's sake, he'd held back as much as he could so, although their union was now complete, he was still wakeful, his desire slightly quenched but not fully satisfied.

How had it been for her? She had not uttered a sound, which had discomfited him slightly. He was used to women taking their delight too, for he knew he took the time to please as much as be pleased, and he flattered himself that he was a considerate lover when he indulged himself, which had not been so often in recent times.

Not only had she been silent, her face had remained passive, still, eyes closed, almost as though she was not really there. Yet, he had seen her lips part slightly, fancied he'd heard a faint sigh. He hoped it was pleasure, not pain. And the feel of her fingers in his hair had delighted and reassured him. She would not have done that if she did not want him just a little, would she? It must be a good sign. Pray God it was, for if he'd not been able to convince her the act should be one of enjoyment, not pain, what would the rest of their years together be like?

As he lay there, propped on one elbow, her eyes flickered wide. He expected her to clamp her lids shut again when she realised he'd noticed, but she turned her head to meet his gaze, and for the first time, he saw an unforced smile on her face. Just a small one which was quickly gone, but he took it as encouragement.

He broke the silence that gaped between them with a yawn. Much as he would like to, he could not lie here looking at her for the whole night.

The sheepskin which covered the blankets had slipped and Giles pulled it back up, tucking it around her tenderly.

He had been going to try to sleep, but the softness of her skin as his hand brushed it kindled a fresh hunger inside him. He would not slake it, for that would be to undo all he hoped he had achieved, but he groaned audibly. The rest of the night would be long.

Wide awake again now, he slid one arm beneath the coverings, feeling the cool silkiness of her bare shoulder where the neck of her shift gaped.

She turned her head and looked at him; he could not read the expression on her face. That was something he hoped to change.

"Don't be afraid, I'll not trouble you more. I simply wish to hold you."

Still, she said nothing but shifted her body slightly towards him, and there was silence. Giles closed his eyes, but sleep would not come no matter how hard he sought it, and thoughts swirled around his brain, tormenting him, teasing him. At length, he opened his eyes again. "Isabella, do you think we might find love together?"

Her eyes were uncertain, her lower lip drooping like the petal of a rose. "I don't know, my lord."

"Then, if not love, might we try for freond-scype between us?" He knew a few Saxon words, and he used this one deliberately now to see if he could provoke a reaction from her, some curiosity, something to take the conversation to safer ground.

It worked. Instead of a small careful smile, her brow wrinkled. It was the first real sign of animation he had seen from her in days. "Fr…?" She stumbled over the unfamiliar word.

"Say it like this: fray ond shippa." Obediently, she repeated it after him.

"It means something more than friendship, yet less than love. Affection; warmth of a sort. Would that not be worth the having?"

She considered. For a moment, he thought she would say nothing. Then, she put one hand to her face. Tears started to her eyes, hovering on her lashes before they brimmed over, and his heart sank.

As he was about to turn from her, she spoke. Her voice was still quiet but steady as she said, "I…should like that, my lord."

It was just a small step forward, but it made his heart sing.

Isabella lay with the unfamiliar weight of Giles' arm heavy across her. She had turned away from him, not in rejection but to allow him to wrap himself around her, and she felt his arm tighten. Did she like that? She thought maybe she did.

It was not something Baldwin had ever done, and not something she'd wished from him. When he'd finished with her, all she wanted was to curl herself in a ball, as far away from him as possible, nursing her bruises while he snored, oblivious to her tears.

She knew Giles had held himself back. Coupling with him had not been what she was expecting. She shook the thought out of her mind – she did not want to remember, let that be consigned to the past, for this was very different. There was a gentleness she had not anticipated. Tenderness, as he had promised. It was far from unpleasant.

No, she did not dislike it. Indeed, she might grow to enjoy it, to want it, even. Her lips curved upwards as she remembered how he had called her name for he *had* needed her. Her, not just any woman. The helplessness she'd always felt before was gone, and something new had taken its place. Her smile increased for, in his need was power of a sort.

She knew he would have liked to do it again but was relieved he'd not tried. Her emotions were raw, her nerve endings sensitive, and there were so many unfamiliar sensations swirling through her at the moment. She could not bear to be touched intimately again until she'd come to terms with what had happened.

And now, she felt the warmth of his body against hers. It was cold even with the blankets and sheepskins; if only she had the courage to move a little closer, but she did not wish to awaken him, to risk his annoyance with her. The glimmer of confidence which had started to flicker like a newly-lit candle would be snuffed out if that happened, and then she doubted she would ever feel anything again. Besides, he might mistake her intention, might think she wanted more of him. And she did not, did she?

It might be that, as *he* – she would not often allow herself to think of him by his name yet – had said, they could find a form of contentment together. If so, it would be more than she had dared to wish for since her first wedding night. Her eyelids grew heavy as the bell for Matins sounded faintly, far away; her last conscious thought, *I hope so. Oh, I hope so.*

Isabella was fathoms deep in sleep when her nose started to itch. She half woke and lifted her hand to scratch it. Still, it itched. She brushed at it again with no better effect. Finally, she gave in to the irritation and managed to prise her eyelids open, to find her husband propped on one elbow, tickling her nose with a lock of her own hair. She blinked the sleep from her eyes and greeted him with a small smile.

"Good morrow, my wife," he said heartily. Too heartily, in Isabella's opinion. Whilst last night had held something unexpected, she was not yet in any rush to repeat the experience, and her heart sank at the playful expression on his face. If she believed in this man and he proved to be like Baldwin in the end, she would break. Best not to put her faith in him, not yet, anyway. In the cold light of the morning, the events of the night seemed like a dream, something not quite real which might shatter if she grasped it too tightly.

On the other shoe, she had to live with him, and to rile him, or to withhold herself, might make him turn against her. While he was treating her thus, happen it was wise to humour him. She forced herself to smile a little wider, bracing herself in case he took it as further invitation.

He let go of her hair and stroked her face. She held her breath but he merely kissed her on the tip of her nose before pushing the covers back. Isabella's shift had ridden up to the top of her thighs, and she saw the flash of desire in his eyes, followed by disappointment as she pulled it back down, but he did not move closer.

She didn't know whether to be relieved or disappointed herself. The neck of her wretched shift had slipped yet again and she rearranged it quickly, tying the laces, tensing as she did so, for at this point, Baldwin would have ripped it from her.

Giles, however, merely chuckled lazily and climbed from the bed. He strolled to the table and poured her a glass of wine, passing it to her, pouring one for himself before he peered out of the shutters. Immediately, a howling gale filled the room. Isabella shuddered and pulled the covers up around her.

De Soutenay also shivered and slammed the shutter closed. "And still it snows, Isabella. I fear we may be here for some time, for I'll not risk setting forth in this." He poked at the brazier, trying to bring the ashes back to life, shrugged, picked up his wine and got back into bed. "Ah well, I'm in no hurry; it will be good to take this chance to better acquaint ourselves, do you not think? For when we're home, there will be duties. Here we may take our leisure, enjoy each other without distractions."

Did she want that? Would it not be better to remain as acquaintances? At least, then, the disappointment – if he turned out to be less than he seemed – would not be so great. Yet, she remembered his words from last night. It might be comfortable to count him as a friend. Did she dare to trust? She tilted her head in agreement and heard the bells sound for Prime.

Giles finished his wine. "And it is pleasant to lie here, but I'm famished. What say you? Shall we see what the abbey can fill our bellies with?"

She went to nod, caught his eye and changed her mind. She'd treated him to her silence long enough. Yes, it had mostly been fear, but she had to confess, some of the reason had also been a punishment, and that for his being a man, which after all, he could not help. In all honesty, she could not really blame him for wedding her either. It would be a foolhardy man who turned down a bride suggested to him by the queen. He'd tried his best; it was time she gave a little, too. "I confess, I do seem to have a hunger this morning, my lord." She hid her face, grimacing. Now, she'd made it sound as though her hunger was caused by desire.

His eyes crinkled in acknowledgment, and he pushed down the covers, kicking his long legs over the edge of the bed. Taking her hand, he pulled her after him.

"As you have no maid, will you let me assist you?" Giles' words were slightly stilted, but she supposed, with longer acquaintance, they might become more at ease with each other – possibly. For the time being, she allowed him to help her on with her stockings, refusing to react as his hands brushed her skin. He took her garters and fastened them below her knee, saying, "No need for you to wear my hose today." He gave a snort of laughter. "We don't wish to scandalise the good sisters. But promise me you'll wear them when we travel."

She made a non-committal noise in the back of her throat, which he took as an answer, turning to take up her gown, frowning. "I begin to wish we'd brought your travelling chest with us. At any rate, I hope we may send for it soon. Where did you move your bags to?"

Isabella averted her gaze, uncomfortable with him in this state of undress. "Over there." She pointed to a coffer, and he rummaged inside, pulling out a warm woollen gown in her preferred shade of bright tawny. She took it from him, and he waited until her head popped through the neck before tying the laces. Then, he pulled his own hose and shirt on, to Isabella's relief. Clad, he looked less...less of a threat to her peace of mind.

He opened his bag and pulled out a serviceable russet-coloured tunic and a thick mantle in a shade of vert.

More comfortable now, she peered at him from beneath her lashes, deciding she quite liked what she saw. Although not handsome, his face was not uncomely, his body well-muscled and lean; she blushed at the thoughts that came unbidden into her head.

He raked his fingers through his hair until it looked a little tidier, then taking up her comb, started to sweep it down her tresses. She winced as he caught it in a knot, then her body tightened in case she had displeased him.

It seemed she had not. "I'm sorry, Isabella, I should take more care, but I'm out of practise these days, although I probably should not tell you that." He kissed the top of her head, then took up his task again, more slowly this time, until he'd smoothed out all the tangles. Finally, he lay the comb down.

"I dare not risk trying to braid it; if I do, it will be in worse knots that it was before I started."

She smiled absently, plaiting it, coiling it up into a silken net and pulling on her linen wimple. Then, she pinned her veil on. All the time, he watched her.

"Such pretty hair. A shame custom decrees it must be covered. But then, it makes the uncovering of it so much more fun." He winked, which so disconcerted her, she stuck the second pin into her scalp and yelped as she felt the sharpness of it.

As she removed both veil and wimple, inspecting them to see whether she had bled, there was a knock at the door. Giles opened it, and

Sister Joan came into the room with a ewer of water from which steam was rising. They washed their hands and faces while the nun raked the brazier over.

"I hope you slept well." The nun did not look at them, which made Isabella blush; she could feel the fiery heat rising up her throat and hastily donned her head coverings again.

De Soutenay gave her a grin. "Thank you, Sister, yes." Then, he held out his arm to escort Isabella from the chamber, saying, "Come, wife, let us break our fast."

She placed her hand along his arm and felt the tension in him. So he was not quite as at ease as he appeared. Somehow, the thought reassured her, and she felt her own strain start to abate again as they found their way to the refectory.

They stepped inside, and he was greeted as boisterously as usual by his men. Today, Isabella was very aware of the difference in herself but, thankfully, none of them seemed to have noticed aught amiss and their talk did not include any ribald comments. The relief lasted until she saw his youngest knight watching her with an indefinable expression on his face. Her husband pulled out the bench for her, and she sat, as the lay sister placed bowls of pottage before them. Silence fell, as the men devoured the contents.

CHAPTER 16

The wind howled and wailed along the cloister as Hildegarde sped through, threatening to tear the cloak from her back. Wrapping it more tightly about her, she dashed into the warming room.

Sister Grecia was huddled by the brazier within, her nose red, her fingers almost blue. Sister Aldith was crouched next to her, sniffing dolefully, Sister Felicia had given up all pretence of working at her sewing, having dropped her needle, and elderly Sister Benedicta had a hacking cough. Enough was enough. Hildegarde found her prioress, Sister Ela, shivering in the library and drew her aside.

"Dear Sister Prioress, I know this should wait until we can bring it up in Chapter, but do you not think we should use the sense we were born with?"

Sister Prioress, who had been massaging her hands surreptitiously, stilled them and looked up with a baffled expression. "Abbess?"

"This cold! I know the rule says we must not have heating except in the calefactory, but I do not believe this type of suffering makes our souls richer. Rather, it makes our bodies weaker."

The prioress goggled at her, mouth agape.

"Well, Sister Prioress, I know your chilblains are paining you. Do you not find it easier to praise when your fingers are less afflicted? Do you not find unnecessary suffering distracts you?"

Sister Prioress tucked her purple, swollen fingers inside her sleeves and said nothing, blinking at her as Hildegarde continued remorselessly. "When suffering cannot be avoided, then yes, I believe we should use it to glorify God, but when it is pointless and needless and endangers lives, do you not think the rule should be tempered with kindness?"

"Well, I..."

"Of course you do. No sane person would not." Hildegarde was well aware that to the religious of this century, her thoughts were scandalous. Sometimes, it was difficult to suppress her twentieth-century background, but on this, she was prepared to take a stand.

"And so, how would it be if we were to light braziers in the dorters and other common rooms? Just while this dreadful weather continues?" she wheedled, seeing Sister Ela beginning to consider such a radical notion. "It would help if you were to back me up, dear Ela. I'm sure Ursel will agree, for if less of us become ill needlessly, it will make her work easier."

At the mention of Ursel's name, Sister Ela brightened but still hesitated. "Well, I..."

Hildegarde beamed at her. "I knew I could rely on you, Sister Prioress. Come, let us tell our dear sisters and relieve their suffering immediately."

Let some sniff and condemn her if they dared; she did not care. And, had she but known it, her nuns blessed her for her tender care of them. Even the most pious did not complain.

Thus, as the weather became more severe, ice froze the fishponds, and the cold seeped into the bones of both young and old, whilst in other religious houses, many perished, the nuns of Sparnstow were among the few who did not suffer serious hardship.

"And I'm glad to see the frost between Sir Giles and his wife has thawed," Hildegarde remarked to Ursel as they left Prime together and headed towards the infirmary, "for the ordeal of dining with them was freezing me nearly as cold as the snow. Now, I can invite the other sisters to join us, although, I'm afraid, dear Ursel, I dare not ask you again, for I don't wish it to seem as though I favour you.

"It does look as though our visitors will be with us for some time yet, so there is opportunity aplenty to make up for my neglect. Although," and her forehead wrinkled, "I must find out how our supplies are holding up."

"Aye, my lady. I know Sister Joan is worried they're getting low." Ursel's face was creased. "She intends to bring the matter up in Chapter."

"Hmm, it is a concern for me, also. I believe we have enough for now, but as soon as the spring comes, we'll need to restrict our diets considerably. I do think we need to pray about this, dear Ursel, for so many are relying on our aid."

"I'd never intended to stay this long," muttered Giles, as he and Isabella hastened from the guest house to the refectory, their cloaks covered with snow, and a gust of wind swirling after them, drawing glares from those who huddled within. "But, in truth, to travel in this would be perilous." He took Isabella's cloak from her, shook the worst from it and lay it over a trestle table. "You do not mind the delay?"

She accepted a cup of warmed ale from a lay sister and moved further into the room. "Not at all, my lord." She shivered as the door banged open again, admitting another refugee from outside.

Someone moved from beside one of the several braziers Hildegarde had ordered lit, and Giles, seizing the opportunity, drew Isabella to the vacated place on the bench before anyone else could beat them to it. One of the other travellers, a stout merchant who had also been heading for the same spot with his equally stout wife, gave Giles a wry nod, acknowledging his greater right to the seat. Giles grinned at him, then turned his attention back to Isabella, who sat close to him, her elbows on her lap, hands held out to the warmth. Giles watched the glow of the flames reflected in her eyes.

For him, their prolonged stay had been a blessing. The stony-faced woman he had arrived with had turned into flesh and blood. And, at night, the cold had been his friend as they clung to each other seeking warmth, for even though she was still the passive recipient of his passions, in her unguarded moments, when he had nuzzled her earlobes and lipped at the tender skin at the hollow of her neck, she had made small noises in her throat, and her fingers had clawed the sheets as though she would have liked to respond in kind. Yes, the nights alone were worth the inconvenience of staying longer.

He put an arm about her waist, and she leaned into him slightly, indicating a couple of jongleurs who were pulling out a psaltery and shawm.

As they began to play some popular lays, the other guests accompanied them, singing with enthusiasm. A few pulled out eating knives and began to tap out the rhythm. Isabella listened for a short while, then sang too, her voice low but tuneful, and even Giles, who knew he had a voice like a half-dead crow, could not resist the urge to join in. However, he was glad his men were seated at a distance, for he knew they would not be able to forbear enjoying themselves at his expense.

The hosteller frowned, but the jongleurs wisely kept their entertainment to innocuous songs which could offend no one, and Giles grinned as he noticed Sister Joan's hand tapping rhythmically against her habit as she went about her business.

And no wonder she was looking concerned before, he thought as she supervised the ladling of pottage into bowls. *There are so many of us, this must be straining their resources to the limit.* There were twenty sisters, five lay brethren and the priest already, plus a few lay sisters and servants. The guest hall itself was accounting for about fifteen poorer travellers, all of whom were sleeping in the big barn and those more noble or wealthy visitors who stayed in the guest house.

As Giles and Isabella were among the most noble, if not the wealthiest, Sister Joan had hesitantly offered to ask the merchant, a trader in fine rings and precious stones, to change rooms. Giles had refused the offer to the worried nun's evident relief. The merchant might, if the abbey nuns were lucky, offer more alms than Giles could afford.

A well-to-do pilgrim and his son occupied another of the rooms and a fairly unimportant knight and his wife. The other guests had not mingled, preferring to keep to their chambers.

Giles left Isabella on the bench and found his way to Sister Joan's side. She turned as he stood there, and he saw close to the lines of worry about her eyes, the deep furrow between her brows.

"Sister Joan," he murmured, "this is a large number you are forced to feed. I hope your stores are not running too low."

She gave a laugh which seemed strained to him. "Indeed, it is making somewhat of a hole in them, but," she shrugged, "what else can we do?

We are bound to care for those who seek shelter here."

He felt for the purse which hung at his waist and pulled a handful of coins out, offering them to her. "It would mean much to me if you would accept this donation to help your charitable efforts."

Joan gasped when she saw how much was there, one hand flying to her mouth, the other half reaching, half hesitating to take what was offered. He pressed them into her palm, then turned before she could thank him.

At last, the thaw came. Cold it still was, but less bitter, and the rest of their journey could be made without danger now. If truth be told, Giles longed for Thorneywell; thoughts of it tugged at him. His people, his home.

As they dressed for the chill weather, he held out a pair of hose to Isabella. "Will you wear these, my wife?"

She paused in the act of pulling on her fur-lined boots. "I…"

"It would please me to know you are warmly clad."

She flushed but held out her hand. He did not give them to her, but pushed her gently onto the bed and, removing the boot she had already put on, he pulled them up himself, stroking her legs as he did so. She lowered her gaze but not before he noticed the kindling of desire there. He was tempted to take her but resisted and replaced her boots. Just as well, he realised, as Alan, one of his senior squires, knocked and opened the door, which he'd forgotten to secure.

Alan shuffled his feet, and Giles beckoned him in impatiently. "Why are you hovering there like some crow who suspects the carrion is a trap?"

Alan swallowed and looked sheepish. "I beg your pardon, my lord. I did not wish to…"

He trailed off, and Giles swallowed a grin. The lad was not used to the protocol of his lord having a wife. "Continue," he said, keeping his face straight.

Alan held out his hand, and Giles was startled to see a missive sealed with John's ring. Curse him, was there to be no peace even here? And how had John even known where to find him? Although it was a simple enough deduction, he supposed. He took the letter, broke the seal and read slowly, feeling his face settle into grim lines as the details unfolded. Alan watched and waited; Giles dismissed him and turned to Isabella. "It seems our plans must change," he said, his heart sinking, for this was not news his wife would be gladdened by.

Isabella, still sitting on the bed, turned her face up to his, a question in her eyes, and Giles realised there was no way to break this to her gently. "It seems John has need of me at Aylesbury."

She frowned. "Now, husband? But…"

He nodded. "Immediately. I cannot escort you home."

"Then what do you wish for me to do, my lord? Will you send me with an escort?"

"I wish I could. That–" He caught himself and rephrased it. "He wishes me to bring my men with me."

"Then what shall I do?" Her face paled to the colour of new cheese. "You do not wish me to accompany you to Aylesbury, my lord?" She bit her lip and swallowed visibly.

He did. Now they had better come to know each other, he did not want to risk losing what he had gained, but how could he, knowing John would probably take every opportunity he could to torment her?

He had not forgotten the exchange between Isabella and John when John had kissed her, neither his wife's look of disgust nor John's response.

John would not easily forget that insult. Taking Isabella to court with him now, exposing her again to John's unpleasant games, would be unfair.

He reached for her hand. "Do you wish to accompany me?" Her eyes wide, she shook her head. "Then how if I leave you here at the abbey? The abbess will find a woman to act as your maid, I'm sure. And I'll return to you as quickly as I can."

Her breath came out almost on a sigh. "My lord, I thank you."

Tilting her head, he bent and kissed her. "I'll not stay longer than necessary."

She smiled. A warm, generous smile. *Probably relief*, he told himself but added, "I'll miss you. I hope you'll also miss me."

The colour back in her face, her tones were as heartfelt as he could have wished as she replied quietly but convincingly, "I believe I shall, my lord."

"Then I'll speak to the abbess and ask her to make arrangements for you. I'll leave her enough to pay someone to attend on you." He pulled her gently to her feet and put his arms around her. He kissed her again, and her arms wound more tightly around him, tempting him to delay, but he must not. He freed himself, and she gazed at him as though memorising his features. Small wonder. They'd barely had time to get to know each other even slightly, and now he was bound to John for who knew how long?

"Go with God, husband."

He took her hand and kissed the palm, folding her fingers inward over the place he'd kissed, then turned and strode from the room, glancing back to see her holding her hand to her face.

Left alone, Isabella removed her boots and Giles' hose since she would not now need them. She would miss him. Never before had she known anything like this relationship. She could barely remember her mother, her father was not some-one she had any liking for, and as for Baldwin and his mother…

She dashed moisture from her lashes with an impatient hand. It was not as though either she or Giles had any choice in the matter, and the depth of her gratitude for not insisting she join him was fathomless. But now she had become used to spending her days and nights with him, the thought of him not being there gave her a hollow feeling. And she would need a maid if she were to be left alone, for company as much as aid.

She slipped her feet into her soft house shoes and waited to see what would happen next, picking up her book of hours and trying not to wonder how long she would be here. The irony of the fact that last time she was at Sparnstow she'd hoped to find sanctuary did not escape her. Suddenly realising she would have one more chance to see Giles before he left, she put the book back down, caught up one of her ribbons and hurried to the stables.

She was not too late; he was still there and walked Troubadour towards her. Leaning from the saddle, he caught her up to him, kissing her hard, his arm like an oak girder around her. As he released her, she called, "May God go with you, my lord. I pray you return to me soon," and pressed the ribbon of yellow silk Marie had given her for a wedding gift into his hand. He held out his wrist, and she bound it there like a favour, then watched it flutter in the wind as he turned and trotted Troubadour out through the gates at the head of his men.

Isabella watched until he was out of sight and Sister Berthe had closed the gates, then stayed staring at nothing until the cold from the ground seeped into the soles of her shoes. Shivering, she turned back to the guest house, surprised at how bereft she felt.

CHAPTER 17

Giles allowed Troubadour to break into a canter. The big sorrel had been cooped up long enough and shook his head, whinnying as he was given free rein. Giles himself felt an emptiness. In the short time he and Isabella had finally crossed the distance between them, his emotions had become engaged and now he felt the loss of her. He gave a wry laugh; a little late to discover the perils of allowing access to his heart.

They reached Aylesbury Castle in time for the noon meal. John, however, was not there. Neither was the castellan. Giles asked the constable for his whereabouts and was given some nonsense about hawking.

Then why the urgency for me to come to him? A lurking suspicion assailed him. Was John punishing him and Isabella by separating them? Of a certainty, John usually avoided him as one might a leper except for his regular covert Whitsuntide duty to John. The very fact that he was the only one apart from Eleanor who knew John's secrets made Giles suspect in John's eyes, and Giles knew he hated to be reminded of his vulnerability.

Then, too, if Isabella had offended him at their wedding, and Giles was well aware something had passed between them, some undercurrent, she was equally likely to become subject to John's revenge.

He kicked his heels until it was growing dark without, and eventually a commotion caught his attention as John and his company clattered in through the bailey. Giles awaited his summons. It did not come.

A sennight later, Giles was full of misgiving. He had tried approaching John, only to be fobbed off with excuses every time he got near. The urgent business John had summoned him on had failed to materialise, and the man himself was hardly on the premises. When he was, he idled around gaming and drinking. Giles, at the tight end of his temper by now, insisted the steward take him to John's private quarters.

John, tossing the dice from one hand to the other, eyed him, one side of his mouth quirking up as Giles knelt before him. "Oh, rise, de Soutenay. Have a drink, man. Wash that sour look from your face. I have an excellent wine here you may like. Would you care to hazard your luck against mine? Mayhap that wife of yours has made fortune smile upon you."

The quirk became a smirk, and Giles itched to smash John's teeth down his throat. A muscle twitched in his jaw. John must have noticed; he said, "I believe our friend here is missing his wife. Myself, I'd sooner bed with a block of marble, but I suppose some have to take what they can get, eh?"

Giles ground his teeth and ignored the re-mark, saying. "My lord, you summoned me, and I await your pleasure."

"Indeed you do, de Soutenay, indeed you do. And when I have time, I will speak to you, but for the moment, as you see, I am occupied with matters of importance."

He flicked an offhand dismissal, and Giles had no option but to leave, swallowing his ire with difficulty. If only John were not a prince! He held all the advantages and would not hesitate to pay Giles back summarily for any perceived slights. All that was left for him to do was pretend he was as unconcerned as John appeared. And he doubted either of them were deceived.

A further week and Giles' temper was at breaking point. His men were avoiding him. The only person who actively sought his company was Mazalina, and her presence he did not want. Not only were her favours expensive, but her face, sharp and painted too gaudily, had never appealed to him, and even less so since he now had Isabella. After such a difficult beginning, he'd not thought his wife could touch him, but once they had reached understanding, she had found her way beneath his skin, and he now discovered the longer he was absent, the more he missed her.

Mazalina, never one to take a hint at the best of times, hovered around him like some gnat hoping to find a place to land, whispering into his ear, her heavy perfume cloying, while she hung on his arm. It was beyond his understanding; she knew he lacked the wherewithal to pay her, and surely he could not make his disinterest any clearer. Unless…

Then he noticed her sidling up to John, giggling as he fondled her. When Giles saw John's sly glance in his direction, he knew his guess had been correct. John wanted him here only to separate him from Isabella. His hands curled into fists for a moment, then he let them hang loose. He would not give John the satisfaction.

From then on, Giles laughed and joked, drank and diced like a man with nowhere he'd rather be. John continued to avoid him, and he wondered how long he could keep this up.

At the end of the third week, he asked again to be taken to John. The steward looked at him in surprise. "Have you not heard? John left to go to France two days ago. He received news his brother was planning a meeting with Geoffrey's widow. John wished to offer support." Support to whom, he did not say.

Giles' first reaction was an urge to smash something against the wall. His second was relief that he was not now needed. John would certainly want to make sure Richard came to no agreement with Constance, his brother's widow. Geoffrey, younger than Richard but older than John, had a son, Arthur.

Giles cursed. If Geoffrey hadn't felt the need to continually prove himself at those damned tourneys, he wouldn't have been killed. Now, with Richard not yet having an heir of his own body, he constantly dangled the kingdom between John and Arthur. Not that Arthur would care at present, being too young. But if John had got wind of some negotiation with Constance, he would want to ensure it was unsuccessful.

Ah well, he shrugged. It was all speculation at the moment. And if it got John off his back, then at least it had worked to his advantage this time. Likely John had completely forgotten about Giles. He could go home.

Hildegarde had been able to spend time with Isabella when Giles had first gone, but after that, she'd had to leave her somewhat to her own devices, so Isabella was delighted when the other knight's wife, Lady Ada, had seen fit to befriend her. Giles knew her husband, although not well, and they had spoken a few times when Giles was there.

Lady Ada had seemed assured and confident to Isabella at the time. The other knight's wife, Lady Estrilda, had barely stepped outside her chamber, giving Isabella and Ada the merest nod when she passed, to Ada's oft-voiced dismay. "For the last time we met, she would hardly leave my side. We were the greatest of friends. I worry in case she might be ill, though more likely that husband of hers is being disobliging. But it's a pleasure to have now made your acquaintance," she assured Isabella. She accompanied her to meals and admired the embroidery Isabella was working on, and together, they sat and picked over the silks deciding which were best to use.

Today, Ada advanced with a beaming smile, taking Isabella's arm possessively and drawing her into a corner of the guest house which was sheltered from the draughts and close enough to one of the braziers to be comfortable. Her maid carried an armful of small cushions appropriated, by the look of them, from her chamber, and strewed them over the wooden bench before bustling off to fetch them spiced wine, then she retreated out of hearing and settled to some sewing.

"Have you heard from your husband yet, Isabella?"

Isabella strove to hide her embarrassment. "Nothing yet, my lady."

"Oh, tush! Enough of 'my lady'. Have I not told you to call me Ada?"

Isabella smiled. "Indeed, Ada, I'll try to remember. And no, I've heard nothing from him." She added, feeling somehow the need to excuse him, "It's likely the count is keeping him too busy."

Ada raised her eyebrows until they disappeared beneath her veil. "And he cannot find time to dictate a few short words to a scribe? Fine behaviour! But they're all the same, these men. Doubtless, he's found time to warm his bed with some harlot at the court."

When Isabella opened her mouth to protest, Ada tapped her on the arm and said, "Don't fear, my dear. You need not scruple to tell me what he's like. My own Henry cannot be trusted the moment he's away from home. Like as not with my own maids, too, if I did not watch them carefully." She shrugged a plump shoulder. "Ah, it's the way they are, is it not? And what can we poor womenfolk do but bear their children year after year? At least, if my Henry is wearing himself out elsewhere, he's not invading my bed. But take heed of me, dear. Don't trust him over-much, for that way hearts get broken."

Isabella tried to make her excuses and leave for this talk was neither what she wanted nor needed. Having only just learned to be comfortable with Giles, Ada's words felt like poison to her, and it would not take much for doubt to rise up and overcome her. She would have got up, but Ada had hold of her hand and she couldn't tug it away without being rude.

Ada continued to pat her hand as though she was Isabella's mother, saying, "Ah, but you're young and newly wed. When I was young, I believed the sun shone out of my Henry's eyes." She pulled a face. "Now I know it's not the sun, merely false reflection. Oh yes, I believed in all the jongleurs' tales. He'd be true only to me, he would face death rather than allow me to be dishonoured. Ah, what fools we women are."

Isabella's face was stiff from trying to smile. Any moment now, she felt she would spit and snarl instead. Did this stupid woman really think she wanted such tittle-tattle so early in her marriage?

Surely Giles wasn't like that. He'd made inroads into a heart she'd thought was too frozen ever to feel again. Surely he'd not turn out to be just the same as Ada's man. She shuddered. Ada noticed and said, "But there, I should not be speaking this way, I suppose. Only, you must know it's so, for he's not your first husband, is he?"

"No." Isabella gave a clipped answer in cool tones hoping Ada would take her hint and change the subject, or better yet, go away, but the woman seemed determined to cling like the ivy on the guest house walls. This was the first time Ada had spoken of such things, and Isabella decided she did not care to spend more time with her if this was how it would be. But how to keep her at a distance now she'd given her friendship?

Surely all men were not alike. She didn't want to believe Giles was like Ada's Henry, yet the woman had far more experience than she.

Isabella tried to close her ears, tried to discourage the wretched woman by replying in monosyllables, focussing her thoughts on the design she was embroidering as a gift to the abbey, but the insidious words invaded her consciousness. Oh, if Giles would but send a note. He may not have noticed her books or even realised she could read but he would know someone at the abbey could read it for her, surely.

In desperation, she allowed her gaze to rove the room until she spotted Sister Joan, sending her a pleading glance, hoping the nun would read her situation and join them. Sister Joan nodded and started towards them.

Ada was still talking when the hosteller reached their corner. Sister Joan stood for a few moments listening, her expression inscrutable, then said with the slightest hint of asperity, "My dear Lady Ada, does not Holy Scripture say women should respect their husbands? This is not speech to be having here."

Ada pressed her lips together mutinously as she glared at the nun who continued blithely, "Come, let us turn our talk to better things. Let me show you a fine new piece Sisters Felicia and Aldith have worked for our abbey." To have the hosteller paying them such personal attention seemed to mollify Ada, and as Sister Joan inclined her head, she got up and followed happily enough. Once into the abbey, the holy atmosphere silenced her.

Isabella was so grateful, she could have hugged Joan. When the nun had walked them down the length of the abbey as far as they were permitted to go, pointing out the fine stonework, the embroidered hangings, the wall paintings of scenes from the scriptures, she finally took them back to the hall, depositing Ada in a high-backed chair with panelled sides, which was such a seat of honour, the woman was unlikely to move until supper.

Then, tucking Isabella's hand firmly into her arm, she took her to Hildegarde's private chamber, saying, "Lady Isabella, please don't let her words upset you. I should not gossip, but it is well known she loves her husband not, nor he her. They are both dreadfully unsuited; nothing like you and Sir Giles. Don't let her dismay you or cause you to doubt him. He's a good man and will be a good husband to you." She hesitated then repeated again, "He *is* a good man, and our blessed Lady was smiling on you when you wed him. Believe me, for it's true. I'm sorry we did not realise she'd got her hooks into you earlier, for she does like to complain about her lot, bless her. We were so busy, it slipped my notice. Still, we will try to keep her from you now. Our abbess has desired you to sup with her after Vespers, and I think you would do well to await her here."

Isabella sank onto the cushioned bench which ran along the wall and rested her aching head on the hanging there as the nun left her, grateful beyond measure for the peace. Her pleasure in her new friendship quite destroyed, she determined to avoid the woman as much as possible, though she had a sinking feeling Ada would not be easy to elude.

After a supper with Hildegarde which helped clear her head, Isabella felt more positive again. She would not allow Ada's complaints against men to taint her marriage. She must take Giles on trust, for now, at least. And if he should warm his bed elsewhere, what of it? It was an acknowledged part of life that men would scratch their itch when opportunity presented itself, nothing more than that, she told herself, although she did not truly believe it. But as long as he treated her well and did not shame her or beat her, she would find what happiness she could. And after all, maybe Henry had his reasons, for it was possible Ada was not faultless. Nevertheless, she could not entirely put Ada's words out of her mind.

As Isabella lay on her bed, Agnes, the maid Hildegarde had found for her, a pilgrim staying at the abbey who was more than glad to line her purse given the chance, bustled around ensuring her mistress was comfortable, then sat sewing as Isabella tried to read by the light of a candle.

Squinting in the flickering light, she was about to give up and put the book aside when, to her dismay, there came a tap on her door. Surely Ada would not seek her out in her chamber at this hour?

Agnes tilted her head questioningly, and Isabella whispered, "If it's Lady Ada, tell her I have a headache, but for the love of our blessed Lady, don't let her enter."

The maid twisted her lips in wry acknowledgement and went to the door, opening it a sliver. Isabella heard soft murmurs, and Lady Estrilda slipped quietly into the room. She wore no wimple and her hair of silver-gilt shade was loosely braided, covered with a veil of gossamer mauve silk.

Isabella came to her feet, and Estrilda held her hands out to her saying, "Lady Isabella, you must forgive me for not speaking to you earlier. I should have liked to make your acquaintance but you were always on the arm of that dreadful woman."

Isabella's eyes widened as Estrilda gave an impish grin. "I'm afraid I've been taking care to discourage her approaches. She befriended me some months ago and clung so tightly, I almost thought I should have to cut my arm off to rid myself of her."

Isabella was dumbfounded as she continued, "I thought at first you were close friends but Sister Joan has asked me if I might seek you out and give you my company. I'll not accompany you in the guest hall, but her chamber is below ours, and I know she sleeps early so she's unlikely to haunt us up here. Do you mind if I join you? Between you and me, the woman is such a harbinger of misery, I cannot tolerate her without finding myself becoming quite shrewish, so my dear husband is happy for me to keep to my chamber." She tilted her head conspiratorially and said, "But I've become so bored. To tell truth, I hope you'll allow me to visit you."

Now she had Estrilda to spend time with, Isabella followed her tactics and avoided Ada as much as possible, dining in her new friend's larger chamber frequently, but at night, Ada's doom-laden words still haunted her sleep and she only dozed fitfully, waking heavy-eyed and still weary. When *would* Giles return?

At last, Alan arrived one morning after Prime with a scrawled piece of parchment, the writing almost illegible to Isabella, who had a neat hand. Giles wrote as though his hands had been bound, and his words were brief and to the point. Frowning, she managed to decipher it enough to know he would arrive within the hour. He did not wish to linger, wanted her to be ready to leave. There were few words of endearment, but never had a letter been so welcome. Sending Alan to find refreshment, she asked Agnes to bring her some sustenance. Having eaten, while Agnes took over the packing, she sat on the bed and pulled on Giles' hose.

She'd expected Agnes to look at her askance, but the sensible dame nodded with approval, saying, "A wise precaution, my lady. The snow may have gone but it's not much warmer for all that."

She was ready long before Giles arrived. She would have waited by the gate had she not been determined to keep out of Ada's sight, but as it was, as soon as Alan came for her bags, she went to find her husband.

Giles was dismounting when she came round the corner of the stables and caught her as she ran towards him. She looked up, knowing her face was unbecomingly flushed but not caring.

Giles was surprised but delighted as she lifted up her face for his kiss. His arms tightened around her and he kissed her like a man who had been in a drought before realising they had amused eyes watching them. His men were not bothering to hide their grins, which was to be expected, but beyond them, Hildegarde and Ursel were also watching with satisfied smiles.

Giles harrumphed and said, "My wife, I've missed you, but we're providing too much entertainment here." Then he whispered mischievously in her ear, "We'll continue this when we get home," and was further delighted when she chuckled.

Holding her at arm's length, he saw she was already dressed for travel, and Alan was busy loading her bags onto the horses. "Well, my wife, shall I take you home?"

She nodded, still blushing like a rose, and he mounted his horse, holding out his hand. She set her foot on his, and Miles lifted her up behind where she wrapped her arms around his waist, resting her head against his back.

Hildegarde came and blessed them, bidding them farewell, Berthe opened the gates, smiling benignly upon them, and they were on their way. He felt Isabella tighten her grip and snuggle against him, and he sighed with pleasure. Maybe it was just practicality – for warmth – but he hoped not.

CHAPTER 18

They'd turned off Akeman Street some miles back, well before Alchester, and the air was now perceptibly colder; pockets of freezing fog had started to drift, stretching out ghostly tendrils through the air. Grass, bushes and trees were rimed with frost. Their noses turned red, hoods were tugged more closely about faces, and when they came across an inn, Giles saw the longing in the eyes of his men.

He halted them, and they dismounted, rubbing hands, stamping the ground. Giles threw open the door and escorted Isabella to a bench as close to the fire as he could find. His men took their horses to the stables before bursting through the door into a welcoming fug of warm air, wet dog, stale bodies and smoke that had failed to escape through the roof vent.

"It's a poor sort of alehouse," he said beneath his breath as Isabella threw back her hood, "but I think we'll find the rest of the journey easier if we warm ourselves and fill our bellies here. Can you bear it?"

She said nothing for a moment, and he wondered what she was thinking. Then, she tilted her head to one side and murmured, "I was so cold, I was praying you'd stop however mean the fare. The fire alone is worth it."

He let out his breath in a gust of relief as his men joined them at the trestle. The proprietor hurried over to them, eyes gleaming at the sight of such patrons, followed by his wife and a couple of slatternly serving girls in none-too-clean aprons, all carrying food.

Giles' men shovelled up the bowls of stew which were dumped unceremoniously before them, eyeing the women with distaste.

Miles took a swig of ale, wiped his mouth with the back of his hand and guffawed. "Are you not going to bedazzle these fair demoiselles with your charms, Adam?"

Adam glowered and snorted in disgust before tossing back his own ale and demanding another.

Amused, Giles dug into his food. If the meat was stringy and tough, and the stew itself greasy, it warmed his belly and put fresh heart into him, although he was still worried Isabella would be offended by the undoubted squalor. Despite his concern, she didn't appear to be, ignoring her surroundings, spooning up the unidentifiable contents of her bowl and swallowing them with a will.

"I'd hoped we might have found somewhere we could stay overnight," he said conversationally to Isabella as they scraped the last of the food from their bowls and drank from their cups of ale. She wrinkled her nose and indicated the floor rushes, strewn with bones, stinking and unspeakably filthy, and he laughed in acknowledgement. "Yes, I thought so too. If the accommodation is like this, we'll need to swamp the whole company in stavesacre baths to kill the vermin we'll pick up."

Now, when she returned his smile, her eyes crinkled at the corners, and she blushed as he added, "Here, unlike the abbey, I think we'd spend more time scratching bites from lice than enjoying other delights."

Isabella pointed into the corner where a scruffy dog was defecating into the rushes. "And the manners of the company leave much to be desired."

It was the first time she had attempted to make a joke, and his mirth was tinged with pleasure as he realised that, finally, he could look forward to contentment with his new bride. Then, he wrinkled his brow.

"I must warn you, my wife," the word still sat oddly on his tongue, but he rather liked the feel of it, "that my dwelling is no castle. It's not even large for a manor. I fear, after your previous home, it might not fulfil your expectations."

Isabella froze, her cup halfway to her mouth, and, unaccountably, he was offended. Castle it might not be, small the house most definitely was, but it was his *home*; she might allow him some pride. Then he realised she was prickling like a hedgehog, and he tilted his head at her enquiringly.

"I had thought you would realise, my lord, I have neither need nor desire for castles or large houses." Her voice was quiet, but the earlier light had gone from her face. "If I did care for such things, I could have screamed 'disparagement'." She looked down, across the room, at her bowl, anywhere, it seemed, but at him.

Giles shifted on the wobbly bench and decided to open his heart. "It's not that I thought you cared, Isabella, merely I did not want you to be disappointed. And, in truth, I was afraid you might judge it and find it wanting, for however mean it might be, it's my home, and I have pride in it, even if that pride is unwarranted."

"And, in my turn, I was disappointed you thought so little of me that you would suppose it carried any import."

He stretched out his hand for hers, and she responded without hesitation. "Then shall we put this misunderstanding down to the fact that we still do not know each other well? Shall we each forgive the other for our assumptions?"

She flushed again, but this time, Giles did not think it was with embarrassment. Her mouth curved upwards generously, her eyes glowing as she nodded at him. He rubbed his thumb against the base of hers and her fingers curled around his.

The dog had finished its business and came to sniff them before raising its leg against the trestle table. Giles pushed it away with his foot, and Isabella laughed lightly as she said, "My lord, if you don't allow your dogs to behave as this one, I think I should like to go home, now."

As they reached the top of the steep incline, Giles cursed and reined Troubadour back. He sensed Isabella straining to see past him, heard her gasp of horror and felt her grip tighten around him, for the scene ahead of them was one of utter carnage. Men sprawled across the ground, a wain was overturned, its contents strewn around it, and a horse was struggling to rise to its feet, its cries of bewildered pain pitiful, broken reins and harness entangled around an obviously shattered foreleg, one of the shafts impaled through its belly.

Giles cursed again, for he could not ignore this, yet his instinct was to protect his wife. He called to Miles who was at his side in an instant, helping Isabella down, lifting her onto his own bay. Giles ordered the two youngest squires to wait with them, called "Good man. Keep her safe," over his shoulder to Miles as he kicked Troubadour into a gallop, his other men and older squires at his back.

Reining to a halt as he reached the first body, he looked around warily, but whoever the attackers were, they had gone, disappeared into the greenwood like wraiths. They must have had a guard posted and seen his party coming, he conjectured. Still, his shoulder blades prickled, and he posted Gareth and Alan to stand watch as he and the others scouted around them.

As soon as he was sure they were in no danger of another attack, he yelled to Miles who came at the canter.

Giles studied the bodies. Dead, mostly, or dying. Eight of them, stripped of weapons and outer garments. Fulke went to the injured horse and efficiently put it out of its misery.

While Giles had been occupied, Isabella had been helped down from Miles' horse and now took off her fine cloak. Laying it to one side, she shivered before bending over one of the men, closing the eyes that gazed stonily skywards and making the sign of the cross over him, lips moving in silent prayer.

Having finished there, she rose and went to another. Giles draped his own cloak around her shoulders, and she glanced gratefully up at him before kneeling to see what could be done for this poor soul, ignoring the blood puddling around him. Giles was astounded. He would have wagered his sword on the sight turning her sick; instead, here she was, behaving for all the world as though this was an everyday occurrence.

She bent her head over the unfortunate man, checking, Giles guessed, whether there was any life in him, closing his eyelids with a soft sigh.

Meantime, his men had been busy examining the condition of the other victims. Two still lived. One, a wealthy merchant by the looks of him, had a severe wound across his belly and his guts were exposed. He breathed faintly, but death would soon claim him, and that, Giles thought, would be a mercy. The second had major wounds to his legs and chest. God alone knew how he still lived, but if he could survive the journey to Thorneywell, he might stand a chance, albeit a slender one.

A lad was sitting propped upright against a tree, clutching his arm from which protruded the shaft of an arrow. Isabella had gone to one of the other two and was slashing at the hem of her shift with a small sharp dagger which Giles had not realised she was carrying.

As he watched, she managed to rip a strip of fabric and set about binding the fellow's wounds, her manner competent and calm. In truth, the injured would need dealing with properly once they reached home but for now, little could be done. There was not even water or wine to wash their injuries with.

Having done her best with the man she had been tending, Isabella moved on to the merchant. Giles searched her face but could see nothing more than tenderness as she knelt; no disgust, no sign of horror.

The upturned cart that had obviously been the draw for the plunderers lay across the track. Giles, accompanied by Eudo, went to inspect it. The dead horse would need to be dragged aside; he motioned for a couple of men to start that task. A pity they did not have time to butcher the animal for the meat would have served to feed the dogs, at least.

Giles turned his attention back to the cart. "If it's not too damaged, we could use it to convey the injured," he suggested.

"Likely it'll be more badly broke than we can tell, my lord." Eudo gave his opinion gloomily as he walked around it, inspecting it from every angle. "Can't see why they'd have left it, else."

Giles could see no real damage, but Eudo was not given to optimism. In Giles' opinion, the outlaws had only taken what they could carry, would have had no use for being slowed down by a clumsy cart, had no intention of staying on tracks or easily travelled roads, and had melted away into the woods with their ill-gotten spoils. If they had posted a lookout, when they saw his party coming down the road, they would not have wasted time making good their escape, for, unlike these poor wretches, his men were well trained and unlikely to be overcome with such ease.

"It looks sound enough to me," he said.

Eudo gave a lugubrious sigh. "Like as not, there'll be some damage we can't see."

"Then help me right it, Eudo. Let's see how it looks when it's right way up. Hoy, Miles, Guy, come over here and aid us."

They were heaving at it when a mound of fabric just visible beneath it suddenly moved, almost causing them to drop it again. "Hold!"

Giles yelled, forcing every muscle to shift the damned thing to one side without damaging whatever wriggled under there. Guy swore as he took the weight, and cords of sinew bulged at Miles' neck, as he too struggled to keep it from toppling again. Eudo braced himself and heaved, his face red with effort.

Sweating and straining, they managed to shift it, and Giles paused, mopping his brow with his arm before turning to see a pointed elfin face peering from beneath a bright purple shimmer of cloth. As they stared, a young woman emerged, dishevelled and dirty, with a smear of blood on her cheek. She looked up at them, chin trembling, pupils dilated, whispering, "Have they gone?"

Before he could answer, she hurled herself at him, wrapping herself around him, pressing a soft, pliant body to his.

In truth, she clung like ivy, and he felt for her, but she was impeding the work. Finally, he managed to prise her from him, holding her at arm's length, and she clutched, instead, at his hands.

"Oh, my lord." Her voice was breathy. "Thank the blessed Virgin you were passing. Had you and your men not come to our aid, we'd all be like to have died." She stopped, raising a hand to her throat, and gazed around her before her face crumpled, and she ran to the man whose innards were spilled out, pushing between him and Isabella, crying out before casting herself down beside him. Although, Giles noticed, she made sure to keep her person well clear of the blood; no mean feat considering how much there was.

She smoothed her hands over his forehead, cradling his head against her and raining kisses down upon him.

"Oh, my husband! My dear, dear lord!" She flung her head upwards, her face accusing. "Can none of you help him?"

Giles made to move, but Adam was before him, urging her away from the dying man. Isabella knelt beside him again, looking to see whether he still breathed. She bent her face close to him listening, her brow furrowed. Giles went to her as she got up, wiping her hands on a piece of torn shift, shaking her head.

"He's dead, my lord husband." She looked at him with an indefinable expression, murmuring so only he could hear her, "He said something. I will tell you later," before handing back his mantle and retrieving her own. She looked over at the youngster who lay beneath the tree and, before Giles could speak, picked up her skirts and ran to him, grasping the arm of the young woman, who was now bent over him, and tugging her away. He heard her outraged cry as she did so.

The young woman responded with a glare at first but as Isabella said, "You could have killed him!" she put her hand to her mouth, stepping backwards as though horror-stricken.

"My lady, I'm sorry. I thought only to aid him." She knelt back beside Isabella, helping to stem the flow of blood as Isabella ripped yet another strip from her shift and began to bandage his injured arm tightly. Beside her lay the arrow which had been pulled from his arm, the pool of red on the ground a testament to why Isabella had not removed it earlier.

"We should have waited until we reached home to remove it. I only hope I've managed to stop the bleeding." Isabella pushed aside a few strands of hair which had worked loose. Her bloodstained hands left a small trail of red and she tutted, wiping them on her already ruined shift.

"I'm so sorry!" The young woman sat back on her heels, weeping and wringing her hands. "I didn't know."

Giles moved to intervene. His men had righted the cart and were hitching one of their spare horses, adapting as best they could a makeshift harness and quickly mended shaft. "Well, what's done is done," he said, and Isabella gave him a blank look. She watched as the two casualties were lifted onto the cart, before bending to help the girl gather up its scattered contents.

Giles took her arm, saying, "Leave that. We must be on our way."

Her eyes were pools of sorrow as she gazed around her. "Are we to leave them here, then? Unburied and unshriven. Can we not at least take their bodies back? And should we not salvage what we can?"

He indicated his men, who were already bending to that task. "As for the dead, of course we'll not leave them. They can go over the spare horses. If you look, you'll see Miles is arranging for that."

"And the sheriff?"

Already concerned about the delay and the injured men, Giles' irritation spilled over before he could stop himself. "You need not lecture me. I know what must be done, but he'll not come out tonight. I'll send a messenger to him on the morrow, if the weather allows, but I will not risk the lives of my men sending them now."

Isabella said no more, casting her gaze downwards, but he felt as though she disapproved. Angered, he snapped, "Well, Madame, who would you send? Nothing can be done tonight. Would you wish for another death to come from this?"

She flinched as though to fend off a blow, and guilt shamed him. He should have controlled his temper. She'd done well; doubtless she was chilled and wearied and, by the looks of her, reaction was starting to set in.

Still, the words could not now be unsaid, so without further ado, he went to get Troubadour. The horse snorted, and Giles patted him absently before turning to see the young woman had already been set pillion behind Adam. Her demeanour surprised him; she did not look as perturbed as he might have expected, bearing in mind the dead men they bore with them, one of whom was her husband. She'd been weeping copiously enough earlier, which was hardly surprising, but she seemed to have recovered herself completely now.

Giles shook his head; the workings of the female mind were a mystery to him. He should just be thankful she was not impeding their progress with hysterical screams. Ah, let the poor soul be. Doubtless she was too exhausted to cry more.

Regretting his earlier temper, he held Isabella for a little longer than necessary, kissing her cheek before mounting. She returned his embrace, for which he was thankful, but he felt her tremble, and again, remorse flooded through him.

When he mounted, lifting her up behind him, she shivered, clinging to him, and he heard her voice soft against his ear. "Husband, I'm not sure she's what she seems."

There was no time to find out what she meant. He did not wish to expose her to the foul weather any longer than he must. Already, sleet was starting to dash at their faces; if he was any judge, there would be snow before long, and they would make but slow progress with the injured men in the cart.

The light was beginning to fade. He wanted to get Isabella to his home before conditions became intolerable. Besides, if the living victims were to stand any chance of survival, he must get them under cover as soon as possible.

CHAPTER 19

The last of the light was dying from the sky as the horses were halted. Isabella, squinting into the dusk, could barely make out what was before her. Because of the stop they had made at the alehouse, she was less frozen than when they had arrived at Sparnstow, but nevertheless, cold enough and aching from head to toe.

Giles gave a yell and dismounted, hammering on the closed gates before them. The others, tired and hungry, took up the cry. After some moments, they swung open, and the horses surged in, knowing their reward awaited them.

Troubadour, ever obedient, stood still whilst Giles lifted Isabella down, holding her close for a moment, then, as his groom took the big horse, he urged her up the steps.

She was surprised to see the main part was of stone but did not linger as Giles hurried her inside where the warmth wrapped itself around her like a blanket.

Once in the hall, she had a jumble of impressions: no central hearth but a fire set against the wall, no chimney but a metal hood over it, directing the smoke out through a hole or slit in the stone, she guessed. Braziers stood against the other walls. Trestles were being set up as servants scurried about, torches blazed brightly from wall sconces, and cresset lamps and rush lights glimmered dimly in darker corners, their smell mingling with the aromas of food and sweat. It was cleaner than she'd expected, more ordered.

Faded hangings were against two of the walls almost hiding the limewash, the others had been painted yellow with designs in red marked out along an upper border.

As she stared, taking everything in, a small man, about her own height, wearing good quality hose and tunic, gaped at her before bowing to Giles. "My apologies, my lord. We did not know when to expect you or–"

"No matter, Oswin," Giles cut in. "You aren't possessed of the ability to read my mind. I did not expect to be gone so long myself."

"Just so, my lord."

"And I bring you news, Oswin." He indicated Isabella, taking her by the hand and leading her forward. "For, whilst I was away, I managed to get myself wed."

"My lord?" The flash of shock that flared briefly in Oswin's face would have amused Isabella had she not been so exhausted.

"Indeed, I surprised myself quite as much as I've surprised you. This is your new mistress, Lady Isabella. I'll introduce her to Nan and Filbert and the rest of the household when we're settled but, for now, as you see, we have two wounded men with us. Can you find somewhere to put them?"

"Of course, my lord." Oswin turned, then, seemingly, thought better of it and swivelled back, bending his knee to Isabella. "My lady, welcome."

Isabella heard approval in his voice and felt encouraged, for this was her home too, now, was it not? And for better or worse, her husband's people were also hers. If Oswin was an example, it would not be so hard. She returned his greeting, saying. "Thank you, Oswin."

Giles let go of her hand, saying, "I'm afraid, apart from my steward, your introduction to my household will have to wait. I'll show you to our bedchamber, then I must see to our guests – assuming they still live."

Isabella stripped off her cloak, folding it over her arm. "Husband, let me attend to them. You have much to occupy you, and I'm more than capable, although," she stood for a moment, undecided, "have you a woman who can help me? And a couple of men?"

Giles looked about the hall before calling, "Nan, come here, if you please."

So he was courteous even to his servants. Perhaps he really was as good as they had all told her.

A large woman, solid and brawny, came bustling over to them, and Giles introduced her, saying, "Nan, this is my wife, Lady Isabella. Isabella, this is Oswin's redoubtable helpmeet." He grinned. "Without her ministrations, doubtless my own hall would more resemble that miserable inn."

Nan's eyes had widened, and her gaze was curious as she came over, but now, she laughed. "Someone has to keep these churls in good order. At least, they did." She paused, looking Isabella up and down before dropping into a curtsey. "My lady, I hope you'll be happy here." Glancing up at Giles, she added, "My lord could do with a good woman, Mistress, as I keep telling him. Now," she said, rolling up her sleeves, revealing dimpled white forearms, "what's to do?"

"We have wounded." Giles gave a jerk of his head to where Miles and Fulke were carrying in the most hurt of the two. Guy was aiding the arrow-shot boy to the wooden staircase which ran along the far side wall. Of the woman and Adam, there was no sign.

"The poor things. Come, my lady." Nan hurried to the stairs, Isabella in her wake.

The stairs led to a gallery with two curtained chambers and two with doors, mirrored by an identical gallery at the opposite end of the hall. The smallest of them was being set with two cots for the injured men. Miles and Fulke laid down their burden, and Nan, who was surely not a woman to be put out of countenance by rank, tsked at them before ordering them to fetch hot water and bandages. "And send Edith and Molly to me. Tell them to bring my simples and unguents."

With that, she set about dealing competently with the older man, although she turned aside to Isabella, shaking her head, after she had tended him. "No need to trouble him with overmuch care; he's not long for this world, poor soul. I'll send one of the men to find the chaplain. Can you deal with the other one, my lady?" Isabella nodded, and Nan rushed away.

Isabella knelt beside the younger one, stroking the damp hair off his face tenderly. He, at least, was conscious, although grey with pain, his teeth chattering. Isabella's heart sank as she carefully unwound the bloodied bandage and inspected his wound – raw and jagged, blood still oozed from it, albeit more sluggishly now. Did they have some aqua vitae she could use?

She went to the top of the stairs and saw a young woman in dull green clambering towards her, wispy corn-coloured hair pulled into a braid and covered with a white cloth, tied at the nape of her neck. "My lady, I'm Molly. Is there aught I can do?"

"Do we have any aqua vitae?" The girl looked at her blankly, and Isabella, exhausted, lost her patience and snapped, "Well, go and ask. And fetch me some more bandages." She got a sullen glare in response and regretted her irritable tone, but it was too late. Besides, she was worn to the bone. *Although I don't wish to make enemies before I've barely arrived. Still, I'll be sweeter when she returns.*

While she waited for Molly, a servant brought a bowl with a ewer of hot water and a linen towel. Isabella poured a little of the water over her hands which still bore traces of dried blood, wiping them dry on the towel.

When Molly came back, mouth twisted in a downward arc as she handed over bandages and a small flask, Isabella remembered to smile. "Thank you, Molly."

The young woman eyed her with suspicion before apparently deciding it was politic to treat her new mistress with respect, assaying a small smile in return.

Isabella knelt again beside the youngster. "Does it pain you much?"

"Aye, lady," he stammered.

"Then, let us see if I might be able to make you more comfortable. What is your name?"

"J...Jerold, my lady."

"Well, then, Jerold, take a little of this." She poured some of the spirit into a cup which Molly held out, and Jerold took it, tossing it back quickly, choking as it hit his gullet.

"Molly, will you go behind him and hold his shoulders, please? Hold him lightly," she added, wondering whether the girl would have the strength and wishing Miles had stayed to help. She looked at Molly's thin wrists. "No, that will not do. Can you bring one of the men up, please? Someone strong. And bring bread, mouldering bread," she amended, "and a needle and thread. We'll have need of them."

Molly nodded and was gone in a swirl of skirts, while Isabella tried to give the older man a small nip of the strong spirit. It dribbled from his lips. Still, he was probably beyond pain by now.

As Fulke's head appeared at the top of the stairs, Isabella gave a sigh of relief. He was followed by Molly and another girl, escorting a tall, cadaverous priest, who sniffed and sneezed. She indicated the dying man, then left them to it, explaining to Fulke what she needed. He inclined his head grimly and took young Jerold by the shoulders, holding him steady. She poured the remainder of the aqua vitae over the wound. Jerold had borne up bravely until then, but now he jerked violently and screamed before collapsing unconscious in Fulke's arms. Fulke kept a tight hold in case he came around, and Isabella decided against stitching the wound which would allow the poultice she would place on it to be more effective. She sniffed the ointment Molly had brought to ascertain it was what she needed then smeared it on the bread and bound it to his arm.

"It might help prevent wound sickness," she said doubtfully. "We can but try."

She turned her head as Giles came up the steps to stand beside her. "Have you done with him?" He jutted his chin at Fulke, who, in turn, looked at Isabella for the answer.

"For now."

"Then, off with you, man. Get some hot food inside you."

Fulke grinned and lurched down the stairs. Giles turned to the priest who had finished his task and was putting away his flask of oil. "Were you able to shrive him, Father?"

"Indeed. I managed to rouse him enough to hear his confession. He will fail fast now, but at least his soul's safety is assured."

"Good. So now you've done your duty by him, come and sup with us."

The priest gave a twitch of his lips and nodded. "Thank you, my lord." He bowed his head to Isabella. "I bid you welcome, my lady. And before I go, I'll pray with this one, too, shall I?"

Jerold, who had just recovered consciousness, looked alarmed, but the priest tapped him lightly on his sound arm, saying, "Don't fret, fellow, you'll not be dying tonight by the looks of you. They'll not be readying a shroud for you," before dropping to his knees in prayer.

Isabella schooled her face not to show her surprise. The priest had not looked to be so kindly, yet he could not help his gaunt features, she supposed, and his cold wasn't improving his looks.

Giles touched her shoulder. "Have you done here?"

She considered. "For the present, I think."

He drew her away from the small chamber, shutting the door firmly. "Then come and warm yourself and change into dry garments."

She'd been so busy, she'd not even felt the cold dampness of her clothes, but now, she found she was starting to shiver.

"Come to our bedchamber; your belongings are all there. You may eat up there if you wish; it's late and you're weary." He looked rueful. "I'm afraid this is not quite the homecoming I had in mind."

CHAPTER 20

Giles led her to the opposite end of the hall, steering her around bodies, dogs and trestles, up the wooden steps to the other gallery, opening a door into a much larger chamber than the one they had just left. Inside, the alcoves were lit with cresset lamps, and two candles stood on a carved table at the end.

From the dim light they provided, Isabella could see two shuttered windows and chests along the wall with cushions on them, on top of which her bags had been laid.

The walls were partly covered by faded hangings, and where there were no hangings, she could see equally faded paint with decorations similar to those in the hall.

The room was divided by a heavy curtain which Giles swished back to reveal a sturdy bed covered in blankets and pelts. Isabella longed to throw herself down onto it and sink into oblivion as the exertions of the day finally overwhelmed her.

Giles grunted, and Isabella glanced fearfully up at him. Had she displeased him in some way? She was aware she had spoken out of turn at the scene of the attack earlier; was he still angry with her? Her stomach muscles contracted, only unknotting when he said, "I have no women suitable to attend you. I did not think, did not expect to be bringing home a wife. And I'd not realised, either, that your own maid would not accompany you."

Touched by his care for her, relieved he'd not found something to blame her for, she ventured, "Could not Nan, or maybe Molly or another girl be spared? If one of them will help me, I can make shift."

Giles looked doubtful. "Nan cannot really be expected to, and the others are not the quality of women you've been used to."

"As to that, if they have merry faces and good hearts, what does it matter? I've had my fill of women of higher birth, I thank you. In almost three years, barely a kind word did Lady Adelaide's women give me. Even when she died, Evalina was the only one who treated me with anything bordering on respect, and she was not of good birth, just one of the village girls. The women you have here will be sufficient to meet my needs."

"I'll see to it." Giles nodded and went to leave the room, only to turn at the door and say, "The young woman we rescued. I think we must offer her a pallet in our outer chamber until the weather improves. In addition to that, she'll have been shaken badly by her ordeal. We cannot ask her to travel again so soon, and, as she is not precisely a guest, I prefer her to be here rather than in one of the guest chambers."

Isabella, who had bent to the bags, raised her head slowly, the smile fading from her face. Certainly, the woman had undergone a terrifying ordeal, and yet, what with the way she had pulled the arrow from Jerold's arm and those words the merchant had whispered, something about her disturbed Isabella. It was irrational, she thought, and Giles was right; it was only common decency to offer her a bed. The merchant had been wealthy by the looks of it; she could not be expected to sleep with the maids. He was right, too, about the guest chambers – it might be lonely there for her.

Isabella shuddered at the thought of her fate had they not disturbed the outlaws. She could not have remained hidden beneath that cart for long.

Giles looked serious, and she guessed he was thinking the same. He nodded and said, "I'll have her brought here, and I'll ask Nan to choose a maid for you. Stay you here whilst I arrange matters."

Obediently, Isabella sat on a chair and waited. She had almost dropped into a light doze when the girl who had escorted the priest to the injured men came trotting in. She dipped a curtsey saying, "I'm Edith, m'lady. Dame Nan sent me to assist you." Isabella gave her a smile and was rewarded with a bright grin. Freckle-faced Edith, with her hazel eyes and snub nose, was cheerful and down-to-earth, and once the maid had stopped being overawed by her new position, Isabella felt comfortable with her.

After most of the unpacking had been done, Edith helped her into fresh garments, not commenting on the hose she wore beneath her gown, merely helping Isabella remove them, replacing them with her stockings. Isabella, despite knowing nothing at all of Edith yet, was convinced she'd made the right decision.

As Edith fastened the lacing of her gown, the door to the outer chamber opened, and Nan escorted their guest in, smiled at Isabella and bustled back out again. Isabella, forgetting her doubts, held her hands out in greeting. "I bid you welcome, Mistress. I imagine you're still shaking after such a terrible event."

The girl seemed to hesitate before grasping Isabella's outstretched hands, gripping them with surprising strength. "Indeed, my lady. And I do not know what would have become of me if you had not come along when you did. As it is…" She paused and gave a gulp before continuing, "As it is, I have lost my own dear husband." She wiped her eyes with the back of her hand and sat on the bed as though her legs would not hold her. Isabella bade Edith fetch her some wine.

Edith laid down the shift she was folding and went out as Isabella said, "You must long for your family."

A tear appeared from beneath the girl's black lashes and trickled down her cheek leaving a sooty trail, and she covered her face with her hands, whimpering, her slender shoulders shaking, before saying in a trembling voice, "My lady, I cannot even remember if I have a family. All I can remember is my name, Clarice. I cannot even remember that of my husband's, only that I loved him dearly."

Isabella was appalled. As she racked her brains for something comforting to say, Giles returned, followed by his youngest knight. Adam, she thought his name was. Adam came past Giles and offered the girl a scrap of linen to wipe her face.

She took it from him distractedly, mopping her tears, giving him a wan smile before turning her face up to Giles. "Oh, my lord, I do thank you for your kindness to my husband, but what am I to do now?" The last word came out on a wail, and Clarice cast herself on the floor before Giles, crying, "I must throw myself on your mercy, my lord, and beg for shelter."

Isabella frowned slightly. The gesture was overly dramatic and totally unnecessary, and it added to her feeling of unease.

Giles took the girl by the elbows and raised her up, easing her towards the chair, but she gave another wail and buried her head in his chest. Self-consciously, he patted her shoulder. Isabella looked on, unsmiling, lips compressed.

Giles managed to prise the weeping woman from him, and she clasped Adam round the neck instead. Adam led her to one of the chairs and bade her sit. Giles stood before her, and she gazed up at him. Her eyes, Isabella noted, did not appear to have reddened even slightly, her nose was not pink. Most women turned into sodden, blotched wrecks when they wept. In fact, the only other one Isabella knew who could cry so prettily was Rosamund.

"We're sorry for your loss, Mistress," said Giles. "Do you have kin nearby? I can arrange escort for you within the week, weather permitting, although you'll have to speak to the sheriff, or at least let us notify him of your whereabouts."

Clarice gave another wail. "I can't *remember*!"

"You can't remember?" Giles sounded startled.

"N…n…no, my lord."

"Yet, you remembered your name." Isabella spoke before thinking, and the girl must have taken her words as reproof, for she turned to her, holding her hands out as though in supplication.

"Oh, my lady, don't be angry with me. I can remember my name, I remember my husband, but apart from that – nothing!" She covered her face with her hands once more.

Giles ran his hands through his hair. "Come now, demoiselle. Surely you remember something. Take your time and cast your mind back."

She screwed up her face as though lost in thought, then said, "Oh, my lord, I wish I could. I remember hiding under the cart, I remember those wicked men, and I remember being so very terrified. I wanted to help my husband, but he had bid me stay where I was, and I had to watch as they k…k…killed him!" As she sobbed, she threw herself into Adam's ready embrace. "I was so f…f…frightened. And now I cannot remember anything. I do not even know where my home is. And I've thought and thought until my head aches from trying. All I can remember is my name, my lord. Clarice," she added forlornly as she rubbed her head and winced. "I think I hit my head. I could find no blood, but it hurts."

Adam, who seemed much more comfortable with a weeping woman than did Giles, soothed her saying, "Hush, sweeting. My lord has offered you shelter. You'll be safe here and cared for, and with time, you will remember." He turned to Isabella and Giles. "Do you not think so, my lord, my lady?"

Isabella looked at Giles, who appeared to be studying the ceiling. She awaited his response for she did not feel it was her place to answer; it was barely her home yet, after all.

Giles peeled his gaze from the ceiling with obvious reluctance, went to Clarice and took her hand. "Adam is right. We'd not turn you out. And even if you wished to leave, you'd not want to travel in this. I would have sent a messenger to your family, but…" his voice trailed off.

Isabella felt a sudden slight frisson of concern. How long would they house Clarice for? Certainly, she would have to be escorted to the sheriff, but presumably, after that, Giles would have to bring her back here. It would be discourteous, inhuman even, not to. And she felt desperately sorry for her, yet, there was something about her she could not quite put her finger on. A niggling suspicion that she was not all she seemed.

She shut her eyes for a moment, pondering. Rosamund! It was not just the same ability to cry without reddened eyes. Something about Clarice reminded her of Rosamund. She shook her head impatiently. It was unreasonable to judge her when they knew so little of her, even if the merchant's last words did not quite match Clarice's story. And maybe she had misunderstood him; he had been barely coherent.

While she was still lost in her thoughts, Giles beckoned her from the room, leaving Clarice with Adam. "I would know your thoughts, Isabella. Your face gives nothing away, yet you seem distracted."

She shrugged. "It's merely that I'm a little uncomfortable with her, my lord. It's nothing, and as you say, we have little choice but to house her."

Giles nodded gravely. "It's to be hoped her memory returns, otherwise it looks as though my household will be extended by one more than I had expected."

Isabella hesitated, then spoke. "The one thing that does concern me, my lord," in truth, it was more than one thing but this was a legitimate worry, "is that we know nothing of her."

"All the more reason to have her sleep in our outer chamber, then, lass. That way, both you and Edith will be able to keep an eye on her."

Isabella sighed. Having come to terms with being married, she'd had expectations for her new life. They had not included Clarice, but what must be, must be. She had a sudden thought and brightened. "I'll ask Jerold tomorrow. Surely he'll be able to tell us more. Her husband, if that's who he really was–" She broke off as Giles raised an enquiring eyebrow. "I'll tell you more of that later," she murmured, pursing her lips.

Giles pulled her towards him in an approving hug as Edith came back with the wine. As she entered the chamber, they heard Clarice snap, "You took your time, girl."

Isabella's eyebrows nearly disappeared beneath her veil. Edith's reply could not be heard, but when she emerged from the room, her face was rigid. Isabella could not resist saying to her quietly, "Don't let her upset you, Edith. Likely, she's not thinking straight just now, but anyway, you are my maid, not hers. Don't feel obliged to wait on her."

Edith's snub nose was pink. Whether with upset or annoyance, it was hard to tell. However, her voice was respectful when she answered

Isabella. "Thank you, m'lady. I told her I had things to do for you. I said it nice, but, m'lady, and pardon me if I'm speaking out of turn, don't you leave her in there alone anywhen, else she'll be nosing into your things."

Isabella glanced at Giles. He was straight-faced, so all she said was, "Thank you, Edith. She'll be sleeping in the outer chamber with you. I trust you to keep a watch on her, but do remember, for the moment, she is our guest."

Edith nodded, and Giles said, "Good. Then, let us join my household for supper. I was going to eat alone with you, but my people are eager to meet their new mistress, and since–" He broke off, gesturing to the bedchamber. "I'll allow Adam to escort our guest." He called to Adam, then held his arm out for Isabella. As she placed her arm along his, she thought on the matter of Clarice. Unwilling though she felt to have to share their chamber with someone from outside the household, there really was no option. Had the girl truly believed that to attempt to remove that arrow from Jerold's arm would do no harm? At all events, Isabella would prefer to keep her eye upon her and to keep her away from the boy. Maybe she would ask Molly to keep a watchful eye on him. Just in case. If she got the opportunity, should she mention her concerns to Giles? Or would he think she was merely being foolish? Well, for now, there was naught she could do.

As Isabella took her place on the dais next to Giles, the smell of spices and cooked meats were filling the hall, and her stomach gave a low growl. Until now, she'd been so caught up in dealing with the injured and trying to remember who was who, she'd not given food a thought. Now hunger gnawed at her insides.

Even though she still felt like a stranger here, Giles was a good table companion, courteous and attentive. He glinted a smile at her as he handed her their shared cup of wine, wiping it first, and as she drank, then turned her attention to the food, Isabella's courage was bolstered.

Raising a spoonful of chicken to her lips, she savoured the aroma, closing her eyes briefly as she swallowed, feeling the warmth of it run from her gullet to her belly.

This was a well-run hall. The servants moved swiftly to intercept need; the hall was clean and homely. The stew was hearty, the pot-au-feu good and fiery, the way she liked it. There was not an abundance of dishes, but those there were had been well cooked.

She slid her gaze to Giles' face. "Your cook is to be commended, my lord."

He acknowledged her with a contented nod as he speared a piece of meat on his knife. "I'm glad he meets with your approval. We feast but sparingly; a well-cooked simple meal suits me more than all your fancy peacocks and dolphins. My household is not large compared to some, but these are people who have served my family all their lives; I wish to do well by them."

Again, an improvement on Baldwin, who feasted grandly himself, but cared little about those who served him. And she noticed, although those on the lowest tables did not have wine to drink, they had almost the same food as was served further up. Even in the short time she'd been here, she could see they held de Soutenay not just in esteem but affection. Happen that was why the hall seemed to be run so well.

Lost in her thoughts, she suddenly realised Giles was looking at her, a quizzical expression on his face. "Well?" he said.

She blushed. "I'm sorry, my lord, I wasn't paying attention."

"So I observed." His tone was grave. "And do you like what you see?"

"Indeed, my lord. I see a well-appointed household, with servants who hold their lord in due respect and do his bidding without complaint. The rushes are clean, as is the table-linen;

your servants are well fed, your food well cooked." Feeling a flicker of courage, she found the nerve to add impishly, "Indeed, it seems you scarce have need of a wife," although she quaked after she'd said it. How would he respond? Had she been too daring?

Tensing, she flicked a sideways glance at him and almost sagged with relief as he laughed, wiped his mouth on the linen napkin and kissed her fingers. "True, my household is well run, but think you that's all I desire in a wife? If so, Nan would be sufficient for me. And yet, I cannot see me taking her to my bed, can you?"

Emboldened again, she considered for a moment. Dare she? Why not? After all, thus far, he had not been displeased. She said in innocent tones, "Oh, I don't know. I think she might make a cosy armful, my lord."

Giles, who had just set his cup to his lips, choked on a mouthful of wine. When he'd regained his composure, he said, "Belike she would, but I think, steward or not, Oswin would spit me on his dagger if I tried it. And, to tell truth, I think I prefer tender lamb to tough mutton."

He chuckled, and Isabella laughed with him. It had been worth the risk, although she would not often so dare. But it pleased her to know that here her attempts at humour were appreciated, and she herself treated with respect, unlike Baldwin's hall, where her presence had barely been tolerated. Here, maybe, she could feel as though she had a purpose.

After preserved fruits had been served with custards, Giles took her arm. "Come, love, let me show you your new home properly."

'Love'? He called her 'love'? Yet, that must just be a courtesy, for love did not sprout overnight. For all she knew, love did not sprout at all, rare plant that it was. Liking maybe, but love?

Still contemplating the endearment, she followed him. The exhaustion she had thought might fell her had been dispelled, at least for the moment, by the hot food, and she felt revived, although doubtless it would not last long. However, for the moment, it had given her renewed strength, and the bright faces about her made her confidence swell slightly.

He led her around the trestles which were being dismantled, to a thickset man with a weathered complexion and a youth of medium height wearing a tunic of good cloth and a hat with a liripipe. His hair was fair and curled crisply about his neck, his beard was sparse. He greeted her with a courtly bow, as Giles said, "Nan you have met, and Oswin. This is their son,

Filbert, who acts as bailiff for me, and Arnulf, my reeve."

Arnulf smiled and dipped his head respectfully, but Filbert took her hand, touching his lips lightly to her fingers with all the grace of an earl's squire. His gaze was frank and approving, and his grin was such that Isabella found herself responding.

Giles took her around the hall, introducing her to everyone from the most senior of his men to the lowliest spit boy, then gazed about him as though looking for someone. "Where's Adam?"

"That lad's brains are in his braies," Fulke muttered, downing his ale.

Miles laughed. "You have a new woman in your hall, my lord; where she is, that's where you'll find Adam."

Giles' lips thinned slightly. "And that would be where?"

Fulke was scornful. "Belike he's gone to count the stars with her if that's what they call it now."

Isabella touched his arm. "My lord, see; there they are." He followed the line of her pointing finger and saw Adam seated on a bench in a dark corner beneath the stairs at the far end of the hall, knee to knee with Clarice, who was giggling at something he had said.

As though she'd become aware of them watching, Clarice looked up, her face changing from laughter to tragedy, fluttering her eyelashes at Giles before turning back to Adam.

"It seems Adam is helping our guest overcome her heartache," Giles said with what Isabella thought was a smile in his voice.

She looked at Clarice with narrowed eyes. *So much for the forlorn waif in our chamber. She seems to have recovered quickly enough now.*

Giles' hand tightened its grip on her arm, and she bared her teeth in what was close enough to a smile at the girl. It didn't matter; Clarice was again absorbed in her conversation with Adam.

Giles, looking down at Isabella's set face, was bemused. Who would have thought she would have a temper that could flare white hot? But he needed her to at least preserve the household harmony for now and behave as though she liked their unexpected guest. Could he trust her to do that? He hoped so. He put an arm around her shoulders, drawing her away to show her the layout of the manor house.

"At this end, as you know, lies our chamber. There is one room beyond – my privy chamber – and in a corner, behind the hangings, our garderobe. That is for our use only." He indicated the opposite staircase, the one Adam was seated beneath. "You see the gallery above the hall?" She nodded. "There are more chambers there.

241

Two are where the womenfolk sleep; two are for guests, though one holds Jerold for now, but when they are free, Fulke, Guy, Adam and Miles sleep there. When we need the rooms, they become hearth knights again."

He led her back to the dais, on which the two high-backed chairs they had used for dinner stood, both with embroidered cushions on the seats. If they were a little worn, it did not matter; they softened the hardness of the wood adequately. Going behind them, he rattled back another dividing curtain, revealing Nan, busy at some sewing. "This was where my grandparents used to sleep. We have built more chambers since, and now my steward and his family use this, and beyond that, the household linens are stored. Nan keeps those in good order, do you not, Nan?"

She nodded, her eyes twinkling, screwed up in her face like two currants. "That I do. Heavy on his household linen, is Sir Giles, my lady. Haply, with you around, he'll do less damage to it."

Giles patted Nan's shoulder. "As if you have not been keeping me in good order these past years, Nan, my sweet."

He gave her a smacking kiss on the cheek, and she flicked her mending at him. "Oh, go on with you. You'll not need me to keep you out of trouble now you've a sweet young wife. Go on, get out of my hair and let me be doing my work."

Giles turned to Isabella, laughing wryly. "You see? She is only too ready to wash her hands of me."

How would she react? He was heartened when Isabella gave a small quirk of her lips and rejoined with, "So if you do not do my bidding, my lord, do I send you back to Nan like a naughty page?"

Nan chuckled richly. "Aye, you do that, my lady. I'll make him mind his manners."

Giles spread out his hands. "I see my position here as lord of this manor is worth less than a clipped penny now there are two women to chivvy me. Ah well, I can always take refuge in the stables. Leofwine will be only too willing to share an ale with me and commiserate at how badly life is using me."

He pulled back the curtain and turned again to Isabella. "Make no mistake, Nan is all cheer but rules the women with a rod of iron. She looks to their welfare but expects obedience. Oswin is of like character, and Filbert is shaping up well under his tutelage. They've been invaluable to me; I trust they will serve you as well. They are dear to me, as you can tell, for I've known them most of my life. Oswin's father served mine,

Nan's mother ran the hall. I hope you'll come to feel as much fondness for them as I do.

"Now, below the hall, the cellars, and outside, the stables, barns and outbuildings. Nan will show you those on the morrow, and Oswin will make his accounts available to you if you would like."

Her head went up, a look of pride on her face. "I should like, my lord. I was taught by the nuns. I can read, write and supervise a household. Although," her lips curved into a smile, "it would seem there will be little for me to do here."

He nodded, but said, "True, but a household always runs better with a woman at the helm, or so my mother was used to say. Oswin needs little supervision, as does Nan, but it is better you know how the whole runs."

Isabella suppressed a yawn, covering her mouth with her hand, and Giles cursed himself for forgetting how tired she must be. She was white with exhaustion. The trestles were already moved, and pallets were being laid out in the hall, and she was looking longingly at them as though she would like to collapse into the nearest one and sleep until noon.

"I'm a fool, and an ill-mannered one at that. Come, my lady wife. It's time we went to bed."

Isabella nearly wept with relief. In truth, she was so tired, she didn't know how to keep the smile pinned to her face. If he found aught else to show her or anyone else to introduce her to, she would be hard pushed not to cry. At least in bed, even if he wanted her, she could rest her weary body. Even the irritation of having Clarice beyond the curtain was as nothing if she could but lie down.

She followed him willingly, just barely managing to give a polite response to the cheerful souls who wished them a goodnight. As she reached the wooden staircase, she stumbled over a dog who had lain down right in her path, and before she could regain her balance, Giles swept her into his arms and carried her up to the bedchamber where Edith lay curled up on one of the two pallets in the outer room. She started to throw back her covers as Giles entered, but he shook his head, and she lay down again, covering her face with the blanket,

Once inside, he set Isabella on the bed, lit the night candle which sat on its nail in the wall niche and pulled the curtain across the room to allow them some privacy. She sat, unprotesting, too tired to lift a finger, only blinking when he removed her veil and wimple.

Giles stripped her to her shift, hanging her gown on the clothes pole and placing the rest neatly on one of the chests, smoothed her hair and kissed her on the brow before tucking the covers around her. Then, without more ado, he stripped himself and climbed in beside her, pulling the bed curtains about them, cocooning them in darkness.

He slid one arm around her and turned her towards him but made no move to touch her other than that. She nestled her head into the crook of his shoulder, something she had not done before. This intimacy, with no demands on her body, was more than she had ever dared hope for, and she felt an ember of warmth stir within her.

The day had been an education, unlike anything she'd known before. His easy manner and his care to his household had impressed her; now, a new sensation filled her. Was this the beginning of affection? Or even desire? She slid one hand daringly across his chest, feeling the dark, springy hair growing thickly there, and he murmured, his breath tickling her cheek, "If you don't have a care, I'll forget how bone-tired I am."

Did she want that? Even more daringly, she whispered back, "If *you* don't have a care, happen I'll also forget."

She felt him reach for her and braced herself. He had been going to let her be. Why had she been so stupid? But as he started to unbraid her hair, the outer door creaked open. Isabella held her breath, and Giles stilled, as Nan's voice came, quietly but clearly, "In this house, Mistress, the women do not count the stars with men. After dark, we go to bed in our own chambers, like decent folk."

The door shut with a bang, and from the other side of the curtain came a huff, and what sounded like, "Old cow!"

Isabella smothered a giggle. Nan was surely a match for Mistress Clarice. She turned back to Giles, expecting him to comment. She waited in vain, for all she heard was a muffled snore.

CHAPTER 21

Isabella surfaced from a dream in which Giles had been stroking her neck to discover it was no dream. He was propped on one elbow, his head bent over hers, his breath on her cheek.

She blinked at him, and he lowered his head, kissing her full on her mouth. Her lips parted involuntarily, and his kiss deepened in intensity. Still half-asleep, Isabella wove her hands through his dark hair, twining her fingers in it, then lowering them to the nape of his neck.

His breathing ragged, he wrapped his arms tightly around her, crushing her to him, and Isabella found he was not the only one filled with desire. She wound her arms around him as though she would draw him even closer, and gave herself up to him, uncaring of anything beyond the privacy of their bed.

Afterwards, in the half-light filtering through a gap in the bed curtains, she saw a glint of satisfaction in his eyes. She smiled at him, unwilling to move.

"Maybe I should ask you to help me dress, my lord."

He laughed, but before he could act on her words, they heard the curtain swish back and the clatter of something. Isabella parted the bed hangings a hand's breadth to see Edith placing laver, pitcher and towels on the table and Clarice bearing a tray with platters and cups. That was not what Isabella had expected. It seemed their guest had chosen to make herself useful – or had Nan decided to keep her occupied?

As Isabella peered out, Clarice's attention flew to the gap, looking beyond Isabella, searching for Giles. Isabella let the hangings fall back into place abruptly, her contentment replaced by indignation. Giles looked at her quizzically, and she swallowed her ire, not without difficulty, hissing beneath her breath, "Clarice, trying to see what goes on within."

She popped her head back out again and dismissed the women who disappeared back into the outer chamber, Edith with alacrity, Clarice following reluctantly, swivelling her head to see more as she left.

Giles pulled a face, stretching one hand out for his shirt. It lay beyond his reach, and he gave a grunt of annoyance before rising, pulling the hangings right back and stepping lazily from the bed, picking up the tray and bringing it back to Isabella.

He sat beside her and placed the platter of bread, cheese and sausage between them, pouring wine into the cups, handing her one, saluting her with the other. "To you, my wife, who I think just might be an unexpected treasure."

Isabella felt her cheeks pink and lowered her gaze to hide her pleasure. Perchance, she could leave her shields down more often in this marriage, for it seemed her sister-by-marriage had not deceived her when she had said Giles was a good man. She looked at him beneath half-closed eyelids, raising her own cup in return, saying softly, "And to you, my husband, who I believe might be an unlooked-for gift."

"Then let's hope we'll both be well satisfied. And today, since it's our first one together beneath this roof, let's enjoy breaking our fast in private." He took a mouthful of sausage and one of bread and saluted her again, but before he could take a sip of his wine, the outer door slammed.

Giles swore and rose, cramming some cheese into his mouth with one hand as he pulled back the dividing curtain. Edith was there, Clarice was not. Isabella scrambled inelegantly from the bed, and Edith helped her on with her gown.

"Where is she?" Isabella demanded of Edith, as she bundled her hair into a net and pinned on her veil.

"She said she thought she should see how Jerold was doing, m'lady, seeing how he was of her own household."

Isabella gave a muffled oath, before making haste to follow Clarice, aware that Giles was close behind her.

She sped across the hall and up the other stair, throwing open the door to the chamber where Jerold was ensconced. He was pressed against the back of his cot, licking his lips, and Clarice sat beside him, holding his hand, murmuring something while she sponged his face with a damp cloth.

When she heard the door open, she swivelled to face them. Her eyes grew round; her voice was honey-sweet.

"My lord." She rose from her seat and curt-seyed, then flicked a glance at Isabella. "My lady, I thought it my duty to see how my injured servant was doing. Is that not so, Jerold?" She turned back to Jerold, whose expression was ghastly. "I fear he is very much worse. I do hope he'll survive."

Isabella swept past her, very much on her mettle, saying, "Well, as you see, he seems to be living still. Pray, do not trouble yourself; I will check on him." She stood between Clarice and Jerold's pallet, daring Clarice to defy her.

Clarice eyed her uncertainly, assessing her, before dipping her head and moving to the door, where she paused, her voice all concern. "Now, Jerold, remember what I told you, and you'll be better the sooner."

Jerold, freckles standing out stark against his pallor, nodded, breathing rapidly. Isabella pulled up a stool and sat, pressing the back of her hand to his forehead. He burned with fever, his breathing rasped, and her heart sank, but not only for the lad, despite the sorrow she felt, for if he died, they would never get to the truth about Clarice.

Giles also pulled up a stool and sat, legs splayed, arms folded across his chest. His face was unreadable.

Jerold broke into Isabella's thoughts, voice wavering, as he croaked out, "Am I d...dying, my lady?" He choked on the last word, and she realised with a jolt of pity just how very young he was. Surely no more than fifteen summers at most.

She gave him what she hoped was a re-assuring smile as she unbandaged his wound, her heart sinking when she saw the signs of suppuration. As she turned to Giles, the smile dropped from her face, and she said, "Husband, would you ask Nan to come to me, please?" Then, she bent her head over Jerold's arm, hiding the fear she felt.

Jerold coughed and pushed himself forward, croaking, "Water, *please*," before he fell backwards muttering incoherently and plucking at his blanket. His eyes glazed as he sank back into semi-consciousness. Isabella went to fetch him a cup of watered wine from the table, stopping in astonishment when she realised there was nothing there. Surely, *surely*, they had left him something to drink, the poor lad.

While she gazed in disbelief at the empty table, Nan came bustling in. Isabella turned on her, biting down her fury, saying in tones that were just the right side of polite, "Nan, did no one leave this boy anything to drink?"

Nan bristled, and Isabella made haste to sound more conciliatory. "Only," she swept her hand around the room, "there is nothing here now."

Nan followed the arc of her arm, eyes widening, a flush deepening her already florid cheeks. "There most certainly was, my lady, I made sure of it myself, yestereve. It had a dose of my own making in it, too. I don't know what's happened to it – belike some 'helpful' fool has cleared it. I'll go and get more immediately."

As she turned to leave, Isabella stayed her, her hand on the woman's arm. "No, Nan, I'll go. I suspect you know more of healing than I do, and I confess, I'm worried for him."

Nan took her place beside Jerold and said, "Don't you fret, my lady, we can mend him." Then, she looked away from the boy and towards Isabella, the light gone from her face, as she mouthed, "I hope."

Isabella hoped so, too. He was too young to have his life snuffed out like this, and surely he had a family somewhere who cared about him. As she stepped outside, Giles took her arm, leading her back to the other side of the hall and upstairs into their chamber, dismissing Edith. Clarice was nowhere to be seen.

Giles put the bar across the inside of the door and moved to the far side of the room, beckoning her to join him. The window was unshuttered, the thin plates of horn allowing weak light into the room, and he leaned against the wall next to it, stroking his neat beard, his grey eyes dark and troubled. "You've not told me what her husband said to you before he died."

She flinched; she had forgotten about that. Was he angry with her? She twisted her veil, and her voice quavered. "He said...but it wasn't clear...I thought he said, 'Not my wife. Har–' the rest, I could not hear properly."

"I see." He spoke curtly, before turning on his heel, jerking the bar upwards, then dropping it with a clatter before leaving the room, and Isabella sank onto the chest, her knees weak, wishing she could read his face better. What would he do next? What should she do? Well, one thing she could do, and that was to ensure the wench would not come near Jerold again. Had Clarice really been trying to help? And what had happened to the watered wine Nan swore had been left for him?

Isabella would not bother Giles further, but she would keep Clarice busy and as far away from Jerold as possible until he was recovered enough to sleep in the hall, where he would be more difficult for her to get to. She would tell Edith to keep a watch on her, too. She didn't think the servants would gossip to Clarice, at any rate, although she suspected Adam might be a different matter.

Still, all this was conjecture, and Jerold's need was more urgent than her speculations. She found Molly and asked her to fetch watered wine, then took it up herself, relieved to see Nan cleansing his wound again using her simples.

Isabella pulled a stool closer and watched, asking Nan about the poultice the woman was preparing. It was similar to the one she had used, but Nan had added some unguent of her own making.

Nan answered her questions sparingly while she worked, and Isabella resolved not to distract her again until she'd finished. As the steward's wife wrapped a clean bandage around Jerold's arm, she gave Isabella a look of assessment before clearing her throat and saying, "If it doesn't offend you, my lady, I'd be happy to teach you what I know."

Isabella had no false pride. What she did not know, she needed to learn. "I'd be most grateful, Nan. Perhaps you'll show me some of your nostrums when you're done here? And teach me how they are made and used?"

As she finished speaking, Jerold ceased his wild mutterings and came back to his senses, watching them, his face filled with fear.

Nan brushed the hair off Jerold's face tenderly and bade him sleep, "For sleep is also a healer, my lad, and you'll do well enough now."

He gave a relieved sigh and closed his eyes, and Nan motioned Isabella outside. "I'll send Molly in to watch him now," she said. "The girl is good with sickness. She's patient, and she's blessed with calm common-sense. And you may come to my herbarium, and I'll start to show you. Although, don't you be expecting to learn it all at once, my lady. I learnt this at my mother's knee, and it's taken me years." She hitched her bosom with her forearms, straightened her veil and said, "But if you bear with me, I daresay you'll learn quick enough. Come, then." And she led the way down to her own domain, where her jars and flasks filled the wooden shelves and dried bunches of herbs hung from the walls. "Doubtless you'll know these and their uses, my lady, but I'll run through them anyway. Vervain, that's to clear the blood of poisons, and fenugreek seeds – just a few, for they are expensive and hard to obtain. I shall try to grow some, I think, although I'm not sure whether they'll like our soil. I add them to the vervain to calm inflammation along with wine vinegar and yarrow and agrimony. Yarrow also calms and stops the bleeding, agrimony in the poultice cleanses the wound."

She moved from one to another, talking all the time, and Isabella concentrated, trying to commit Nan's teachings to memory.

She was beginning to wonder how much more she could take in when Nan put down the pestle she was using and said, "Here I am going on as though you needed to know everything immediately. You'll struggle to remember what I've taught you already, without me trying to cram more knowledge into you today."

"Belike you're right, Nan. My head feels as though it might burst if you tell me one more thing."

"Well then, you go off to your own concerns, my lady. I'll teach you no more today."

Brushing some dried petals from her gown, Isabella turned to leave. As she did so, Nan called after her, "You spend some time with me every day, my lady, and we'll make a herb wife of you yet."

To Isabella's annoyance, as she entered her chamber again, Clarice was sitting on their bed. She stood quickly when she saw Isabella and dropped a curtsey, saying, "My lady, I'm concerned about Jerold. He's the last of my household." She paused, pressing her fingers to her forehead, "At least, he must be. Oh, why can I not remember? And yet, he does not seem to like me, and I don't know why." She looked piteously at Isabella. "I only wish to help him, yet he turns from me."

She wandered to the wall, leaning her face against the stone. "It is so difficult, my lady. I do not know my station, I do not know my kin, I can barely even remember my husband, although I know he was a good man, and I loved him dearly."

Isabella regarded her with suspicion; she was showing a different face now than the one she wore with Adam last night. Yet, the soft underbelly of her emotions felt a tug of compassion, and, she reasoned, if she at least appeared to believe Clarice, she would eventually gain her trust. And then, maybe she could winkle out the truth.

She held out her hand in a gesture of friendship, and the girl clung to it. "I'm truly sorry for your loss, Clarice. Perhaps, if you start trying to recall small things, the rest will come with time. Or it might be that, when you try less hard to remember, the things that are evading you now will return."

Clarice gazed back, her whole demeanour one of earnest hope. "Oh, my lady, I do pray so."

Isabella's heart softened. After all, she had suffered much. If she could be put at ease, she might remember something. And if she was not who she seemed to be, then she would surely slip eventually.

Clarice, still clinging to her, laid her other hand on Isabella's sleeve. Isabella looked at it with detached interest – it was small and square with some oval-tipped nails and some ragged ones, but then, in her fear and haste to hide from danger, she may have torn them – while Clarice continued, "My lady, I'm so grateful for your help. Yesterday, I was so overwrought, in truth, I barely knew what I was about. Your husband has been kind to me, as have you, and I want to assure you, now I'm recovering a little, I'm fully aware of that."

Isabella felt her face flame. As though Clarice had read her thoughts, she gave a small, tight smile. "You don't have to feel embarrassed, my lady. I treated your maid badly, yesterday, and I'm ashamed of the way I threw myself at your husband, yet only because," her voice wobbled, "I was so afraid, and I could sense the gentleness in him. I won't do so again." She looked down, and her voice was low. "I only hope I've not filled you with disgust, for," that treacherous wobble was back in her voice, "I have nowhere else to go until I know who I am."

Clarice gave a sniff and let go of Isabella, wiping a tear from her face with the back of her hand, and Isabella, not knowing what else to say, responded, "Of course you may stay here. We would not cast you adrift."

She hoped she'd not have cause to regret that. She smiled as genuinely as she could manage at Clarice, who watched her hopefully. "Come, let us go down to the hall. I have much to discover

here, and if you help me, we can learn together."
And you'll be where I can keep an eye on you. If this is all a sham, I want you in my sight.

The day was busy. Isabella met with Oswin, who showed her his accounts and explained to her the ways of the household; with Nan, who took her around her domain, and with Filbert, who showed her the areas beyond that; the work-rooms, the barns, the mill, and the chapel, which nestled against the stone wall of the house.

With Filbert, she did not linger. It had begun to snow again, fine snow which stung her face. The wind tugged at her mantle and hood, catching at her hair, pulling it free from its confines, blowing it into her eyes so she could not see.

She wished she had sturdier boots; the ones she had were soon soaked through, and her toes were numb. Cutting the tour short, she returned to the shelter of the hall to ponder on the problem that was Clarice.

Clarice was a complete enigma. Although rude to Edith yesterday, she seemed eager to please now, submissive, helpful. She spoke more politely to Edith, had stopped behaving as though the maid was there to serve her personally, although Isabella judged from Edith's expression that she was not the only one who wasn't entirely convinced about Clarice's change of attitude. Still, she was one of the household for the foreseeable future. If she was prepared to make herself useful, it would help.

Isabella saw nothing of Giles during the rest of the daylight hours; he and Fulke were preparing to ride out to the sheriff to report the deaths. Molly nursed Jerold, with Nan checking on him from time to time.

The wall hangings, Isabella noted, were frayed around the edges and a little moth-eaten in places. Although most of her possessions were still in the chest at Berkhamsted Castle, she'd brought her sewing and embroidery necessities with her, and she believed the hangings could be repaired until she had time to make more. It would give her something useful to do, make her feel less of an outsider.

One of her husband's household servants was passing, and she stepped out in front of him, racking her brains to remember his name. "Simkin? It is Simkin, is it not?"

"Aye, lady." Simkin bowed his head, not quite hiding a smirk, which Isabella hoped was pleasure that she'd called him aright.

"Well then, Simkin, can you take this down for me? I wish to restore it." She leaned to touch one of the more faded parts, pointing out a couple of holes. "As you see, it's in need of some repair."

Simkin's watery green eyes regarded her. "Aye, lady, that piece was stitched by my lord's mother, it was, the dear lady. It's bin a sorrow to me to watch it fall into tatters."

She gave him her most dazzling smile. "Then, if I have your help, Simkin, I will endeavour to bring it back to its former condition."

Simkin shuffled, a beatific expression spreading across his face, then clambered onto the bench, reaching for the hanging on unsteady legs. Isabella held her breath. Why had she not asked one of the younger men? If Simkin fell and hurt himself, she would be to blame. But, tense as she was, she had just grasped at the first person she saw, not even thinking about whether or not he was suitable for the task.

Her nerves were taut as a stretched thread while he wobbled precariously on the bench, and she could almost hear them twang with relief when he had detached the hanging and climbed down, holding it out to her like a trophy.

The pride she saw on his face, though, made her glad after all that she had asked him for aid. Perchance not many asked him to do much, deferring to his antiquity. She, too, knew how it felt to be patronised and unimportant. And, after all, he was safe down now.

"I thank you, Simkin. That was kind of you." She inclined her head graciously towards him, and the old man beamed.

"Where d'you want me to tek it to, lady?" he asked. "To your solar?"

Again, Isabella felt a qualm. Was he fit to climb the solar stair? But she had not the heart to give the task to another, so, nerves taut again, she allowed him to carry it upstairs, almost trembling herself when he grasped the guardrail firmly and, with wavering steps, hauled himself up.

Once in the solar, she took it from him hastily, insisting he sit down for a moment, as he wheezed and panted. She poured him a cup of wine. "Drink this, my good Simkin. And thank you for your aid." Clarice looked on, and Isabella was disturbed to see a slightly scornful look on her face. Clarice saw her watching and her expression seemed to melt into concern until Isabella wondered if she had imagined it. She turned again to Simkin.

His face, already bright, lit up still more as he took the wine from her, and she knew she had won a heart today.

When he recovered, she sent him on his way, then examined the hanging more thoroughly. The light which came through the horn panes of the window was weak, and she didn't wish to use too many candles, not knowing how many Giles would think of as extravagance, so she ordered rushlights and torches lit, and another brazier, for her fingers were nearly too cold to sew. Then she positioned herself so she could see to work, laid out her silk embroidery threads, and considered how she might best make a start.

Clarice pulled up a stool next to her, helping her to sort the threads, and Edith followed suit, since it turned out, she had a good eye for colour and was skilled with a needle.

The activity seemed to draw them together, although before long, a tear dripped onto the hanging. Isabella looked up to see Clarice wiping her eyes again, and raised her brows.

"I'm sorry, my lady." The single tear became a flood, and Edith twitched the fabric from her before it could be spoiled. "I just wondered, might it be possible for me to see my husband? I...I never got the chance to say farewell. They won't..." She sniffed. "They won't just bury him, will they? Not without telling me?"

"I'm sure they won't. There will be an investigation, for certain. But, Clarice, you do know he's not prepared, don't you? The bodies have been wrapped ready to take to the sheriff, and anyway, they could not bury him at the moment; the ground is too frozen."

Clarice ripped her veil from her head, tore at her hair and dropped to her knees on the floor, wailing. Isabella and Edith left their needles and knelt beside her, coaxing and cajoling until she'd regained some composure, their eyes meeting over her head with a mix of compassion and doubt.

Clarice eyed them through the tangle of her fox-red hair. She'd not been herself yesterday. It was the shock. Now, she realised how important it was to play her hand carefully. Their goodwill was equally as important as that of the menfolk, but she had always been one who preferred the company of men. For the time being, though, she must appear to be a respectable married woman of substance and consequence.

She hated Isabella, hated women born to privilege, while she had nought but her wits and her ability to slake men's thirst. Women had one weakness; they were harder to fool than men, yet once they trusted you, they could sway the household in your direction. She dug her nails hard into her palms, and the pain made it easy to squeeze out more tears.

She did not like any of them, vain, silly, simpering things, and she had every intention of ousting this one, who had been so contemptuous of her. Isabella appeared to sympathise, but it was only an act; Clarice was familiar enough with mistrust. For now though, she would play her part with more care. Already, it was beginning to work. Now, if she could be absolutely sure that youth of Walerin's employ could be convinced, she could stop fretting about him.

She had thought to do away with him, but that might now make her suspect. Anyway, he was looking so frail today, her hand in his demise might not be necessary. He would say nothing at present. She'd made sure of that. As long as he remembered when he regained his strength.

She smiled weakly up at the maid and Isabella, who were both watching her with what she hoped was anxiety, and gulped, drying her eyes on her veil as she picked it up from where she had cast it. "I'm so sorry, my lady. Sometimes the grief is too much to bear. If I might have a sip of wine?"

Isabella helped her to her feet and nodded to Edith, who brought her a cup.

Clarice made sure to stagger slightly, as Isabella supported her to a stool near the bed. It was a good bed. Richly polished wood with a solid frame, and comfortable. One day, she would have one like it, maybe even this very one.

She held out a shaking hand, and felt Edith push the cup into it. Taking a sip, she allowed the rich warmth of it to linger on her tongue. She had ever been one to enjoy the finer things of life, once she'd discovered them.

That fool merchant whose mistress she'd been had no finesse in himself, but his home had been sumptuously furnished, his gifts generous. If she was not mistaken, he had more wealth than this knight. She had not missed the shabby hangings and furnishings scattered throughout the house. Now, though, she could claim Walerin the Fleming's wealth, and so long as she had that, she could live without his pudgy hands fumbling at her.

Giles de Soutenay! He was one she would take without the other trappings, for to be his mistress – she had no expectations of more, but then, who knew? – would afford her infinitely more pleasure. Besides, wealth was not everything, consequence was equally important, and perhaps he would rise to greater things. That she found him attractive, intriguing, was a further incentive.

And Adam had told her de Soutenay served John, Count of Mortain, the king's brother, so there was always the possibility de Soutenay might take her to court. She almost purred at the thought. She'd heard Prince John was not averse to having a mistress, and Clarice was very sure she could arouse his interest in her. Once there, the world was open to her. There were many ways a valued mistress could rise, and she would explore all of them.

A sigh of pure avarice escaped her. No matter, it would be taken for one of despair.

She closed her eyes to hide the gleam of triumph that flashed there, lest they guessed her thoughts, and set her mind to winning them both over. Betrayal had always been her game, and this time would be no exception. She just needed to be very sure of her tactics, for only a fool would not see this happenstance as an opportunity, and she was no fool.

Isabella had not been completely convinced. She could not shift a lingering suspicion, and she did not like the expression in the girl's eyes when she looked at Giles. When she was alone with Clarice, she found her easy enough to get on with, but she still did not entirely trust her near Jerold, and she was beginning to trust her even less near Giles.

CHAPTER 22

Giles was taking good care to remain distant from Clarice, for he felt she would become more reliant on him than he was comfortable with. As it was, his wife seemed to tighten her jaw whenever she saw the girl speaking to him. He began to have the suspicion that Isabella might be jealous of her. It irked him, for he could not bear to see all his progress with her undone. The best course of action, he thought, was to avoid Clarice. Unfortunately, it meant he had to keep his distance from Isabella, too, and that, he did not want.

At least, beneath the hangings of their bed, they could find privacy when they came together at night, though he cursed the fact that Clarice had to share their chamber.

Isabella appeared able to tolerate the girl better when he was not near. He glanced across to where his wife sat by the hearth sewing industriously at a wall hanging pegged to her embroidery frame.

As the firelight flickered, casting light and shade upon her face, he leaned back on his bench, long legs stretched to the fire, hands clasped behind his head, watching the look of concentration she wore as she pushed her needle in and out of the fabric.

She paused from time to time to exchange comments with Nan and Edith; Giles realised her inevitable shadow, Clarice, was no longer with her. Glancing around the room covertly, he could see no sign of Adam, and for once, blessed the lad. His eagerness to slope off from his duties and dally with the women of the household normally earned him a curse, but this time…

Soon, he would have to despatch the bodies to the sheriff. The weather had eased again, and he had no further excuse for delay, but he did not want to go.

By rights, he should have done so earlier, but since they'd arrived here, the weather had been vile. Also, he'd not wanted to leave Isabella until he was sure she was at ease with both home and servants and had convinced himself a day more or less would make no difference.

However, he could no longer use either as an excuse, for Isabella seemed settled enough, and today the sun shone weakly in a sky that was palely blue, streaked with one or two wisps of white, and he could put it off no more.

Giles pushed himself from his bench and ambled over, pausing to pick up a platter of dried fruits and some cheese from the kitchen along with a costrel of wine. He deposited them in the solar and returned, laying his hand on Isabella's shoulder. She started, stabbing her finger with her needle, winced and held it aloft, examining the blood welling from it.

He took her hand and held the finger to his mouth, licking the blood from it, a deeply intimate gesture, and noticed how her breathing quickened. Giving her a look of invitation, he jerked his head upwards, and she rose, her face fiery red, her pupils growing huge and dark.

She allowed him to lead her away, and his lips twitched with amusement at her obvious embarrassment, although he was pleased her discomfort did not seem to make her reluctant to join him.

Giles felt like a boy caught filching honey cakes as he opened the door to the solar. "At last, I have you to myself." It was hardly original, but now, of a sudden, he found his mind a blank.

Her face crinkled into an open smile, and his heart sang to see it. Sometimes she still flinched if he spoke too sharply, but he was beginning to learn to keep his tone more even, mostly finding the reward was worth the effort.

He sat, pulling her to his lap, pushing her veil to one side and burying his face in the nape of her neck, for here, at her home, she wore no wimple. Inhaling deeply, he caught a hint of the rose petals and cloves which she kept in the folds of her chemises in her clothing chest. She leaned into his embrace, winding her arms around his neck, saying with a laugh in her voice, "My lord, if you sniff much harder, I'll disappear up your nose."

He groaned, said, "Bella, I've missed you," caught the plaintive tone in his voice and felt abashed.

"Missed me?" She let go of his neck and looked at him with an impish expression. "But I've been in the hall."

Taking her wrists and moving her arms back around his neck, he said, "Foolish wench. I mean I've missed being able to be with you."

Her eyes glinted at him, amber fire in their depths flashing through her half-closed lids, her lower lip in a sultry pout. "But my lord, you had only to cross the hall."

Was she toying with him, or did she truly not know? "And have Clarice cast herself at my feet again?"

A small gurgle of laughter came from her as she hid her face in his tunic, and he wrapped his arms around her and drew her close, tugging off her veil, nuzzling the ties at her neck, pulling at them with his teeth to loosen them. She made a small sound deep in her throat and slid one hand down the nape of his neck.

As he began to unbraid her hair, the door swung open, and she all but leapt from his lap as Clarice sidled into the room.

Giles bit back a curse; Isabella, flushed and dishevelled, grabbed for her veil. Clarice's gaze swung sharply between them, and for a moment, Giles recoiled at what he thought he saw there. Then, the girl dropped into a curtsey and said apologetically, "Your pardon, my lord. I came to tell you the horses are saddled and the cart ready."

Giles swore openly this time, and Isabella clasped her hands before her, knuckles white, biting her lip. Damn his temper! And damn FitzAubrey. Damn Clarice too. He tilted his head in dismissal, but the girl stayed where she was, her head bowed. Irritably, he snarled, "Tell them I'm on my way."

She raised a limpid gaze to him. "Yes, my lord. Do you wish me to help you arm?"

Giles' brow furrowed. Help him arm? How in Hell would she know how to do that? She'd been wed to a merchant, not a knight.

Isabella, standing rigidly by the bed, cut in before he could open his mouth. "I thank you, Clarice, but no, I am perfectly capable of that. Do you go and pack supplies for my lord. Ask Edith and Molly to help you."

Clarice gave them a slightly wounded look. "I have already done so, my lady. I thought you might be able to use my help here."

"Well, as you see, we do not." Isabella's lips had thinned. Giles saw a pulse throbbing in her throat. "Thank you for your kindness." But she did not sound very grateful.

"Very well, my lady." At last, Clarice turned and left, glancing over her shoulder as she walked away, not quite closing the door behind her.

Giles strode to the door, kicking it shut, dropping the bar across it. "Does that woman never take a hint?" Isabella flushed again, whether with embarrassment or annoyance, he could not tell. "Now, where were we?" he said, catching her to him, but the moment had fled, disappearing through the door along with Clarice just as surely as if she had picked it up and taken it with her. Isabella put her arms around his waist, but her earlier promise of passion was gone.

He kissed her, but her lips were cool and he had no time. "Do you really wish to help arm me, love? Or should I call one of the lads?" He doubted she could do it but if she truly wished to try, he would not stop her.

She stepped from his embrace and pulled his gambeson from the pole where it had been airing; the weight of it made her stagger. He thrust his head into it and she pulled it down around him. When she attempted to pick up his hauberk, she nearly dropped it, and he took it from her. "I'll call Alan and Eustace to help, it's not a job for a woman; it will take the both of them. Come, kiss me." He pulled her to him again, and this time, she pressed herself tight against him, seeking his mouth with lips slightly parted. He returned the kiss with enthusiasm, but as his tongue sought hers, she pulled back and stepped away from him.

Her face puckered a little, but all she said was, "Take care, my lord." Then, she went to lift the bar at the door. Opening it, she left quickly, and he heard her calling the squires.

As they assembled, Giles ran his gaze over his men. He had Eudo and Humphrey, his serjeants, his two older squires, Alan and Gareth, two of his knights, Fulke and Adam, plus a few more of his mesnie. If they met with the outlaws, assuming they were local and not miles away by now, he hoped it would be enough.

It was unlikely they would attempt the house in his absence – the thorny thicket around its perimeter would discourage them, but he must leave enough here to protect his people. Guy and Miles, plus the armed guard he had left behind, along with Oswin and his son, both capable of fighting if the need arose.

His two younger squires, Thomas and Eustace, were too inexperienced to be of much help, but the rest should be enough. God grant the weather held so he need not be gone long.

The women came to see them safe away. Adam caught Clarice by the hand before he mounted Blaze, murmuring something into her ear. Clarice responded briefly then swatted him away, all the time watching Giles from beneath her lashes. Giles embraced his wife before swinging himself onto Troubadour.

He raised one hand to Isabella as the gate was opened, and she made a small moue with her lips. His heart misgave him. She would be safe, would she not? Then he chuckled at his fears. He did not usually behave with such maudlin sensitivity, but then, he had not left behind a wife ere this.

He turned his head for one last glance. Isabella's raised hand trembled a little. Clarice stood beside her, casting him a look which promised things he did not wish to think on. Nan waved, and they rode out, Giles praying devoutly that all would be well in his absence and chiding himself for his foolishness.

CHAPTER 23

Within the hour of their leaving, the weather turned again. Giles ignored the first flakes of snow, but as it started to swirl about him, he pushed a lock of wet hair from his face, pulling his hood further down. All around him, his men were doing the same thing until little more than their noses could be seen.

Surely no outlaws would be lying in wait in this. But still, Giles felt a prickling at the base of his neck. Nothing could be done however. He'd taken precautions; each man carried a mace, axe or spear along with his sword. To be seen bristling with weapons would, he hoped, deter anyone both foolish enough to be out in this weather and desperate enough to think of attacking them.

Simon de Beauchamp, Bedford's sheriff, was renowned for his dedication to upholding the king's peace, and a band of outlaws so close to home was something Giles wanted dealt with urgently. He hoped they were long gone from the area.

As the cart rumbled along, Leofwine doing his best to avoid the ruts in the road, Giles kept his senses alert for trouble, straining his eyes to see through the dizzying white dance as the snow fell more heavily.

The horses had plumes of steam rising from their nostrils, and Giles' fingers were almost numb inside his gauntlets. Fulke's eyes were red-rimmed as he turned his head this way and that, and Adam's face was grim. In places, the trees were beginning to encroach too near to the road, and Giles could hear Eudo cursing beneath his breath.

Thoughts of Isabella warmed his blood, but at the same time distracted him, so he forced her regretfully from his mind, trying not to linger on the curve of her hip, the softness of her mouth, the honey-depths of her eyes, until he realised he was doing it again. He shook his head hard to dispel the images that tantalised him, fixing his gaze firmly on the road ahead, and was half pleased, half dismayed, to see an alehouse looming dimly before him. His men, however, responded with such enthusiasm, Giles allowed the halt.

The warm air hit their frozen bodies, and too-cold extremities tingled as they jostled to the fire, the men who had been seated there moving hastily out of the way when they barged in, darting resentful glances at them.

"We must look like desperate men," Adam muttered through chapped lips, turning his back to the fire and raising his cloak and tunic to warm his buttocks.

"Well, I am, if you're not. Desperate to get warmed and fed. I wouldn't let a dog out on a day like this." Fulke grabbed one of the mugs of ale the serving wench brought over on a tray.

As the tray emptied, Adam lunged at the girl, pulling her close to him. She squealed in protest, but he plumped himself down on a stool and pulled her to his lap. "Now, this is the best way to warm myself." He chuckled as she squirmed to get free. "Come, sweeting. Save me from freezing to my death."

He smacked a kiss on her cheek at the same time as slipping his money pouch onto the table. She giggled and wrapped her arms around him, nuzzling her face into his neck as his hands wandered over her, only pulling away when an older girl tugged at her, reminding her of her duties. Adam snatched a final kiss before she scurried off.

Giles snatched up Adam's purse and threw it at him, snapping, "Don't make yourself more of a fool than you were born, Adam." Adam scowled, and Giles indicated the crowded hostelry, lowering his voice. "Any of these could be the outlaws we seek. Do you truly wish to make us a target? I am aware you believe your skills to be superlative, but we have no idea how many of them there are. Yes, we can probably take them, but if not, I have no wish to make my lady a widow just yet."

Adam opened his mouth, but Fulke cut in. "Like I said, brains in his braies. One nice armful, and his wits fly out the window. I've a sweet lass of my own back at Thorneywell. I've no intention of replacing her arms with a shroud just yet. Be patient, Adam. When we get to Bedford Castle, de Beauchamp will likely send his own men out with us to find them. There's trouble enough just getting the dead there without bringing outlaws down on us. After that, you can cozen as many women as you wish. For now, let's just get the job done."

He glared at Adam, who, outfaced by the older knight, hastily scooped up the contents of his purse before burying his nose in his cup. Fulke, having said his piece, ignored him, finished his ale and held out his cup for refilling as a different girl brought pies and bowls of pottage over to them.

Leofwine joined them, holding his hands out to the fire. "Wain's in the barn. They're rubbing the horses down and feeding them, my lord."

"Good man. Here's food and ale; get it down you and warm your innards."

Leofwine pulled up another stool and fell upon the food like a starving man, licking his lips as he wiped the bowl clean with a piece of bread, laughing and jesting with the others.

Giles allowed Leofwine time to eat and take his ease for a while, then tossed back the last of his ale, slamming the cup down onto the trestle. "We should be moving. We have far to go, and while we can still see, we need to get going."

He was met with grimaces and acknowledged them with a wry quirk of his face but his tone brooked no argument. "Indeed, I feel the tug also, but I intend to make progress while we may, for who knows how much worse this will get?"

Leofwine grabbed another cup of ale and swallowed it in swift gulps. Fulke sighed and made to rise, Adam groaned audibly.

Eudo, seizing a piece of bread and cramming it into his mouth, said indistinctly through the crumbs, "Aye, you're in the right of it, my lord; best to be on our way before it grows too dark."

The others grumbled and muttered as they donned cloaks which had not had time to dry, but at least their bellies had been filled, their blood warmed, and, reluctantly, they left the alehouse behind them, mounting their horses. Leofwine climbed onto the wain, and they set out again.

Giles reckoned there was about an hour until Vespers when they spied another hostelry. Although the snow had eased again, the light would soon be gone, and he called a halt. Dismounting wearily, they trudged in, glad of the roaring fire and enticing aroma of hot food.

As some of those inside moved back to allow the newcomers access, Giles' men draped their cloaks around the fire and flopped down on benches, glad to be done for the day. Once fed and warmed through, they stayed awhile taking their ease before they found space in the barn for the night. They burrowed into the hay, pulled their still damp cloaks over them and most were soon snoring. If soft noises and murmurings came from Adam's direction, Giles was too intent on sleep to care. The boy would learn soon enough.

Next morning, rousing just before dawn from a dream where Isabella was curled up beside him caressing his chest, beginning to move her hands over his belly, Giles woke with a jolt to realise a young woman was kneeling by his side, her hands running along his belt, reaching down to where his purse hung. He grabbed her wrists in a vice-like grip, and she muttered what might or might not have been an obscenity before rubbing her face against his, saying, "I just wondered if you needed any comfort, my lord."

"Wondered if I had anything you could help yourself to, more like." He flung her from him, and she landed in a heap on top of Adam, who mumbled and pulled her close. Like lightning, Giles rose, ripping her from Adam's arms. As the younger man opened his eyes wide, Giles said acidly, "If this is the wench you were coupling with last night, I suggest you check your pouch."

Adam, still on his back, felt along his length, swearing viciously when he realised it was gone. He leapt to his feet, striking the girl hard across the face. She screamed and would have fallen had Giles not been holding her. Adam ferreted in her skirts and found his purse, and Giles cast her from them. She landed in a heap, her lip bleeding from Adam's blow, glaring up at them with a feral expression, part hate, part fear.

Adam went to kick her, but Giles caught at him. "Enough! If you couple so carelessly, what do you expect? You have your money back. And you!" She scooted backwards, and he grasped her by the arm, dragging her behind him into the inn as she protested her innocence. "Let's see what your mistress has to say about you robbing travellers while they sleep."

He forced her into the inn, ignoring her wails, and thrust her before the alewife. "Is this trull one of yours?"

"That she's not!" The alewife put her hands on her hips, looking the girl up and down before boxing her ears and striking her across the face. The slap rang out, silencing those who had been talking and eating as all swivelled to watch. Her handprint was left clear on the girl's cheek.

The girl spat and swore as Giles let go of her, crumpling to the ground, then pushed herself backwards, rose, gathered her skirts and ran.

The alewife cursed. "I'm goin' to have to deal with that thievin' little cow. I've kicked her out before, but she keeps tryin' to slip back in. She must have crept into the barn when my man's back was turned."

Or smuggled herself in with Adam, thought Giles. "Yet you haven't reported her. Why is that?" Was the alewife as genuine as she appeared? Or did they work together?

"Nay, lord, for truth to tell, I'm a bit sorry for her. Her ma was no good, an' the lass never stood a chance. We did employ her a while back, for I thought she'd be grateful enough to keep her sticky paws to herself, but I was wrong. Now I can't seem to get rid of her." She sighed gustily. "I'm that sorry, my lord. I'll put the fear of the devil into her next time she shows up, an' if all else fails, she'll have to go before the bailiff, but, well, you know how it is, my lord. Likely, she's just trying to survive."

Giles frowned. "Maybe so, but if this happens to your customers often, it may be you who's summoned before the bailiff. And you've your reputation to think of. Robbing your patrons blind is not a way to keep that intact."

Her face reddened, and she drew herself up to her full height, stretching her neck like an enraged goose, ruffled feathers quivering with indignation. "Aye, I know, my lord. An' like I say, I'll deal more sternly with her if I catch her at it again. But, I can't do more than say sorry, an' at least you got your money back, so no harm done, eh?

"Tell you what, to show you my good faith, I'll take no payment for your food this morning. Can't say fairer than that, now, can I?"

Giles said gravely, "Indeed. But again, I warn you, take care. You never know who she'll rob next. We're on our way to meet with the sheriff as it is. I'm a reasonable man, but you may not be so lucky next time."

"Quite so, my lord. An' I'm grateful." She backed away, anxious for the conversation to be over. Giles sat himself down at the long table, joined by his men as they trickled into the room, and the woman sent a girl over bearing a tray piled high with bread, cheese, ale and pottage.

Adam rode balefully behind them as they continued on their way. The snow had eased up, the sky was brighter, and they bantered cheerfully as they rode. Two more days it took, lumbering with the wain, but they eventually reached Bedford Castle without incident.

Simon de Beauchamp was away, but his under-sheriff, Randolf du Beke, tugged at his short beard thoughtfully as he watched his men lifting the bodies and laying them in the chapel crypt. "Ground's too hard to bury them. Anyway, we need to keep them until we can identify them. At least in this weather, they won't raise a stink. They'll do well enough here; the cold will keep them from decay."

Their clothing and boots had mostly been taken, but he examined whatever had been left on each one. "This one's well fed and wealthy to go by the state of him. Was there evidence of horses?"

"I believe so. The ground had been churned up. As many horses as men, I'd say."

"Looks as though he wore rings, too. Skin's torn where they ripped them off, see?" He held a pudgy hand up; Giles observed it with distaste. "Was anything left?"

Giles nodded. "I think they may have had a lookout posted. At any rate, they were gone by the time we came across the bodies. There was one cart. Not much left in it but a couple of lengths of silk and some other fabrics, although they'd be worth a fair bit. They must have left in a hurry and not had time to finish their plundering. We salvaged what we could.

"There's only two survived. One's a mere boy – about fifteen summers, I would guess, and," he paused for effect, "we found a woman hidden under the cart."

The under-sheriff looked up sharply. "A woman? His wife? Daughter? Whore?"

"No idea."

Du Beke ran his gaze over Giles' face. "Well, man, did you not think to ask her?"

Giles smiled grimly. "She claims she was his wife."

"Claims? At any rate, surely she told you who they are."

"She also reckons to have lost her memory."

Randolf pushed his tongue around his teeth as though dislodging a crumb, taking his time before saying, "I suppose it could be the case. Do you believe her?"

"Not sure. It's hard to tell."

"Was she raped?"

"Not that I'm aware of."

"Does she appear to be telling the truth about anything else?"

"Again, I'm not sure."

Du Beke searched his face. "Not sure of much, are you, de Soutenay? You didn't bring her with you. Why?"

"In these conditions, she'd just have slowed us down further. She's perfectly safe at my manor for now, my lord."

"As long as she remains there until I've spoken to her. You're certain she'll not run off?"

"In this weather? Besides, she begged me to let her stay until she remembers who she is, which does lend a little credence to her story."

Du Beke's eyes narrowed. He tugged his beard again while he considered. "Very well, then. And you say there's an injured boy? Can he not verify her claims?"

"Indeed. He took an arrow to his arm. He was fevered before I left and making little sense. My wife is tending him, and like Mistress Clarice, he'll be quite safe where he is." Giles frowned. "Well, as long as the outlaws don't take the opportunity of my absence to attack. By your leave, we'll not remain long. My manor is small, and although I've left men there, it's somewhat vulnerable if this band of outlaws is large. I don't wish to be gone for too great a time under the circumstances."

Du Beke's tongue worried at his teeth again, his brow furrowed. "We'll expect your help to search for them, and we'll need you to show us exactly where the bodies were found, but I'll send men back with you; one of my constables, too. You may leave some of them to guard your hall whilst you hunt. There will be room to sleep them?"

"There will, my lord. My servants can remove to the barns if necessary."

"Well and good, then." He rubbed his hands together. "Now, come you in and warm yourselves. You're in time for supper, and we'll find you some space at the hearth." He tilted his head. "I understand your haste; however, you can remain a couple of nights?"

"A couple, no more, unless you have need of us." It was a lie, for he was itching to return, worried about his own people, longing for his wife, but he must at least sound willing.

"Very well. I'll get things arranged as quickly as possible. Now," he opened the door and led Giles out and towards the castle, "a wife, eh? I heard rumours you were recently wed. Le Gris' daughter, they say." He laughed, looking much less officious now business had been concluded.

Clapping Giles on the shoulder, he said, "I bet that made the old man swear. Come and eat. I'll speak more with you on the morrow."

CHAPTER 24

Giles had been gone seven full days. The snow had started again within hours of his departure, at first intermittently, as though it could not make up its mind, while a weak sun tried to push through the clouds. Then, the sky turned an ominous shade of yellow. Little flurries of snow whirled around doors like down, creeping into the hall as men came in or out. That lasted for a few hours. Then, it began to fall in earnest, swirling into vast swathes of white, blotting out all vision.

Few ventured out unless they must, preferring to stay snug in the hall, gossiping, gaming and drinking. Those who had skills on instruments brought them out, and folk joined in, singing and clapping lustily.

Isabella sat on a bench before the hearth, tapping her foot in time with the music, but pursed her lips as she sewed. How long would it be before Giles returned? He surely would not attempt the journey home in this. Now she was used to his presence beside her, the bed felt cold and empty without him.

Nan paused in her mending to reassure her. "He'll have taken shelter somewhere, my lady. That lad knows how to take care of himself. He's not lived this long serving Prince John by taking foolish risks."

He still serves Prince John? That was why John had attended their wedding, then? She hadn't realised, and her heart gave a sickening lurch. Did that mean they would have to dance attendance on him when he was in England? Which, as far as Isabella was concerned, was very much too often. Did Giles have to travel over the narrow sea with him? She knew so little about him or about his terms of service as John's liege man.

Thinking of John, remembering his vile touch, she shuddered, then shrugged off the idea of him, put aside her sewing, stood and held out her hands to the fire to warm them. The flames made them tingle but could not reach the chill that gripped her heart.

As she turned back to Nan, a sudden dizziness caught at her, and she swayed slightly. Edith leapt to her feet to steady her but was elbowed aside by Clarice, who put an arm about her, leading her back to the bench.

Isabella was about to shrug her off politely when her stomach gave a heave, and she tore herself free, running wildly for the latrines. Nan heaved her bulk from where she sat and lumbered after her, swatting Clarice away like some troublesome fly.

She stood placidly by as Isabella bent over the privy, the foul stench which rose from its depths making her retch more than she had thought possible. When she sat back on her heels, wiping her mouth, Nan said, "Have you had your flux this month, my lady?"

Isabella felt her mouth gape. She had not. Indeed, she had forgotten in all the upheaval since her wedding, and her linens lay, unused and unremembered, in one of the chests.

A babe! She had not thought. Could she have quickened so soon? And yet, Giles had made full use of their leisurely time at the abbey. A thrill of triumph started to rise, it seemed from her toes, until it enveloped her, and despite the nausea that still threatened to overcome her, she filled with a simple pride. Baldwin had called her a dried-up thorn; now, she had proof that she was not.

Nan, watching her closely, said, "Aye, my lady, I thought I'd seen it in you. You've caught quickly, lass." She hesitated, then continued, "You don't mind me calling you lass, do you? Only, sometimes, I forget Giles is now my lord. I've known him since he was nought but a little tacker, you see."

Isabella smiled shyly. "I should like it, Nan."

"Only, I'll give you all due respect before the others, my lady. I'd not want them to be forgetting themselves. And now, would you not rather be sitting in your own chamber, where the garderobe will smell a lot sweeter than this if you should need it? Reckon these need cleaning out again, but it won't be this side of the month. Come now, lass, and I'll fetch you a ginger tisane. And don't be worrying about being sick, for it just means the babe is settling itself strong in your womb."

As she spoke, she led Isabella from the latrines, sweeping all before her as she drew her mistress through the hall, holding her arm to steady her up the stairs. She settled Isabella in a chair, pulled up a log for her to rest her feet on, put more wood on the brazier, and sent Edith, who had hurried after them, to fetch, "One of my infusions. The ginger one. Molly knows where it is. Stir some of it into some hot wine with lots of honey and bring it back here." And as Edith opened the door, she called after her, "And bring some of the sweet wafers, too. Best thing for nausea. You'll find Molly looking after that poor lad. Make haste."

Jerold! Isabella had not given him a thought for several hours. She turned to Nan, her face full of concern. "How does he do? Is he any better?"

Nan shook her head. "I'm sorry, my lady. I've done all I can, but I'm not sure he'll make it. I don't understand it, for I thought he was on the mend. Molly managed to get some broth down him, but he took another bad turn after." Her voice was dismal. "It's not the wound fever, and it doesn't look like the stiffening sickness, but then, he's weak and there's many a fever will cause problems in the sickly that the strong can just shrug off."

Isabella made to rise, and Nan pressed her down again. "A little longer will be neither here nor there, la–"

She broke off as the door opened, and Clarice came into the room bringing cup and platter. "Where's Edith?"

"She took sick, Dame Nan."

Nan raised her head, eyes sharp. "What? But she was well only a few moments ago. How sick?

This is of a suddenness, Clarice. Does she need my attention?"

Clarice, her face innocent of anything but concern, said, "Did you not notice she was looking pale, Dame? She told me she'd been feeling poorly this while since, but she'd not wished to worry you. She was struggling to do her duties, but I saw she had a fever and told her she must take to her bed. I told her I should be happy to help you."

Isabella shook her head briefly to clear it, which was a mistake. Swallowing bile, she said, "If she is that ill, Nan, you must go to her. I insist."

"I think I must, my lady. Edith never ails. I–"

"No need, Dame Nan," Clarice cut in. "To me, it seems naught to worry about. If she rests, I'm sure she'll be well again. I'll tend her for you."

Nan eyed her suspiciously. "If she's not well enough for her duties, I should see her."

Clarice ignored her, tilting her head towards Isabella and adding guilelessly, "It could be what ails you, my lady, also ails her."

Nan gave a snort of derision and opened her mouth to reply, but Isabella, fearing she'd tell Clarice about her pregnancy, gave her a pleading glance. Nan gave an almost imperceptible nod before saying irritably to Clarice, "You say she's taken to her bed, but she's not here. Which bed?"

Clarice smiled, which made Nan narrow her lips. "She did not wish to disturb Lady Isabella. I took her to the other chamber. I thought while Fulke and Adam are gone, she could sleep there until she recovers. I did right, did I not, my lady?" she appealed, her gaze sliding past Nan to Isabella.

Isabella could not think. Her head seemed as though it was filled with wadding. She opened her mouth to try to say something useful but Nan cut in, much to her relief. "I suppose you did what you thought best. Although I'm sure I can't understand this. She was not ailing just now, I'd stake my life on it."

Clarice said nothing, just waited, head bowed, hands folded before her, the picture of sweetness.

Nan cast her hands upwards. "Well, that's neither here nor there. If she's ailing, she's ailing. Go to her and tell her I'll be with her as soon as I've settled my lady. I'll be no more than the shake of a lamb's tail. And when you've done that, my girl, you can take yourself back to the hall – there's plenty of mending in my basket by the fire."

As Clarice flounced from the room, Nan grumbled, "Thinks a sight too much of herself, does that one. Still, she's improved, I'll give her that. I'll not ask what plans you and my lord have for her; I dare say I'll find out in good time.

"Now, you rest, my lady. We want to look after that youngling of yours. Sip on my remedy and nibble on those wafers and just stay here where it's quiet. If Edith's still not well when Fulke and Adam return, they can sleep in the hall like Guy and Miles are having to; it'll do them no harm." She stroked Isabella's brow, still talking. "I'll send young Thomas to build up that brazier. I think he and Eustace can pull another one in here, too." She touched the water in the ewer with her finger and tsked. "That there water is ice cold. You'd be warmer in the hall, but you need a little quiet, in my opinion. Besides, you can't keep dashing off to those latrines, and they young squires will get lazy without their knights to serve. It'll do 'em good to do some work. Warm them up, too."

She wrapped Isabella's mantle around her, saying, "In fact, why don't you get into bed, my lamb? You'll be a sight warmer in there," and whisked back the hangings, before she took herself from the chamber, leaving Isabella to her thoughts.

The movement from chair to bed set Isabella's head spinning again. She pulled a sheepskin over her, her fingers burrowing into the soft wool, and closed her eyes in an effort to stop the room from whirling about her.

Despite the nausea, inside her heart a bud of contentment started to bloom, and she slid her hands over her flat belly. How would it feel as the life inside her grew, swelling into fecund fullness? With such pleasurable thoughts, she turned onto her side, drifting into oblivion with a smile playing gently around her mouth as she slept.

Isabella awoke with a numb arm where she had lain on it awkwardly. She could hear sounds of stealthy movement; was that Nan? Opening her eyes, she saw Clarice, head bent over an opened chest. She lay there silently, unwilling to shift herself until she had ascertained what the girl was doing, but Clarice, alerted perhaps by her fixed gaze, looked up with no hint of awkwardness.

"Do you feel better now, my lady? I was just looking to see if you had any linens I could use." She held her stomach and grimaced. "My flux has just started and all mine are gone."

Isabella sat, rubbing her arm, forcing herself to keep her tones even. "Then go to Dame Nan and ask her for some. You should not be rooting in our private coffers."

Clarice looked as though sweet wafers would not melt on her tongue. "Oh, I would have, my lady, but she was so busy running between Edith and Jerold, I didn't want to bother her."

It sounded reasonable enough. However, Isabella thought she could have tried harder. "Then ask Molly to get you some from the household linens, Clarice."

Clarice clapped her hand over her mouth. "How stupid of me, my lady, I hadn't thought of that. Truly, when my flux arrives, my wits fly out the window. Forgive me." And she fluttered out of the room like some gaily-attired butterfly. Isabella frowned. Clarice had been wearing more serviceable garments thus far from a chest that had been missed by the outlaws; now, she was wearing a finer gown than Isabella would have, apart from her wedding gown, until the rest of her possessions arrived from Berkhamsted. She was shocked to feel a worm of jealousy stir within her. She would feel dowdy when Giles returned, for how could she compare if Clarice had more of those?

She turned the thoughts over in her mind. Mayhap she could buy one of those lengths of fabric from the girl. *I have coin; I'll broach the subject when she returns, for surely she'll have need of money now she has no husband.*

She would need some new garments anyway, for who knew when her own would arrive? Even had the weather been clement enough to visit a market, she would not like to ask Giles to take her, nor did she wish to bother him about her possessions just yet, but having had the idea of purchasing cloth from Clarice, she lay back, satisfied. She could quickly sew something up, and she could leave room for her soon-to-be expanding girth. With that in mind, she dozed again.

When Isabella woke next, stiff and cold, the darkness was lit only by the flames flickering in the two braziers. The rush lights and torches had gone out, and the room was empty. Shivering, she pulled her mantle around her and sat up cautiously. Her nausea was gone, and her stomach growled in protest at its emptiness.

She touched one foot to the sheepskin on the floor and groped for her shoes. Shoving them on and fastening them, she stood, stretching, arching her back, before going to the door. Why had Nan not woken her?

As she ventured out, the smell of fish rose from the hall, and she clapped her hand over her nose, trying not to breathe it in. Sweet Virgin, her stomach was churning again; she'd forgotten it was a fast day. Still, there would be bread and dried fruits. She could take some back to the solar and eat away from the smell.

The trestles were laid, but her place had not been set. Isabella wrinkled her brow. What was going on? She may not wish to eat down here, but since she had not given orders to bring food up, she expected her place on the dais to be prepared. She squared her shoulders and descended, curiosity vying with indignation.

Stalking down the hall, head high, very much on her mettle, she changed her mind about not eating here. Where were the faces she expected to see? Nan and Oswin? Filbert? She caught one of the harassed servants by the elbow as he lay a bowl of preserved eels on the table, averting her gaze so the eels, chopped and served in broth, were not in her sight. What was the man's name? Oh yes, Hubert.

He jerked and whirled round, a curse on his lips as he steadied the bowl, which changed to a look of surprise when he saw her. "My lady! I'm sorry, I didn't expect to see you here. I'd have laid your place, else."

"You did not expect me? And why would that be?"

"She," he jutted his chin in the direction of Clarice, who was sitting by the hearth with her feet on a small stool, "said you were ill. She said you wouldn't want supper."

Isabella stared at him. "Well Hubert, as you see, she was wrong."

"Yes, my lady. Sorry, my lady."

"And Hubert, why did you take orders from her? Where is Nan? Oswin?"

He looked crestfallen. "I'm so sorry, my lady. They've all taken ill. She… Mistress Clarice… She said she'd been left in charge."

Isabella was torn between fury at Clarice taking control, and worry about Nan and Oswin. "What's wrong with them?"

He looked at his feet. "I dunno, my lady, some kind of sickness."

"I see." Although she did not. "Well, then, carry on as you were, and certainly set my place, for as you see, I am here. But," she wrinkled her nose, "no fish. Just bring me bread, a bowl of pottage, and some fruit, please."

Hubert nodded and scuttled away. Isabella, all her dignity offended, slipped around the hall, coming up behind Clarice, who jumped when Isabella laid a hand on her shoulder. Swivelling her head, she saw Isabella standing over her and stood quickly, banging her knee on the bench as she turned. She yelped and rubbed it. Isabella stood quietly, waiting for her to explain herself.

Clarice peered at her through long lashes. "How are you, my lady? Do you feel well again now? Only Mistress Nan said not to waken you. She said you wouldn't be hungry."

Oh, she did, did she? Isabella doubted that very much. "And where is Nan?"

Clarice played with the fringe on her ceinture. "Oh, she's got a sickness. She's gone to bed. Oswin has it too."

"What sickness? This is news to me."

"It was after you'd gone to sleep, my lady. She was looking after Edith and Jerold. Worn to a frazzle, she said she was, and suddenly, she put her hand to her head and just keeled over. I reckon she has the same as Edith. Oswin and Fulke helped carry her to her bed, then Oswin came over all queer, too. I sent him to join her. And, I thought, since Molly was busy with Jerold, I'd better oversee supper myself. I didn't do wrong, did I?"

Clarice's dark blue eyes, innocent as a babe's, were big with concern as she wiped her brow with her forearm as though exhausted. "I just sat here for a moment to get my breath. I've been that busy, you wouldn't credit. No need to thank me, my lady. You've been good to me, and someone had to look after things. I'm only too willing to help."

Isabella studied her gravely. How much of this was truth? Yet Nan and Oswin were indeed missing from the hall. She looked around her. Filbert, too.

Clarice interrupted her thoughts. "That lad of hers!" She put her nose in the air and sniffed. "The one who thinks he's too good for the likes of me, for all he's naught but the son of a servant. He's looking after them. I tried to help, but he'd have none of it so I left him to do as best he might and did what I could out here."

Her face was full of concern, but Isabella was not entirely convinced. Still, if they were sick, then she supposed someone had to take charge. And from Clarice's appearance and the fact that she was filling the position of her personal maid, Isabella supposed the servants would assume it was the girl's duty to do so.

She bit the inside of her cheek, determined to say nothing until she knew more, contenting herself with, "Well, under those circumstances, Clarice, I would have expected you to wake me. Bear that in mind, please. Now, come, the table is set, the food is ready. And," she forced it out unwillingly, "thank you for your efforts."

Clarice gave a jaunty bob. "You're welcome, my lady. I mean to make myself useful. You rescued me, after all, so I do owe you for that."

Most of the servants joined them at the table; it seemed only a handful were affected so far.

Isabella prayed that would continue to be the case.

Giles' chaplain said grace, and Isabella found her appetite was fully restored. Even the smell of the eels did not upset her, although she did not eat them. The pottage, however, was good and satisfying. She nibbled on dried fruits afterwards, and as the servants cleared the trestles away, rose to check on Nan and Oswin.

She coughed delicately outside their curtained alcove, and Filbert pulled back the hangings. His cap was askew, his tunic stained. Beyond him, in the bed, Oswin was puking into a chamber pot, and Isabella's stomach roiled afresh.

"Best you don't come in, my lady. Mam's telling me what to do. She's got her potions in here, and I can look after them." He bowed and pulled the curtain shut. Isabella was only too glad to leave him to it, but she felt bereft and disjointed, still too new to the household to be entirely comfortable without the solid authority of Nan to back her up. *Stupid,* she told herself. *You were born to this.* She put her chin up. She could do this. Where was her backbone?

Remembering Jerold, she hurried up the other staircase, opened the door and peered in. Molly was mopping the boy's brow and looked up.

"How is he, Molly?"

The maid shook her head. "Not well, my lady. I've tried to get something down him, but it's doing no good." Her mouth puckered. "Can I leave him and get something to eat, please? I've had nothing since morning."

"Nothing?" Isabella was appalled. "Has no one brought food or taken your place?"

Molly's chin wobbled. "No, my lady. And I've been stuck here all that time. I mean, I grabbed something from the kitchen when I had to use the privy, but apart from that…" She trailed off, her face downcast.

"Of course you may, Molly. I will sit with Jerold; you go and get something. The tables have been cleared but tell Amos I sent you."

The maid's face crumpled with relief. "Oh, thank you, my lady."

"And send someone to aid me, will you?"

Molly nodded and left, carrying a covered chamber pot with her. By the smells coming from it, Isabella assumed it contained vomit and urine, and she held her breath until the door shut behind the maid.

The chaos was worse on the morrow, as more of the household were taken ill. To keep the hall from reeking with their vomit, Isabella arranged for those who were worst afflicted to sleep in the rooms in the gallery. The men were laid where

Giles' senior knights normally slept; Edith, who was beginning to recover, moved to the chamber where the women of the household usually slept, and the other women who were most ill in with her.

The rest of them had to be reorganised, then. For now, the unwed women could sleep in the outer gallery while their dormitory was otherwise occupied. Clarice, she would keep under her own eye, and Molly was willing to sleep on a pallet in the chamber where Jerold lay.

Isabella resolved to have Molly, too, as one of her personal maids later, if Giles and Nan both agreed. She was certainly working hard without complaint. Harder, she thought, than Clarice, however much that young woman declared her weariness. Molly's eyes were sunken, black circles beneath them showing how tired she was. Clarice, unaccountably, looked fresh as a spring morning, despite the amount of work she said she was doing.

Isabella herself was run ragged trying to supervise the kitchen, the laundry and those who remained untouched by the sickness. The stench from the latrines was becoming a major problem, and she asked Arnulf if he could arrange for them to be cleaned. He shrugged on his thickest cloak and rounded up some of the serfs from the estate, and she breathed a literal sigh of relief as the putrid contents were removed.

Struggling to fight off her own nausea, she managed to keep things running, if not smoothly, at least reasonably, for Nan and Oswin were still ailing, and a few more of the servants started to sicken. At least, though, when she dropped into her lonely bed at night, she was too tired to fret, sleeping soundly until cockcrow, when she staggered to her feet and started again.

At last, the illness ended. One by one, the servants returned to their duties. Nan had lost weight and her face was gaunt but she insisted she was well despite Isabella's protests. Since she could not convince Nan to take her ease, there was no choice but to let the steward's wife take up the reins of the household again, and although Isabella was concerned, she had to admit to a sense of relief. Clarice and she had been amongst the very few who had not suffered, and she felt worn to the bone.

Nan was all apologies, almost weeping with mortification.

"But it was not your fault," Isabella assured her. "You did not choose to be ill, did you?"

Nan shook her head until the folds of loose skin about her jowls quivered.

"Well then, don't be so foolish."

Nan sniffed, and her brow puckered. Isabella watched horrified as a tear ran down her cheek. "I'm that sorry, my lady. I still feel a bit low in spirits." She managed a watery smile. "Seems like the least little thing sets me off, as it is. Don't pay me no mind, I'm just being a foolish wight."

She sniffed again and wiped the back of her hand across her nose, the resolution settling on her face as she hitched up her bosom in business-like fashion. "And don't you go urging me to rest again, my lady. I've had more than enough of that. I'll be better once I'm occupied.

"Now then, my lamb, you look all in. I reckon you should stay in the solar today until I've got this household back under control."

Isabella was only too pleased to do so, for she had a dull ache in the small of her back and down her flanks. Should she be feeling like that? She shrugged. It was likely down to tiredness.

"You lie down, my lady, and I'll be back with you as soon as I can."

Isabella wanted to tell Nan she shouldn't be overdoing it until she was fully well, but she knew better than to argue, and, in truth, she felt as though she was weighted down today. A weight, almost a lassitude, seemed to be creeping over her. Wearily, she crawled into bed, propped her needlework over her knees and settled down to enjoy some longed-for rest.

CHAPTER 25

To Giles' annoyance, he had been left cooling his heels at Bedford a full sennight whilst du Beke made painstakingly slow enquiries. His return journey with du Beke's men was no faster than the outward one, for at each village they passed, enquiries and investigations were made. Otto, du Beke's constable, was infuriatingly thorough.

Now, fourteen days after he had departed, he rode into the forecourt at Thorneywell. His heart at first swelled with contentment to be home, then, as he searched the doorway where his people stood waiting to welcome him, sank back to his boots.

Nan was there, smiling and bustling, and Oswin, hurrying to greet him and ready places in barns and hall alike, his grooms and servants busying themselves with their allotted tasks.

Clarice curtseyed deeply, eyes gleaming like sloes beneath half-closed lids in the fading light, watching the men who accompanied him with interest.

And Isabella? She was there, walking towards him, but slowly, listlessly, almost heavily, eyes deep-shadowed and rimmed with red, dressed in drab colours which made her skin appear tinged with grey.

She held up her face dutifully for his kiss, but he could detect no real enthusiasm, and, as he reached out to clasp her tightly to himself, she slipped from his grasp, evading him like a shadow. He cast a questioning glance at Nan, who pursed her lips and shook her head. Doubtless she would tell him later; for now, there was no time.

The ten men from Bedford Castle who had accompanied him jostled into the hall, exclaiming at the warmth, shedding cloaks rimed with snow, holding cold hands out to the fire and drinking the ale thrust at them by giggling maidservants. His own men entered with no less enthusiasm, greeting friends and family as the trestles, which had been half dismantled, were speedily replaced, and the cook raced back to his kitchen to see what food could be found to fill hungry bellies.

Isabella had slipped away to the kitchens too, Giles supposed to confer with Amos, who ruled his domain jealously. Nan was moving hither and thither efficiently, speedily, arranging, organising. Only Clarice hovered at his elbow, her hands held out, waiting to take his cloak, sliding her gaze sideways to Bedford's constable, dipping her head to him, if not her knee.

Since there was no way to avoid her, Giles gave Clarice his mantle, expecting her to take it to the bedchamber. She did not, thrusting it into the hands of a passing maid, remaining at his side. Moistening her lips with the tip of her pink tongue, like a cat, she waited, her face hinting of secrets to be told.

He studiously ignored her for as long as he could, but when she planted herself before him, catching his arm, drawing him to a corner, he capitulated, still glancing round for his wife, who had not reappeared. After one last searching look, he sat himself down on the bench beneath the stairs and called for Thomas to help him off with his hauberk and gambeson.

Thomas came scuttling over, to be dismissed by Clarice. Giles opened his mouth to remonstrate, but she placed her finger on her lips, and as Thomas scuffed away again, she said, "I will help you, my lord. I may look slight, but I'm strong, and I have news I must tell you about the Lady Isabella."

A deep sigh, almost a groan, forced itself from Giles' chest, but, with the rest of the household busy with other tasks, it seemed he had no option. Clarice helped him out of his armour without stumbling or dropping it, and he saw she was indeed stronger than she appeared. Then, she called Thomas back, saying as he returned, "Take my lord's equipment and see you do your duty, boy."

Thomas, mouth agape, looked at him in confusion, waiting, Giles supposed, for confirmation, since the order came neither from himself nor Isabella. He gave the lad a curt nod. Best get this over with, then he would find his wife. He was weary and chilled to his marrow, but that could wait; Isabella, he knew, could not. The very fact that she was avoiding him spoke of problems which he needed to discover and resolve.

Dropping back onto the bench, he looked up at Clarice. "Sit then, and say what you have to say. I cannot afford to give you long."

She remained standing, her hands held out as though she would take his. Her eyelids fluttered. "Oh, my lord," she said breathily, "your lady lost…" She gulped but not in such a manner as one overcome with emotion. To Giles, it seemed her appearance of sorrow was but a veneer covering something else simmering below the surface. Ach! He had no patience for this game she played.

"She lost…" Clarice gave a hiccupping breath as though about to cry, which Giles very much doubted. She mopped at her eyes, and his temper, already exacerbated, snapped.

"What did she lose? Spit it out, girl!"

Clarice gave a gasp and spilled out the words. "She lost the baby! It's so sad. And now–"

She had no time to say more; Giles stood, thrusting her away from him firmly, pushing his way past her, striding to the kitchens, where Isabella stood aimlessly against a wall as the spit boy and scullions rushed about, and the cook swore over his cauldrons.

She whimpered when he appeared before her and pulled away from him as he sought to draw her from the kitchen. "My lord," she protested, white to the lips, "we are too busy. All these men you've brought with you." She gestured, blinking rapidly. "Leave me to get this done. We can speak later."

Giles looked around him. "They seem to have no need of you here, at any rate, wife, and I do."

She drooped, defeated, and allowed him to lead her from the place, easing through the surging hall like thread through a needle, pulling her gently up the stairs to their chamber, where he sat her down on their bed. Kneeling before her, he took her small hands and folded them between his large, calloused ones.

When she did not respond, he pulled her head down onto his shoulder and heard her make a small sound in her throat as though she was choking back tears. "Now, my heart, what's this I hear?"

At that, her head raised up. She pulled away and glared at him. "You know?"

He nodded.

"Who told–" She broke off as understanding dawned on her, then said bitterly, "Clarice!" She gave him a baleful glare as though it was he, not Clarice, who had offended, then burst out with, "That bitch! I should have known. It was for me to tell you, my lord, not her. But always she meddles in that which does not concern her."

Giles was taken aback by the venom in her voice but did not show it, merely seating himself beside her, placing his arm around her shaking shoulders, saying, "You were with child?"

Head down, she nodded mutely, before looking up at him with dead eyes. "I was. I lost it. It's gone."

But she could hardly have known she was pregnant; it was too soon. This grief was too heavy a response. Still, he supposed her hopes had been dashed. Perhaps that was what she mourned rather than the babe, which could not have been near formed at this stage.

He put his hand gently beneath her chin and kissed her forehead. "Then, I'm sorry, with all my heart, love. But come, you must have barely known you were carrying before you lost it. Do not grieve, we can make other babes. There's time aplenty."

He was aghast when she ripped herself from his arms and stood, staring at him with something – surely not – akin to hate, before whisking herself out of the room, heading back to the main hall.

Giles remained where he was, bewildered. What had he said to warrant such a reaction? He had not blamed her, had tried to give her comfort. He let out a long, slow breath. *Women!* How was a man to know what they wanted? Well, if she didn't need his comfort, then his belly was empty, his throat dry, and there was food and drink below. He shrugged his shoulders in hurt confusion, pushed himself from the bed and went to join his men, avoiding his wife in the same way she was avoiding him.

As he sat around the hearth – no formality tonight, the men had shunned the trestles, wanting only to warm and feed themselves before rolling out the straw paillasses provided and falling asleep – Clarice slithered onto the bench beside him, touching his arm, her eyes offering him consolation, even as his wife ignored him from the chair where she'd seated herself, far from the fire. Beneath the light from a wall sconce, which threw dark shadows on her face, Isabella was embroidering as though her life depended on it, and his resolve hardened.

By all the saints, he'd been gone a fortnight! He wanted a welcome, wanted to feel as though he belonged in his own demesne. This was not the homecoming he'd been dreaming of every day since he'd left. Of a surety, Bella was upset, yet he had tried offering her sympathy and un-derstanding, and she'd rejected him. What did she expect him to do?

Clarice, smiling enigmatically, served him herself, bringing him hot stew and a cup of ale, seating herself at his feet, leaning against him as he devoured it.

He spooned it into his mouth, barely tasting what he ate or drank and was just sinking into an exhausted stupor when Nan surged over, stand-ing before him with arms akimbo.

Clarice shot her a challenging look. It had no effect. Nan hauled her to her feet, scolding, ex-claiming about work to be done, pulling her away, and Giles' legs felt cold from the lack of a warm, pliant body against them. Ach! There was no point in remaining here!

He dumped his cup and bowl down on the bench, checked his own servants had found room enough, made sure of the comfort of their guests, all of which Oswin and Filbert had already done, and went up to his bedchamber with leaden feet. If he could not have the comfort of his wife's body, then at least he would have that of his bed.

Isabella had dashed from the solar, her chin trembling, blinking hard to hold back the flood of tears which she felt would drown her if she let but one of them fall. She shook with a mixture of fear, misery and fury. How could he even think to try for another babe without grieving for this one first? Yes, it was not even formed yet, but she was convinced she had felt the life within her, despite Nan's telling her it was too early for quickening.

She wrapped her arms around her belly as though the babe was still safe within, slumping against the wall, determined she would not weep. And if she had angered him, and if he whipped her for it, what did she care? Almost, she hoped he would; it might ease the awful emptiness inside her. The pain of that would give her a reason to hate him.

She stood there, not caring if anyone saw her, lost in grief until she could pull the drawbridge up over her feelings and cover them from sight. Then, steeling herself, she stood straight, letting her mask of indifference fall back into place. She could do this; she had managed without feeling for long enough when wed to Baldwin. Compressing her lips tightly as though daring anyone to question her, she moved back to the hall, a shell with no spirit, face blank.

As the hall cleared and men started to snore on their pallets, she had no choice but to return to her chamber, tiptoeing around the sleeping forms of Edith and Clarice, moving quietly behind the dividing curtain, removing her gown but not her shift, and climbing stealthily into bed. Giles was already beneath the covers. Asleep, she thought, and she lay on the edge of the feather-filled mattress as far away from him as she could get. She did not want his caresses, for what could he understand of her pain?

She heard him sigh softly, felt him move one hand towards her, stroking her belly, but rolled away from him, then lay there feigning sleep, rigid and wakeful.

She must have slept, finally, for when she woke, Giles was gone. Part of her was relieved, part bereft. How could he have left without waking her? She did not even know for certain why he'd brought such a large company of men to their home. His home, for she did not feel as though it was hers now.

She guessed they must be here to search for the outlaws, for the sheriff would expect Giles to do his part, and he would need the men provided. All to the good then. It would be easier to busy herself and easier to avoid her husband.

She rose listlessly, shaking her head as Edith held out her red gown, taking up the one she had worn yesterday – a serviceable but plain one of dark grey wool. Edith looked as though she might remonstrate, but Isabella took the red gown from her, throwing it to the floor, where it lay like the puddle of blood that had seeped from her womb, bearing away her child.

Edith, mouth tightly shut, laced the grey one, and Isabella reached for the wimple she had stitched herself whilst she lay abed recovering from her miscarriage. Stark, severe, uncompromising.

Edith tsked under her breath and said quietly, "M'lady, don't you wish to wear something more appealing now your lord husband is returned?"

Isabella rounded on her, her usually gentle voice harsh now. "Would you also not have me mourn the child?"

Edith caught her lip between her teeth and turned to pick up the red gown but not before

Isabella had seen her pity. Then, faces grim, lady and maid quit the room, together, yet miles apart.

When Isabella set foot in the hall, it seemed as though the servants parted before her like the Red Sea before the Israelites, but as she moved, wraithlike, round the room, she heard their soft murmurs of sympathy. Unable to bear it, she snatched up the sewing she had been working on and took it back to the solar.

She would not cry, would not break!

As she sat by the cresset lamp, screwing up her eyes the better to see what she was doing, she heard scuffling outside and whispering voices. She paused, needle part in, part out of the fabric, straining her ears to hear what was being said, and then wished she had not.

When the voices died away, Isabella's heart was even bleaker than before. It had gone unremarked, for she'd told no one; after all, what was there to celebrate? But today was her birthday. She was seventeen.

CHAPTER 26

Clarice watched slyly, veiling her triumph beneath her lashes as the gulf between Isabella and Giles widened. She had been sure to drop the idea into Isabella's head that, once Giles did not believe she could bear him a living child, he would turn elsewhere. Not that she'd said it directly, just discussed it in audible whispers when she knew Isabella was within hearing.

She noticed Giles standing by himself and dragged Agnes, the skinny brat who crept timidly about the hall doing her duties like some small mouse, over to a place out of his sight but within his hearing. She'd not normally bother with such as Agnes, but for now, she would do.

"So sad, he looks," Clarice said, her voice oozing with sympathy. She spoke just loudly enough to be overheard, and Agnes looked about frantically, imploring her to shush. Ignoring her desperate entreaty, Clarice continued ruthlessly, "And he must feel so alone, now, mustn't he? My heart aches for the poor lord. Does not yours, Agnes?"

Agnes muttered something inaudible.

"If you ask me, she blames him."

Agnes squeaked a reluctant response.

"And he's suffering too. You can see that, can't you? She's being unfair. Not that I blame her for her sorrow, but she's making his pain worse, turning away from him as she is."

Agnes took a step away, but Clarice caught her arm and held her. "Yes, Agnes, it's turned her against him, that's what. You can see it in her eyes. Blank, they are. Before long, she'll be going about with her hair in tangles, spending all her time in prayer, turning away from him in bed. I pity her, for there's a darkness about her soul, but I pity him the more.

"Poor lord, he doesn't deserve such treatment. It's not natural, Agnes, you mind my words. Small blame to him if he looks elsewhere for comfort."

She let go of Agnes, who was still trying to back away, turning her head fearfully this way and that, whispering, "Oh hush, Mistress Clarice. He'll hear you. Do hush."

Once released, Agnes almost ran back to her duties, and Clarice smiled like a lazy cat, satisfied the job was done. A few more words in a few more ears, and she'd convince Giles de Soutenay he needed to look elsewhere.

He would surely warm to her soon – she thought he already was, but if not – if not, then she was also working to bedazzle the constable from Bedford Castle. For all he was lower than she aimed, it was inevitable she'd be questioned about Walerin, and she needed him on her side. Anyway, if she could not soon win Giles – she tossed her head – then once she reached the castle, her charms would take her to greater heights than he could ever hope to reach.

Things were all progressing very nicely. It had been a flash of brilliance that had made her think to induce sickness at the hall, easily achieved when one had the stealth of hand she possessed. Start with Jerold, and if he died in error, what matter?

And since he had lived, she'd now convinced him it was through her care, even though the work of looking after him had been down to Molly. The poor wretch was so befuddled with the herbs she kept administering to him that, now he was on the mend, he'd been brought to believe her marriage to Walerin was fact, not lie. Aware that Molly had at first watched her movements, she'd taken the effort to win the girl's trust which had made it much easier to gain access to the boy.

So humbled was Jerold by his brush with the Angel of Death, so grateful for what he thought was her care, he now fully believed everything she said, which was why she'd decided he could live. She was not so hard of heart, after all. And he would back her story, she was sure.

She approached him now, her expression friendly, and to her satisfaction, he raised his head, watching her with hunger poorly disguised on his face as she sat down beside his cot.

Smiling at him brilliantly, she said, "You're getting so much stronger now, dear Jerold. Come, try to take a few steps. I'll aid you."

She helped him from the bed and placed an arm around his waist as he took unsteady steps around the room, then assisted him to lie down again, saying, "I do believe you'll be much better very soon now. I've nursed you well, I do think. Should you like me to speak to Sir Giles and ask him if he can find a place for you?" How fortunate that he was an orphan with no kin and no ties. Clarice allowed her face to pucker. "As for me, I shall soon have to go to Bedford Castle to speak to the sheriff about my poor lord. Folk consider me hard but I've tried not to let myself think of him for fear my heart would break."

She broke off with a small choke in her throat and held a hand to her eyes. "Alas that he wed me in secret and with such haste, for it makes my truth seem like lies." She wiped her face with her hand again and twisted her fingers in the blanket that covered Jerold, drooping her head.

Jerold put a tentative hand out, and Clarice clasped it with both hers, holding it to her, sighing.

"At least I never forgot my dear husband, even though my memory still fails me in part. I wonder if I shall ever remember where my home is." She allowed a tear to glisten on her lashes. "You believe we were wed, do you not, Jerold, after Walerin's wife died? For if *you* do not, how shall anyone else? My case is indeed sorrowful, for not only have I lost my heart's treasure, I may lose all else."

Jerold stuttered his belief, and she kissed his cheek, allowing her mouth to linger warmly on his skin. When she moved away, he gawped at her like one who beheld a vision.

"Thank you, my dearest Jerold. No wonder my lord treasured you so much." She stroked his brow. "Oh, I know he did not seem so. I know he beat you oft-times, but it was only because he wanted you to grow straight and true, knowing the difference between right and wrong. He would not have done that, had he not cared for you." *Careful. Best not to lay it on any thicker.* "And soon, I'll have to leave you. Although, who knows? Maybe I'll be able to return, some day."

She patted his hand again. "The constable says there's no need for you to travel to Bedford, now whilst you're so sick, for I told him such a journey would likely be the death of you. And when he tried to question you, you were quite out of your wits. He understands you can remember nothing with any certainty."

She slid her gaze sideways to watch his face as she added, "Indeed, I don't know whether you'll ever be quite the same again, for I'm afraid, dear Jerold, there's a dullness about you now, which makes me sad. Be glad you'll be well cared for here and don't strain yourself to remember, my dear, for it will only distress you and bring on a brain fever. And that, you know, might kill you."

Jerold's expression was one of horror. Good. She'd kept him addled so long, he'd never trust himself to recall his past correctly anyway, but best to be safe.

She kissed his forehead. "It does me good to know at least one of my dear lord's household has survived with me. How lonely I should have been without you to care for." And she drifted out of the door, safe in the knowledge she had won another conquest.

The constable, too, was more than halfway to being smitten with her. She would far rather have Giles, if she could get him, but if not, then she had to take care of herself, after all.

A pity de Soutenay was so short a time at the hall while the search for the outlaws continued, but when he was there, weary, disheartened and shunned by his wife, she made sure to be the one to serve him, offering warmth, comfort and understanding in equal measure. He was beginning to lean towards her now. Just a few more days, and she would have him.

Although, if Nan stood in her way, the woman would likely have another bout of illness, Clarice thought grimly, fingering the string of amber beads which hung around her neck, disappearing beneath the opening of her shift. Depending from it, hidden from sight, tucked away beneath her garments, hung a small ampulla of fool's funnel essence. She grinned. Fool's funnel for an old fool, what could be more suitable?

Clarice was not the only one who saw the gulf widening between Isabella and Giles. Nan was keeping her eye on things, too, albeit with a sinking heart. She had her suspicions of Clarice, but could pin nothing to her yet, however carefully she watched.

The girl tried hard enough to convince her, and certainly, she'd been a help while that murrain had been upon them, but there was something Nan couldn't quite put her finger on.

Such a pity Isabella had miscarried of the babe, for it would have been the making of them. Nan had not expected it; she had seemed well; her vomiting had not been the ailment that afflicted the others, for there was no purging of Isabella's bowels, just the morning sickness. And that had not been extreme, just within normal expectations. But then, there was always the possibility of loss so early on; she'd seen it happen many a time.

Nan herself was still feeling less well than she let on. Each time she thought she'd regained her strength, she seemed to have another setback.

She frowned fretfully for it wasn't like her. Almost never was she ill, and even when she was, she recovered more quickly than anyone else she knew. Still, she would not give in to it, even when Oswin and Filbert urged her to take things more slowly.

Hitching her bosom, she went up the stairs, grabbing hold of the guard rail to help her on the ascent. She entered the solar to find Isabella sitting by the window, sewing, her face withdrawn and remote. She did not even look up as Nan entered but continued to push her needle in and out, in and out, stitching and snipping as though the work was the only thing she had left to her.

Nan steeled her courage and approached. Isabella looked up at her without interest, then turned her head away.

"My lady?"

Isabella ignored her. Nan felt her legs trembling and sat heavily on the footstool at Isabella's feet, although how she would get herself up again was anybody's guess. Likely they'd have to send for Oswin to lift her.

She steadied herself and tried again, louder this time. "My lady!" It came out more sharply than she'd intended, and Isabella raised her head to face her, eyes full of resentment.

Nan softened her tone; no good antagonising the lass or she'd never hear her out. "My lady, I'm concerned about this coldness between you and Sir Giles." There, she'd said it. She was committed now.

Isabella gazed stonily at her. "You need not trouble yourself, it is of no consequence," she said tonelessly.

Nan almost raised her hands in despair, but restrained herself. Instead, she leaned forward, taking Isabella's sewing from her. Isabella held it with a death grip, and Nan found herself in a tug-of-war. Giving up, she heaved herself painfully to her feet, then stood over Isabella, her hands either side of her on the sill, imprisoning her mistress, praying this would not end with her and Oswin being cast from the manor.

Isabella, with no escape, glared. Nan took no notice, saying with determination, "My lady, you must stop this ere it's too late."

Isabella placed the sewing carefully on her lap. "Stop what?"

"Stop withholding yourself from your husband. If you do not take care, you'll lose his love." Nan was almost breathless with the risk she was taking.

Isabella's face was as rigid as if it had been set in stone. "Dame Nan, you forget yourself."

Nearly weeping with frustration, Nan said, "My lady, I know I'm speaking out of place, but it's because I care about you, and I care about my lord. It's breaking my heart to see things go so badly wrong between you."

Isabella gave a gasp, and Nan began to believe she was getting through to her.

"And do you not believe it breaks my heart, too, Nan?" Isabella's voice cracked. "Do you not know I'm dying inside? But he doesn't care that I've lost the babe." She put her hands to her face. "He'll look elsewhere now. He doesn't want me, just an heir, and I've proved I can't give him one." She pushed Nan's arms away and ran to the bed, hiding her face in the covers, her slight frame heaving with sobs.

Oh, the foolish wench. Nan's own eyes filled, as she forgot her stiffness and dropped to her knees beside the bed. "Oh, my dear lady, of course he won't. Can you not see he loves you? And he did not even know you were carrying. It often happens with a first babe; you should not allow yourself to get into such a state. You can always try again."

Isabella reared up. "That's what he said! And he didn't even mourn for it." Her face was stormy with grief and anger, tears coursing down her cheeks.

"You silly lass. What else would he say? He didn't even know you were expecting his child, so how could he mourn it? You barely knew yourself. You're being unreasonable, if you'll pardon me for saying it. You're all out of sorts, all mixed up, and making a mountain out of everything. It's often so when a woman has just miscarried; believe me, for it's the truth.

"And my lord? He's just a man. They always say the wrong things, as well you know, so there's no point in expecting him to get it right. There's no unkindness behind it, my lamb. He just thought to comfort you in his unwieldy way and got it all wrong. Now, he's fretting because he thinks you don't want him, and you're all upset because you think he doesn't want you."

Isabella listened, eyes wide with shock, then cast herself at Nan, who wrapped her arms round her as Isabella wept, almost weeping with relief herself.

It seemed to Nan, they sat there an age. She stroked her mistress's hair as though she were a child whilst Isabella shuddered and gasped, clinging to her as though she was the one sure thing in a maelstrom.

Thank goodness the tears had come. As it was with a boil, to keep the misery and resentment pent up inside her would do naught but spread poison and pain. Lancing it, letting the bitterness out, was, in itself, healing. Nan's relief was great – the more so since it had taken her great courage to broach the subject.

As the storm died, Isabella slowly regained control, easing herself out of Nan's motherly embrace.

Nan struggled to get to her feet, pushing her bulk against the bed, and Isabella, stifling a watery giggle, made to help her, tugging at her until she could lever herself up.

Nan sat on the bed, huffing and puffing with the effort, waiting until she'd caught her breath before saying, "That's better, my lady. You've been burying it all inside you. You'll feel better now you've let it out."

Isabella surveyed her, mopping at her eyes. "I think I do already." Her voice quavered. "It still hurts but not quite so much."

"That's always the way when you hide your grief, my lamb. You'll start to mend now. If you don't let it out, you'll never stop the pain."

Isabella gave a sniff and blew her nose on a crumpled piece of linen. "But Giles doesn't want me." She blinked another tear back. "He turns away from me."

"And whose fault is that, my lady?"

Isabella gazed blankly at her. Nan continued remorselessly. "Yes, my lady, I know you've been pushing him away. Never tell me he didn't seek to mend matters, for I'll not believe you." She crossed her arms, a note of warning in her voice, and Isabella sniffed again, her chin wobbling.

Nan relented; she'd made her point. "Now, don't you take on so, my lamb. It's not too late. Yet! But now, you must stop rejecting him, my lady, else you'll push him too far, and there's one not a hundred miles from here who'll be only too quick to offer her own form of comfort."

Isabella's eyes flashed. With fury or jealousy, Nan didn't know, but it heartened her to see it. She patted the girl's hand. "So, now you know what to do, if you don't want to lose his love, don't you?"

Isabella gulped and nodded and made as though to get off the bed. Nan pushed her down again. "Not right this moment, my lamb, and not like that. You stay here, and Nan'll bring you a nice tisane and a bowl of water to bathe your face. You don't want *her* seeing you with those red eyes, do you?" And without waiting to see how Isabella responded, she left, pausing only to send Edith to guard the door and let nobody but Nan herself in.

CHAPTER 27

Isabella had managed to get her tears under control when Nan came back in. As she glanced up, she was shocked to see rivulets of sweat on the older woman's face. Nan's eyes were heavy and moist, her skin pale, and, far from bustling as she usually did, she trod heavily, placing the cup, ewer and basin down with an effort, before gasping and wrapping her arms around her middle.

She staggered, and Isabella forgot her own woes as she rushed to help, taking Nan's weight. She'd thought the steward's wife would resist her aid; worryingly, Nan leaned into her. Isabella braced herself, expecting to feel the strain of Nan's not inconsiderable weight, but discovered, to her further concern, that she was not as heavy as expected, as though the ailment had sucked the very flesh from her bones.

She guided Nan to the bed. Nan rallied briefly, but as Isabella helped her sit, she sank backwards with a whimper, curling into a ball.

Isabella grabbed the basin and placed it next to Nan on the bed before laying her hand on the older woman's forehead. The skin was clammy to her touch. Nan gave a small moan and attempted to rise, then gave up and fell backwards, her eyelids closing.

"Rest, Nan," murmured Isabella, removing the sweat-sodden wimple and bathing her face with a napkin dampened with water from the ewer.

Nan opened her eyes and muttered something which Isabella couldn't quite hear. She bent lower, but by now, Nan was incoherent, and moaned as she writhed on the bed.

Thoroughly alarmed, Isabella forgot her own swollen eyes, forgot she had been avoiding Giles, and went down to the hall to find him and Oswin. She had no idea why Nan had suffered more setbacks than anyone else who'd been ill – it might be that she had driven herself too hard and not allowed herself sufficient time to recover. Or, and she shuddered at the thought, the sickness had gone deeper with Nan. At any rate, Oswin and Giles had to know.

As she reached the foot of the stair, she swept her gaze around the hall until she found Oswin. Giles, she could not see immediately.

When she told him about Nan's relapse, the steward's face crumpled. "She pushes herself so, my lady. I entreated her not to get up for a few more days, but you know how she is. She'll have none of it."

Isabella knew all too well. Guilt consumed her, for had she been stronger, less easily overset, Nan would not have felt the need to rise from her bed so soon.

As if he'd read her thoughts – although Isabella supposed Nan had confided her worries in him – Oswin said, "And don't go blaming yourself, my lady. If she thinks you do, she'll not rest even now."

"You're a good man, Oswin. Now, go to your wife. She lies in our chamber. I'll find my lord husband and go to her myself as soon as I have her simples. She'll have something there which will help, I've no doubt."

Oswin nodded. "She will, my lady. Edith knows what everything's for."

"Then go, Oswin, before she tries to come downstairs. I'll manage."

He turned, brow furrowed with anxiety, and Isabella searched for Giles, her heart contracting when she spotted him in a dark corner of the hall, cup in hand, being fawned over by Clarice.

Isabella's mouth tightened as she advanced, but when he looked up at her and she saw the shadows of pain on his face, she knew they were caused by her rejection. A bitter smile played around her lips; Nan was right, she had driven him away. Small blame to him for seeking solace elsewhere when she had turned from his every touch. Cursing herself for a fool, she placed a hand on his shoulder, subtly edging Clarice out of the way as she moved between them.

Giles' eyes were cold, no flicker of warmth there. Isabella forced herself not to recoil, for that would be to drive the wedge even deeper between them. Hers was the fault, and she must be the one to mend it.

"My husband?" The words were softly spoken, but she had no doubt Clarice would hear – as she was intended. Giles looked at Isabella dully, and she reached out to take his hand. It lay like a dead thing in hers, but she stroked her thumb over the palm. "I do not wish to worry you, but Nan is ill again. I thought you'd want to know."

He blenched and rose from his seat, staggering slightly. How heavily had he been drinking? She could smell the wine on his breath as he said, "Ill?"

"She's collapsed in our chamber, my husband." If she kept emphasising the word, it would remind both Giles and Clarice whose he was.

He pushed past her, and Isabella, ere she moved to follow him, thought she caught a flash of triumph in Clarice's eyes before that young woman smiled demurely, saying, "Can I be of any help, my lady?"

Isabella fought her anger down, saying with a calm smile, "Thank you, Clarice, yes. You may find Edith and send her to me, if you will, please. I will be with my lord." *In case there's any doubt in your mind,* she thought, turning on her heel and following Giles.

Catching up with him, she reached for his hand again, but he brushed her aside. She felt the colour stain her cheeks but stayed close behind him as he surged up the stairs, bursting through the door, then slowing as he moved across the room, beyond the dividing curtain to the bed. The smell of vomit and purged bowels hung foetidly in the air.

Oswin was on his knees, one hand stroking Nan's dishevelled hair. As Isabella came in, he swivelled round, his face filled with fear. "My lady," he whispered, "I cannot wake her. And…" He gulped. "I cannot lose her."

Isabella pushed up her sleeves. "Has she vomited much, Oswin?"

"Yes, my lady. I disposed of it."

"And her bowels?"

He nodded. "Yes. She roused for that, but now, she…" He choked and wiped his hand over his eyes. "My lord, will you help me remove her to our own bed? She'd not wish to be here. In our chamber she'll be more at peace, and I can…" He paused, fighting for control, "I can take care of her the better."

Isabella chewed her lip. "Are you really sure, Oswin? Would she not be more comfortable to lie here undisturbed? Edith and I can take care of her."

Oswin shook his head. "No, my lady. I know what she'd want."

"Very well, then." She looked at Giles. "My lord, is there a physician nearby? Would someone come to her? For I do not know what ails her."

Giles was haggard. "The nearest would be–"

Oswin interrupted. "She'd not want that, my lord. No one knows more about simples than my Nan. And I've watched her. I know what to do."

Giles, face bleak, went to the bed and lifted Nan in his arms, holding her as though she weighed no more than a child, carrying her down the stairs and through the hall, taking no notice of the worried faces staring at them. Proceeding to the chamber behind the dais, he laid her tenderly on Oswin's bed, while Oswin went to her chest of nostrums. Filbert had followed them and put his arm around his father's shoulders.

Giles mentioned the physician again, but Oswin was firm in his rejection.

Giles splayed his hands. "If you're sure that's what she'd want, Oswin. But if she's no better on the morrow, I will fetch a physician with or without your yeasay. Is that understood?"

Oswin bowed his head in acquiescence.

"Then I'll leave her in your hands, for I must join the hunt for the outlaws." Giles turned and strode from the room, ignoring Isabella who went after him, almost running in her attempt to keep up with his long stride.

She shivered in the chill wind as she followed Giles to the stables, watching, hands clasped before her as he saddled Troubadour. As he went to mount, she caught his arm.

He looked down at her, and she quailed at the expression he wore, but before she could lose her courage, she leaned into him, stood up on her toes and grazed his neck with her lips. "Take care."

He nodded curtly, then swung himself onto Troubadour and rode out. Isabella, left behind in the stables, fell to her knees in the straw, not caring who might see her, praying she had not left it too late.

CHAPTER 28

Clarice considered her options. How much did she want Giles? Was it just that he appealed to her? Or that he was a challenge, not succumbing easily to her wiles? And what was the more important? Appeasing her desires, or trying her luck at Bedford Castle?

Nan had been barely conscious for the past two days. The leech had been. He'd sniffed at her urine and examined her stools, bled her and applied a poultice to her abdomen, then left, shaking his head.

De Soutenay, when he was there, went about with a grim face, and his wife's seemed bleached of all colour. He'd taken to sleeping in the hall with his men. Clarice would have gone to him, but Isabella barely slept and woke at the slightest sound, as Clarice had discovered. Still, each night spent apart would deepen the chasm between them, and when the time was right, she would know.

She sat idly at Nan's bedside, hands in her lap, trying to discern what she wanted most.

If she only aspired to Otto, Bedford's constable – senior constable, so he said – he was hers for the lifting of her finger. But did she? She shook her head resolutely, as though to dislodge the cobwebs of having family and home which seemed to lurk in the depths of her mind. That meant, if not actual poverty, a far lower position than she sought, although the man himself was fairly appealing.

Her lip curled. *I don't think so.* No, best to keep him dangling, go with him to the castle, get the matter of Walerin the Fleming, and more importantly, what remained of his possessions, settled once and for all. Then she would see. She might be able to convince Giles to accompany her, for *if* she wished to return to Thorneywell, she would need an escort.

She had no fears about trouble falling upon her. As long as she behaved as though she believed Walerin had been free to marry her, who could prove otherwise? If the fat fool's wife showed up – and how would she know where to find him? – but *if* she did, Clarice could still play the deceived innocent, and by then, she would have found a richer, more important lover, no doubts of that. She did not underestimate her charms; she did not need to. The gazing glass Walerin had given her told her all she needed to know. And none could prove he'd not given her the ring she wore. The ring the outlaws had dropped. She'd seen it glinting in the mud as it rolled beneath the cart where she hid and scooped it up.

So much could be won or lost on a turn of fate's wheel, and those who dared take a chance, who dared play the game, could make their fortune. Clarice had ever been a gambler.

A small sound from the bed distracted her. Nan was gazing up with fear-filled eyes. Clarice smiled brightly, enjoying her power. The only reason she was allowed to sit with Nan was because Clarice had assured Oswin that she recognised the symptoms and knew how to treat them. And, of course, the remedy was simple when you knew the cause. A few drops of nightshade and all would be well. Probably. As long as she did not give Nan too much.

Oswin had been so easy to convince, despite Filbert glowering in the background. Which left Isabella with no choice but to acquiesce to the steward's wishes. The look on her face had made Clarice want to smirk. Well, now she would prove she could heal, she thought benignly, since now, she had other fish to fry.

She patted Nan's hand. "Don't fret, dear Nan. You've been deathly ill." Her voice was sweet as honey. *That'll give the old crone a fright.* "But we've prayed for you, and I've been tending you with care." No matter this was the first day Clarice had been long at her side. She wanted to be away from the duties of the hall, and thus far, Isabella had not bothered her.

Here, it was quiet, and she could think. In the hall, the hustle and bustle as Isabella took her temper and frustration out on a frantic bout of cleaning was distracting. And Isabella could scarcely drag her away now she had Oswin's blessing.

Nan was trying to speak, and Clarice lifted her as tenderly as though she actually cared, feeling the lightness of her. The solid flesh seemed to have melted from her bones.

She held a ginger tisane sweetened with honey to Nan's lips, and although resisting her at first, the woman soon gave in and drank thirstily. "There, Nan. That feels better, doesn't it?"

It amused her to be playing the nurse. It would be fun to change the old cow's opinion of her. Let Isabella notice Nan's change of attitude and tremble, for Clarice knew she could convince the steward's wife she'd misjudged her. She damped a linen napkin in a laver of water and sponged Nan's face with it.

"You've done too much, my dear. That's why you were ill again, you know. Did not your husband and son beg you to rest yourself until you were fully well?" Nan's eyes watched her warily. "But never fear. You will be well soon enough. Only, this time, you must promise to rest if you wish to recover. And I'll stay with you and take care of you, don't you worry."

Nan opened her mouth and closed it again. *Good! That's left her with nought to prate on about.* "Would you like me to fetch you something to eat?" *As if she would.* And fasting was best for her, it would help her insides rest and rid themselves of the last of the fool's funnel. It never killed. Well, almost never. But she'd given Nan more doses than the others.

Nan shuddered and shook her head, closing her eyes as though to shut out the sight of Clarice. Clarice sponged her face again and crooned, "No, I thought not. Well then, I'll stay with you my dear, just in case you have need of anything."

She watched Nan's lips tighten and almost laughed aloud. To change her mind would be a challenge. Well, she was not one to shirk from those.

In the hall, Isabella ordered the scouring of tables and floors with an energy which was almost fury. The old rushes were swept up and the stone flags scrubbed until it seemed they would dissolve, before dried herbs and fresh rushes were taken from the undercroft and strewn over them.

Maids scurried around trying to avoid her eye, keeping busy so they did not feel the lash of her tongue, shocked at the change in her.

She prowled like a foraging wolf, cleaning everything that could be moved, venting her fears in furious activity, checking stores, accounts, even venturing into the kitchens, to the silent rage of Amos.

She poked her head into Nan's domain, the worry in her heart intensifying when she saw Clarice sitting there, eyes closed, hands in her lap. Nan gave a weak smile, and Isabella had to admit Clarice's remedy, whatever it was, seemed to be working, for at least Nan was conscious now.

Oswin had followed her and went to Nan, holding her hands, pouring out thanks to Clarice as that young woman opened her eyes. Isabella left them, shaking her head, for she did not have the right to remove Clarice if Oswin wanted her there.

The men would likely be back soon, she reminded herself, ordering a tub brought to the bedchamber. While it steamed, she sprinkled rosewater into it, then stripped and submerged herself in the scented water. She scoured her body with the same fervour she had displayed in the hall, then stepped out and wrapped herself in the linen towel Edith held out.

Once she was dry, Edith helped her into the gown she had worn for her marriage, before rubbing more rosewater into her hair, and if the maid had a satisfied tilt to her lips, her mistress affected not to notice.

Isabella looked with disdain at her discarded linen wimple before pinning on the sheerest veil she possessed, ordering the tub to be refilled as soon as Giles arrived.

Then, she stalked the hall, biting her lip, pulling at her gown, constantly turning her head to listen for the men and horses returning, so sharp-tempered that most stayed well out of her way.

After what seemed an interminable time, the shouts from outside confirmed they were back. Isabella's legs almost gave way as she went to the door to welcome them.

Giles dismounted, face drawn. The day had been long, he was worried sick about Nan, and he had no wish to have his wife spurn him yet again. Best to stay well clear of her. But it made what had been a happy household seem cold and cheerless. He cursed as he stepped in dung, wiping his boot with straw.

Otto was grinning beneath his fatigue; for him, the day had been good. They had followed a tip from the brother of Giles' groom's uncle-by-marriage, who'd had a large group of men in his hostelry the night before. Walter, the groom, volunteered to visit and keep an eye on them whilst the others had set up camp a couple of miles away waiting for word.

As soon as the messenger had arrived, labouring his sweating horse, they'd set off at the gallop, catching the miscreants in the act of robbing another merchant.

The merchant had been grateful and indignant by turns, and it had taken long to pacify him. Now the outlaws sat tied on their horses. They would not be allowed to escape; Giles must find a safe place to keep them overnight and post guards on them.

He hissed between his teeth as he saw Isabella waiting at the door. What did she want of him? He had offered her his comfort, had he not? His every step towards her had been rebuffed. Why the change now? His breath rose in white puffs in the frigid air. In truth, it felt as warm out here as did his hearth. Well, enough. He'd not offer his heart for her to trample on again.

Having ordered his servants to clear one of the storerooms in the undercroft, Giles saw the outlaws secured, then, leaving both his men and Otto's to share the watch, he emerged into the forecourt and, ignoring Isabella, led Troubadour to the stable, spurning Walter's attempts to unbridle and unsaddle, sending him for a hot bran mash for the horse.

When Troubadour had his nose in his reward, Giles tended him, taking comfort from the horse's warmth, putting all his energies, all his confusion, into the long, sweeping strokes. Troubadour, as though sensing his unhappiness, whickered softly, nuzzling into him, and Giles rubbed the soft ears and fondled his long nose. "Never mind, boy, you eat your supper. Happen your appetite's better than mine."

He leaned his head against the horse's mane, starting as he felt a hand on his arm. Swearing, he spun on his heel to see Isabella standing behind him, blinking nervously.

"What?" Even Giles was surprised at the harshness of his tone.

Isabella wrung her hands before reaching out to him again. He shrugged her off, but she did not go.

"My lord." Her voice was pitched so low, he could hardly hear it. She took a step nearer. Behind him, Troubadour snorted. Giles smelt the rosewater she'd anointed herself with, and his resolve broke. By the saints, he needed her.

He met her across the small gap between them, catching her to himself, almost crushing her. He heard a muffled groan and let her go again. Her eyes were wet with tears. "What do you want of me, wife? When I come to you, you spurn me; when I seek to console you, you turn on me like a harpy. What more do you want from me?"

Her face crumpled. He expected her to turn and run, but she threw herself at him, wrapping her arms round his neck, straining to reach his lips, and he forgot everything except his need of her.

Later, as Isabella clung to him, still shaken by the strength of their mutual passion, he stroked the contours of her face, picking a piece of straw from her lips.

She gazed up at him, honey-coloured eyes shining with moisture. "Giles?"

"Yes, my heart."

Her lower lip trembled, and he resisted the urge to cover it with his own, for he needed to hear what she had to say if he was ever to understand her. "Giles, I'm sorry I was such a shrew."

"So am I." His gaze slid sideways, eyes gleaming at her in the dark of the stables, and she gave a wobbly laugh.

"Only…" She swallowed.

"Go on."

"It's just that I've never conceived before. Baldwin cursed me for it. When my flux came each month, he beat me for being barren, so when I knew I was carrying your child, you can imagine how I rejoiced. And then…" The tears sparkling in her eyes started to spill over, and he traced her lids as he wiped them with the tip of his finger. "And then…to lose it." She gulped. "My mother only conceived twice. What…what if it does not happen again for me?"

Giles shifted so he could cup her face in his hands, kissing her cheeks, her lips, her eyelids. "My heart, you may not have conceived with FitzAubrey, but," his voice was smug; he knew it but did not care, "with me, you must have conceived almost immediately."

She pulled back a little and chewed her fingertip, considering. Almost he could see her mind processing the thought, see the hope starting to light her face.

"So, sweetheart, it seems to me, your womb is fertile enough. Indeed, after this, you may have already done so again." He grinned wickedly. "And if not, we can keep trying for, unless I misread the situation, it seems you took more than just a little pleasure in it."

Her face flushed a fiery red, and she buried her head in his chest, muffling her reply, for she had quite forgotten herself in this coupling. Her enjoyment had been all too evident, to Giles' great delight. Then, she raised her head again, an impish smile playing around her mouth. "We could indeed keep trying, my lord, if it would please you."

"Indeed, wife. And," he paused, studying her. She did not avert her eyes, which now shone like stars, "It does seem to me you also took much pleasure in our joining," he repeated, his heart swelling.

Keeping one arm about her, he pulled himself to his feet. "Come. If we're absent much longer, they'll be like to raise the hue and cry."

She giggled, and he stood away from her, dusting the straw from her gown. As he bent to retrieve her veil from where he had cast it, light footsteps pattered into the stables and stopped abruptly. He looked up to see Clarice, staring slack-mouthed.

As the girl went to speak, his wife surprised him, for she cut in before Clarice could get a word out. "As you see, Clarice, I have been helping my husband to, er, tend his horse. Pray you, go back to the hall. It is not meet you should be out here so late."

Giles suppressed a choke of amusement as Clarice gasped. With fury? From the glitter of her eyes and the hectic flush on her cheeks, he thought so. Then, she recovered her equilibrium, dropped a none-too-respectful curtsey and was gone in an indignant swirl of skirts.

Repressing a smirk, Giles held out his arm, Isabella laid her hand along it, and they walked back to the hall in stately fashion, as though attending a banquet.

Clarice watched through her lashes as they entered the hall, her lips moving in a silent curse. She'd lost her chance. She could not understand how, when she'd taken so many pains to sew discord between them, and a pang went through her as she considered Giles' lithe, well-muscled body. A shame she would never taste it.

Had she been a fool not to dispose of Isabella when she had the opportunity? No, for she could not afford suspicion to taint her. A pity though. A great pity.

Still, if milk-and-water was the way his tastes ran, he deserved to lose the opportunity to lie with her. She smiled slyly. She could have kindled a blaze in him that would have seared his very soul, but he'd taken the safe option. Well, he was nothing to her, after all.

She tossed her head, mind made up, and watched the hall until Otto entered, going to him, offering him wine, putting her arm through his and drawing him to a bench near the fire.

"And so, you caught them. How courageous of you." Clarice's eyes glowed as though she thought him the most fascinating man in the room. The constable's chest swelled visibly, and Clarice clasped her hands before her. "I wish you would tell me what happened."

He favoured her with a wink, puffed out his cheeks and told the tale, giving himself much of the credit. But then, she had that effect on men; they wished to impress her.

Tomorrow, she would leave with him and make what opportunities she could at the castle. If fortune favoured her – and she was good at encouraging fortune's smile – Prince John might be present. From what Otto had let slip, John was generous to women who pleased him, and she could be very pleasing. If not, there were fine lords aplenty. She could take her pick.

She allowed her gaze to drop and let her lower lip tremble slightly. "And now, you must return and take me with you, for I must speak to the sheriff and tell him about my husband. Now, I find I'm quite fearful. Is he very daunting?"

The constable took possession of her hand again, stroking it. "He can indeed be a daunting man, Mistress Clarice, but only to wrong-doers. To innocent victims such as yourself, he'll be gentle. You've done naught wrong by all accounts, so no need to worry. And, of course, I'll vouch for you."

Clarice dimpled up at him. "It will be such a comfort to have you by my side."

She flirted with Otto for the rest of the evening, allowing him to stroke her hand, laughing at his feeble jokes, almost, but not quite nestling into his side. He responded with flattering enthusiasm, but she poured him more wine, making sure he kept his cup filled. She would ensure he drank too much to try his luck with her, for she would not waste herself on such as he. She was made for greater things.

Encouraging him to talk, she made a mental note of any information she could glean, for knowledge was always power, and Clarice enjoyed power.

On the morrow, she took her leave of Giles and Isabella with becoming gratitude, trying one last attempt to make him desire her. She smiled up at him prettily, for he should be made to understand what he'd lost, then less daintily at Isabella, for she need not think she'd won; it was merely that Clarice had now decided what she wanted, and that was not Giles.

She waited for Otto to help her mount and sat behind him, dreaming and scheming, relieved to be putting distance between Thorneywell and herself. For once, she had nearly let her bodily desires subdue her ambitions. It would not happen again.

Jerold had risen from his bed today and now stood watching her leave. Isabella wondered at the look of desolation in his eyes. Although, she reminded herself, Clarice had probably had the same effect on him as Adam, Otto and whomever else she had chosen to bewitch. A youth of Jerold's age would all too likely be overwhelmed by her charms, even if those bestowed upon him were of the most minor.

He moped around for several days, getting in the way of various members of the household, drooping in corners and generally looking woebegone. Giles seemed not to notice. Isabella, reluctant to interfere but not caring to see the boy looking so unhappy, finally intervened when he wandered in front of Nan, who was now beginning to take up her duties again, making her drop some of the napery she was carrying. For that, he was subjected to a scolding which turned his ears red.

As Nan turned away, muttering, "Great daft lummox, he is," Isabella caught his eye and beckoned him to her. He came, face as fiery as his ears, stumbling over his feet like the adolescent he was. Although, indeed, he was not so very much younger than she. Still, she was his lady, and thus, in part, responsible for him. Besides, she felt years older.

"Aye, lady," he mumbled, looking at the floor as though it might hold inspiration.

"Look at me, Jerold." Isabella had no intention of talking to someone who was gazing anywhere but at her face. He raised unwilling eyes to her.

Now she had his full attention, she spoke more softly. "Jerold, is there aught amiss?"

"No, lady." He scuffed one foot in the rushes.

"Then why do you look so downcast?" His mouth turned down even further. Isabella would swear that if he were not of an age to be beyond such nonsense, he was near to tears. He remained silent. She waited a moment longer then prompted him. "Well?"

"It's nothing, my lady."

She drew an exasperated breath. This was like drawing teeth! But then, he was a man – even if a very young one. And if he wasn't to be coaxed, then he would be ordered. "Jerold," she said, her voice compelling his obedience now, "do not insult my intelligence, please. It is very evident things are not as you wish them to be. I am not able to see your thoughts, and if you will not tell me them, how can I help you?"

He shuffled, then looking her straight in the eye, blurted out his words as though if he didn't hurry, he might change his mind. "The Lady Clarice. She said, she said she'd ask your lord if I might have a place here. But now–"

He broke off and started scuffing his feet in the rushes again.

"I see. And she went without keeping her word, did she?" The cat! Jerold's plight had likely vanished from her mind before she'd even left the manor.

He nodded dolefully. "My lady, I'm well now; I can work. But I don't 'ave nowhere to go. I was hopin'…"

"You were hoping you might find employment with my lord?"

"Aye, my lady."

"Should you like me to ask him?"

The sullen look was wiped from his face. One side of his mouth twisted up in the beginning of a hopeful smile. "Would you, my lady?"

Her own heart sank at the optimism in his voice, for now, she would have to approach Giles. Would he think she was meddling? Ah well, she had talked herself into this situation. She stiffened her spine. And after all, it was foolish still to be fearful of doing wrong. He was not likely to beat her, she acknowledged. His disapproval, although she would not enjoy it, was something she must face, if, indeed, he did disapprove. And she did not think he would cast the boy out.

Shrugging her shoulders, half amused at the plight she had landed herself in, she went off to find her husband.

Giles was deep in conversation with Oswin when Isabella approached him. She hovered uncertainly, not sure whether he would be angry with her for interrupting. It might be better if she approached him when he was relaxed. Maybe when they dined. She was about to move quietly away when he raised his head, saw her and held up a hand to his steward.

"The rest can wait, Oswin. I see my wife comes to find me. It would not do for her to think I put my business matters above her."

"Not when you're so newly wed, my lord." Oswin's eyes crinkled in shared amusement. "The time for that comes later."

"Indeed. But let her not hear you say so."

He seemed in high good humour, and Isabella took courage from that. Oswin collected up his tally sticks and accounts, and Giles took her hands. "Well, love? Have you tired of the company of your women?"

She smiled absently, wondering how to approach the matter, and Giles sat himself down on a bench, drawing her to him, serious now. "What is it, Bella? You look worried. Does something trouble you?"

"Not me, my husband, but there is something I've promised to ask."

"Oho! Who in my household has taken fright of me and sent you to bear the brunt of my surliness?" He growled, but his eyes twinkled.

Isabella felt some of the tension drain from her. After all, he could but say no. He was in good spirits, so now was the best time. She peeped at him from below the edge of her veil. "My husband, it concerns Jerold."

He looked at her appraisingly.

"He is very young, my lord."

Giles had just raised a cup of ale to his lips. To his credit, he managed not to spit it out when he choked on it.

Isabella drew herself up to her full height. "My lord, I know he is near of an age to me, but he seems so very much younger. And he did not come to me. I saw his distress and asked what ailed him."

Giles paused and seemed to master himself, and Isabella's indignation melted away as he said, "That was well done of you, Bella. I confess, I've had little time to think about the lad. Is he worried about what's to become of him?"

Thankful he'd guessed by himself, she found it easy to tell him the rest, ending with, "And, I think he expected Clarice to deal with it for him. Now she has gone, and he is no wiser."

"He felt the effect of her, too, did he? Well, as you say, he is young and less aware of the ways of women like her. I suppose the poor lad was blinded by her; she does seem to dazzle the susceptible."

Isabella forced herself not to ask if he also had been dazzled, and waited while he considered. "I don't have the time to speak to him just now. However, tell him he may stay. Filbert will assess him to find out what tasks he may be suitable for – or has he already told you where his talents lie?"

She shook her head forcefully. "He has not, my husband. And I think you are laughing at me again."

"Ah, but it's so irresistible to see you ruffle your feathers like a chicken."

Isabella could not help herself. The full vision of a hen wearing veil and wimple hit her, and she hid a grin behind her hand. Then as the image in her head cackled, she sat down next to Giles and rocked with mirth. Giles took one look at her and joined in, his deep chuckles turning heads. When she finally mopped her streaming eyes, she saw half the household were gaping at them as though they had run mad. "M...my lord," she said unsteadily, "your people will be thinking we're most unseemly."

"That's only because they don't know what amused us. Should you like me to tell them?"

Isabella started to bridle, then became aware she was doing it again and gave a small giggle. "Perhaps this is something we should keep to ourselves, my lord. How shall they respect me if every time I have need to scold them, they see naught but a hen?"

"How indeed?" His voice still held a tremor in it. "Go you and put the poor lad out of his misery. Try not to cluck at him." His voice broke, and Isabella bit back another giggle and fled while she could still keep her countenance. How she was going to face Jerold now, she could not imagine. In her head, the hen broke forth into renewed cackling, and she decided Jerold must wait a little longer. She would take a few moments in the solar while she composed herself.

That night as they were preparing for bed, Isabella stopped in the middle of undressing, holding one stocking, the other still gartered about her leg, a pensive look on her face. Giles beckoned to her, but she did not see it, so lost in thought was she.

He lay back, his arms behind his head, pillowing it. "What addles your brain at this late hour, love?"

She shook her head. "It's nothing," she responded, laying the stocking down and untying the binding of the other.

His curiosity roused, Giles tilted his head to one side. "What kind of a nothing?" She looked him full in the eye, and he began to wish he'd not asked. The workings of women's minds could still mystify him at times, even when they explained themselves. But still, he said, "Come to bed and tell me your nothing, then."

She slid in beside him, laying her head on his chest, her fingers entwining in the dark curls that grew there and he stilled her hand, clasping it in his own, for it tickled. Then, she raised herself on one elbow, gazing at him, her eyes reflecting the light from the candle which stood on its pricket at the side of the bed. "Do you really see me as little older than Jerold? For I feel full five years older than he."

Giles considered for a moment. "In truth, I do not. Until a few days ago, I'd not been aware of your age, assumed you were older. And even now I know, you do still seem older to me, if that does not offend you. I did but say it to tease."

She gave a satisfied smile, pinched out the candle, drew the bed hangings close about them and lay back down beside him, pulling the covers up. He wrapped her in his arms and drew her close, nestling his face in her hair.

CHAPTER 29

No one, it seemed, not even Adam, felt the loss of Clarice. Within a week of her departure, it was as though she had never existed. The poisonous miasma she had fostered between Giles and Isabella had disappeared as completely as the morning mist once the sun has warmed the earth and the wind dispersed it.

Nan was still not quite back to her usual self. Isabella made her rest in the solar for a full candle notch each day after dinner. The fact that Nan did not object proved she was not quite as well as she would have them believe.

Isabella's coffers had been collected from Berkhamsted and she had arranged her few treasures about the chamber. A small psalter, ivory bound, lay open on the carved table. A book of hours on a shelf, her reliquary next to it.

And now she had her workbox, she had a full complement of her embroidery silks again rather than the small selection she had packed so hurriedly when she'd left the castle.

Her gowns hung on clothing poles in a corner of the room, hidden behind another curtain, her other garments stowed in the chests which stood around the walls, and a small casket, which held the few other items that she possessed: her cloak brooches, her comb made of polished antler and the ivory one from Maude and Petronilla, her needle-case and a silver thimble, the only things she had left of her mother's. The paternoster her sisters-by-marriage had given to her, she wore attached to her ceinture.

The betrothal and wedding rings bestowed upon her by Baldwin she had wrapped in a scrap of cloth and poked into a small hole in the corner of the casket. To tell truth, it made her feel sick to look at them, but Giles might someday find a use for them. That, or she could use them as a gift if the occasion arose or sell them if there was ever need. For now, they would remain hidden from her sight.

Isabella sat often in the solar where the light was brighter than the hall, candles and rushlights aiding her, working on a worn hanging from the hall. Always her stitchery had soothed her. Now she was content, her needle fairly flew through the fabric.

When the repair was finished. Isabella put down her needle and stood, releasing it from its frame, laying it across the bed the better to admire her work. The small holes had been repaired, the frayed edges bound. The dust had been carefully brushed from it for she had not dared to risk treating it vigorously. The other stitching, so faded, she had sewn over, keeping the colours the same but with fresh thread which made it look, if not new, near as good as it must once have been. It also had the effect of making the fabric thicker – the better to keep draughts at bay.

"Shall I tak' it to the hall and get someone to rehang it, m'lady?" Edith whisked away a stray piece of silk thread.

Isabella considered a moment. Simkin was far too old for the exertion, yet he'd been so proud to be asked for aid. Surely he should be honoured with some part in its rehanging. She touched a fingernail to her teeth, tapping them, while she thought the matter through.

"No, Edith, but, think you Simkin would be able to mount the stair without doing an injury to himself?"

Edith screwed up her nose. "Simkin? But he's too old, m'lady, no one expects any work of him these days. Surely someone younger? Neither his eyes nor his legs are what they were."

"Ah, do not look like that, Edith. He was so pleased not to be overlooked when he helped me take it down."

Edith was aghast. "M'lady?"

"Yes, I know I ought not, but I was not thinking at the time. And his old face shone to be asked. Think you we could find a way to include him?"

Edith screwed up her nose again, then caught Isabella's eye and straightened her face. "I s'pose he could instruct someone else where to hang it. I know it'll go back where it was, but if he's got the ordering of it, that would satisfy him, I think.

"I'll fetch him. I'll give him my arm to help him climb the stairs. An' I'll ask Thomas to help him – no, Alan, he'll be more careful. Thomas is too young and heedless."

She left the chamber, and Isabella sat down to await Simkin. He arrived on Edith's arm, blowing with exertion, but his eyes were bright, and he puffed his chest out like a robin when Isabella asked Edith to seat him and pour a cup of wine.

"Ah, that does my 'eart good to see, lady," he squeezed out between wheezy coughs. "Looks as good as it did when my lord's sainted mother, bless 'er soul, first sewed it."

Isabella smiled. "Well then, Simkin, since you were the first to help me take it down, I thought you were the person to supervise its rehanging."

A grin spread slowly across his face. "Me, lady?"

"You, Simkin."

He blinked, eyes shining. "It'd be an honour, lady."

"Good." As she spoke, Alan tapped on the door and entered. Isabella acknowledged him, tilting her head. "And here's young Alan, who'll be your assistant, dear Simkin. Alan, you carry this downstairs–"

"Carefully, mind," Edith cut in, admonishing him. "M'lady spent long hours on this, so no foolishness, if you please."

Alan glanced from one to the other, then nodded and picked up the hanging, folding it carefully over his arm. Edith tutted impatiently and straightened it. "You take that downstairs and Simkin'll join you when he's finished his wine."

"Ah," wheezed Simkin. "That'll not tek long." He picked up his cup, draining it, and Edith helped him to his feet. "Will you 'elp me downstair again, lass? I'm not so good as I used to be."

Edith took his arm and most of his weight, and he bowed his head to Isabella. "I thank you, lady. You're good to an old man who's 'ad 'is day long since."

His simple dignity touched Isabella, and she was glad she'd thought to ask him. "And, Simkin," she said, as he reached the door, "Perhaps you'd be kind enough to tell Alan which one needs my attention next."

His face turned pink as a rose. "Aye, I'll do that, lady. I'll choose for you."

Edith helped the old man from the room, a merry word for him on her tongue, and shortly afterwards, Alan carried the next hanging into the chamber.

Slowly, the worn embroidery in the hall was restored, bright, vibrant colours glowing from the walls.

Isabella glowed too, as she marvelled on how her life had changed. At night, she responded to Giles' caresses with increasing enthusiasm; during the day, she sought his company as often as possible. Something within her seemed to have thawed and disappeared even as the snow was now beginning to melt, releasing her, giving her the freedom to trust in her feelings, to trust in the man by her side.

A stiff north wind blew, howling round the outer walls. It blustered and demanded, forcing its way through shutters, slamming any doors left ajar.

In the manor house, noses were red with cold and raw from sniffing. Fingers throbbed where chilblains tormented them, but slowly, the days brightened. Buds began to bulge on branches, a tracery of leaves spread like green filigree on trees; small green shoots broke through the frozen soil.

As the days lengthened, the sun shone with more zeal. If occasional flurries of snow skittered across the sky, they did not settle. Warmth began to creep back across the land.

Isabella yearned to see daylight. *Well, why not?* Still cold it might be, but they could light more braziers. She reached for her mantle, and Edith looked up questioningly.

"I think we shall remove the oilcloth from the other window, Edith. My eyes ache for a sight of daylight, do not yours?"

Edith's needle hovered above her sewing for an instant before she laid it aside and jumped up, face bright and eager. She hesitated, though, as she raised her arms to remove the oilcloth, which let the outside brightness in but dimly. "Will you not be cold, m'lady?"

Isabella thought not. "Even with the cloth there, Edith, the cold gets in. Short of closing the shutters, there's no way to keep it out. We'll light another brazier anyway."

Reassured, Edith took down the fabric. Day-light streamed in, and Isabella, wrapping herself more warmly, leaned on the narrow ledge, holding her sewing in one hand, observing the scene outside.

Giles' older knights and squires were not within sight; Isabella guessed they might be at the ground beyond the stables which was used for swordplay by the older men. His youngest knight, Adam, was leant against a wall, laughing at the efforts of Thomas and Eustace as they trained. Considered too young to practice with the others, they would be allowed to join them only when they were more proficient. Eustace showed some promise; Thomas, as yet, had not acquired the skill of wielding either sword or knife, but the lad's face was red with effort, and as he managed a lunge which had Eustace leap-ing away, Adam applauded him. Thom's face lit with pleasure, and Eustace gave him a good-natured clout on the shoulder which nearly had the boy reeling.

As Isabella watched, amused, the gates swung open, and her face lit up. Giles was back. She turned aside and went downstairs to greet him.

He swept into the hall brimming with boyish exuberance, and she laughed as he grasped her hands and tugged her towards the door, saying, "My lord, what's to do? Why the hurry?"

As he neared the door, he let go of her and, instead, stepping behind her, covered her eyes with his hands. She groped in front of her, then tried to pull free, exclaiming with indignation. Giles merely laughed, saying, "I have a surprise for you."

Isabella made one more unsuccessful attempt to free herself, before saying, "My lord, am I not to be allowed to see this surprise, then?"

Giles crowed in amusement. "Patience, Bella." He kicked open the door and steered her down the steps, and she clung to him, afraid of missing her footing, protesting and complaining, but he would not relent.

At last, she stood on solid ground. He guided her a few more steps, then left her, saying, "I trust you to keep your eyes shut," and she recoiled as something large and solid bumped her shoulder.

"You may look now, Bella." His voice was breathless and grinning, and she opened her eyes to see a dainty grey jennet whiffling at her, silver bells tinkling on a red leather harness.

"Here," Giles said, thrusting a piece of dried apple at her. "Give her this."

Isabella, baffled but laughing, held out her hand, and the mare gently lipped it from her.

"An elegant lady, is she not?" Giles' eyes were creased with delight.

"Indeed, my lord, she is charming."

"Do you like her?"

Did she like her? The horse was beautiful. "She's lovely."

"Good." Giles looked thoroughly pleased with himself. "She's yours."

"Mine?" Isabella was confused.

"A birthday gift. Belated, but that was hardly my fault. How could I have known?" He stood close, his breath warm on her cheek. "Would you like to learn to ride properly, Bella?"

The horse watched them with liquid eyes, as though she too would like to know the answer.

Isabella didn't know how to respond. Riding pillion or on a leading rein with a lady's sideways facing seat, being led by a dutiful groom, was one thing. That she could do without being taught, although she didn't much enjoy it, but she did not think that was what he meant. Did he want her to ride astride? Like a man? Surely not.

Confused, she stuttered something unintelligible, but Giles must have taken it in the affirmative, for he beamed at her. "You may still ride aside when it is politic to do so, but you cannot properly control a horse seated like that." Then, he paused, eyes shining. "However, if you wished it, I could also teach you how to ride astride. Then we could hunt together."

"But...but..."

"It is a useful skill to acquire, love, in case you should ever have need. And a few of the women at court do ride to the hunt, Bella, so it would not be unseemly. If you ride with a divided skirt, it would be acceptable. And if not, do you care?" He grinned like a youth half his age. "I do not."

She could not bring herself to blight his pride. Still, she quailed at the thought of wearing such a garment. But then, if it was just in their own demesne... Still somewhat stupefied, she gave a reluctant nod. As though she understood, the mare came to her and rubbed her long nose gently against Isabella's shoulder. Isabella patted the horse, and the jennet leaned against her, snorting with pleasure.

Giles stroked the mare's neck. "Her name is Merlin, although I hope her manners will be better than the bird of the same name."

Isabella was confused. "Merlin? But, she's a mare!"

Giles looked a little sheepish. "I named her after the bird because of its grace. Do you wish to call her something different?"

She forbore to chuckle. And it would not be a gracious way to accept the gift. "Then I will think of her as a bird, my lord. And she is an elegant creature; the name is perfect." Now the shock had faded, she was overwhelmed. No one had ever thought to give her something just for the

joy of it, apart from her wedding gifts, but this…
She stepped back and stood on tiptoe, pressing
her lips to his, and he caught her round the
waist. The horse thrust its nose between them,
and Giles chuckled. "I believe Merlin may be
jealous."

"You rate yourself too highly, my lord."
Isabella laughed, stepping neatly from his grasp
and standing just out of his reach.

Giles pulled a face at her and she dipped her
head, but he caught her hand and kissed it.
"Come, love, let's introduce her to her new
quarters. As soon as you've altered one of your
gowns, I'll begin your lessons, but for now, I
have a saddle made for you. It's to my own
design."

He indicated the low-backed padded seat
which lay in the stable, and Alan picked it up,
showing it to her before he strapped it onto the
mare. The contraption faced sideways, in the
same way as she had travelled to Berkhamsted
Castle with the palfrey borrowed from Mabille
de Bourne, except that, when she examined it
more closely, it seemed skewed a little forwards.
Not much, but it would allow her to more easily
face ahead.

Giles grinned, clearly delighted with himself,
and Isabella felt a faint stirring of excitement
when he said, "Do you wish to try her paces?"

Did she? The mare whinnied as though eager to show off, and Isabella steadied her nerves and nodded.

Giles boosted her onto Merlin, who stood quietly. "See how gentle she is? Not at all skittish. Walter will lead you, won't you Walter?"

He mounted Troubadour, and Isabella clung to her seat as Walter led Merlin back out through the gates.

CHAPTER 30

The weather had not held. Icy rain drizzled incessantly from the skies, and, as a precaution, Giles ordered the sheep brought in from the fields to lamb in the barns. Whilst the ewes complained, indignant at the change in their circumstances, the lambs bounced around in their confined quarters, thrusting their noses hard into their dams' udders, greedy, demanding, before sleeping, their bellies full for now.

Despite the inclement weather, each time there was a brief dry spell, Giles insisted Isabella have her riding lesson and took her on small outings around the manor, still walking, still led by Walter, but she needed to gain her confidence before he would allow her to try without leading reins, for which she was glad.

Returning from a lesson on one of the rare days when the sun decided to shine, Giles, riding side by side with Isabella, halted Troubadour and looked up startled as two labourers and a couple of lads walking ahead of them on the path stopped and turned.

"Your pardon," said the shorter one, giving him the briefest of bows. "Are you my Lord de Soutenay?"

"And if I am, what of it?" Giles was not going to tell them anything until he knew what they were about.

"My lord," said the taller one, "we've been sent to put glass in the window of yon manor house."

"A window? Are you crazed?"

The shorter one beamed, unperturbed. "Aye, my lord. Your brother said as how you'd react like that. He said to tell you it was all arranged."

Giles was stunned. *Glass?* "I hesitate to disappoint you, but I'm not wealthy. I cannot afford glass."

The man's grin grew broader. "Nay, my lord. Sir Ralph said to tell you as how it was Lady Maude who done it. He said it's to be a wedding gift, ain't that so, Clem? Nothing for you to pay." Giles gaped like a stranded trout, as he continued, "And if you're worried about noise or damage, my lord, you needn't. We're skilled craftsmen, we are, ain't we Clem?"

Clem nodded. "Won't find none better than us, my lord. We can do it so quick, you'll hardly notice we was there, will 'e, Robin? Skilled, we are. We were hired to put the glass in the windows at Aylesbury Castle, and Sir Ralph had us put glass in two of his solar windows." He stood, legs apart, hands out as though waiting for acclaim.

Giles couldn't help but smile. Trust Maude to have wheedled glass out of Ralph. Glass windows! In their solar! Would that he had seen Ralph's face. And from what he'd heard, there had been more than just these two putting glass in the windows at Aylesbury Castle, an unnecessary conceit in Giles' opinion. He wondered just where they had fitted into the scheme of things. However, there was something disarming about the pair, and if Maude had sent them, what choice did he have? He inclined his head gravely. "Then, I bow to your skills."

Robin's smile was now so broad, Giles felt it might almost split his face. "So, my lord, where do we go? The lady said it would be in your solar. Can someone show us the way, like?"

Giles splayed his hands in an attitude of submission. Since Maude was involved in this, he might as well give in now. "When you arrive, ask for my steward; he'll show you where you're to go. I'll leave it to his good judgement and that of my wife."

"Right you are, my lord." Robin bent to pick up the bag at his feet. Clem shouldered the other one without discernible effort and, singing a jaunty lay, they trudged along the path towards the manor, moving to one side to allow Giles and Isabella and the others to pass.

Giles, almost too bemused for speech, turned to Isabella, whose face brimmed with laughter. "Well, my lady, think you this will make me worthy of you?"

She bowed her head graciously. "Indeed, my lord, I think it might."

He chuckled as the horses walked on and sought out Oswin as soon as they arrived home, noting with amused satisfaction that the steward looked as shocked as he himself felt.

Shortly afterwards, Jerold came running through the hall, skidding to a halt as he reached Giles. "They're here, my lord. They just came through the gates."

Giles all but groaned as heads turned. Still, he beckoned Filbert and instructed him to meet them and take them to the solar, following them himself. As much as he'd been going to leave it to Isabella and remain downstairs, he found himself unable to hide his curiosity.

Robin walked over to the windows, pushed back his cap and scratched his head as Clem got string and started to measure them. Isabella, entering the solar, hid a smirk as Giles caught her eye, and Robin and Clem muttered to themselves, making incomprehensible comments as they worked out which window opening would be the best.

They looked at each other, then at the windows. "Will this one suit?" Clem indicated the window in the outer part of the solar, beyond the dividing curtain. "That'd be better. Well, in my opinion. And you've already got horn panes in the other."

Giles quirked his lips. "Then I'm sure you're right. Do you require anything else?"

"No my lord, you just leave it to us. Of course, we won't be putting the glass in today, will we, Rob?"

Robin shook his head. "That we won't. We'll just be measuring up today. Then, we have to make them." He sucked his teeth. "Can't tell you exactly when we'll have them ready, but we'll be as quick about it as we can. Do you have a place we can work, begging your pardon?"

Giles glanced at Filbert, who nodded assent, saying, "When you're done here, I'll show you."

"Just about finished, my lord. By your leave, we'll get started."

"Very well, then."

Isabella had seated herself by the other window, ostensibly doing her embroidery. Edith, with sewing on her lap, sat opposite. To his amusement, Giles saw Edith biting her lip and Isabella trying not to catch her eye. If she did, the giggles they were both trying to hide would surely erupt from them. He snorted. Glass in his window! Whatever next!

The day the window was fitted, the entire manor was in a state of excitement. The consequence of having such a luxury would affect them all.

Giles groaned. Folk would think him richer by far than he actually was. Pray God, it would not cause him complications; he could only imagine John's face if he found out. What on earth had possessed Maude, he could not imagine. Ralph too. But then his brother could never withstand Maude's wiles. Still, if glass he must have, then he may as well stop worrying and enjoy it.

Robin and Clem had insisted only one of his men stayed in the solar while the window was fitted. Apparently, the viewing was to be a moment of high drama and celebration. He was aware every member of his household would want to see it, and would likely be coming to the chamber with the flimsiest of excuses until their curiosity was satisfied. Better by far to indulge them for the next few days, or doubtless, they would find illicit ways of inspecting it.

He resigned himself to constant interruptions until the wonder had died down and focussed, instead, on his wife. FitzAubrey had not had glass in his windows, so she was as excited as the others, cocking her head every few moments until the summons should come from upstairs

Giles winced as a clatter and a ripe curse came from above. Isabella started to her feet, and Edith dropped her spindle. All eyes, it seemed, were on the upper gallery. Even Amos kept finding excuses to come into the hall, which did not auger well for dinner.

Finally, Filbert's head popped out of the solar door, and Isabella leapt again to her feet. Filbert hung over the gallery rail, grinning. "My lord, my lady," he called. "It's done."

Almost before he'd finished, Isabella's feet were on the bottom step, with Edith and Nan close behind. Unwilling to look so eager, Giles sauntered up behind them, though as he heard their gasps, which he hoped were of delight, he quickened his own steps.

At the top of the stair he paused before following them in. He caught his breath as he beheld the window. Today, the sun had again broken through the clouds, and although still narrow, the panes of glass allowed so much more light it seemed the window blazed with it.

Used to the dimmer light as he was, the solar seemed almost bathed in brightness, at least around the small area of that particular window. The other, with its horn panes, was dull in comparison.

Isabella beckoned him. "Look, Giles." In her excitement, she used his name instead of her usual formal speech. "You can actually see through it. Is it not marvellous?" She gazed up at him, face glowing. "It's as good as Berkhamsted Castle."

She shrugged. "Well, maybe a little smaller," she added, laughing, "but still, you can see so much. I used to delight in looking through the windows there. Now, we have our very own. Imagine it! Even in winter, we'll be able to see outside without getting cold."

It was true. The landscape lay before them, albeit slightly distorted by the varying thickness of each pane, but clearly visible. The small panes varied in colour from almost clear to a pale yellow, like weak sunlight, to those with a hint of green, like seawater. Light bounced into the room and spread the colours across the floor so that it was almost as though the rushes were alive.

Robin and Clem watched, huge grins plastered across their faces, while the two lads they'd brought with them to do the more menial work gathered tools and debris from the floor, and Nan looked on, arms akimbo. She would permit no mess to be left behind.

"Do you like it, my lord?" Robin spread his hands in appeal.

Giles was still lost for words. Robin and Clem looked at him anxiously, and he dredged his brains. At length, in the face of their mute concern, he managed to croak out, "I am dumbfounded." He struggled to keep his gaze from the window as he added, "You have done wonders."

"Gives you a lot more light, doesn't it? You'll be glad of that, come winter. You'll not need near so many candles now, nor braziers. It's a..." He paused, and Giles could almost see him groping in his vocabulary for the word he wanted, nodding in satisfaction when it came to him. "A...an investment," he concluded triumphantly. "It'll save money in the long run, it will, my lord."

Clem was already picking up his bag. Robin looked at Giles hopefully.

"Indeed, such excellent work deserves recompense." Giles gestured to Oswin. "I trust you'll see they are suitably thanked." He could rely on

Oswin to remember they had already been paid, but in truth, such work was worthy of a little extra.

Clem picked up his bag and tugged Robin, who was still expounding on the wonders of glass, from the room, followed by Oswin, who, like Giles, had seemed reluctant to tear himself away from the window.

That night, they did not close the bed hangings, nor yet the dividing curtain. From where they lay, they could just see the moon casting its light across the room, the soft gleam making Edith's sleeping face glow palely, and they held hands, watching until a cloud blew across it, plunging the room into darkness.

Isabella heard Giles give a sigh, felt his grasp loosen on her hand, and he turned away, his breathing deepening into a soft snore. Closing her eyes, she let her mind drift until sleep overcame her.

Just after cockcrow, she woke and gasped aloud as the panes rippled with red and gold. Were they afire? She was about to raise the alarm when she realised it was just the light of dawn, the colours of the sky, which although beautiful, betokened ill for the day, flickering across the glass. It was something she had not noticed at court for, being winter, they had shuttered the windows each night.

"It's a wondrous sight, is it not?" Giles voice was thick with sleep. She turned, gave a squeak, quickly muffled, as one hand found her thigh, and the sight was forgotten as his free arm wrapped around her waist, drawing her gently towards him.

CHAPTER 31

Isabella laid her needlework aside and leaned idly on the sill of the new window, which was a constant source of delight to her. The last few days, there had been respite from the rain, and the wind was drying the mud in the forecourt as the sun made a determined effort to break through the leaden skies. Below her, making the most of the opportunity, the men were training – not at the ground beyond the stables today for that was too much of a quagmire.

Giles was spending time with Eustace and Thomas, observing as they wielded their swords, then stopping them so he could instruct and demonstrate. As they followed his directions, he turned to speak to Miles, then disappeared in the direction of the hall.

Isabella, balked of her view of her husband, went to turn away, but paused as she saw the palisade gates flung open and a group of riders trot in and dismount. Guests?

She was about to tidy herself and go down to greet them, when she noticed the eldest horseman. Her hand flew to her mouth, and she drew back from the window, her legs turning to straw beneath her.

Edith, all solicitous, came to her. "M'lady?"

"It's nothing, Edith." Isabella forced a smile. "Merely, it appears that my father has decided to pay us a visit. Tidy the solar, please, and arrange for water so he can bathe. I must go and greet him."

Her smile faltered, and she fled, ignoring her maid's questioning eyes. She stopped at the top of the gallery, grasping the handrail, gripping it until her knuckles turned white. Then, breathing deeply, she tidied her veil, straightened her gown, and moved slowly down the stairs with a composure she was far from feeling.

As she arrived in the hall, she collided with Giles, who took one look at her face and steered her into a corner, demanding to know what was wrong.

"My lord, it's my…my father."

His face darkened. From the few words he had spoken of her father, Isabella knew her husband held no high opinion of him. Giles took her hand, kissed the palm and folded her fingers over the kiss, imprisoning it in his sturdy grip. "Then, we'll meet him together. Courage, my heart, he has no power over you now. He gave that to me, remember."

"He gave it unwillingly, husband."

His smile glinted at her. "Nevertheless, he gave it. And I take care of what is my own."

He drew her through the hall, and with his strength at her side bolstering her courage, she paced beside him, trying to ignore the sick feeling in the pit of her stomach.

Her father was still in the forecourt ordering the care of his horses when they went forward to greet him, and acknowledged them coolly. "De Soutenay. Daughter. I trust I find you well."

Isabella curtseyed deeply to him, unable to find her voice, relieved when she heard Giles replying, "Well enough, my lord. To what do we owe this pleasure?"

She heard the irony in his voice; if her father did also, he took no notice. The likelihood was, he did not, so overweening was his own sense of self-worth.

Le Gris looked the pair of them up and down, the vestige of a wintry smile on his face, mere courtesy, quickly gone.

"I have news for you. Shall we go within?"

"Indeed."

Giles led le Gris to the solar where Edith was supervising the tub. Steam rose from it scented by the bay and rosemary scattered on the surface. Soap and a linen towel were laid to one side.

Le Gris arched his back, yawning, and stretching, then began to disrobe. Isabella excused herself on the pretext of fetching wine as he dropped the last of his garments onto the rushes for his squire to pick up and stepped into the tub.

When she returned, her father was leaning back in the steaming water giving himself up to Edith's ministrations, speaking sharply to her when she did not follow his instructions quickly enough.

Giles seated himself on the chest beneath the window and waited for him to speak as Isabella set the wine on the table and poured a cup for her father, passing him a platter of cold meat which he eyed with disfavour.

"Fowl, Daughter? In Lent?"

Giles responded, "Barnacle goose." His tone was curt.

Isabella cringed, for surely her father knew exactly what it was. Although, he would doubtless have found fault with whatever she served, and he loathed fish. She held out a second cup of wine to Giles, and he took it from her, caressing her palm with his thumb, holding her hand for a moment or so longer than necessary. It gave her confidence, and she sat quietly next to him, hands in her lap, her hips and shoulders almost touching him, as though she could draw strength from his proximity.

Le Gris ignored Giles and took a gulp of the wine, rolling it around his tongue before swallowing. Apparently satisfied, he poured the rest down his throat and handed the empty cup to Edith before taking a leg of goose and biting into it with teeth that were stained and beginning to crumble. Wincing, he probed his mouth with a finger, pulling out a piece of meat which had lodged awkwardly, viewing it with disfavour before placing it back in his mouth.

Gesturing towards their window, he said, "I see you have been quick to waste your new wealth, de Soutenay."

Isabella blenched as she saw Giles swallow a sharp retort. "In fact," he replied blandly, "it was a wedding gift from my brother."

Le Gris raised his eyebrows. "A generous gift."

"Just so. My brother is one who believes wealth should be enjoyed."

"And how is he to enjoy it when he squanders it thusly on others?"

"Perhaps the enjoyment is sometimes in the giving." Giles' voice was still even, but his jaw had tightened and Isabella could see the throb of a pulse in his temple, a sure sign his temper was rising. God grant he did not lose it.

Le Gris ignored him, his gaze roving round the room. "Although, it seems my daughter has not wasted your gold with expensive hangings and tawdry finery." The sneer in his voice was barely there, but Isabella saw a tic in Giles' eyelid and knew the effort it was costing him to sound cordial.

She took a deep breath. She'd decided to work first on the wall hangings and cushions in the hall, and their chamber, although it had hangings, was a little shabby. The paint on the walls was faded, too, but she had not liked to ask Giles if they could redo it, not wanting him to see her as greedy.

She thought about saying so, but before she could, Giles' voice cut in. "Indeed." His tone was dry. "My wife has been attending to other matters, for, as you stated, we do not wish to squander what wealth I have on 'tawdry finery'. Doubtless, she will attend to this chamber in due course. I leave such housewifely decisions entirely to her, for, since John is my liege lord, I have more pressing matters to concern me."

Le Gris raised his chin, still looking down that long nose of his. "You give her great freedom, de

Soutenay. Let us hope she does not disappoint you."

Giles gave her a fond look. "I doubt that will happen. I have a great trust in her."

Isabella's heart swelled until she thought that she might burst. To know he thought of her so highly, to have his trust, that was riches indeed. Well had Hildegarde prevented her from considering the convent. To think she might have missed all this. Inwardly, she sent up a prayer of thanks, her faith restored. Eleanor had known what she was about, after all. Or, maybe God had guided the queen, for Isabella could never have dreamed to have such happiness.

Meanwhile, her father continued his litany of disapproval. "As I rode through your demesne, de Soutenay, I noted your tenants appear to be overfed."

How like him to comment on that.

Giles had relaxed again. Isabella noticed a gleam of humour in his eyes. Surely he was not beginning to enjoy himself at her father's expense, for now, he said smoothly, "I consider it good husbandry. Underfed men produce less work. Dead men produce none."

Thwarted again, le Gris snorted and tried a different line of attack. "I wonder why it is you should hold for John rather than Richard. I hope you've backed the right horse, there."

Isabella was hard put to disguise her sharp intake of breath, for the last she'd heard, her father also stood for Prince John. What was his game, now? Was he trying, too late, to win back Eleanor's approval? Or was he just using any weapon which fell into his mind to raise Giles' hackles?

It did not seem to have had any effect. Giles said mildly enough, although Isabella detected a hint of malice, "Sometimes, the choice is not ours. It all depends on how the dice fall. Indeed, I seem to remember you were keen to aid my liege lord yourself some years ago."

Le Gris muttered something and changed the subject, calling for Edith to hand him the towel. His squire had laid out fresh raiment for him: a soft linen shirt, a fur-trimmed tunic of fine wool, dyed madder-red, richly embroidered, a mantle of soft blue. A large gold cloak brooch set with a ruby was beside them; the finishing touch.

Isabella averted her eyes as her father rose dripping from the tub, draping the towel around his spare frame. Even he could not spoil what she had now. She would not let him disturb her.

Her resolve was strained to the limit over supper. Le Gris talked loudly and at length about his manors and wealth, then harrumphed and with an expression on his face which Isabella could only read as malicious, said no more until he had the full attention of her husband. Then, he continued, "No doubt you've been wondering why I'm here."

In the blandest voice Isabella had yet to hear Giles use, he replied, "I'd assumed your visit was for the pleasure of seeing your daughter."

Le Gris curled his upper lip. "Just so. And to pass on my news, which will affect you both substantially."

Giles raised an eyebrow, Isabella felt herself grow cold. Then le Gris dropped his thunderbolt. "You will be interested to hear I am to be wed."

She caught her breath. Wed? Her father? This, she had not expected. But she should have, she acknowledged. He had not wanted her marriage, had been balked by the queen's command, and this was how he would circumvent it.

Giles said dryly, "My congratulations, le Gris. Who is the fortunate lady?"

Isabella didn't hear her father's answer. Her blood seemed to be roaring in her ears. She reached an unsteady hand for her cup and drained it.

As the roaring subsided, she listened with fury as her father talked on and on, rubbing their noses in the fact that he was soon to be married.

At length, he turned to Isabella with a satisfied twist of his lips that might be mistaken for a smile. "And, of course, when my new wife bears me a son, you, Daughter, will no longer be my heiress. Not that you will mind, of course, for it seems your tastes run to lower things. From castle to manor again, despite my efforts."

He gestured with his cup, which Isabella refilled hastily, praying he would soon drink himself insensible, for she could not stand much more of this.

Le Gris continued, "Well, let it not be said I did not do my best for you. Had you done your duty and borne sons to FitzAubrey, I daresay the queen would have provided you with another more worthy husband on his demise."

Isabella winced. Without the likelihood of her father's money, would Giles even have considered marrying her?

She saw Giles stiffen and laid her hand over his, saying, "I am quite content with my lot. I know that seems strange to you, but wealth and position do not always bring happiness."

Le Gris snorted into his wine. "Happiness, Daughter? It is meet that you do your duty, not spend your life searching for 'happiness', which is a most illusory and ephemeral thing."

The meal dragged interminably on, and Isabella's head ached with the effort of ignoring the shafts and spears of her father's conversation; her jaw was stiff from smiling, her neck from nodding. She hadn't trusted herself to speak again after her remark about happiness, not wishing to be the recipient of more advice. From the look on Giles' face, he was feeling the same.

Her father drank deeply and often until his head was drooping and he was near to snoring in his platter of wafers. At last, at long, long last, he placed both hands flat on the table, heaving himself to his feet.

"Well, de Soutenay, I trust you'll hold me excused. I've travelled far, and I will sleep now. I'll leave here on the morrow, for I have other matters to which I must attend."

The tension began to drain from Isabella. She had feared his stay might be indefinite.

Giles moved to take his arm and lead him to their chamber, which manners decreed they give up to him. Tonight they would sleep on a couple of pallets in one of the small chambers in the gallery opposite. Le Gris shook him off with all the charm of a cornered boar, stumping his way up the stairs, retiring, kicking the door closed behind him.

Isabella stood there, hands on the table, eyes closed, until she felt Giles' arm about her shoulders. She leaned against him, so grateful for his support, and he looked down at her tenderly. "Well, Bella, shall we away to our own rest?"

She nodded wordlessly. What would his feelings about her be now? Giles took her hand, leading her across the hall and to the upper chamber. Tomorrow, she decided, she would change their bedlinen whether that was considered overly fastidious or not, for she could not bring herself to sleep in the same sheets which had covered her father. Bad enough he slept in their bed.

As Giles closed the door behind them, he leaned on it, running his hands through his hair. "I do not know how I managed to keep from throttling him," he said, rolling his shoulders and stretching. He yawned, his mouth gaping so wide she thought his jaw would crack. "I regret to have to say this, love, but I find your father is one of the most cantankerous old goats I've ever had the misfortune to meet."

Isabella said nothing. If her father were just cantankerous, she could have borne it the more easily. She closed her eyes, remembering how many times she'd felt the lash of his belt. Giles had not seen the worst of him. Pray God he never would. She eyed her husband, hoping he would tell her how he felt about her father's marriage, for he would surely speak of it, wouldn't he?

He did not. Silently, but by mutual consent, they took their straw-stuffed mattresses from the single pallets that had been hastily pushed together, upending those against the far wall, and spreading the palliasses on the floor where the pallets had stood.

No reeds here to soften the floor, but it was planked with wood, so less cold than the stone flags of the hall, and the straw was thick enough to cushion them. She spread one sheet beneath them and one on top, piled blankets on those, then she clung tightly to Giles, too consumed by her need of him to care about any lack of comfort, as she strove to forget le Gris, snoring in their bed across the hall. And it seemed to her that her father's revelations had not diminished her husband's desire. She shut her mind to the fact that it was sin to take each other during Lent. Time enough to confess on the morrow.

CHAPTER 32

Isabella awoke before cockcrow, wishing she could stay beside Giles for longer. But her father would be making his preparations to leave and would be slow to forgive any lack of courtesy on his daughter's part. At least he would soon be gone from them, hopefully, too caught up in his own concerns to make their lives miserable again in the foreseeable future.

She leaned over and kissed her husband, who mumbled in his sleep and buried his head deeper under the blankets. Then, rising, she shivered as the morning air chilled her bare skin. Still, Isabella was grateful there was no crusting of ice on the water in the ewer. It was still frigid to her touch, but she did not wish to call for hot water. Doubtless the servants were up; they rose betimes. But she wanted to hold off the moment when she must face the world for just a little longer.

She washed herself swiftly, scrambling into her shift and gown without assistance, tidying her hair and rebraiding it as best she might. Bundling it into a net, she covered the whole with a demure wimple and secured her veil with two precious crystal-headed silver pins Giles had given her. Although doubtless, her father would think those a waste of his wealth, too. On the other hand, he would not wish her to look as though Giles did not have coin to spend on her, for that also would reflect badly on his own prestige.

She sighed heavily, then held her breath as Giles muttered and turned over. It would not matter what she did, her father would find reason to complain, but for the sake of her own pride, she wished to look as well-valued as possible.

With that in mind, she pinned her silver-gilt brooch to her favourite mantle – the one Eleanor had given her. Even her father could find no fault in that, surely. And with one last longing look at her husband, she slipped from the room and went downstairs with a heavy heart.

The hall was busy as she trod across. Palliasses were being tidied away, benches moved towards the fire already stirring in the hearth.

The trestles were being set up. A few of the servants called out greetings to her as she moved through, and she answered them with more cheer than she felt, stopping to load a tray with bread, pottage and ale.

As she went up the wooden steps the other side, she reminded herself the ordeal would soon be over.

She entered timidly, loath to disturb him if he still slept, but her father was already up, the signs of his heavy drinking last night barely visible as he strode about the chamber, his squires nowhere to be seen. He turned as she entered, barking a greeting at her, and she laid the tray down on the table, forcing a smile to her face.

Le Gris harrumphed, clearing his throat and spitting into the rushes, then sat down before the table, legs spread wide, tearing into the bread with his teeth. He spooned up the pottage, clearing the bowl, and tossed back his ale, before he said, "I trust I find you well, this morning."

"Yes, Father. And you?" She knew her voice was toneless, but not for all the treasures in Christendom could she conjure up any enthusiasm.

"Tolerable, Daughter, tolerable. Although I found your wine disagreed with me during the night, but I daresay it's the best your husband can afford." He hawked and spat again.

He wouldn't have done that in his own chamber, she thought resentfully. And had he not over-indulged, she doubted the wine would have disagreed with him. He'd certainly drunk enough of it yestereve.

"Well, what are you standing there for? Sit, girl!" Aware he was watching her, she forced the smile back to her lips. He grunted. "So, my daughter, have you got yourself with child yet?"

She hadn't expected that, and it disconcerted her, leaving her with nothing to say. Shaking her head dumbly, she looked down, hiding the hatred she felt for him.

"And, I hear tell you've already lost one."

She jerked up her head violently. How in Heaven's name had he learned that? She gritted her teeth as he continued, "Just as I suspected. Weak stock. Comes from your mother's side."

Isabella took a deep breath, trying to stem the rage building in her, but he wasn't done yet.

"Years I wasted, ploughing an empty furrow. I hope you'll serve your husband better than your mother served me, may God assoil her."

Isabella rose with dignity. Her time with Giles, although not long, had given her more confidence, and now, the words were out before she could swallow them. "Had you served her so less often, Father, maybe she would have been better able to."

As she heard herself speak, she flinched. How had she dared? It was this life. Her opinion was valued here, and, for one short, dangerous moment, she had forgotten how to behave herself before her father.

Le Gris spoke softly, enunciating each word clearly. "How dare you, Daughter? I see your husband has been too soft with you."

She bowed her head, awaiting the explosion of his wrath; it didn't take long. He pushed his chair back, and it clattered as it fell against the wall before toppling into the rushes. Then he grasped her arm and smacked her hard in the face with the back of his hand. Her head snapped to one side, and she felt her lip split where his ring caught it. He hit her again on the other side of her face, harder this time, palm first, and she whimpered. Once more, then he threw her from himself.

She landed against the table, cracking her head on the side of it, crumpling almost senseless onto the floor. Le Gris kicked her in the ribs. She moaned and rolled herself into a ball. One more kick landed at the base of her spine, jarring her bones, and she bit back a scream as more pain ripped through her. She heard him gather his things and slam from the room, but could not move. She lay there, tears seeping from beneath her closed lashes, stinging her torn mouth as they rolled down her face and dripped to the floor.

Giles, waking to find his wife gone, dressed quickly and headed out to find her, calling cheerful greetings to the household as he crossed the hall. Remembering his annoyance of the previous day, when he met le Gris on the stair, he found himself struggling to resist the temptation to throw him over the handrail. Reining in his temper with difficulty, he turned to accompany him back down to the hall, noting le Gris was wearing his cloak.

"Are you leaving us so early?" He hoped so. By all the saints, he hoped so.

"There is no reason to stay longer; I must be back for my wedding. I would invite you, but the occasion is to be small, and I do not see the need."

He wouldn't! But his parsimony relieved Giles. It would be no celebration for Isabella having to return to her father's roof even for one night, and Giles himself would risk biting through to his jaw if he had to hold his tongue again so soon.

As he escorted le Gris from the hall, he spoke banal trivialities which largely went unanswered.

On the threshold, le Gris turned and, staring down his nose at Giles – no mean feat, for Giles was a handspan taller – said in repressive tones, "You would do well to remind your wife to keep to her distaff, de Soutenay. Women should be encouraged to speak less and serve more. My daughter may have married below her status, but that's no reason to allow her too much freedom. Like all her kind, she's a weak vessel and requires much discipline."

Giles raised his eyebrows, raking his gaze over the supercilious fool, fighting the urge to knock his teeth down his throat before saying in carefully measured tones, "I would remind you, le Gris, that when you handed her over to my keeping, you passed ownership of her to me, and I'll 'discipline' her as I see fit." He bared his teeth in the semblance of a smile, repressing a snarl of rage.

"Well, see that you do, de Soutenay, see that you do. There's nothing more unbecoming than a woman who cannot control herself. I've taken it upon myself to lesson her already this morning, and the day has scarce begun."

Control herself? Isabella's icy control of herself had nearly broken him. What had she said to le Gris in his absence? An awful premonition swept over him, and it was all he could do not to race back to the solar. Instead, he braced himself, bidding le Gris God speed, forcing himself not to strike him, and accompanied him and his men to their waiting horses, curbing his impatience until they had ridden out and the gates were closed behind them. Then, he strode back to the hall in a fury of concern, the set of his face such that the servants got out of his way speedily.

His mind churning, he took the stairs two at a time, hurtling into the solar, to stall abruptly, aghast at the sight that met his eyes.

Isabella was curled in a ball against the far side of the room, her arms wrapped around herself, hands clenching convulsively, shudders running through her body. In swift strides, he was at her side, but as he put his arm around her, she flinched from his touch.

He swore, and she cowered further away from him. Crouching in front of her, he said quietly, compellingly, "Isabella. Bella, my dearest love, look at me. Your father has gone. It's me, Giles."

Wincing, she turned her head, looking up at him with terrified gaze through eyelids that were swollen slits. The imprint of le Gris' fingers were livid on her face, and her lips were torn and bleeding. Appalled, Giles tried to draw her to himself, but she cried out in pain as he touched her.

He poured out the water which lay in the laver, not wanting anything le Gris had touched to touch her, then refilled it from the ewer which stood beside it. Moistening a clean napkin, he dabbed gently at her swollen mouth.

She whimpered as he sponged her face, but did not withdraw from him, for which he thanked God.

"Where else has he hurt you, my heart?" He wanted to hold her close, but dared not until he knew where else she had been injured. His ire rose, but he forced it down. If he thought on le Gris at all, he would combust, and above all, she needed calm and peace.

She murmured something, and he bent his head closer to hear. "My ribs, husband, and my back."

Curse the hellspawned churl. Although he knew it would cause her more pain, he couldn't leave her lying there. With infinite care, he slid his arms beneath her shoulders and knees. She moaned at his touch, a low keening noise which made the hair on the back of his neck rise.

As he set her on the bed, she grasped his arm, face wet with tears. "My fault," she muttered indistinctly, and he strained to make out the words. "I forgot myself. I forgot his temper." Then, the dam broke, and she wept, clinging to him as though she would never let go.

He held her gently to himself, afraid of hurting her, stroking her hair with the lightest of touches, until her sobs ceased. She curled up against him, and her awful shuddering eased. Hearing the door to the solar open, he held his finger to his lips when Edith poked her head around the curtain. She took one step closer, unnoticed by Isabella, then stopped, a look of horror etched on her face when she saw the state of her mistress.

"Fetch Nan," he mouthed, and she nodded once and left, forgetting to close the door in her haste.

Nan came, sleeves rolled up, her bag of nostrums slung across her shoulder, face full of pity, and between them, they unlaced Isabella's gown, easing it from her, and treated her hurts as gently as possibly. Edith wept openly, and Nan's eyes brimmed over as she saw the livid marks on Isabella's body, but she probed carefully at the bruises that spread across her mistress's back and ribs like some evil stain. Isabella's muted groans of pain cracked Giles' heart, and it tore at his senses that all he could do was sit helplessly by.

Nan completed her examination, dabbing the bruises and abrasions with vinegar before smearing comfrey and marigold in goose grease over them, and bandaging her ribs, saying, "At least nothing's broken, poor lamb. This will help, but you'll be in pain awhile yet. And how you're to drink through your poor mouth, I don't know.

Lucky you've lost none of your teeth, though I misdoubt me they'll feel loose for a few days."

She gave Isabella a small amount of poppy juice in wine to drink, pouring it into a spoon so as not to hurt her swollen lips, and covered her with the blankets before addressing Giles. "Best you leave her to rest now. While she's sleeping, she's not hurting. If I had the…" she pursed her lips, not saying the word Giles could almost hear formed in her head, "If I had him in here, I'd have a thing or two to say."

"Better you haven't then, Nan, for if you did, no doubt you'd be in the same case as she. The man's no better than an animal."

"Huh!" Nan sniffed. "Given the choice of him or a wild boar, I'd take my chances with the boar every time. All that polish is worth nothing if the man is a brute beast beneath it. I'd not have to open my mouth to make him suffer. If he shows his face here again, I vow he'll rue the day. I know my simples, I do. I know well how to cure, and," her mouth was grim, "I know more than that. Le Gris would be wishing he was dead by the time I'd finished with him."

Giles was equally grim. "Almost, I wish I could send you as a gift to him, Nan."

Nan's eyes blazed as she said, "Almost, I wish you would."

Giles got to his feet carefully so as not to waken Isabella. His horror at seeing her lying there, injured and mute with fear like some terrified fawn, which he had forced down so as not to cause her distress, was now turning into a rising tide of fury that threatened to swamp him. He would see to it le Gris never touched her again.

He buckled on his sword belt, then snatched up his weapon, thrust it into the scabbard, grabbed his cloak from the chest and strode to the door spitting a particularly foul epithet. His overwhelming desire at the moment was to beat le Gris to a pulp. He called over his shoulder, "Look after your mistress," and strode from the chamber, storming into the hall, calling his men. They came quickly. It was not often his temper was so roused, but when it was, a wise man did not irritate him further.

As Giles flung himself on his horse, he cleared his mind of the image of Isabella bleeding on the floor, for if he did not, he surely would kill le Gris. But his honour, his wife's honour, demanded he did not sit tamely by. And how would she be able to trust him if he did not avenge her.

When he returned some hours later, he barged up the stairs, pausing to compose himself before he opened the door to the solar. His blood-lust mostly cooled now, he breathed deeply, then reached for the door, noticing his grazed knuckles for the first time.

As the door creaked open, Nan peeped round the curtained bedchamber, her face clearing at the sight of Giles. "Oh, my lord, it's you," she said, somewhat unnecessarily in Giles' opinion.

He detected relief in her tone and eyed her. "My lady has been distressed," she whispered. "I couldn't calm her."

Distressed? He knew she was distressed. It was why he had paid le Gris in kind. He took Nan's arm and moved her out of his path, walking quietly to the bed.

Isabella, eyes swollen with weeping as much as bruises, looked up at him, the tragic expression on her face dissolving into fresh tears when she saw him. "Oh, my lord!" She held her hands out to him. "You're safe. He didn't kill you." He took her hands and she stroked the grazes.

Giles didn't know whether to be moved or offended. "No, he did not kill me. Did you think he might?"

She hesitated, then spoke as though choosing her words with care. "You've not seen his temper, my lord. And his men would not hesitate to do murder if he ordered them." She looked down, then raised her gaze to him again. "I did not want you to go after him."

Her voice was no more than a murmur and her words were muffled by her swollen mouth; Giles was not sure he'd heard her aright.

"Does he mean that much to you even now, my heart?"

Her voice, though weak, was filled with loathing. "He means *nothing* to me." She gulped and wiped another tear from her face. "But you do, my husband. I was afraid. This," she indicated herself, "is nothing. I can bear it. I could not bear to lose you."

Giles stroked the hair tenderly from her face, where it clung to the wetness of her cheeks. "Well, sweetheart, he has not killed me. Neither have I killed him, much though he deserves it. But, and this I promise you, it will be a very cold day in Hell before your father lays his hands on you again."

She tried to smile, and her brave attempt almost broke his heart. Then, she gripped his hands until her knuckles turned white. "I thank you, my husband. It wasn't necessary, but I do thank you."

He left unsaid the words, *But it was necessary for me.*

It took two weeks for the bruising to fade. Two weeks, during which time she hid herself in their chamber, attended only by Nan and Edith, for she refused to allow anyone else to see her.

Giles spent what time he could spare with her. He would have spent more, but Isabella chivvied him to eat in the hall, "Else, they'll think I'm at death's door, my husband."

His eyes were tender. "Will you not feel too alone, my heart?"

She shook her head, wincing a little as she moved too suddenly. "No, for I have Nan and Edith to bear me company."

"And I flattered myself you'd miss me." He pulled a face at her.

She flushed and started to stutter a reply, but he forestalled her, laying his finger on her lips. "Don't distress yourself, Isabella. I do but jest. And if I deprive you of myself now, you'll be all the more glad to see me later, no?"

He saw the tension drain from her, then bent to kiss her forehead before leaving her.

As the evidence of her father's rough treatment was erased from her face, she regained her confidence. That her husband had been prepared to avenge her hurts made her heart swell with pride. She was gazing out the window when Giles entered.

He stood beside her, tilting her chin gently towards him, inspecting her. "I think, my love, you could grace the hall again now, do not you? The marks have faded, the swelling gone. Will you rejoin the household tomorrow?"

She leaned against him, as though to draw from his strength. "If that's what you wish, my husband. If the bruises have truly gone."

"I swear to you they have, and I think it time your 'ailment' is cured before my people really begin to believe your sickness is mortal." He took both her hands and pressed them to his lips. "Come, Bella, no one will think aught of it except to be glad you're able to join us again."

Her mouth trembled slightly. "Giles, I'm so ashamed."

"Sweetheart, there's no shame for you in this. The shame is upon your father. He's the one who has besmirched his honour, if he ever had any. And none but Nan, Edith and I know. Nan swears to me she's not even told Oswin and Filbert. You surely will believe her? And if not, believe me when I say no one will guess what happened."

She'd been looking at her feet. Now, she raised her head as though summoning up her courage. Giles put his arm around her. "And I won't leave your side."

She smiled wanly at him. "And now I have no secrets from you. But, do you see? Do you under-stand why I was so afraid when you wed me?

How could I know you'd not be of the same cut? Baldwin was."

Giles kissed her softly; her lips were warm and pliant on his. "So now do you believe I'm truly of different cloth?"

She nodded, then looked up, her face clouded with concern. "But Giles, what if he did speak true? What if I cannot bear you children? Will you want to be rid of me? For if you might, then tell me now, once for all. If I learn to trust you wholly, and then I lose your love, I may as well be dead. You won't even have the consolation of inheritance at his death if his new wife bears a son. And that, my lord, was what you expected when you wed me."

Giles' gaze held hers, his soul in his eyes. "My heart, his money is nothing to me. The queen warned me this might happen. But you'll keep your dower lands, she saw to that. And that is enough for me, I promise you. I will vow on the reliquaries at St. Alban's if you wish. I'll vow on any reliquary you choose, be it at Compostela, Walsingham, Vézelay, Cluny, Rome. I will even vow on the very altar in Jerusalem, if you desire it."

As he spoke, the worry had lifted from her face, and now, she gurgled with laughter. "I'd only ask that if I wanted to be rid of you. I'll take your word for it, only, please, let me know if you start to tire of me." She moved to the bed and sat, head tilted upwards, gazing at him.

Giles knelt, took her hands and placed his own between them. "I promise, by all the saints who ever lived, there will be no secrets between us." Then, thinking of those things he could not share, he hesitated, suffused by doubt and guilt, but only momentarily – they were not his to tell. As a sop to his conscience, he added, "At least, not those secrets which are my own. Secrets which belong to others – those I cannot promise. But beyond that, I do so swear."

She sighed and laid her head on his chest. He drew her closer, then released her, but only to draw the hangings about the bed.

CHAPTER 33

August 1195

"Come, love, I want to show you something." Giles held his hand out to Isabella, who sat at the solar window with her sewing. She looked up at him, at the face which had become dear to her, and smiled. "Then you must wait while I ease myself to my feet, husband. I feel like a porpoise or a fat old badger."

Giles grinned. "Only somewhat less hairy and smelly, I hope."

She tapped his arm playfully. "That's not for me to say. You're the one who can best judge."

Giles chuckled, then came to her and helped her to her feet. In truth, she was not huge yet. The pregnancy barely showed, but she had been so afraid she would never be fecund that she almost flaunted the slight bulge of her abdomen, the extra curve of her breasts. And she needed no help to rise; she was still lithe enough but made a pretence of heaving herself up, levering herself against Giles' outstretched hand as he groaned. "Before this babe comes, I think I shall have arms like some mythical beast – long enough to touch the ground."

She liked that he teased her and indulged her whim of heaviness, but she hid a niggle of worry, for so much could yet go wrong. Still, she pushed away the dark cloud that hovered at the back of her mind and leaned against him.

The faint fluttering sensations she felt in her womb reassured her. It was not what she'd felt last time. This was more definite, so perhaps she had only imagined it before – certainly Nan had told her she was mistaken, but Isabella had not wished to believe her. And whether or not, she would forever hold a place in her heart for that first unborn child.

Giles put his arm around her waist, and they walked down the stairs together. So much safer than the castle steps, this wooden staircase. So much less likelihood she would fall down these or be pushed, as she had feared Baldwin might do in the worst of his rages. Giles, she knew now, would never give rise to such fear in her. Even if he felt the need to berate her, she had no doubt he would never harm her. It was a good feeling, this cocoon of safety which wrapped itself around like strong arms enfolding her. Giles' arms, she thought, leaning her head against his shoulder.

They wandered through the hall where Nan was chivvying the servants, Oswin had his head bent over his accounts, and several children chased a chicken that had somehow found its way in. It was a domestic, harmonious scene, with cheerful voices raised in jokes and con-versations; the difference between this and the day-to-day life with Baldwin was immeasurable. Isabella heaved a great sigh of contentment.

Giles laughed. "Wearied already? At this hour? What will you be like come Martinmas?"

"Not weary, my lord. Happy."

He brushed her lips with his own, lightly, like a butterfly's wing. "Then, I'm happy, also."

As they reached the forecourt, he turned to a small track which ran away from the manor to the west. Isabella hadn't noticed it before. It was narrow and surrounded by brambles, their flow-ers open and glowing in the brightness of the day. The earliest small fruits, destroyed by un-seasonable rainfall before they'd had chance to fully grow or ripen, were rotting on the thorn, but now, it was as though the later blooms were bursting with renewed vigour, making up for the lack of sunshine earlier in the year.

"Gather your gown close to you, Bella. I need to have this cut wider now I have a wife, I think. I have deliberately kept the path narrow, but the thorns are sharp. If they catch the fabric of your gown, they'll damage it."

"Happen it's a good job you did not wait until I am grown even larger."

He acknowledged her jest absently, saying, "I've only waited this long in the hope the track will not be too muddy."

The sun was warm on her face, and she wore no wimple, just a light veil. She lifted her face to the sky and closed her eyes briefly. The song of a lark was loud, and Isabella searched until she found the small, dark speck that hung, suspended, over the fields beyond.

The joy of the life she now led was so great, she felt as though she had been reborn.

Giles tugged at her hand. "Come, wife. We're not yet where I wish to go."

"No? Then, lead the way."

He turned again to kiss her. "Now, it's my turn to dally." Then, he moved on, and Isabella, her hand still captured, followed. After a miserable summer, the weather had finally improved. Butterflies flitted across the path, bees buzzed about their business, and the shouts of the labourers in the fields could be heard faintly even at this distance, along with the lowing of the oxen. In good times, this would be a bountiful land, and now, she too, bore fruit.

At last, Giles came to a small clearing, where a stone well stood, partially surrounded by more brambles and dog-roses, all with wicked thorns. "Here it is. This is the place for which the manor was named. Thorneywell. The well is not used often now, but sometimes, women come to draw water, for the old legends say it was blessed by Saint Rumwold after his death, and to drink from it is supposed to ensure lifelong health, wealth and happiness. We have a new well at the hall, the one you have seen, but this is ancient; it's been here, so they say, for centuries.

"The thorns protect the well. And in summer, as you see now, the blossom is bountiful. Some of the berries and rose hips we use at the hall, but there are so many, the villagers come here and pick their fill."

And he let them. That was the measure of this man; he gave freely. Baldwin would not have allowed them to pick any fruit without demanding a tax on it. Baldwin had taxed everything, then squandered it all while his people starved.

They stood in the gap between the brambles, side by side, hands on the rough stone of the old well. Isabella leaned over it and could see a faint sparkle of sunlight on water in its dark depths.

Giles picked up a rope that lay alongside, pulling at it until a bucket appeared. He let it down into the well, and she heard the splash as it hit the water, then he was bringing it up again, offering it to her, tilting it so she could sip at it, before taking a deep draught himself.

It tasted clear and clean, at least as good as the water they had at the manor, if not better. "Only our own people know this is here," he said. "I thought it time to share it with you."

Turning, she leaned against the rim, tilting her head back, breathing in the fragrance around her. Giles did the same, saying, "In winter, this is a forbidding place. With no blossom, the thorns are bare and jagged. It looks barren and ugly, then. But now, as you see, the thorns are covered with flowers. Do you not think it beautiful?"

She nodded silently. It was the way Baldwin had made her feel; dry, barren, and sharp as an old thorn. She'd forgotten thorns could also flower. And now she, like the roses and brambles, would soon also bear fruit. In truth, she'd found the blossom on the thorn.

Giles held out his hand again, and she took it, following him as he led her home.

AUTHOR NOTES

Although readers of my previous novels will know Giles is fictitious, I used a knight who had actually lived to base his land holding on. The record book of a petty knight called Henry de Bray, lord of Harlestone in Northamptonshire survives, showing that he had twenty-four tenants sharing five hundred acres (Daily Life in Medieval Times, Frances and Joseph Gies) and, although Giles is not a wealthy knight, I didn't want him to be too lowly, so I allotted him something similar.

Not many people had glass in their houses at this time in history, and Giles would certainly not have been able to afford a glazed window, but I imagined his brother and sister-in-law might delight in buying one as a wedding gift. The scene I describe of the rays of the rising sun looking as though the glass was on fire was described to me by the owner of Long Crendon Manor, a medieval manor house with a twelfth century hall, where my husband and I stayed for two nights in September 2017. Although the glazed windows there would have been of a slightly later date, apparently, the imperfections in the glass do have that effect when the sunlight catches it. Sadly, it rained most of the time we were there, and I never got to experience it, but I thought it would be nice to include that in my story.

Simon de Beauchamp was the Sheriff of Buckingham at this time but would probably have been located at Bedford Castle, so although the outlaws had attacked nearer Buckingham, I think the administrative district would have been Bedford Castle. I may be wrong, but if I am, please don't let the error stop you from enjoying the story which of course is fiction.

There is some dispute over whether there were snowdrops in England in the twelfth century, although the general belief seems to be that they were not introduced in any quantity until the sixteenth century. However, since they were known in Italy during the time my story is set, and since it is recorded that Eleanor was at the inauguration of Pope Clement III in 1191, it seems possible he might have given her some snowdrop bulbs as a gift. Luckily for me, they thrived! There is also dispute about whether they would have flowered this early. The ones in my garden have certainly flowered quite early in January some years.

Eleanor would not have been at Berkhamsted Castle during Christmas 1194, and it's extremely unlikely John would have been either, but for the sake of my plot I allowed them an unscheduled visit.

As for the location of the fictitious Sparnstow Abbey – this has always been a mystery to me. However, with the aid of various Anglo-Saxon and medieval maps, and using the timespans for various journeys in the book, my husband managed to pin it down to a location between Aylesbury Parkway and the medieval settlement of Eythrope, which seems to have disappeared sometime between the fourteenth and fifteenth centuries.

In the twelfth century the manor belonged to D'Arches family. You can read more about the fascinating history of Eythrope and surrounding area on www.historicengland.org.uk. However, since my story is fiction, my imaginary Abbey of Sparnstow, which was situated in close prox-imity to this location, is nothing to do with the D'Arches, nor yet the village of Eythrope. It is just nice to have an approximate location.

The mushroom used by Clarice to produce sickness – fool's funnel – doesn't usually cause death, although very small amounts cause sweating and sickness. It can occasionally be fatal, so it seemed likely that the prolonged doses Nan was subject to might have brought her close to death.

I couldn't find whether or not fool's funnel was a native British mushroom, so I contacted the British Mycological Society who told me that although it wasn't formally described until 1801, it is a very common native British species and it would have been growing here in the twelfth century. They say they have no reason to suppose people would not have known about its poisonous properties.

Saint Rumwold, who blessed the well in my story, actually existed. He was a medieval saint, supposedly the grandson of Penda of Mercia. Born in 662, he lived for only three days. According to legend, at birth, he cried out three times, 'I am a Christian,' and requested baptism. Immediately after that, he was said to have made a profession of faith and preached a sermon, reciting scriptures. Then, he predicted his death and gave instructions for his burial. Pretty impressive for one so young! There are a couple of wells associated with Rumwold, so, since everything about him seems rather far-fetched, I thought it wouldn't strain things too much further to add another well not too far away from where he was buried in Buckingham.

With reference to the word 'freondscype' which Giles translates as a kind of love, I found this definition in a translation of The Husband's Message edited by Murray McGillivray in the Online Corpus of Old English Poetry – friend-ship, a love relationship. My friend, author Annie Whitehead, who specialises in the Anglo-Saxon period, was kind enough to find an ap-proximate pronunciation for me.

With reference to Isabella's saddle – I've tried to be logical with the riding aside scenes, but the actuality of it as far back as the twelfth century is not conclusive. Thanks to the wonderful Helen Hollick and her daughter Kathy Hollick Blee, who competes 'aside', for their help and advice on this matter. You can find more on Helen's website, Helen Hollick's World of Books

I hope you enjoyed reading Blossom on the Thorn as much as I enjoyed writing it. I am no historian, but I do my best. If you found any anachronisms, I do hope they didn't spoil the story for you.

As an independent author, I rely very much on reviews and word of mouth, so if you enjoyed my story it would mean a lot to me if you would spare a few minutes to write a review on Amazon, Goodreads or other websites.

BOOKS BY LORETTA LIVINGSTONE

Novels

Out of Time (Book 1 – Out of Time – 1191)

A Promise to Keep (Book 2 – Out of Time – 1197)

Blossom on the Thorn (Book 3 –Out of Time – 1194/95)

Short Stories

Beautiful and Other Short Stories

Four Christmases

Where Angels Tread

Three for Hallowe'en

Poetry

Rhythms of Life

Jumping in the Puddles of Life

Hopes, Dreams and Medals volumes 1 & 2

ABOUT THE AUTHOR

British author Loretta Livingstone lives with her husband and cat in the beautiful Chiltern Hills. She started writing poetry but progressed first, to short stories and now, to full-length fiction.

Her first historical novel, Out of Time, was shortlisted by the Historical Novel Society for the 2016 HNS Indie Award.

Loretta suffers from ME so it sometimes takes her longer than she would wish to complete books, but she considers she is blessed just to be able to write at all, since a few years earlier, it would have been impossible for her to write anything of any length.

You can find more about Loretta on her website, www.treasurechestbooks.co.uk and she can also be contacted on Twitter, Goodreads or Facebook.

Printed in Poland
by Amazon Fulfillment
Poland Sp. z o.o., Wrocław

50230597R00263